Nancy Mitford

THE PURSUIT OF LOVE

Nancy Mitford, daughter of Lord and Lady Redesdale and the eldest of the six legendary Mitford sisters, was born in 1904 and educated at home on the family estate in Oxfordshire. She made her debut in London and soon became one of the bright young things of the 1920s, a close friend of Henry Green, Evelyn Waugh, John Betjeman, and their circle. A beauty and a wit, she began writing for magazines and writing novels while she was still in her twenties. In all, she wrote eight novels as well as biographies of Madame de Pompadour, Voltaire, Louis XIV, and Frederick the Great. She died in 1973. More information can be found at www.nancymitford.com.

THE PURSUIT OF LOVE

Nancy Mitford

THE PURSUIT OF LOVE

Foreword by Jessica Mitford

Introduction by Zoë Heller

Vintage Books
A Division of Penguin Random House LLC
New York

FIRST VINTAGE BOOKS EDITION, AUGUST 2010

Library of Congress Cataloging-in-Publication Data
Mitford, Nancy, 1904–1973.
The pursuit of love / by Nancy Mitford ; foreword by Jessica Mitford ; introduction
by Zoë Heller. — 1st Vintage Books ed.
p. cm.
1. Upper class—Fiction. 2. Country life—Fiction.
3. England—Fiction. I. Title.
PR6025.I88P87 2010
823'.914—dc22
2010021926

Vintage Books Trade Paperback ISBN: 978-0-307-74081-6
eBook ISBN: 978-0-307-74136-3
TVTI ISBN: 978-0-593-46727-5

www.vintagebooks.com

Printed in the United States of America
10 9 8 7 6 5 4 3 2 1

FOREWORD

"THE MITFORD INDUSTRY" is a phrase cleverly coined by the odious London *Evening Standard* (ever the bane of our family) circa 1979, when the English reading and telly-viewing public were subjected to an unprecedented barrage of Mitfordiana: Harold Acton's memoir of Nancy, David Pryce-Jones's book about Unity, Diana's book about Diana, mine about me.* BBC produced two hour-long documentaries about Nancy and me, soon followed by Thames Television's six-part dramatization of *The Pursuit of Love* and *Love in a Cold Climate*. As I write this the Industry rolls on with Ned Sherrin's and Caryl Brahms's musical show, *The Mitford Girls*, featuring six dancing and singing actresses who alternate period songs of the twenties and thirties with snippets of conversation from the aforementioned books. My sister Deborah has cruelly dubbed this show "La Triviata."

It was, of course, Nancy who started it all. Without her, there would be no Mitford industry. If only she could have lived to see

---

*Nancy Mitford: A Memoir, Harold Acton. Harper & Row, 1976. *Unity Mitford: An Inquiry into Her & the Frivolity of Evil*, David Pryce-Jones. Dial, 1977. *A Life of Contrasts*, Diana Mosley. Times Books, 1978. *A Fine Old Conflict*, Jessica Mitford. Knopf, 1977.

the unlikely fruits of her early endeavors. "*How I* shrieked," she would have said.

And how *I* shrieked when I first read *The Pursuit of Love*, which clattered into my postbox in California some time in 1945. Because there we all were, larger than life, Mitfords renamed Radletts, reliving our childhoods as seen through Nancy's strange triangular green eyes.

Some contemporaneous family reactions: My mother (*alias* Aunt Sadie in the book) wrote to say *she* thought it very amusing, but she doubted if anybody outside the family would want to read it because they wouldn't understand the jokes. (In the event she was proved wrong. According to Harold Acton, it has sold over a million copies.) My sister Deborah (*alias* Vicki) was vastly annoyed at Nancy's saying that she and I (*alias* Jassy) had called our secret society "The Hons" because we were Honourables, when in fact the name derived from the sweet hens we used to keep, whose eggs were the mainspring of our personal economy: we sold them at a slight profit to my mother, and then ate them for breakfast. This distortion persisted in translation; in the French edition, the Hons' Cupboard is "la Cave des Nobles." Debo was pleased when later I made a public correction (in *Hons and Rebels*)* of wicked Nancy's misrepresentation.

To what extent, then, are the characters in these novels drawn from life? Almost entirely, I would say, with, of course, the novelist's propensity to merge and distill characters: Linda, for example, seems to me to be a composite of my sisters Diana and Deborah, with a splash of Nancy herself thrown in.

Before the war, Nancy had written three novels, all pretty much based on family and friends. Her first was *Highland Fling*, in which our father is felicitously named General Murgatroyd, later to become the terrifying Uncle Matthew of *The Pursuit of Love* and

---

*Published in this country as *Daughters and Rebels* and previously available in paperback from Holt, Rinehart and Winston.

Love in a Cold Climate. His distinctive argot—"Damn sewer" or "Stinks to merry hell"—his violent outbursts against those unfortunates to whom he had happened to take a dislike, are drawn to the life. In fact, so accurate was Nancy's portrayal of my father that after his death in 1958, even the London *Times* obituary writer seemed confused as to whether he was describing Lord Redesdale or "the explosive, forthright Uncle Matthew" of her novels.

To supply further clues to the reader: Lord Merlin is Lord Berners, who really was a neighbor of ours and who really did have the cable address of "Neighbourtease." Lady Montdore is partly drawn from Violet Trefusis, of whom Harold Acton writes: "One can almost hear Violet remarking, like Lady Montdore, 'I think I may say we put India on the map. Hardly any of one's friends in England had ever even heard of India before we went there, you know.'"

But—what of Nancy herself? Ah, that was the real puzzler. To what extent did that intensely private character let down her comedian's mask to reveal herself in these novels?

As soon as I had finished reading *The Pursuit of Love*, in which Linda after many a false start finds true bliss with a hero of the Free French resistance movement, I sat straight down and wrote to Nancy: "Now Susan [we called each other Susan—why, I can't remember], we all know you've got no imagination, so I can see from yr. book that you are having an affair with a Frenchman. Are you?" She wrote back, "Well, yes, Susan, as a matter of fact I am."

Jessica Mitford
November 1981

INTRODUCTION

SOME NOVELISTS EMERGE, as if from the head of Zeus, with their talents fully formed, their distinctive styles already in place. Others shilly-shally for a couple of books until, for reasons that have as much to do with chance as with effort, they happen upon an idea, or a character, or even an opening sentence, that liberates whatever is most interesting in their writing selves. Mitford had produced four works of fiction by the time *The Pursuit of Love* was published in 1945, but it was only in this novel – her first attempt to capture the sui generis oddities of Mitford family life – that her genius finally declared itself.

The Pursuit of Love may be reasonably described as a comic novel – a light comic novel even – but it is too spiky and intelligent, I think, to qualify as an altogether cosy or comforting novel. I have revisited it many times over the last thirty years and if I have been drawn back in most instances by a slightly lazy desire for familiar, reliable pleasures, the actual experience of reading the book has never failed to surprise that complacent expectation. The jokes are peerless, yes. I doubt I shall ever tire of reading Linda's horrified account of housekeeping or Uncle Matthew's outraged review of *Romeo and Juliet* or Davey's devastating analysis of the Radlett family's "museum-quality" mineral collection. But beneath the brittle surface of this novel's wit there is something infinitely more melancholy at work – something that is apt to snag you and pull you into its dark undertow when you are least expecting it. In contrast to some of the more obviously serious novels that impressed me in my youth, whose depths have since proved disappointingly plumbable, this unassuming bit of mid-century "chick lit" has not only held up beautifully over time, but continues to yield riches.

Years of pressing the book enthusiastically on friends and loved ones have taught me some caution, however. Mitford's fiction is strong meat. Readers who appreciate it at all, tend to love it with a dotty passion; others, who escape the enchantment, are apt to despise it with almost equal fervour. The decisive factor, in either case, would seem to be the voice – the unmistakable, arresting Mitford trill, in whose light, bright cadences, an entire hard-to-shock and easy-to-bore view of life is made manifest. This voice is not *actually* a voice, of course; it is the illusion of a voice, painstakingly created in prose. The narrator of this novel, Fanny, writes with such immediacy and casual fluency – her tone is so natural and true – that it is easy to forget this fact. "The charm of your writing," Evelyn Waugh once wrote to Mitford, "depends on your refusal to recognize a distinction between girlish chatter and literary language." Indeed, if Mitford has never quite received her due as a stylist – if even her devotees are inclined to classify her as a "guilty pleasure" – it is perhaps because the sound of light, extemporaneous chatter in her prose is too convincing.

Such attention as her style has received over the years, has tended to emphasize its documentary value. It has been praised as a peculiarly vivid example of how the *jeunesse dorée* spoke in 1930s England, or, even more narrowly, as a charming demonstration of Mitford family idiolect. The achievement, in other words, has been understood to be one of transcription rather than of writing. But the felicities of Mitford's style cannot, in fact, be reduced to class or period, or even to Hon-ish locutions. There is care – there is art – in the most artless-seeming passages of this novel. Examine the insouciant sentences, the frothy dialogue, carefully, and you will find that they are as precise as algebraic equations: you cannot tinker with their syntax or vocabulary without irrevocably harming the result. Here is Linda, describing to Fanny, in typically breathless fashion, the man who will become her second husband: "Well, he's heaven. He's a frightfully serious man, you know, a Communist, and so am I now, and we are surrounded by comrades all day, and they are terrific Hons, and there's an anarchist. The comrades don't like anarchists, isn't it queer? I always thought they were the same thing, but Christian likes this one because he threw a bomb at the King of Spain; you must say it's romantic. He's called Ramón, and he sits about all day and broods over the miners at Oviedo, because his brother is one."

This is an impeccable spoof on a young woman's dizzy, paratactic speech patterns but it is also a rather deft dramatization of the speaker's complicated attitude towards her new social circle. Linda is in love with Christian – eager to love what he loves – but at the same time, she detects something absurd in the deadly seriousness of the comrades and in her unlikely involvement with them. The tonal distinction between her genuine reverence ("He's a frightfully serious man . . . they are terrific Hons") and her sly amusement (". . . but Christian likes this one because he threw a bomb at the King of Spain") is a subtle one – not least because Mitford's characters have a tendency to sound most wide-eyed when they are at their most satirical. (In her novel *The Blessing*, Mitford sums up the typical English joke as, "naive but penetrating.") Even so, by the time we get to the account of the lugubrious Ramón, and the inspired silliness of the final clause, "because his brother is one," there can be no doubt that Linda has succumbed to the temptation of a classic Mitfordian "tease."

Linda's amused response to Communist earnestness is not untypical of this novel's attitude towards any number of grave causes and important historic movements. Various political philosophies are

adumbrated in the course of the plot, but, with the possible exception of Linda's dreamy defences of England's ancien régime, none
of them are taken remotely seriously. The seminal lesson of Linda's
two failed marriages – the first to a Tory with Nazi sympathies, the
second to Christian – would seem to be that equal degrees of
absurdity and dullness exist at either end of the ideological
spectrum. The only point at which Linda can be said to lose her
intense charm is when she tries, briefly, to take politics seriously.
(Much to Fanny's relief, the experiment is doomed by Linda's constitutional inability to feel "wider love for the poor, the sad and the
unattractive.")

For some, Mitford's brazen indifference to big ideas, coupled
with her minute attention to the sex and love lives of the privileged
upper class, condemn this, and all her other novels, to inconse-
quentiality. Fanny's husband, Alfred, speaks for generations of Mitford's detractors when he rebukes his wife in *Love in a Cold
Climate* for the triviality of her preoccupations: "[G]eneral subjects
do not amuse you, only personalities."

Of course, Alfred and his fellow critics tend to take a rather narrow view of what constitutes the "general." There is, after all, a long
and honourable history of women writers who have used small can-
vases and gossipy plots in the service of expansive moral themes.
(Jane Austen, lest we forget, devoted the entirety of her estimable
oeuvre to posh people's love lives and never once got round to
mentioning the French Revolution or the slave trade.)

I am not sure, however, that we serve Mitford well by attempting
to shoehorn her into this tradition. She is too devoted to making
fun of everything, too allergic to any admission of moral seriousness. If she is flippant about political causes, she is not, in any obvious way, earnest about her characters either. She tends to keep her
protagonists at a coolly amused distance – focusing on their public
performances of themselves and declining to ferret about in their
private emotional states. Even the heroine of this novel remains
largely opaque to us – a "flat" character in Forsterian terms, as

opposed to a "round" one. Fanny offers breezy, rather banal speculations on how ghastly it must be to be married to Tony, or how blissful it must be to have an affair with a Frenchman, but we see for ourselves almost nothing of Linda's interior life – despite the many occasions on which her feckless behaviour cries out to be mitigated by some insight into her conscience.

Any number of modern novelists might take on the daring task of depicting a heroine who rejects her newborn, but the chances are that they would psychologize the act – would ask the reader to enter into the horror and shame of not wanting one's child and so on. Mitford does none of that. She asks us, instead, to laugh at Linda's jokes about the hideousness of little Moira and to accept that in the long run, the child will be much better off with her stepmother, the ghastly, blue-haired Pixie Fairweather. (Children in Mitford's fiction are remarkably hardy, cynical little creatures.)

The writer Andrew O'Hagan is among those who find something ultimately repugnant in such show-off cruelty. He identifies Mitford's style as an exemplar of the "posh aesthetic" – a beguilingly witty school of English prose at whose centre lies a moral void. "The posh aesthetic appeals to people who want life's profundities to scatter on the wind like handfuls of confetti. The great enemy of the posh aesthetic is effortfulness, which is why aristocrats find the middle classes so absurd. All that labour, all that seriousness: so much more stylish to laugh at death, etc . . . For the devoted toff, effort and compassion are embarrassing in life and horrific on the printed page."

There is no use disputing that Mitford's levity, her undisguised preference for amusing sinners over virtuous dullards, her highly stylized complacency in regard to social injustice and class inequities, are all potent provocations. And it may be that an era like ours – an era that sets such store by the uncomplicated generosity and "big-heartedness" of its popular writers – is particularly ill-suited to appreciating her astringent pleasures. Even so, O'Hagan's account of Mitford's style does not seem to me entirely accurate. If Mitford's heart does not lie moistly on her sleeve, it is a mistake to conclude that it is nowhere about her person. And if her humour often flirts with facetiousness, it does not, in the end, I think, represent a dismissal of "life's profundities," so much as a rigorously unsentimental way of coping with those profundities. It would be a very obtuse reader who failed to notice the murmur of pain in this novel, the hints of desolation lurking within its merriment.

The novel begins, in fact, in explicitly elegiac mode, with the contemplation of an old Radlett family photograph. "There they are, held like flies, in the amber of that moment – click goes the camera and on goes life; the minutes, the days, the years, the decades, taking them further and further from that happiness and promise of youth." Fanny moves the narrative along quickly, thrusting us into the gay doings of the young Radlett girls, but the muted note of anguish that is struck here – the minatory intimation of life's pain and disappointment and brevity – continues to sound throughout the novel. We hear it, not in spite of the jokes, or as some sort of pious addendum to the jokes, but resonating from their very centre. Think of Davey and Linda and Fanny in the linen cupboard at Alconleigh, wittily forecasting the way in which their interwar generation will be traduced in future decades. Somewhere in the course of this breezy exchange, the perspective telescopes and we find ourselves glimpsing the skeletons beneath the skins of these gorgeously alive people.

A reader might wish that Mitford wrote passionately and expansively about the miseries of war, and the outrage of death, and the sadness of being in a bad marriage. But it is simply wrong to read her teasing prose as a denial of those experiences. Nor is it quite accurate to say that Mitford is embarrassed by earnestness and effort: she is embarrassed by the *advertisement* of these things, certainly, but the hard work that it takes to keep up a "good shop-front" is something she admires very much. Linda's lover, Fabrice, who speaks so eloquently in defence of *"les gens du monde,"* does in fact have principles for which he is prepared to risk his life: he simply wouldn't dream of boring a lady with those principles at luncheon. Linda herself has plenty of private sorrows: it would just never occur to her to whine about them publicly.

It is the elegance of this discretion – the courage of it – that ultimately redeems Mitford's heroine. More than her beauty or bouquet-like charm, what we are asked to admire in Linda is the bravery with which she pursues her rackety course. Unlike Fanny, who has found in her marriage to Alfred "a refuge from the storms and puzzles of life," Linda has dared to stay out on the romantic heath. And if she is buffeted by the high winds of fleeting passions – if she falls in love with asses and often makes an ass of herself in the process – she has the good sense and the guts to never apologize, never explain. "Don't pity me," she tells Fanny when she returns from France, still married to Christian and pregnant with another man's child. "I've had eleven months of perfect and unalloyed happiness, very few people can say that, in the course of long long lives, I imagine."

Whether it is better to hold out, like Linda, enduring loneliness and infamy in return for the occasional feast of transcendent pleasure, or to settle like Fanny for a steady but uninspiring diet of marital contentment, is one of the great questions of the novel. Fanny envies the glamour of Linda's adventures, but she has too much sense not to be appalled by the radical uncertainty of a life lived according to sensibility. The possibility that her friend will end up with "nothing to show" for her troubles, frightens her. And when she asserts, at the end of the novel, that Linda has found true love with Fabrice, this seems to be her way of reassuring herself that Linda's existence has, after all, had meaning, that her pursuit of love has not been in vain. Fanny's mother, the Bolter (who knows quite a lot about the ways of men like Fabrice), is doubtful. But if her sceptical words – the final words of the novel – seem to point to an utterly comfortless conclusion, Linda herself has shown us one further possibility: that a life lived with passion and brio may have beauty and value, even if one ends up with "nothing to show for it" and that the search for true love is a noble endeavour, whether or not it concludes in domestic bliss.

Zoë Heller is is the author of three novels: *Everything You Know*, *Notes on a Scandal* (shortlisted for the Man Booker Prize), and *The Believers.*

THE PURSUIT OF LOVE

TO GASTON PALEWSKI

Chapter 1

THERE IS A photograph in existence of Aunt Sadie and her six children sitting round the tea-table at Alconleigh. The table is situated, as it was, is now, and ever shall be, in the hall, in front of a huge open fire of logs. Over the chimney-piece plainly visible in the photograph, hangs an entrenching tool, with which, in 1915, Uncle Matthew had whacked to death eight Germans one by one as they crawled out of a dug-out. It is still covered with blood and hairs, an object of fascination to us as children. In the photograph Aunt Sadie's face, always beautiful, appears strangely round, her hair strangely fluffy, and her clothes strangely dowdy, but it is unmistakably she who sits there with Robin, in oceans of lace, lolling on her knee. She seems uncertain what to do with his head, and the presence of Nanny waiting to take him away is felt though not seen. The other children, between Louisa's eleven and Matt's two years, sit round the table in party dresses or frilly bibs, holding cups or mugs according to age, all of them gazing at the camera with large eyes opened wide by the flash, and all looking as if butter would not melt in their round pursed-up mouths. There they are, held like flies in the amber of that moment—click goes the camera and on goes life; the minutes, the days, the years, the decades, taking them further and further from that happiness and promise of youth, from the hopes Aunt Sadie must have had for them, and from the dreams they dreamed for themselves. I often think there is nothing quite so poignantly sad as old family groups.

When a child I spent my Christmas holidays at Alconleigh, it was a regular feature of my life, and, while some of them slipped by with nothing much to remember, others were distinguished by violent occurrences and had a definite character of their own. There was the time, for example, when the servants' wing caught fire, the time when my pony lay on me in the brook and nearly drowned me (not very nearly, he was soon dragged off, but meanwhile bubbles were said to have been observed). There was drama when Linda, aged ten, attempted suicide in order to rejoin an old smelly Border Terrier which Uncle Matthew had had put down. She collected and ate a basketful of yew-berries, was discovered by Nanny and given mustard and water to make her sick. She was then "spoken to" by Aunt Sadie, clipped over the ear by Uncle Matthew, put to bed for two days and given a Labrador puppy, which soon took the place of the old Border in her affections. There was much worse drama when Linda, aged twelve, told the daughters of neighbours, who had come to tea, what she supposed to be the facts of life. Linda's presentation of the "facts" had been so gruesome that the children left Alconleigh howling dismally, their nerves permanently impaired, their future chances of a sane and happy sex life much reduced. This resulted in a series of dreadful punishments, from a real beating, administered by Uncle Matthew, to luncheon upstairs for a week. There was the unforgettable holiday when Uncle Matthew and Aunt Sadie went to Canada. The Radlett children would rush for the newspapers every day hoping to see that their parents' ship had gone down with all aboard; they yearned to be total orphans—especially Linda, who saw herself as Katie in *What Katie Did*, the reins of the household gathered into small but capable hands. The ship met with no iceberg and weathered the Atlantic storms, but meanwhile we had a wonderful holiday, free from rules.

But the Christmas I remember most clearly of all was when I was fourteen and Aunt Emily became engaged. Aunt Emily was Aunt Sadie's sister, and she had brought me up from babyhood, my own mother, their youngest sister, having felt herself too beautiful and too gay to be burdened with a child at the age of nineteen. She left my father when I was a month old, and subsequently ran away so often, and with so many different people, that she became known to her family and friends as the Bolter; while my father's second, and presently his third, fourth and fifth wives, very naturally had no great wish to look after me. Occasionally one of these impetuous parents would appear like a rocket, casting an unnatural glow upon my horizon. They had great glamour, and I longed to be caught up in their fiery trails and be carried away, though in my heart I knew how lucky I was to have Aunt Emily. By degrees, as I grew up, they lost all charm for me; the cold grey rocket cases mouldered where they had happened to fall, my mother with a major in the South of France, my father, his estates sold up to pay his debts, with an old Rumanian countess in the Bahamas. Even before I was grown up much of the glamour with which they had been surrounded had faded, and finally there was nothing left, no foundation of childish memories to make them seem any different from other middle-aged people. Aunt Emily was never glamorous but she was always my mother, and I loved her.

At the time of which I write, however, I was at an age when the least imaginative child supposes itself to be a changeling, a Princess of Indian blood, Joan of Arc, or the future Empress of Russia. I hankered after my parents, put on an idiotic face which was intended to convey mingled suffering and pride when their names were mentioned, and thought of them as engulfed in deep, romantic, deadly sin.

Linda and I were very much preoccupied with sin, and our great hero was Oscar Wilde.

"But what did he do?"

"I asked Fa once and he roared at me—goodness, it was terrifying. He said: 'If you mention that sewer's name again in this house

I'll thrash you, do you hear, damn you?' So I asked Sadie and she looked awfully vague and said: 'Oh, duck, I never really quite knew, but whatever it was was worse than murder, fearfully bad. And, darling, don't talk about him at meals, will you?'"

"We must find out."

"Bob says he will, when he goes to Eton."

"Oh, good! Do you think he was worse than Mummy and Daddy?"

"Surely he couldn't be. Oh, you are so lucky to have wicked parents."

I STUMBLED INTO the hall blinded by the light after a six-mile drive from the station. Aunt Sadie and the children were having tea, under the entrenching tool, just like in the photograph. It was the same table and the same tea-things, the china with large roses on it, the tea-kettle and the silver dish for scones both kept hot over flickering flames; the human beings were five years older. That is to say the babies had become children, the children were growing up. There had been an addition in the shape of Victoria, now aged two. She was waddling about with a chocolate biscuit clenched in her fist, her face was smothered in chocolate and was a horrible sight, but through the sticky mask shone unmistakably the blue of two steady Radlett eyes.

There was a tremendous scraping of chairs as I came in, and a pack of Radletts hurled themselves upon me with the intensity and almost the ferocity of a pack of hounds hurling itself upon a fox. All except Linda. She was the most pleased to see me, but determined not to show it. When the din had quieted down and I was seated before a scone and a cup of tea, she said:

"Where's Brenda?" Brenda was my white mouse.

"She got a sore back and died," I said. Aunt Sadie looked anxiously at Linda.

"Had you been riding her?" said Louisa, facetiously. Matt, who had recently come under the care of a French nursery governess, said in a high-pitched imitation of her voice: "As usual, it was kidney trouble."

"Oh, dear," said Aunt Sadie, under her breath.

Enormous tears were pouring into Linda's plate. Nobody cried so much or so often as she; anything, but especially anything sad about animals, would set her off, and, once begun, it was a job to stop her. She was a delicate, as well as a highly nervous child, and even Aunt Sadie, who lived in a dream as far as the health of her children was concerned, was aware that too much crying kept her awake at night, put her off her food, and did her harm. The other children, and especially Louisa and Bob, who loved to tease, went as far as they dared with her, and were periodically punished for making her cry. *Black Beauty, Owd Bob, The Story of a Red Deer,* and all the Seton Thompson books were on the nursery index because of Linda, who, at one time or another, had been prostrated by them. They had to be hidden away, as, if they were left lying about, she could not be trusted not to indulge in an orgy of self-torture.

Wicked Louisa had invented a poem which never failed to induce rivers of tears:

"A little, houseless match, it has no roof, no thatch,
It lies alone, it makes no moan, that little, houseless match."

When Aunt Sadie was not around the children would chant this in a gloomy chorus. In certain moods one had only to glance at a match-box to dissolve poor Linda; when, however, she was feeling stronger, more fit to cope with life, this sort of teasing would force out of her very stomach an unwilling guffaw. Linda was not only my favourite cousin, but, then and for many years, my favourite human being. I adored all my cousins, and Linda distilled, mentally and physically, the very essence of the Radlett family. Her straight features, straight brown hair and large blue eyes were a theme upon which the faces of the others were a variation; all pretty, but none so absolutely distinctive as hers. There was something furious about her, even when she laughed, which she did a great deal, and always as if forced to against her will. Something reminiscent of pictures of Napoleon in youth, a sort of scowling intensity.

I could see that she was really minding much more about Brenda than I did. The truth was that my honeymoon days with the mouse were long since over; we had settled down to an uninspiring relationship, a form, as it were, of married blight, and, when she had developed a disgusting sore patch on her back, it had been all I could do to behave decently and treat her with common humanity. Apart from the shock it always is to find somebody stiff and cold in their cage in the morning, it had been a very great relief to me when Brenda's sufferings finally came to an end.

"Where is she buried?" Linda muttered furiously, looking at her plate.

"Beside the robin. She's got a dear little cross and her coffin was lined with pink satin."

"Now, Linda darling," said Aunt Sadie, "if Fanny has finished her tea why don't you show her your toad?"

"He's upstairs asleep," said Linda. But she stopped crying.

"Have some nice hot toast, then."

"Can I have Gentleman's Relish on it?" she said, quick to make capital out of Aunt Sadie's mood, for Gentleman's Relish was kept strictly for Uncle Matthew, and supposed not to be good for children. The others made a great show of exchanging significant looks. These were intercepted, as they were meant to be, by Linda, who gave a tremendous bellowing boo-hoo and rushed upstairs.

"I wish you children wouldn't tease Linda," said Aunt Sadie, irritated out of her usual gentleness, and followed her.

The staircase led out of the hall. When Aunt Sadie was beyond earshot, Louisa said: "If wishes were horses beggars would ride. Child hunt tomorrow, Fanny."

"Yes, Josh told me. He was in the car—been to see the vet."

My Uncle Matthew had four magnificent bloodhounds, with

which he used to hunt his children. Two of us would go off with a good start to lay the trail, and Uncle Matthew and the rest would follow the hounds on horseback. It was great fun. Once he came to my home and hunted Linda and me over Shenley Common. This caused the most tremendous stir locally, the Kentish week-enders on their way to church were appalled by the sight of four great hounds in full cry after two little girls. My uncle seemed to them like a wicked lord of fiction, and I became more than ever surrounded with an aura of madness, badness, and dangerousness for their children to know.

The child hunt on the first day of this Christmas visit was a great success. Louisa and I were chosen as hares. We ran across country, the beautiful bleak Cotswold uplands, starting soon after breakfast when the sun was still a red globe, hardly over the horizon, and the trees were etched in dark blue against a pale blue, mauve and pinkish sky. The sun rose as we stumbled on, longing for our second wind; it shone, and there dawned a beautiful day, more like late autumn in its feeling than Christmas-time.

We managed to check the bloodhounds once by running through a flock of sheep, but Uncle Matthew soon got them on the scent again, and, after about two hours of hard running on our part, when we were only half a mile from home, the baying slavering creatures caught up with us, to be rewarded with lumps of meat and many caresses. Uncle Matthew was in a radiantly good temper, he got off his horse and walked home with us, chatting agreeably. What was most unusual, he was even quite affable to me.

"I hear Brenda has died," he said, "no great loss I should say. That mouse stank like merry hell. I expect you kept her cage too near the radiator, I always told you it was unhealthy, or did she die of old age?"

"She was only two," I said, timidly.

Uncle Matthew's charm, when he chose to turn it on, was considerable, but at that time I was always mortally afraid of him, and made the mistake of letting him see that I was.

"You ought to have a dormouse, Fanny, or a rat. They are much more interesting than white mice—though I must frankly say, of all the mice I ever knew, Brenda was the most utterly dismal."

"She was dull," I said, sycophantically.

"When I go to London after Christmas, I'll get you a dormouse. Saw one the other day at the Army & Navy."

"Oh Fa, it *is* unfair," said Linda, who was walking her pony along beside us. "You know how I've always longed for a dormouse."

"It is unfair" was a perpetual cry of the Radletts when young. The great advantage of living in a large family is that early lesson of life's essential unfairness. With them I must say it nearly always operated in favour of Linda, who was the adored of Uncle Matthew.

Today, however, my uncle was angry with her, and I saw in a flash that this affability to me, this genial chat about mice, was simply designed as a tease for her.

"You've got enough animals, miss," he said, sharply. "You can't control the ones you have got. And don't forget what I told you—that dog of yours goes straight to the kennel when we get back, and stays there."

Linda's face crumpled, tears poured, she kicked her pony into a canter and made for home. It seemed that her dog Labby had been sick in Uncle Matthew's business-room after breakfast. Uncle Matthew was unable to bear dirtiness in dogs, he flew into a rage, and, in his rage, had made a rule that never again was Labby to set foot in the house. This was always happening, for one reason or another, to one animal or another, and, Uncle Matthew's bark being invariably much worse than his bite, the ban seldom lasted more than a day or two, after which would begin what he called the Thin End of the Wedge.

"Can I bring him in just while I fetch my gloves?"

"I'm so tired—I can't go to the stables—do let him stay just till after tea."

"Oh, I see—the thin end of the wedge. All right, this time he can stay, but if he makes another mess—or I catch him on your bed—or he chews up the good furniture (according to whichever crime it was that had resulted in banishment), I'll have him destroyed, and don't say I didn't warn you."

All the same, every time sentence of banishment was pronounced, the owner of the condemned would envisage her beloved moping his life away in the solitary confinement of a cold and gloomy kennel.

"Even if I take him out for three hours every day, and go and chat to him for another hour, that leaves twenty hours for him all alone with nothing to do. Oh, why can't dogs read?"

The Radlett children, it will be observed, took a highly anthropomorphic view of their pets.

Today, however, Uncle Matthew was in a wonderfully good temper, and, as we left the stables, he said to Linda, who was sitting crying with Labby in his kennel:

"Are you going to leave that poor brute of yours in there all day?"

Her tears forgotten as if they had never been, Linda rushed into the house with Labby at her heels. The Radletts were always either on a peak of happiness or drowning in black waters of despair; their emotions were on no ordinary plane, they loved or they loathed, they laughed or they cried, they lived in a world of superlatives. Their life with Uncle Matthew was a sort of perpetual Tom Tiddler's ground. They went as far as they dared, sometimes very far indeed, while sometimes, for no apparent reason, he would pounce almost before they had crossed the boundary. Had they been poor children they would probably have been removed from their roaring, raging, whacking papa and sent to an approved home, or, indeed, he himself would have been removed from them and sent to prison for refusing to educate them. Nature, however, provides her own remedies, and no doubt the Radletts had enough of Uncle Matthew in them to enable them to weather storms in which ordinary children like me would have lost their nerve completely.

Chapter 2

IT WAS AN accepted fact at Alconleigh that Uncle Matthew
loathed me. This violent, uncontrolled man, like his children knew
no middle course, he either loved or he hated, and generally, it
must be said, he hated. His reason for hating me was that he hated
my father; they were old Eton enemies. When it became obvious,
and obvious it was from the hour of my conception, that my parents
intended to doorstep me, Aunt Sadie had wanted to bring me up
with Linda. We were the same age, and it had seemed a sensible
plan. Uncle Matthew had categorically refused. He hated my
father, he said, he hated me, but, above all, he hated children, it
was bad enough to have two of his own. (He evidently had not
envisaged so soon having seven, and indeed both he and Aunt
Sadie lived in a perpetual state of surprise at having filled so many
cradles, about the future of whose occupants they seemed to have
no particular policy.) So dear Aunt Emily, whose heart had once
been broken by some wicked dallying monster, and who intended
on this account never to marry, took me on and made a life's work
of me, and I am very thankful that she did. For she believed passionately in the education of women, she took immense pains to
have me properly taught, even going to live at Shenley on purpose

to be near a good day school. The Radlett daughters did practically no lessons. They were taught by Lucille, the French nursery governess, to read and write, they were obliged, though utterly unmusical, to "practise" in the freezing ballroom for one hour a day each, when, their eyes glued to the clock, they would thump out the "Merry Peasant" and a few scales, they were made to go for a French walk with Lucille on all except hunting days, and that was the extent of their education. Uncle Matthew loathed clever females, but he considered that gentlewomen ought, as well as being able to ride, to know French and play the piano. Although as a child I rather naturally envied them their freedom from thrall and bondage, from sums and science, I felt, nevertheless, a priggish satisfaction that I was not growing up unlettered, as they were.

Aunt Emily did not often come with me to Alconleigh. Perhaps she had an idea that it was more fun for me to be there on my own, and no doubt it was a change for her to get away and spend Christmas with the friends of her youth, and leave for a bit the responsibilities of her old age. Aunt Emily at this time was forty, and we children had long ago renounced on her behalf the world, the flesh, and the devil. This year, however, she had gone away from Shenley before the holidays began, saying that she would see me at Alconleigh in January.

ON THE AFTERNOON of the child hunt Linda called a meeting of the Hons. The Hons was the Radlett secret society, anybody who was not a friend to the Hons was a Counter-Hon, and their battle-cry was "Death to the horrible Counter-Hons." I was a Hon, since my father, like theirs, was a lord.

There were also, however, many honorary Hons; it was not necessary to have been born a Hon in order to be one. As Linda once remarked: "Kind hearts are more than coronets, and simple faith than Norman blood." I'm not sure how much we really believed this, we were wicked snobs in those days, but we subscribed to the general idea. Head of the hon. Hons was Josh, the groom, who was greatly beloved by us all and worth buckets of Norman blood; chief of the horrible Counter-Hons was Craven, the gamekeeper, against whom a perpetual war to the knife was waged. The Hons would creep into the woods and hide Craven's steel traps, let out the chaffinches which, in wire cages without food or water, he used as bait for hawks, give decent burial to the victims of his gamekeeper's larder, and, before a meet of the hounds, unblock the earths which Craven had so carefully stopped.

The poor Hons were tormented by the cruelties of the country-side, while, to me, holidays at Alconleigh were a perfect revelation of beastliness. Aunt Emily's little house was in a village; it was a Queen Anne box; red brick, white panelling, a magnolia tree and a delicious fresh smell. Between it and the country were a neat little garden, an ironwork fence, a village green and a village. The country one then came to was very different from Gloucestershire, it was emasculated, sheltered, over-cultivated, almost a suburban garden. At Alconleigh the cruel woods crept right up to the house; it was not unusual to be awoken by the screams of a rabbit running in horrified circles round a stoat, by the strange and awful cry of the dog-fox, or to see from one's bedroom window a live hen being carried away in the mouth of a vixen; while the roosting pheasant and the waking owl filled every night with wild primeval noise. In the winter, when snow covered the ground, we could trace the footprints of many creatures. These often ended in a pool of blood, a mass of fur or feathers, bearing witness to successful hunting by the carnivores.

On the other side of the house, within a stone's throw, was the Home Farm. Here the slaughtering of poultry and pigs, the castration of lambs and the branding of cattle, took place as a matter of course, out in the open for whomever might be passing by to see. Even dear old Josh made nothing of firing, with red-hot irons, a favourite horse after the hunting season.

"You can only do two legs at a time," he would say, hissing through his teeth as though one were a horse and he grooming one, "otherwise they can't stand the pain."

Linda and I were bad at standing pain ourselves, and found it intolerable that animals should have to lead such tormented lives and tortured deaths. (I still do mind, very much indeed, but in those days at Alconleigh it was an absolute obsession with us all.)

The humanitarian activities of the Hons were forbidden, on pain of punishment, by Uncle Matthew, who was always and entirely on the side of Craven, his favourite servant. Pheasants and partridges must be preserved, vermin must be put down rigorously, all except the fox, for whom a more exciting death was in store. Many and many a whacking did the poor Hons suffer, week after week their pocket-money was stopped, they were sent to bed early, given extra practising to do; nevertheless they bravely persisted with their discouraged and discouraging activities. Huge cases full of new steel traps would arrive periodically from the Army & Navy Stores, and lie stacked until required round Craven's hut in the middle of the wood (an old railway carriage was his headquarters, situated, most inappropriately, among the primroses and blackberry bushes of a charming little glade); hundreds of traps, making one feel the futility of burying, at a great risk to life and property, a paltry three or four. Sometimes we would find a screaming animal held in one; it would take all our reserves of courage to go up to it and let it out, to see it run away with three legs and a dangling mangled horror. We knew that it then probably died of blood-poisoning in its lair; Uncle Matthew would rub in this fact, sparing no agonizing detail of the long drawn-out ordeal, but, though we knew it would be kinder, we could never bring ourselves to kill them; it was asking too much. Often, as it was, we had to go away and be sick after these episodes.

The Hons' meeting-place was an unused linen cupboard at the top of the house, small, dark, and intensely hot. As in so many country houses, the central-heating apparatus at Alconleigh had been installed in the early days of the invention, at enormous expense, and was now thoroughly out of date. In spite of a boiler which would not have been too large for an Atlantic liner, in spite of the tons of coke which it consumed daily, the temperature of the living-rooms was hardly affected, and all the heat there was seemed to concentrate in the Hons' cupboard, which was always stifling. Here we would sit, huddled up on the slatted shelves, and talk for hours about life and death.

Last holidays our great obsession had been childbirth, on which entrancing subject we were informed remarkably late, having supposed for a long time that a mother's stomach swelled up for nine months and then burst open like a ripe pumpkin, shooting out the infant. When the real truth dawned upon us it seemed rather an anticlimax, until Linda produced, from some novel, and read out loud in ghoulish tones, the description of a woman in labour.

"Her breath comes in great gulps—sweat pours down her brow like water—screams as of a tortured animal rend the air—and can this face, twisted with agony, be that of my darling Rhona—can this torture-chamber really be our bedroom, this rack our marriage-bed? 'Doctor, doctor,' I cried, 'do something'—I rushed out into the night—" and so on.

We were rather disturbed by this, realizing that too probably we in our turn would have to endure these fearful agonies. Aunt Sadie, who had only just finished having her seven children, when appealed to, was not very reassuring.

"Yes," she said, vaguely. "It is the worst pain in the world. But the funny thing is, you always forget in between what it's like. Each time, when it began, I felt like saying, 'Oh, now I can remember, stop it, stop it.' And, of course, by then it was nine months too late to stop it."

At this point Linda began to cry, saying how dreadful it must be for cows, which brought the conversation to an end.

It was difficult to talk to Aunt Sadie about sex; something always seemed to prevent one; babies were the nearest we ever got to it. She and Aunt Emily, feeling at one moment that we ought to know more, and being, I suspect, too embarrassed to enlighten us themselves, gave us a modern text-book on the subject.

We got hold of some curious ideas.

"Jassy," said Linda one day, scornfully, "is obsessed, poor thing, with sex."

"Obsessed with sex!" said Jassy, "there's nobody so obsessed as you, Linda. Why if I so much as look at a picture you say I'm a pyg-malionist."

In the end we got far more information out of a book called *Ducks and Duck Breeding*.

"Ducks can only copulate," said Linda, after studying this for a while, "in running water. Good luck to them."

This Christmas Eve we all packed into the Hons' meeting-place to hear what Linda had to say—Louisa, Jassy, Bob, Matt and I.

"Talk about back-to-the-womb," said Jassy.

"Poor Aunt Sadie," I said. "I shouldn't think she'd want you all back in hers."

"You never know. Now rabbits eat their children—somebody ought to explain to them how it's only a complex."

"How can one *explain* to *rabbits*? That's what is so worrying about animals, they simply don't understand when they're spoken to, poor angels. I'll tell you what about Sadie though, she'd like to be back in one herself, she's got a thing for boxes and that always shows. Who else—Fanny, what about you?"

"I don't think I would, but then I imagine the one I was in wasn't very comfortable at the time you know, and nobody else has ever been allowed to stay there."

"Abortions?" said Linda with interest.

"Well, tremendous jumpings and hot baths anyway."

"How *do* you know?"

"I once heard Aunt Emily and Aunt Sadie talking about it when I was very little, and afterwards I remembered. Aunt Sadie said: 'How does she manage it?' and Aunt Emily said: 'Skiing, or hunting, or just jumping off the kitchen table.'"

"You are so lucky, having wicked parents."

This was the perpetual refrain of the Radletts, and, indeed, my wicked parents constituted my chief interest in their eyes—I was really a very dull little girl in other respects.

"The news I have for the Hons today," said Linda, clearing her throat like a grown-up person, "while of considerable Hon interest generally, particularly concerns Fanny. I won't ask you to guess, because it's nearly tea-time and you never could, so I'll tell straight out. Aunt Emily is engaged."

There was a gasp from the Hons in chorus.

"Linda," I said, furiously, "you've made it up." But I knew she couldn't have.

Linda brought a piece of paper out of her pocket. It was a half-sheet of writing-paper, evidently the end of a letter, covered with Aunt Emily's large babyish handwriting, and I looked over Linda's shoulder as she read it out:

". . . not tell the children we're engaged, what d'you think darling, just at first? But then suppose Fanny takes a dislike to him, though I don't see how she could, but children are so funny, won't it be more of a shock? Oh, dear, I can't decide. Anyway, do what you think best, darling, we'll arrive on Thursday, and I'll telephone on Wednesday evening and see what's happened. All love from Emily."

Sensation in the Hons' cupboard.

Chapter 3

"Bᴜᴛ ᴡʜʏ?" I said, for the hundredth time. Linda, Louisa and I were packed into Louisa's bed, with Bob sitting on the end of it, chatting in whispers. These midnight talks were most strictly forbidden, but it was safer, at Alconleigh, to disobey rules during the early part of the night than at any other time in the twenty-four hours. Uncle Matthew fell asleep practically at the dinner-table. He would then doze in his business-room for an hour or so before dragging himself, in a somnambulist trance, to bed, where he slept the profound sleep of one who has been out of doors all day until cockcrow the following morning, when he became very much awake. This was the time for his never-ending warfare with the housemaids over wood-ash. The rooms at Alconleigh were heated by wood fires, and Uncle Matthew maintained, rightly, that if these were to function properly, all the ash ought to be left in the fireplaces in a great hot smouldering heap. Every housemaid, however, for some reason (an early training with coal fires probably) was bent on removing this ash altogether. When shakings, imprecations, and being pounced out at by Uncle Matthew in his paisley dressing-gown at six a.m., had convinced them that this was really not feasible, they became absolutely determined to remove, by hook or by crook, just a little, a shovelful or so, every morning. I can only suppose they felt that like this they were asserting their personalities.

The result was guerrilla warfare at its most exciting. Housemaids are notoriously early risers, and can usually count upon three clear hours when a house belongs to them alone. But not at Alconleigh. Uncle Matthew was always, winter and summer alike, out of his bed by five a.m., and it was then his habit to wander about, looking like Great Agrippa in his dressing-gown, and drinking endless cups of tea out of a thermos flask, until about seven, when he would have his bath. Breakfast for my uncle, my aunt, family and guests alike, was sharp at eight, and unpunctuality was not tolerated. Uncle Matthew was no respecter of other people's early morning sleep, and, after five o'clock one could not count on any, for he raged round the house, clanking cups of tea, shouting at his dogs, roaring at the housemaids, cracking the stock whips which he had brought back from Canada on the lawn with a noise greater than gun-fire, and all to the accompaniment of Galli Curci on his gramophone, an abnormally loud one with an enormous horn, through which would be shrieked "Una voce poco fa"—"The Mad Song" from *Lucia*—"Lo, here the gen-tel lar-ha-hark"—and so on, played at top speed, thus rendering them even higher and more screeching than they ought to be.

Nothing reminds me of my childhood days at Alconleigh so much as those songs. Uncle Matthew played them incessantly for years, until the spell was broken when he went all the way to Liverpool to hear Galli Curci in person. The disillusionment caused by her appearance was so great that the records remained ever after silent, and were replaced by the deepest bass voices that money could buy.

"Fearful the death of the diver must be,
Walking alone in the de-he-he-he-he-epths of the sea"
or "Drake is going West, lads."

These were, on the whole, welcomed by the family, as rather less piercing at early dawn.

"WHY SHOULD SHE want to be married?"

"It's not as though she could be in love. She's forty."

Like all the very young we took it for granted that making love is child's play.

"How old do you suppose he is?"

"Fifty or sixty I guess. Perhaps she thinks it would be nice to be a widow. Weeds, you know."

"Perhaps she thinks Fanny ought to have a man's influence."

"Man's influence!" said Louisa. "I foresee trouble. Supposing he falls in love with Fanny, that'll be a pretty kettle of fish, like Somerset and Princess Elizabeth—he'll be playing rough games and pinching you in bed, see if he doesn't."

"Surely not, at his age."

"Old men love little girls."

"And little boys," said Bob.

"It looks as if Aunt Sadie isn't going to say anything about it before they come," I said.

"There's nearly a week to go—she may be deciding. She'll talk it over with Fa. Might be worth listening next time she has a bath. You can, Bob."

CHRISTMAS DAY WAS spent, as usual at Alconleigh, between alternate bursts of sunshine and showers. I put, as children can, the disturbing news about Aunt Emily out of my mind, and concentrated upon enjoyment. At about six o'clock Linda and I unstuck our sleepy eyes and started on our stockings. Our real presents came later, at breakfast and on the tree, but the stockings were a wonderful *hors d'oeuvre* and full of treasures. Presently Jassy came in and started selling us things out of hers. Jassy only cared about money because she was saving up to run away—she carried her post office book about with her everywhere, and always knew to a farthing what she had got. This was then translated by a miracle of determination, as Jassy was very bad at sums, into so many days in a bed-sitting-room.

"How are you getting on, Jassy?"

"My fare to London and a month and two days and an hour and a half in a bed-sitter, with basin and breakfast."

Where the other meals would come from was left to the imagination. Jassy studied advertisements of bed-sitters in *The Times* every morning. The cheapest she had found so far was in Clapham. So eager was she for the cash that would transform her dream into reality, that one could be certain of picking up a few bargains round about Christmas and her birthday. Jassy at this time was aged eight.

I must admit that my wicked parents turned up trumps at Christmas, and my presents from them were always the envy of the entire household. This year my mother, who was in Paris, sent a gilded bird-cage full of stuffed humming-birds which, when wound up, twittered and hopped about and drank at a fountain. She also sent a fur hat and a gold and topaz bracelet, whose glamour was enhanced by the fact that Aunt Sadie considered them unsuitable for a child, and said so. My father sent a pony and cart, a very smart and beautiful little outfit, which had arrived some days before, and been secreted by Josh in the stables.

"So typical of that damned fool Edward to send it here," Uncle Matthew said, "and give us all the trouble of getting it to Shenley. And I bet poor old Emily won't be too pleased. Who on earth is going to look after it?"

Linda cried with envy. "It *is* unfair," she kept saying, "that you should have wicked parents and not me."

We persuaded Josh to take us for a drive after luncheon. The pony was an angel and the whole thing easily managed by a child, even the harnessing. Linda wore my hat and drove the pony. We got back late for the Tree—the house was already full of tenants and their children; Uncle Matthew, who was struggling into his Father Christmas clothes, roared at us so violently that Linda had to go and cry upstairs, and was not there to collect her own present from him. Uncle Matthew had taken some trouble to get her a longed-for dormouse and was greatly put out by this; he roared at everybody in turn, and ground his dentures. There was a legend in the family that he had already ground away four pairs in his rages.

The evening came to a climax of violence when Matt produced a box of fireworks which my mother had sent him from Paris. On the box they were called *Pétards*. Somebody said to Matt: "What do they do?" to which he replied: "*Bien, ça péte, quoi?*" This remark, overheard by Uncle Matthew, was rewarded with a first-class hiding, which was actually most unfair, as poor Matt was only repeating what Lucille had said to him earlier in the day. Matt, however, regarded hidings as a sort of natural phenomenon, unconnected with any actions of his own, and submitted to them philosophically enough. I have often wondered since how it was that Aunt Sadie could have chosen Lucille, who was the very acme of vulgarity, to look after her children. We all loved her, she was gay and spirited and read aloud to us without cease, but her language really was extraordinary, and provided dreadful pitfalls for the unwary.

"*Qu'est-ce que c'est ce custard, qu'on fout partout?*"

I shall never forget Matt quite innocently making this remark in Fullers at Oxford, where Uncle Matthew had taken us for a treat. The consequences were awful.

It never seemed to occur to Uncle Matthew that Matt could not know these words by nature, and that it would really have been more fair to check them at their source.

Chapter 4

I NATURALLY AWAITED THE arrival of Aunt Emily and her future intended with some agitation. She was, after all, my real mother, and, greatly as I might hanker after that glittering evil person who bore me, it was to Aunt Emily that I turned for the solid, sustaining, though on the face of it uninteresting, relationship that is provided by motherhood at its best. Our little household at Shenley was calm and happy and afforded an absolute contrast to the agitations and tearing emotions of Alconleigh. It may have been dull, but it was a sheltering harbour, and I was always glad to get back to it. I think I was beginning dimly to realize how much it all centered upon me; the very timetable, with its early luncheon and high tea, was arranged to fit in with my lessons and bedtime. Only during those holidays when I went to Alconleigh did Aunt Emily have any life of her own, and even these breaks were infrequent, as she had an idea that Uncle Matthew and the whole stormy set-up there were bad for my nerves. I may not have been consciously aware of the extent to which Aunt Emily had regulated her existence round mine, but I saw, only too clearly, that the addition of a man to our establishment was going to change everything. Hardly knowing any men outside the family, I imagined them all to be modelled on the lines of Uncle Matthew, or of my own seldom seen, violently emotional papa, either of whom, plunging about in that neat little house, would have been sadly out of place. I was filled with apprehension, almost with horror, and, greatly assisted by the workings of Louisa's and Linda's vivid imaginations, had got myself into a real state of nerves. Louisa was now teasing me with the *Constant Nymph*. She read aloud the last chapters, and soon I was dying at a Brussels boardinghouse, in the arms of Aunt Emily's husband.

On Wednesday Aunt Emily rang up Aunt Sadie, and they talked for ages. The telephone at Alconleigh was, in those days, situated in a glass cupboard halfway down the brilliantly lighted back passage; there was no extension, and eavesdropping was thus rendered impossible. (In later years it was moved to Uncle Matthew's business-room, with an extension, after which all privacy was at an end.) When Aunt Sadie returned to the drawing-room she said nothing except: "Emily is coming tomorrow on the three-five. She sends you her love, Fanny."

The next day we all went out hunting. The Radletts loved animals, they loved foxes, they risked dreadful beatings in order to unstop their earths, they read and cried and rejoiced over Reynard the Fox, in summer they got up at four to go and see the cubs playing in the pale-green light of the woods; nevertheless, more than anything in the world, they loved hunting. It was in their blood and bones and in my blood and bones, and nothing could eradicate it, though we knew it for a kind of original sin. For three hours that day I forgot everything except my body and my pony's body; the rushing, the scrambling, the splashing, struggling up the hills, sliding down them again, the tugging, the bucketing, the earth and the sky. I forgot everything, I could hardly have told you my name. That must be the great hold that hunting has over people, especially stupid people; it enforces an absolute concentration, both mental and physical.

After three hours Josh took me home. I was never allowed to stay out long or I got tired and would be sick all night. Josh was out on Uncle Matthew's second horse; at about two o'clock they changed over, and he started home on the lathered, sweating first horse, taking me with him. I came out of my trance, and saw that the day, which had begun with brilliant sunshine, was now cold and dark, threatening rain.

"And where's her ladyship hunting this year?" said Josh, as we started on a ten-mile jog along the Merlinford road, a sort of hog's back, more cruelly exposed than any road I have ever known, without a scrap of shelter or windscreen the whole of its fifteen miles. Uncle Matthew would never allow motorcars, either to take us to the meet or to fetch us home; he regarded this habit as despicably soft.

I knew that Josh meant my mother. He had been with my grandfather when she and her sisters were girls, and my mother was his heroine, he adored her.

"She's in Paris, Josh."

"In Paris—what for?"

"I suppose she likes it."

"Ho," said Josh, furiously, and we rode for about half a mile in silence. The rain had begun, a thin cold rain, sweeping over the wide views on each side of the road; we trotted along, the weather in our faces. My back was not strong, and trotting on a side-saddle for any length of time was agony to me. I edged my pony onto the grass, and cantered for a bit, but I knew how much Josh disapproved of this, it was supposed to bring the horses back too hot; walking, on the other hand, chilled them. It had to be jog, jog, back-breaking jog, all the way.

"It's my opinion," said Josh at last, "that her ladyship is wasted, downright wasted, every minute of her life that she's not on a 'oss."

"She's a wonderful rider, isn't she?"

I had had all this before from Josh, many times, and could never have enough of it.

"There's no human being like her, that I've ever seen," said Josh, hissing through his teeth. "Hands like velvet, but strong like iron, and her seat—! Now look at you, jostling about on that saddle, first here, then there—we shall have a sore back tonight, that's one thing certain we shall."

"Oh, Josh—trotting. And I'm so tired."

"Never saw her tired. I've seen 'er change 'osses after a ten-mile point, get onto a fresh young five-year-old what hadn't been out for a week—up like a bird—never know you had 'er foot in your hand, pick up the reins in a jiffy, catch up its head, and off and over a post and rails and bucking over the ridge and furrow, sitting like a rock. Now his lordship (he meant Uncle Matthew) he can ride, I don't say the contrary, but look how he sends the 'osses home, so darned tired they can't drink their gruel. He can ride all right, but he doesn't study his 'oss. I never knew your mother bring them home like this, she'd know when they'd had enough, and then head for home and no looking back. Mind you, his lordship's a great big man, I don't say the contrary, rides every bit of sixteen stone, but he has great big 'osses and half kills them, and then who has to stop up with them all night? Me!"

The rain was pouring down by now. An icy trickle was feeling its way past my left shoulder, and my right boot was slowly filling with water, the pain in my back was like a knife. I felt that I couldn't bear another moment of this misery, and yet I knew I must bear another five miles, another forty minutes. Josh gave me scornful looks as my back bent more and more double; I could see that he was wondering how it was that I could be my mother's child.

"Miss Linda," he said, "takes after her ladyship something wonderful."

At last, at last, we were off the Merlinford road, coming down the valley into Alconleigh village, turning up the hill to Alconleigh house, through the lodge gates, up the drive, and into the stable yard. I got stiffly down, gave the pony to one of Josh's stable boys, and stumped away, walking like an old man. I was nearly at the front door before I remembered, with a sudden leap of my heart, that Aunt Emily would have arrived by now, with HIM. It was quite a minute before I could summon up enough courage to open the front door.

Sure enough, standing with their backs to the hall fire, were Aunt Sadie, Aunt Emily, and a small, fair, and apparently young man. My immediate impression was that he did not seem at all like a husband. He looked kind and gentle.

"Here is Fanny," said my aunts in chorus.

"Darling," said Aunt Sadie, "can I introduce Captain Warbeck?"

I shook hands in the abrupt graceless way of little girls of four-teen, and thought that he did not seem at all like a captain either.

"Oh, darling, how wet you are. I suppose the others won't be back for ages—where have you come from?"

"I left them drawing the spinney by the Old Rose."

Then I remembered, being after all a female in the presence of a male, how dreadful I always looked when I got home from hunting, splashed from head to foot, my bowler all askew, my hair a bird's nest, my stock a flapping flag, and, muttering something, I made for the back stairs, towards my bath and my rest. After hunting we were kept in bed for at least two hours. Soon Linda returned, even wetter than I had been, and got into bed with me. She, too, had seen the Captain, and agreed that he looked neither like a marrying nor like a military man.

"Can't see him killing Germans with an entrenching tool," she said, scornfully.

Much as we feared, much as we disapproved of, passionately as we sometimes hated Uncle Matthew, he still remained for us a sort of criterion of English manhood; there seemed something not quite right about any man who greatly differed from him.

"I bet Uncle Matthew gives him rat week," I said, apprehensive for Aunt Emily's sake.

"Poor Aunt Emily, perhaps he'll make her keep him in the stables," said Linda with a gust of giggles.

"Still, he looks rather nice you know, and, considering her age, I should think she's lucky to get anybody."

"I can't wait to see him with Fa."

However, our expectations of blood and thunder were disappointed, for it was evident at once that Uncle Matthew had taken an enormous fancy to Captain Warbeck. As he never altered his first opinion of people, and as his few favourites could commit nameless crimes without doing wrong in his eyes, Captain Warbeck was, henceforward, on an infallible wicket with Uncle Matthew.

"He's such a frightfully clever cove, literary you know, you wouldn't believe the things he does. He writes books, and criticizes pictures, and whacks hell out of the piano, though the pieces he plays aren't up to much. Still, you can see what it would be like, if he learnt some of the tunes out of the *Country Girl*, for instance. Nothing would be too difficult for him, you can see that."

At dinner Captain Warbeck sitting next to Aunt Sadie, and Aunt Emily next to Uncle Matthew, were separated from each other, not only by four of us children (Bob was allowed to dine down, as he was going to Eton next half), but also by pools of darkness. The dining-room table was lit by three electric bulbs hanging in a bunch from the ceiling, and screened by a curtain of dark-red jap silk with a gold fringe. One spot of brilliant light was thus cast into the middle of the table, while the diners themselves, and their plates, sat outside it in total gloom. We all, naturally, had our eyes fixed upon the shadowy figure of the fiancé, and found a great deal in his behaviour to interest us. He talked to Aunt Sadie at first about gardens, plants and flowering shrubs, a topic which was unknown at Alconleigh. The gardener saw to the garden, and that was that. It was quite half a mile from the house, and nobody went near it, except as a little walk sometimes in the summer. It seemed strange that a man who lived in London should know the names, the habits, and the medicinal properties of so many plants. Aunt Sadie politely tried to keep up with him, but could not altogether conceal her ignorance, though she partly veiled it in a mist of absent-mindedness.

"And what is your soil here?" asked Captain Warbeck.

Aunt Sadie came down from the clouds with a happy smile, and said, triumphantly, for here was something she did know, "Clay."

"Ah, yes," said the Captain.

He produced a little jewelled box, took from it an enormous pill, swallowed it, to our amazement, without one sip to help it down, and said, as though to himself, but quite distinctly,

"Then the water here will be madly binding."

When Logan, the butler, offered him shepherd's pie, (the food at Alconleigh was always good and plentiful, but of the homely schoolroom description) he said, again so that one did not quite know whether he meant to be overheard or not:

"No, thank you, no twice-cooked meat. I am a wretched invalid, I must be careful, or I pay."

Aunt Sadie, who so much disliked hearing about health that people often took her for a Christian Scientist, which, indeed, she might have become had she not disliked hearing about religion even more, took absolutely no notice, but Bob asked with interest, what it was that twice-cooked meat did to one.

"Oh, it imposes a most fearful strain on the juices, you might as well eat leather," replied Captain Warbeck, faintly, heaping onto his plate the whole of the salad. He said, again in that withdrawn voice:

"Raw lettuce, anti-scorbutic," and, opening another box of even larger pills, he took two, murmuring, "Protein."

"How delicious your bread is," he said to Aunt Sadie, as though to make up for his rudeness in refusing the twice-cooked meat. "I'm sure it has the germ."

"What?" said Aunt Sadie, turning from a whispered confabulation with Logan ("ask Mrs. Crabbe if she could quickly make some more salad").

"I was saying that I feel sure your delicious bread is made of stone-ground flour, containing a high proportion of the germ. In my bedroom at home I have a picture of a grain of wheat (magnified, naturally) which shows the germ. As you know, in white bread the germ, with its wonderful health-giving properties, is eliminated—extracted, I should say—and put into chicken food. As a result the human race is becoming enfeebled, while hens grow larger and stronger with every generation."

"So in the end," said Linda, listening all agog, more than could be said for Aunt Sadie, who had retired into a cloud of boredom, "Hens will be Hons and Hons will be Hens. Oh, how I should love to live in a dear little Hon-house."

"You wouldn't like your work," said Bob. "I once saw a hen laying an egg, and she had a most terrible expression on her face."

"Only about like going to the lav," said Linda.

"Now, Linda," said Aunt Sadie, sharply, "that's quite unnecessary. Get on with your supper and don't talk so much."

Vague as she was, Aunt Sadie could not always be counted on to ignore everything that was happening around her.

"What were you telling me, Captain Warbeck, something about germs?"

"Oh, not germs—the germ—"

At this point I became aware that, in the shadows at the other end of the table, Uncle Matthew and Aunt Emily were having one of their usual set-tos, and that it concerned me. Whenever Aunt Emily came to Alconleigh these tussles with Uncle Matthew would occur, but, all the same, one could see that he was fond of her. He always liked people who stood up to him, and also he probably saw in her a reflection of Aunt Sadie, whom he adored. Aunt Emily was more positive than Aunt Sadie, she had more character and less beauty, and she was not worn out with childbirth, but they were very much sisters. My mother was utterly different in every respect, but then she, poor thing, was, as Linda would have said, obsessed with sex.

Uncle Matthew and Aunt Emily were now engaged upon an argument we had all heard many times before. It concerned the education of females.

Uncle Matthew: "I hope poor Fanny's school (the word school pronounced in tones of withering scorn) is doing her all the good you think it is. Certainly she picks up some dreadful expressions there."

Aunt Emily, calmly, but on the defensive: "Very likely she does. She also picks up a good deal of education."

Uncle Matthew: "Education! I was always led to suppose that no educated person ever spoke of notepaper, and yet I hear poor Fanny asking Sadie for notepaper. What is this education? Fanny talks about mirrors and mantelpieces, handbags and perfume, she takes sugar in her coffee, has a tassel on her umbrella, and I have no doubt that, if she is ever fortunate enough to catch a husband, she will call his father and mother Father and Mother. Will the wonderful education she is getting make up to the unhappy brute for all these endless pinpricks? Fancy hearing one's wife talk about notepaper—the irritation!"

Aunt Emily: "A lot of men would find it more irritating to have a wife who had never heard of George III. (All the same, Fanny darling, it is called writing-paper you know—don't let's hear any more about note, please.) That is where you and I come in you see, Matthew, home influence is admitted to be a most important part of education."

Uncle Matthew: "There you are—"

Aunt Emily: "A most important, but not by any means the most important."

Uncle Matthew: "You don't have to go to some awful middle-class establishment in order to know who George III was. Anyway, who was he, Fanny?"

Alas, I always failed to shine on these occasions. My wits scattered to the four winds by my terror of Uncle Matthew, I said, scarlet in the face:

"He was king. He went mad."

"Most original, full of information," said Uncle Matthew, sarcastically. "Well worth losing every ounce of feminine charm to find that out, I must say. Legs like gateposts from playing hockey, and the worst seat on a horse of any woman I ever knew. Give a horse a sore back as soon as look at it. Linda, you're uneducated, thank God, what have you got to say about George III?"

"Well," said Linda, her mouth full, "he was the son of poor Fred and the father of Beau Brummell's fat friend, and he was one of those vacillators you know. 'I am his Highness's dog at Kew, pray tell me, sir, whose dog are you?'" she added, inconsequently. "Oh, how sweet!"

Uncle Matthew shot a look of cruel triumph at Aunt Emily. I saw that I had let down the side and began to cry, inspiring Uncle Matthew to fresh bouts of beastliness.

"It's a lucky thing that Fanny will have £15,000 a year of her own," he said, "not to speak of any settlements the Bolter may have picked up in the course of her career. She'll get a husband all right, even if she does talk about lunch, and *en*velope, and put the milk in first. I'm not afraid of that, I only say she'll drive the poor devil to drink when she has hooked him."

Aunt Emily gave Uncle Matthew a furious frown. She had always tried to conceal from me the fact that I was an heiress, and, indeed, I only was one until such time as my father, hale and hearty and in the prime of life, should marry somebody of an age to bear children. It so happened that, like the Hanoverian family, he only cared for women when they were over forty; after my mother had left him he had embarked upon a succession of middle-aged wives whom even the miracles of modern science were unable to render fruitful. It was also believed, wrongly, by the grown-ups that we children were ignorant of the fact that my mamma was called the Bolter.

"All this," said Aunt Emily, "is quite beside the point. Fanny may possibly, in the far future, have a little money of her own (though it is ludicrous to talk of £15,000). Whether she does, or does not, the man she marries may be able to support her—on the other hand, the modern world being what it is, she may have to earn her own living. In any case she will be a more mature, a happier, a more interested and interesting person if she—"

"If she knows that George III was a king and went mad."

All the same, my aunt was right, and I knew it and she knew it. The Radlett children read enormously by fits and starts in the library at Alconleigh, a good representative nineteenth-century library, which had been made by their grandfather, a most cultivated man. But, while they picked up a great deal of heterogeneous information, and gilded it with their own originality, while they bridged gulfs of ignorance with their charm and high spirits, they never acquired any habit of concentration, they were incapable of solid hard work. One result, in later life, was that they could not stand boredom. Storms and difficulties left them unmoved, but day after day of ordinary existence produced an unbearable torture of ennui, because they completely lacked any form of mental discipline.

As we trailed out of the dining-room after dinner, we heard Captain Warbeck say:

"No port, no, thank you. Such a delicious drink, but I must refuse. It's the acid from port that makes one so delicate now."

"Ah—you've been a great port drinker, have you?" said Uncle Matthew.

"Oh, not me, I've never touched it. My ancestors—"

Presently, when they joined us in the drawing-room, Aunt Sadie said: "The children know the news now."

"I suppose they think it's a great joke," said Davey Warbeck, "old people like us being married."

"Oh, no, of course not," we said, politely, blushing.

"He's an extraordinary fella," said Uncle Matthew, "knows everything. He says those Charles II sugar casters are only a Georgian imitation of Charles II, just fancy, not valuable at all. Tomorrow we'll go round the house and I'll show you all our things and you can tell us what's what. Quite useful to have a fella like you in the family, I must say."

"That will be very nice," said Davey, faintly, "and now I think, if you don't mind, I'll go to bed. Yes, please, early morning tea—so necessary to replace the evaporation of the night."

He shook hands with us all, and hurried from the room, saying to himself: "Wooing, so tired."

"DAVEY WARBECK IS a hon," said Bob as we were all coming down to breakfast next day.

"Yes, he seems a terrific Hon," said Linda, sleepily.

"No, I mean he's a real one. Look, there's a letter for him, The Hon. David Warbeck. I've looked him up, and it's true."

Bob's favourite book at this time was Debrett, his nose was never out of it. As a result of his researches he was once heard informing Lucille that "The origins of the Radlett family are lost in the fogs of antiquity."

"He's only a second son, and the eldest has got an heir, so I'm afraid Aunt Emily won't be a lady. And his father's only the second Baron, created 1860, and they only start in 1720, before that it's the female line." Bob's voice was trailing off. "Still—" he said.

We heard Davey Warbeck, as he was coming down the stairs, say to Uncle Matthew:

"Oh no, that couldn't be a Reynolds. Prince Hoare, at his very worst, if you're lucky."

"Pig's thinkers, Davey?" Uncle Matthew lifted the lid of a hot dish.

"Oh, yes please, Matthew, if you mean brains. So digestible."

"And after breakfast I'm going to show you our collection of minerals in the north passage. I bet you'll agree we've got something worth having there, it's supposed to be the finest collection in England—left me by an old uncle, who spent his life making it. Meanwhile, what'd you think of my eagle?"

"Ah, if that were Chinese now, it would be a treasure. But Jap I'm afraid, not worth the bronze it's cast in. Cooper's Oxford, please, Linda."

After breakfast we all flocked to the north passage, where there were hundreds of stones in glass-fronted cupboards. Petrified this and fossilized that, blue-john and lapis were the most exciting, large flints which looked as if they had been picked up by the side of the road, the least. Valuable, unique, they were a family legend. "The minerals in the north passage are good enough for a museum." We children revered them. Davey looked at them carefully, taking some over to the window and peering into them. Finally, he heaved a great sigh and said:

"What a beautiful collection. I suppose you know they're all diseased?"

"Diseased?"

"Badly, and too far gone for treatment. In a year or two they'll all be dead—you might as well throw the whole lot away."

Uncle Matthew was delighted.

"Damned fella," he said, "nothing's right for him, I never saw such a fella. Even the minerals have got foot-and-mouth, according to him."

Chapter 5

―――――――――――――

THE YEAR WHICH followed Aunt Emily's marriage transformed Linda and me from children, young for our ages, into lounging adolescents waiting for love. One result of the marriage was that I now spent nearly all my holidays at Alconleigh. Davey, like all Uncle Matthew's favourites, simply could not see that he was in the least bit frightening, and scouted Aunt Emily's theory that to be too much with him was bad for my nerves.

"You're just a lot of little crybabies," he said, scornfully, "if you allow yourselves to be upset by that old cardboard ogre."

Davey had given up his flat in London and lived with us at Shenley, where, during term—time, he made but little difference to our life, except in so far as a male presence in a female household is always salutary (the curtains, the covers, and Aunt Emily's clothes underwent an enormous change for the better), but, in the holidays, he liked to carry her off, to his own relations or on trips abroad, and I was parked at Alconleigh. Aunt Emily probably felt that, if she had to choose between her husband's wishes and my nervous system, the former should win the day. In spite of her being forty they were, I believe, very much in love; it must have been a perfect bore having me about at all, and it speaks volumes for their characters that never, for one moment, did they allow me to be aware of this. Davey, in fact was, and has been ever since, a perfect stepfather to me, affectionate, understanding, never in any way interfering. He accepted me at once as belonging to Aunt Emily, and never questioned the inevitability of my presence in his household.

By the Christmas holidays Louisa was officially "out," and going to hunt balls, a source of bitter envy to us, though Linda said scornfully that she did not appear to have many suitors. We were not coming out for another two years—it seemed an eternity, and especially to Linda, who was paralysed by her longing for love, and had no lessons or work to do which could take her mind off it. In fact, she had no other interest now except hunting, even the animals seemed to have lost all charm for her. She and I did nothing on nonhunting days but sit about, too large for our tweed suits, whose hooks and eyes were always popping off at the waist, and play endless games of patience; or we lolled in the Hons' cupboard, and "measured." We had a tape-measure and competed as to the largeness of our eyes, the smallness of wrists, ankles, waist and neck, length of legs and fingers, and so on. Linda always won. When we had finished "measuring" we talked of romance. These were most innocent talks, for to us, at that time, love and marriage were synonymous, we knew that they lasted for ever, to the grave and far, far beyond. Our preoccupation with sin was finished; Bob, back from Eton, had been able to tell us all about Oscar Wilde, and, now that his crime was no longer a mystery, it seemed dull, unromantic, and incomprehensible.

We were, of course, both in love, but with people we had never met; Linda with the Prince of Wales, and I with a fat, red-faced, middle-aged farmer, whom I sometimes saw riding through Shenley. These loves were strong, and painfully delicious; they occupied all our thoughts, but I think we half realized that they would be superseded in time by real people. They were to keep the house warm, so to speak, for its eventual occupant. What we never would admit was the possibility of lovers after marriage. We were looking for real love, and that could only come once in a lifetime; it hurried to consecration, and thereafter never wavered. Husbands, we knew, were not always faithful, this we must be prepared for, we must understand and forgive. "I have been faithful to thee, Cynara, in my fashion" seemed to explain it beautifully. But women—that was different; only the lowest of the sex could love or give themselves more than once. I do not quite know how I reconciled these sentiments with the great hero-worship I still had for my mother, that adulterous doll. I suppose I put her in an entirely different category, in the face that launched a thousand ships class. A few historical characters must be allowed to have belonged to this, but Linda and I were perfectionists where love was concerned, and did not ourselves aspire to that kind of fame.

This winter Uncle Matthew had a new tune on his gramophone, called "Thora." "I live in a land of roses," boomed a deep male voice, "but dream of a land of snow. Speak, speak, SPEAK to me, Thora." He played it morning, noon and night; it suited our mood exactly, and Thora seemed the most poignantly beautiful of names.

Aunt Sadie was giving a ball for Louisa soon after Christmas, and to this we pinned great hopes. True, neither the Prince of Wales nor my farmer was invited, but, as Linda said, you never could tell in the country.

Somebody might bring them. The Prince might break down in his motor-car, perhaps on his way to Badminton; what could be more natural than that he should while away the time by looking in on the revelry?

"Pray, who is that beautiful young lady?"

"My daughter Louisa, sir."

"Ah, yes, very charming, but I really meant the one in white taffeta."

"That is my younger daughter Linda, Your Royal Highness."

"Please present her to me."

They would then whirl away in a waltz so accomplished that the other dancers would stand aside to admire. When they could dance no more they would sit for the rest of the evening absorbed in witty conversation.

The following day an A.D.C., asking for her hand—

"But she is so young!"

"His Royal Highness is prepared to wait a year. He reminds you that Her Majesty the Empress Elizabeth of Austria was married at sixteen. Meanwhile, he sends this jewel."

A golden casket, a pink satin cushion, a diamond rose.

My daydreams were less exalted, equally improbable, and quite as real to me. I imagined my farmer carrying me away from Alconleigh, like young Lochinvar, on a pillion behind him to the nearest smith, who then declared us man and wife. Linda kindly said that we could have one of the royal farms, but I thought this would be a great bore, and that it would be much more fun to have one of our own.

Meanwhile, preparations for the ball went forward, occupying every single member of the household. Linda's and my dresses, white taffeta with floating panels and embroidered bead belts, were being made by Mrs. Josh, whose cottage was besieged at all hours to see how they were getting on. Louisa's came from Reville, it was silver lamé in tiny frills, each frill edged with blue net. Dangling on the left shoulder, and strangely unrelated to the dress, was a large pink silk overblown rose. Aunt Sadie, shaken out of her accustomed languor, was in a state of exaggerated preoccupation and worry over the whole thing; we had never seen her like this before. For the first time, too, that any of us could remember, she found herself in opposition to Uncle Matthew. It was over the following question: The nearest neighbour to Alconleigh was Lord Merlin; his estate marched with that of my uncle, and his house at Merlinford was about five miles away. Uncle Matthew loathed him, while, as for Lord Merlin, not for nothing was his telegraphic address Neighbourtease. There had, however, been no open breach between them; the fact that they never saw each other meant nothing, for Lord Merlin neither hunted, shot, nor fished, while Uncle Matthew had never in his life been known to eat a meal in anybody else's house. "Perfectly good food at home," he would say, and people had long ago stopped asking him. The two men, and indeed their two houses and estates, afforded an absolute contrast. Alconleigh was a large, ugly, northfacing, Georgian house, built with only one intention, that of sheltering, when the weather was too bad to be out of doors, a succession of bucolic squires, their wives, their enormous families, their dogs, their horses, their father's relict, and their unmarried sisters. There was no attempt at decoration, at softening the lines, no apology for a façade, it was all as grim and as bare as a barracks, stuck up on the high hillside. Within, the keynote, the theme, was death. Not death of maidens, not death romantically accoutred with urns and weeping willows, cypresses and valedictory odes, but the death of warriors and of animals, stark, real. On the walls halberds and pikes and ancient muskets were arranged in crude patterns with the heads of beasts slaughtered in many lands, with the flags and uniforms of bygone Radletts. Glass-topped cases contained, not miniatures of ladies, but miniatures of the medals of their lords, badges, penholders made of tiger's teeth, the hoof of a favourite horse, telegrams announcing casualties in battle and commissions written out on parchment scrolls, all lying together in a timeless jumble.

Merlinford nestled in a valley of south-westerly aspect, among orchards and old mellow farmhouses. It was a villa, built at about the same time as Alconleigh, but by a very different architect, and with a very different end in view. It was a house to live in, not to rush out from all day to kill enemies and animals. It was suitable for a bachelor, or a married couple with one, or at most two, beautiful, clever, delicate children. It had Angelica Kauffman ceilings, a Chippendale staircase, furniture by Sheraton and Hepplewhite; in the hall there hung two Watteaus; there was no entrenching tool to be seen, nor the head of any animal.

Lord Merlin added continually to its beauties. He was a great collector, and not only Merlinford, but also his houses in London and Rome flowed over with treasures. Indeed, a well-known antique dealer from St. James's had found it worth his while to open a branch in the little town of Merlinford, to tempt his lordship with choice objects during his morning walk, and was soon followed there by a Bond Street jeweller. Lord Merlin loved jewels; his two black whippets wore diamond necklaces designed for whiter, but not slimmer or more graceful necks than theirs. This was a neighbour-tease of long standing; there was a feeling among the local gentry that it incited the good burghers of Merlinford to dishonesty. The neighbours were doubly teased, when year after year went by and the brilliants still sparkled on those furry necks intact.

His taste was by no means confined to antiques; he was an artist and a musician himself, and the patron of all the young. Modern music streamed perpetually from Merlinford, and he had built a small but exquisite playhouse in the garden, where his astonished neighbours were sometimes invited to attend such puzzlers as Cocteau plays, the opera "Mahagonny," or the latest Dada extravagances from Paris. As Lord Merlin was a famous practical joker, it was sometimes difficult to know where jokes ended and culture began. I think he was not always perfectly certain himself.

A marble folly on a near-by hill was topped with a gold angel which blew a trumpet every evening at the hour of Lord Merlin's birth (that this happened to be 9.20 p.m., just too late to remind one of the B.B.C. news, was to be a great local grievance in years to come). The folly glittered by day with semi-precious stones, by night a powerful blue beam was trained upon it.

Such a man was bound to become a sort of legend to the bluff Cotswold squires among whom he lived. But, although they could not approve of an existence which left out of account the killing, though by no means the eating, of delicious game, and though they were puzzled beyond words by the aestheticism and the teases, they accepted him without question as one of themselves. Their families had always known his family, and his father, many years ago, had been a most popular M.F.H.; he was no upstart, no new rich, but simply a sport of all that was most normal in English country life. Indeed, the very folly itself, while considered absolutely hideous, was welcomed as a landmark by those lost on their way home from hunting.

The difference between Aunt Sadie and Uncle Matthew was not as to whether Lord Merlin should or should not be asked to the ball (that question did not arise, since all neighbours were automatically invited), but whether he should be asked to bring a house party. Aunt Sadie thought he should. Since her marriage the least worldly of women, she had known the world as a girl, and she knew that Lord Merlin's house party, if he consented to bring one, would have great decorative value. She also knew that, apart from this, the general note of her ball would be utter and unrelieved dowdiness, and she became aware of a longing to look once more upon young women with well brushed hair, London complexions, and Paris clothes. Uncle Matthew said: "If we ask that brute Merlin to bring his friends, we shall get a lot of aesthetes, sewers from Oxford, and I wouldn't put it past him to bring some foreigners. I hear he sometimes has Frogs and even Wops to stay with him. I will not have my house filled with Wops."

In the end, however, as usual, Aunt Sadie had her way, and sat down to write:

"Dear Lord Merlin,
We are having a little dance for Louisa, etc. . . ."

while Uncle Matthew went gloomily off, having said his piece, and put on "Thora."

Lord Merlin accepted, and said he would bring a party of twelve people, whose names he would presently submit to Aunt Sadie. Very correct, perfectly normal behaviour. Aunt Sadie was quite agreeably surprised that his letter, when opened, did not contain some clockwork joke to hit her in the eye. The writing-paper did actually have a picture of his house on it, and this she concealed from Uncle Matthew. It was the kind of thing he despised.

A few days later there was another surprise. Lord Merlin wrote another letter, still jokeless, still polite, asking Uncle Matthew, Aunt Sadie and Louisa to dine with him for the Merlinford Cottage Hospital Ball. Uncle Matthew naturally could not be persuaded, but Aunt Sadie and Louisa went. They came back with their eyes popping out of their heads. The house, they said, had been boiling hot, so hot that one never felt cold for a single moment, not even getting out of one's coat in the hall. They had arrived very early, long before anyone else was down, as it was the custom at Alconleigh always to leave a quarter of an hour too soon when motoring, in case there should be a puncture. This gave them the opportunity to have a good look round. The house was full of spring flowers, and smelt wonderful. The hothouses at Alconleigh were full of spring flowers too, but somehow they never found their way into the house, and certainly would have died of cold if they had. The whippets did wear diamond necklaces, far grander ones than Aunt Sadie's, she said, and she was forced to admit that they looked very beautiful in them. Birds of paradise flew about the house, quite tame, and one of the young men told Louisa that, if she came in the daytime, she would see a flock of multi-coloured pigeons tumbling about like a cloud of confetti in the sky.

"Merlin dyes them every year, and they are dried in the linen cupboard."

"But isn't that frightfully cruel?" said Louisa, horrified.

"Oh, no, they love it. It makes their husbands and wives look so pretty when they come out."

"What about their poor eyes?"

"Oh, they soon learn to shut them."

The house party, when they finally appeared (some of them shockingly late) from their bedrooms, smelt even more delicious than the flowers, and looked even more exotic than the birds of paradise. Everybody had been very nice, very kind to Louisa. She sat between two beautiful young men at dinner, and turned upon them the usual gambit:

"Where do you hunt?"

"We don't," they said.

"Oh, then why do you wear pink coats?"

"Because we think they are so pretty."

We all thought this dazzlingly funny, but agreed that Uncle Matthew must never hear of it, or he might easily, even now, forbid the Merlinford party his ball.

After dinner the girls had taken Louisa upstairs. She was rather startled at first to see printed notices in the guests' rooms:

OWING TO AN UNIDENTIFIED CORPSE IN THE CISTERN VISITORS ARE REQUESTED NOT TO DRINK THE BATH WATER.

VISITORS ARE REQUESTED NOT TO LET OFF FIREARMS, BLOW BUGLES, SCREAM OR HOOT, BETWEEN THE HOURS OF MIDNIGHT AND SIX A.M.

and, on one bedroom door:

MANGLING DONE HERE

But it was soon explained to her that these were jokes.

The girls had offered to lend her powder and lipstick, but Louisa had not quite dared to accept, for fear Aunt Sadie would notice. She said it made the others look simply too lovely.

AS THE GREAT day of the Alconleigh ball approached, it became obvious that Aunt Sadie had something on her mind. Everything appeared to be going smoothly, the champagne had arrived, the band, Clifford Essex's third string, had been ordered, and would spend the few hours of its rest in Mrs. Craven's cottage. Mrs. Crabbe, in conjunction with the Home Farm, Craven, and three women from the village who were coming in to help, was planning a supper to end all suppers. Uncle Matthew had been persuaded to get twenty oil-stoves, with which to emulate the caressing warmth of Merlinford, and the gardener was preparing to transfer to the house every pot-plant that he could lay his hands on. ("You'll be dyeing the White Leghorns next," said Uncle Matthew, scornfully.)

But, in spite of the fact that the preparations seemed to be going forward without a single hitch, Aunt Sadie's brow was still furrowed with anxiety, because she had collected a large house-party of girls and their mammas, but not one single young man. The fact was that those of her own contemporaries who had daughters were glad to bring them, but sons were another matter. Dancing partners, sated with invitations at this time of year, knew better than to go all the way down to Gloucestershire to a house as yet untried, where they were by no means certain of finding the warmth, the luxury and fine wines which they looked upon as their due, where there was no known female charmer to tempt them, where they had not been offered a mount, and where no mention had been made of a shoot, not even a day with the cocks.

Uncle Matthew had far too much respect for his horses and his pheasants to offer them up to be messed about by any callow unknown boy.

So here was a horrible situation. Ten females, four mothers and six girls, were advancing from various parts of England, to arrive at a household consisting of four more females (not that Linda and I counted, still, we wore skirts and not trousers, and were really too old to be kept all the time in the schoolroom) and only two males, one of whom was not yet in tails.

The telephone now became red-hot, telegrams flew in every direction. Aunt Sadie abandoned all pride, all pretence that things were as they should be, that people were asked for themselves alone, and launched a series of desperate appeals. Mr. Wills, the vicar, consented to leave Mrs. Wills at home, and dine, unattached, at Alconleigh. It would be the first time they had been separated for forty years. Mrs. Aster, the agent's wife, also made the same sacrifice, and Master Aster, the agent's son, aged not quite seventeen, was hurried off to Oxford to get himself a ready-made dress suit.

Davey Warbeck was ordered to leave Aunt Emily and come. He said he would, but unwillingly, and only after the full extent of the crisis had been divulged. Elderly cousins, and uncles who had been for many years forgotten as ghosts, were recalled from oblivion and urged to materialize. They nearly all refused, some of them quite rudely—they had, nearly all, at one time or another, been so deeply and bitterly insulted by Uncle Matthew that forgiveness was impossible.

At last Uncle Matthew saw that the situation would have to be taken in hand. He did not care two hoots about the ball, he felt no particular responsibility for the amusement of his guests, whom he seemed to regard as an onrushing horde of barbarians who could not be kept out, rather than as a group of delightful friends summoned for mutual entertainment and joyous revelry. But he did care for Aunt Sadie's peace of mind, he could not bear to see her looking so worried, and he decided to take steps. He went up to London and attended the last sitting of the House of Lords before the recess. His journey was entirely fruitful.

"Stromboli, Paddington, Fort William and Curtley have accepted," he told Aunt Sadie, with the air of a conjurer producing four wonderful fat rabbits out of one small wine-glass.

"But I had to promise them a shoot—Bob, go and tell Craven I want to see him in the morning."

By these complicated devices the numbers at the dinner-table would now be even, and Aunt Sadie was infinitely relieved, though inclined to be giggly over Uncle Matthew's rabbits. Lord Stromboli, Lord Fort William and the Duke of Paddington were old dancing partners of her own, Sir Archibald Curtley, Librarian of the House, was a well-known diner-out in the smart intellectual world, he was over seventy and very arthritic. After dinner, of course, the dance would be another matter. Mr. Wills would then be joined by Mrs. Wills, Captain Aster by Mrs. Aster, Uncle Matthew and Bob could hardly be counted as partners, while the House of Lords contingent was more likely to head for the bridge table than for the dancing floor.

"I fear it will be sink or swim for the girls," said Aunt Sadie, dreamily.

In one way, however, it was all to the good. These old boys were Uncle Matthew's own choice, his own friends, and he would probably be polite to them; in any case they would know what he was like before they came. To have filled the house with strange young men would, she knew, have been taking a great risk. Uncle Matthew hated strangers, he hated the young, and he hated the idea of possible suitors for his daughters; Aunt Sadie saw rocks ahead, but this time they had been circumnavigated.

THIS THEN IS a ball. This is life, what we have been waiting for all these years, here we are and here it is, a ball, actually going on now, actually in progress round us. How extraordinary it feels, such unreality, like a dream. But, alas, so utterly different from what one had imagined and expected; it must be admitted, not a good dream. The men so small and ugly, the women so frowsty, their clothes so messy and their faces so red, the oil-stoves so smelly, and not really very warm, but, above all, the men, either so old or so ugly. And when they ask one to dance (pushed to it, one cannot but suspect, by kind Davey, who is trying to see that we have a good time at our first party), it is not at all like floating away into a delicious cloud, pressed by a manly arm to a manly bosom, but stumble, stumble, kick, kick. They balance, like King Stork, on one leg, while, with the other, they come down, like King Log, onto one's toe. As for witty conversation, it is wonderful if any conversation, even of the most banal and jerky description, lasts through a whole dance and the sitting out. It is mostly: "Oh, sorry—oh, my fault," though Linda did get as far as taking one of her partners to see the diseased stones.

We had never learnt to dance, and, for some reason, we had supposed it to be a thing which everybody could do quite easily and naturally. I think Linda realized there and then what it took me years to learn, that the behaviour of civilized man really has nothing to do with nature, that all is artificiality and art more or less perfected.

The evening was saved from being an utter disillusionment by the Merlinford house party. They came immensely late, we had all forgotten about them in fact, but, when they had said how do you do to Aunt Sadie and taken the floor, they seemed at once to give the party a new atmosphere. They flourished and shone with jewels, lovely clothes, brilliant hair and dazzling complexions; when they danced they really did seem to float, except when it was the Charleston, and that, though angular, was so accomplished that it made us gasp with admiration. Their conversation was quite evidently both daring and witty, one could see it ran like a river, splashing, dashing and glittering in the sun. Linda was entranced by them, and decided then and there that she would become one of these brilliant beings and live in their world, even if it took her a lifetime to accomplish. I did not aspire to this. I saw that they were admirable, but they were far removed from me and my orbit, belonging more to that of my parents; my back had been towards them from the day Aunt Emily had taken me home, and there was no return—nor did I wish for it. All the same, I found them fascinating as a spectacle, and, whether I sat out with Linda or stumped round the room with kind Davey, who, unable to persuade any more young men to take us on, gave us an occasional turn himself, my eyes were glued to them. Davey seemed to know them all quite well, and was evidently great friends with Lord Merlin. When he was not being kind to Linda and me, he attached himself to them, and joined in their accomplished chatter. He even offered to introduce us to them, but, alas, the floating panels of taffeta, which had seemed so original and pretty in Mrs. Josh's cottage, looked queerly stiff beside their printed chiffons, so soft and supple; also our experiences earlier in the evening had made us feel inferior, and we begged him not to.

That night in bed, I thought more than ever of the safe sheltering arms of my Shenley farmer. The next morning Linda told me that she had renounced the Prince of Wales.

"I have come to the conclusion," she said, "that Court circles would be rather dull. Lady Dorothy is a lady-in-waiting and look at her."

Chapter 6

THE BALL HAD a very unexpected sequel. Lord Fort William's mother invited Aunt Sadie and Louisa to stay at their place in Sussex for a hunt ball, and shortly afterwards, his married sister asked them to a shoot and an Infirmary Ball. During this visit, Lord Fort William proposed to Louisa and was accepted. She came back to Alconleigh a fiancée, to find herself the centre of attention there for the first time since the birth of Linda had put her nose for ever out of joint. This was indeed an excitement, and tremendous chats took place in the Hons' cupboard, both with and without Louisa. She had a nice little diamond ring on her fourth finger, but was not as communicative as we could have wished on the subject of Lord (John now to us, but how could we remember that?) Fort William's love-making, retiring, with many blushes, behind the smoke-screen of such things being too sacred to speak of. He soon appeared again in person, and we were able to observe him as an individual, instead of part, with Lord Stromboli and the Duke of Paddington, of a venerable trinity. Linda pronounced the summing-up. "Poor old thing, I suppose she likes him, but, I must say, if he was one's dog one would have him put down." Lord Fort William was thirty-nine, but he certainly looked much more. His hair seemed to be slipping off backwards, like an eiderdown in the night, Linda said, and he had a generally uncared-for middle-aged appearance. Louisa, however, loved him, and was happy for the first time in her life. She had always been more frightened of Uncle Matthew than any of the others, and with good reason; he thought she was a fool and was never at all nice to her, and she was in heaven at the prospect of getting away from Alconleigh for ever.

I think Linda, in spite of the poor old dog and the eiderdown, was really very jealous. She went off for long rides by herself, and spun more and more fantastic daydreams; her longing for love had become an obsession. Two whole years would have to be made away with somehow before she would come out in the world, but oh the days went dragging by. Linda would flop about in the drawing-room, playing (or beginning and then not finishing) endless games of patience, sometimes by herself, sometimes with Jassy, whom she had infected with her own restlessness.

"What's the time, darling?"

"Guess."

"A quarter to six?"

"Better than that."

"Six!"

"Not quite so good."

"Five to?"

"Yes."

"If this comes out I shall marry the man I love. If this comes out I shall marry at eighteen."

If this comes out—shuffle—if this comes out—deal. A queen at the bottom of the pack, it can't come out, begin again.

Louisa was married in the spring. Her wedding dress, of tulle frills and sprays of orange blossom, was short to the knee and had a train, as was the hideous fashion then. Jassy got very worked up about it.

"So unsuitable."

"Why, Jassy?"

"To be buried in, I mean. Women are always buried in their wedding dresses, aren't they? Think of your poor old dead legs sticking out."

"Don't be such a ghoul. I'll wrap them up in my train."

"Not very nice for the undertakers."

Louisa refused to have bridesmaids. I think she felt that it would be agreeable, for once in her life, to be more looked at than Linda.

"You can't think how stupid you'll look from behind," Linda said, "without any. Still, have it your own way. I'm sure we don't want to be guyed up in blue chiffon, I'm only thinking what would be kinder for you."

On Louisa's birthday John Fort William, an ardent antiquarian, gave her a replica of King Alfred's jewel. Linda, whose disagreeableness at this time knew no bounds, said that it simply looked like a chicken's mess. "Same shape, same size, same colour. Not my idea of a jewel."

"I think it's lovely," said Aunt Sadie, but Linda's words had left their sting all the same.

Aunt Sadie had a canary then, which sang all day, rivalling even Galli Curci in the pureness and loudness of its trills. Whenever I hear a canary sing so immoderately it recalls that happy visit, the endless flow of wedding presents, unpacking them, arranging them in the ballroom with shrieks of admiration or of horror, the hustle, the bustle, and Uncle Matthew's good temper, which went on, as fine weather sometimes does, day after unbelievable day.

Louisa was to have two houses, one in London, Connaught Square, and one in Scotland. Her dress allowance would be three hundred a year, she would possess a diamond tiara, a pearl necklace, a motor-car of her own and a fur cape. In fact granted that she could bear John Fort William, her lot was an enviable one. He was terribly dull.

THE WEDDING DAY was fine and balmy, and, when we went in the morning to see how Mrs. Wills and Mrs. Josh were getting on with the decorations, we found the light little church bunchy with spring flowers. Later, its well-known outlines blurred with a most unaccustomed throng of human beings, it looked quite different. I thought that I personally should have liked better to be married in it when it was so empty and flowery and full of the Holy Ghost.

Neither Linda nor I had ever been to a wedding before, as Aunt Emily, most unfairly we thought at the time, had been married privately in the chapel at Davey's home in the North of England, and we were hardly prepared for the sudden transformation on this day of dear old Louisa, of terribly dull John, into eternal types of Bride and Bridegroom, Heroine and Hero of romance.

From the moment when we left Louisa alone at Alconleigh with Uncle Matthew, to follow us in the Daimler in exactly eleven minutes, the atmosphere became positively dramatic. Louisa, enveloped from head to knee in tulle, sat gingerly on the edge of a chair, while Uncle Matthew, watch in hand, strode up and down the hall. We walked, as we always did, to the church, and arranged ourselves in the family pew at the back of it, from which vantage point we were able to observe with fascination the unusual appearance of our neighbours, all tricked out in their best. The only person in the whole congregation who looked exactly as usual was Lord Merlin.

Suddenly there was a stir. John and his best man, Lord Stromboli, appearing like two jacks-in-the-box from nowhere, stood beside the altar steps. In their morning coats, their hair heavily brilliantined, they looked quite glamorous, but we hardly had time to notice this fact before Mrs. Wills struck up "Here comes the Bride," with all the stops out, and Louisa, her veil over her face, was being dragged up the aisle at double quick time by Uncle Matthew. At this moment I think Linda would gladly have changed places with Louisa, even at the cost—the heavy cost—of being happy for ever after with John Fort William. In what seemed no time at all Louisa was being dragged down the aisle again by John, with her veil back, while Mrs. Wills nearly broke the windows, so loud and so triumphant was her "Wedding March."

Everything had gone like clockwork, and there was only one small incident. Davey slipped out of the family pew almost unobserved, in the middle of "As pants the hart" (Louisa's favourite hymn) and went straight to London, making one of the wedding cars take him to Merlinford station. That evening he telephoned to say that he had twisted his tonsil, singing, and had thought it better to go immediately to Sir Andrew Macpherson, the nose, throat and ears man, who was keeping him in bed for a week. The most extraordinary accidents always seemed to overtake poor Davey.

WHEN LOUISA HAD gone away and the wedding guests had left Alconleigh, a sense of flatness descended upon the house, as always happens on these occasions. Linda then became plunged into such despairing gloom that even Aunt Sadie was alarmed. Linda told me afterwards that she thought a great deal about killing herself, and would most likely have done so had the material difficulties not been so great.

"You know what it is," she said, "trying to kill rabbits. Well, think of *oneself*!"

Two years seemed an absolute eternity, not worth ploughing through even with the prospect (which she never doubted, just as a religious person does not doubt the existence of heaven) of blissful love at the end of it. Of course, this was the time when Linda should have been made to work, as I was, all day and hard, with no time for silly dreaming except the few minutes before one went to sleep at night. I think Aunt Sadie dimly perceived this fact, she urged her to learn cooking, to occupy herself in the garden, to be prepared for confirmation. Linda furiously refused, nor would she do jobs in the village, nor help Aunt Sadie in the hundred and one chores which fall to the lot of a country squire's wife. She was, in fact, and Uncle Matthew told her so countless times every day, glaring at her with angry blue eyes, thoroughly bloody-minded.

Lord Merlin came to her rescue. He had taken a fancy to her at Louisa's wedding, and asked Aunt Sadie to bring her over to Merlinford some time. A few days later he rang up. Uncle Matthew answered the telephone, and shouted to Aunt Sadie, without taking his mouth away from the receiver:

"That hog Merlin wants to speak to you."

Lord Merlin, who must have heard, was quite unmoved by this. He was an eccentric himself, and had a fellow feeling for the idiosyncrasies of others. Poor Aunt Sadie, however, was very much flustered, and, as a result, she accepted an invitation which she would otherwise most probably have refused, to take Linda over to Merlinford for luncheon.

Lord Merlin seemed to become immediately aware of Linda's state of mind, was really shocked to discover that she was doing no lessons at all, and did what he could to provide some interests for her. He showed her his pictures, explained them to her, talked at length about art and literature, and gave her books to read. He let fall the suggestion, which was taken up by Aunt Sadie, that she and Linda should attend a course of lectures in Oxford, and he also mentioned that the Shakespeare Festival was now in progress at Stratford-on-Avon.

Outings of this kind, which Aunt Sadie herself very much enjoyed, soon became a regular feature of life at Alconleigh. Uncle Matthew scoffed a bit, but he never interfered with anything Aunt Sadie wanted to do; besides, it was not so much education that he dreaded for his daughters, as the vulgarizing effect that a boarding-school might have upon them. As for governesses, they had been tried, but none had ever been able to endure for more than a few days the terror of Uncle Matthew's grinding dentures, the piercing, furious blue flash of his eyes, the stock whips cracking under their bedroom windows at dawn. Their nerves, they said, and made for the station, often before they had had time to unpack enormous trunks, heavy as though full of stones, by which they were always accompanied.

Uncle Matthew went with Aunt Sadie and Linda on one occasion to a Shakespeare play, *Romeo and Juliet*. It was not a success.

He cried copiously, and went into a furious rage because it ended badly. "All the fault of that damned padré," he kept saying on the way home, still wiping his eyes. "That fella, what's 'is name, Romeo, might have known a blasted papist would mess up the whole thing. Silly old fool of a nurse too, I bet she was an R.C., dismal old bitch."

So Linda's life, instead of being on one flat level plain of tedium, was now, to some extent, filled with outside interests. She perceived that the world she wanted to be in, the witty, sparkling world of Lord Merlin and his friends, was interested in things of the mind, and that she would only be able to shine in it if she became in some sort educated. The futile games of patience were abandoned, and she sat all day hunched up in a corner of the library sofa, reading until her eyes gave out. She often rode over to Merlinford, and, unbeknownst to her parents, who never would have allowed her to go there, or indeed anywhere, alone, left Josh in the stable yard where he had congenial friends, and chatted for hours with Lord Merlin on all sorts of subjects. He knew that she had an intensely romantic character, he foresaw much trouble ahead, and he continually urged upon her the necessity for an intellectual background.

Chapter 7

WHAT COULD POSSIBLY have induced Linda to marry Anthony Kroesig? During the nine years of their life together people asked this question with irritating regularity, almost every time their names were mentioned. What was she after, surely she could never possibly have been in love with him, what was the idea, how could it have happened? He was admittedly very rich, but so were others and surely the fascinating Linda had only to choose? The answer was, of course, that, quite simply, she was in love with him. Linda was far too romantic to marry without love and indeed I, who was present at their first meeting and during most of their courtship, always understood why it had happened. Tony, in those days, and to unsophisticated country girls like us, seemed a glorious and glamorous creature. When we first saw him, at Linda's and my coming-out ball, he was in his last year at Oxford, a member of Bullingdon, a splendid young man with a Rolls-Royce, plenty of beautiful horses, exquisite clothes, and large luxurious rooms, where he entertained on a lavish scale. In person he was tall and fair, on the heavy side, but with a well-proportioned figure; he had already a faint touch of pomposity, a thing which

Linda had never come across before, and which she found not unattractive. She took him, in short, at his own valuation.

What immediately gave him great prestige in her eyes was that he came to the ball with Lord Merlin. It was really most unlucky, especially as it happened that he had only been asked at the eleventh hour, as a stop-gap.

Linda's ball was not nearly such a fiasco as Louisa's had been. Louisa, a married London lady now, produced a lot of young men for Aunt Sadie's house-party, dull, fair Scotch boys mostly, with nice manners; nothing to which Uncle Matthew could possibly take exception. They got on quite well with the various dull dark girls invited by Aunt Sadie, and the house-party seemed to "go" very nicely, though Linda had her head in the air, saying they were all too impossibly dreary for words. Uncle Matthew had been implored by Aunt Sadie for weeks past to be kind to the young and not to shout at anybody, and he was quite subdued, almost pathetic in his wish to please, creeping about as though there were an invalid upstairs and straw in the street.

Davey and Aunt Emily were staying in the house to see me come out (Aunt Sadie had offered to bring me out with Linda and give us a London season together, an offer which was most gratefully accepted by Aunt Emily) and Davey constituted himself a sort of bodyguard to Uncle Matthew, hoping to stand as much as possible between him and the more unbearable forms of irritation.

"I'll be simply wonderful to everybody, but I won't have the sewers in my business-room, that's all," Uncle Matthew had said, after one of Aunt Sadie's prolonged exhortations, and, indeed, spent most of the week-end (the ball was on a Friday and the house-party stayed on until Monday) locked into it, playing "1812" and the "Haunted Ballroom" on the gramophone. He was rather off the human voice this year.

"What a pity," said Linda, as we struggled into our ball dresses (proper London ones this time, with no floating panels), "that we

are dressing up like this, and looking so pretty, and all for those terrible productions of Louisa's. Waste, I call it."

"You never know in the country," I said, "somebody may bring
the Prince of Wales."

Linda shot me a furious look under her eyelashes.

"Actually," she said, "I am pinning great hopes on Lord Merlin's
party. I'm sure he'll bring some really interesting people."

Lord Merlin's party arrived, as before, very late, and in very high
spirits. Linda immediately noticed a large, blond young man in a
beautiful pink coat. He was dancing with a girl who often stayed at
Merlinford called Baby Fairweather, and she introduced him to
Linda. He asked her to dance the next, and she abandoned one of
Louisa's Scotch boys, to whom she had promised it, and strutted off
with him in a quick onestep. Linda and I had both been having
dancing lessons, and, if we did not exactly float round the room,
our progress was by no means so embarrassing as it had been before.

Tony was in a happy mood, induced by Lord Merlin's excellent
brandy, and Linda was pleased to find how well and easily she was
getting on with this member of the Merlinford set. Everything she
said seemed to make him laugh; presently they went to sit out, she
chattered away, and Tony roared with laughter. This was the royal
road to Linda's good books; she liked people who laughed easily
more than anything; it naturally did not occur to her that Tony was
a bit drunk. They sat out the next dance together. This was immediately noticed by Uncle Matthew, who began to walk up and down
in front of them, giving them furious looks, until Davey, observing
this danger signal, came up and hurried him away, saying that one
of the oil-stoves in the hall was smoking.

"Who is that sewer with Linda?"

"Kroesig, Governor of the Bank of England, you know; his son."

"Good God, I never expected to harbour a full-blooded Hun in
this house—who on earth asked him?"

"Now, Matthew dear, don't get excited. The Kroesigs aren't

30-1815

Huns, they've been over here for generations, they are a very highly respected family of English bankers."

"Once a Hun always a Hun," said Uncle Matthew, "and I'm not too set on bankers myself. Besides, the fella must be a gate-crasher."

"No, he's not. He came with Merlin."

"I knew that bloody Merlin would start bringing foreigners here sooner or later. I always said he would, but I didn't think even he would land one with a German," Uncle Matthew bellowed.

"Don't you think it's time somebody took some champagne to the band?" said Davey.

But Uncle Matthew stumped down to the boiler room, where he had a long soothing talk with Timb, the odd man, about coke.

Tony, meanwhile, thought Linda ravishingly pretty, and great fun, which indeed she was. He told her so, and danced with her again and again, until Lord Merlin, quite as much put out as Uncle Matthew by what was happening, firmly and very early took his party home.

"See you at the meet tomorrow," said Tony, winding a white silk scarf round his neck.

Linda was silent and preoccupied for the rest of the evening.

"You're not to go hunting, Linda," said Aunt Sadie the next day, when Linda came downstairs in her riding-habit, "it's too rude, you must stay and look after your guests. You can't leave them like that."

"Darling, darling Mummie," said Linda, "the meet's at Cock's Barn, and you know how one can't resist. And Flora hasn't been out for a week, she'll go mad. Be a love and take them to see the Roman villa or something, and I swear to come back early. And they've got Fanny and Louisa after all."

It was this unlucky hunt that clinched matters as far as Linda was concerned. The first person she saw at the meet was Tony, on a splendid chestnut horse. Linda herself was always beautifully mounted, Uncle Matthew was proud of her horsemanship, and had given her two pretty, lively little horses. They found at once, and there was a short sharp run, during which Linda and Tony, both in a somewhat showing-off mood, rode side by side over the stone walls. Presently, on a village green, they checked. One or two hounds put up a hare, which lost its head, jumped into a duckpond, and began to swim about in a hopeless sort of way. Linda's eyes filled with tears.

"Oh, the poor hare!"

Tony got off his horse, and plunged into the pond. He rescued the hare, waded out again, his fine white breeches covered with green muck, and put it, wet and gasping, into Linda's lap. It was the one romantic gesture of his life.

At the end of the day Linda left hounds to take a short cut home across country. Tony opened a gate for her, took off his hat, and said:

"You are a most beautiful rider, you know. Good night, when I'm back in Oxford I'll ring you up."

When Linda got home she rushed me off to the Hons' cupboard and told me all this. She was in love.

Given Linda's frame of mind during the past two endless years, she was obviously destined to fall in love with the first young man who came along. It could hardly have been otherwise; she need not, however, have married him. This was made inevitable by the behaviour of Uncle Matthew. Most unfortunately Lord Merlin, the one person who might perhaps have been able to make Linda see that Tony was not all she thought him, went to Rome the week after the ball, and remained abroad for a year.

Tony went back to Oxford when he left Merlinford, and Linda sat about waiting, waiting, waiting for the telephone bell. Patience again. If this comes out he is thinking of me now this very minute—if this comes out he'll ring up tomorrow—if this comes out he'll be at the meet. But Tony hunted with the Bicester, and never appeared on our side of the country. Three weeks passed, and Linda began to feel in despair. Then one evening, after dinner, the telephone bell rang; by a lucky chance Uncle Matthew had gone down to the stables to see Josh about a horse that had colic, the business-room was empty, and Linda answered the telephone herself. It was Tony. Her heart was choking her, she could scarcely speak.

"Hullo, is that Linda? It's Tony Kroesig here. Will you come to lunch next Thursday?"

"Oh! But I should never be allowed to."

"Oh, rot," very impatiently, "several other girls are coming down from London—bring your cousin if you like."

"All right, that will be lovely."

"See you then—about one—7 King Edward Street, I expect you know the rooms. Altringham had them when he was up."

Linda came away from the telephone trembling, and whispered to me to come quick to the Hons' cupboard. We were absolutely forbidden to see young men at any hour unchaperoned, and other girls did not count as chaperons. We knew quite well, though such a remote eventuality had never even been mooted at Alconleigh, that we would not be allowed to have luncheon with a young man in his lodgings with any chaperon at all, short of Aunt Sadie herself. The Alconleigh standards of chaperonage were medieval; they did not vary in the slightest degree from those applied to Uncle Matthew's sister, and to Aunt Sadie in youth. The principle was that one never saw any young man alone, under any circumstances, until one was engaged to him. The only people who could be counted on to enforce this rule were one's mother or one's aunts, therefore one must not be allowed beyond the reach of their ever-watchful eyes. The argument, often put forward by Linda, that young men were not very likely to propose to girls they hardly knew, was brushed aside as nonsense. Uncle Matthew had proposed, had he not? to Aunt Sadie, the very first time he ever saw her, by the cage of a two-headed nightingale at an Exhibition at the White City. "They respect you all the more." It never seemed to dawn upon the Alconleighs that respect is not an attitude of mind indulged in by modern young men, who look for other qualities in their wives than respectability. Aunt Emily, under the enlightened influence of Davey, was far more reasonable, but, of course, when staying with the Radletts, I had to obey the same rules.

In the Hons' cupboard we talked and talked. There was no question in our minds but that we must go, not to do so would be death for Linda, she would never get over it. But how to escape? There was only one way that we could devise, and it was full of risk. A very dull girl of exactly our age called Lavender Davis lived with her very dull parents about five miles away, and once in a blue moon, Linda, complaining vociferously, was sent over to luncheon with them, driving herself in Aunt Sadie's little car. We must pretend that we were going to do that, hoping that Aunt Sadie would not see Mrs. Davis, that pillar of the Women's Institute, for months and months, hoping also that Perkins, the chauffeur, would not remark on the fact that we had driven sixty miles and not ten.

As we were going upstairs to bed, Linda said to Aunt Sadie, in what she hoped was an offhand voice, but one which seemed to me vibrant with guilt:

"That was Lavender ringing up. She wants Fanny and me to lunch there on Thursday."

"Oh, duck," said Aunt Sadie, "you can't have my car, I'm afraid."

Linda became very white, and leant against the wall.

"Oh, please, Mummy, oh please do let me, I do so terribly want to go."

"To the Davises," said Aunt Sadie in astonishment, "but darling, last time you said you'd never go again as long as you lived—great haunches of cod you said, don't you remember? Anyhow, I'm sure they'll have you another day, you know."

"Oh, Mummy, you don't understand. The whole point is, a man is coming who brought up a baby badger, and I do so want to meet him."

It was known to be one of Linda's greatest ambitions, to bring up a baby badger.

"Staggers and ringworm," said Linda, her large blue eyes slowly filling with tears.

"What did you say, darling?"

"In their stables—staggers and ringworm. You wouldn't want me to expose poor Flora to that."

"Are you sure? Their horses always look so wonderful."

"Ask Josh."

"Well, I'll see. Perhaps I can borrow Fa's Morris, and, if not, perhaps Perkins can take me in the Daimler. It's a meeting I must go to, though."

"Oh, you are kind, you are kind. Oh, do try. I do so long for a badger."

"If we go to London for the season you'll be far too busy to think of a badger. Good night then, ducks."

"WE MUST GET hold of some powder."

"And rouge."

These commodities were utterly forbidden by Uncle Matthew, who liked to see female complexions in a state of nature, and often pronounced that paint was for whores and not for his daughters.

"I once read in a book that you can use geranium juice for rouge."

"Geraniums aren't out at this time of year, silly."

"We can blue our eyelids out of Jassy's paint-box."

"And sleep in curlers."

"I'll get the verbena soap out of Mummy's bathroom. If we let it melt in the bath, and soak for hours in it, we shall smell delicious."

"I THOUGHT YOU loathed Lavender Davis."

"Oh, shut up, Jassy."

"Last time you went you said she was a horrible Counter-Hon, and you would like to bash in her silly face with the Hons' mallet."

"I never said so. Don't invent lies."

"Why have you got your London suit on for Lavender Davis?"

"Do go away, Matt."

"Why are you starting already, you'll be hours too early."

"We're going to see the badger before luncheon."

"How red your face is, Linda. Oh, oh you do look so funny!"

"If you don't shut up and go away, Jassy, I swear I'll put your newt back in the pond."

Persecution, however, continued until we were in the car and out of the garage yard.

"Why don't you bring Lavender back for a nice long cosy visit?" was Jassy's parting shot.

"Not very honnish of them," said Linda, "do you think they can possibly have guessed?"

We left our car in the Clarendon yard, and, as we were very early, having allowed half an hour in case of two punctures, we made for Elliston & Cavell's ladies-room, and gazed at ourselves, with a tiny feeling of uncertainty, in the looking-glasses there. Our cheeks had round scarlet patches, our lips were the same colour, but only at the edges, inside it had already worn off, and our eyelids were blue, all out of Jassy's paint-box. Our noses were white, Nanny having produced some powder with which, years ago, she used to dust Robin's bottom. In short, we looked like a couple of Dutch dolls.

"We must keep our ends up," said Linda, uncertainly.

"Oh, dear," I said, "the thing about me is, I always feel so much happier with my end down."

We gazed and gazed, hoping thus, in some magical way, to make ourselves feel less peculiar. Presently we did a little work with damp handkerchiefs, and toned our faces down a bit. We then sallied forth into the street, looking at ourselves in every shop window that we passed. (I have often noticed that when women look at themselves in every reflection, and take furtive peeps into their hand looking-glasses, it is hardly ever, as is generally supposed, from vanity, but much more often from a feeling that all is not quite as it should be.)

Now that we had actually achieved our objective, we were beginning to feel horribly nervous, not only wicked, guilty and frightened, but also filled with social terrors. I think we would both gladly have got back into the car and made for home.

On the stroke of one o'clock we arrived in Tony's room. He was alone, but evidently a large party was expected, the table, a square one with a coarse white linen cloth, seemed to have a great many places. We refused sherry and cigarettes, and an awkward silence fell.

"Been hunting at all?" he asked Linda.

"Oh, yes, we were out yesterday."

"Good day?"

"Yes, very. We found at once, and had a five-mile point and then—" Linda suddenly remembered that Lord Merlin had once said to her: "Hunt as much as you like, but never talk about it, it's the most boring subject in the world."

"But that's marvellous, a five-mile point. I must come out with the Heythrop again soon, they are doing awfully well this season, I hear. We had a good day yesterday, too."

He embarked on a detailed account of every minute of it, where they found, where they ran to, how his first horse had gone lame, how, luckily, he had then come upon his second horse, and so on. I saw just what Lord Merlin meant. Linda, however, hung upon his words with breathless interest.

At last noises were heard in the street, and he went to the window.

"Good," he said, "here are the others."

The others had come down from London in a huge Daimler, and poured, chattering, into the room. Four pretty girls and a young man. Presently some undergraduates appeared, and completed the party. It was not really very enjoyable from our point of view, they all knew each other too well. They gossiped away, roared with laughter at private jokes, and showed off; still, we felt that this was Life, and would have been quite happy just looking on had it not been for that ghastly feeling of guilt, which was now beginning to give us a pain rather like indigestion. Linda turned quite pale every time the door opened, I think she really felt that Uncle

Matthew might appear at any moment, cracking a whip. As soon as we decently could, which was not very soon, because nobody moved from the table until after Tom had struck four, we said good-bye, and fled for home.

The miserable Matt and Jassy were swinging on the garage gate.

"So how was Lavender? Did she roar at your eyelids? Better go and wash before Fa sees you. You have been hours. Was it cod? Did you see the badger?"

Linda burst into tears.

"Leave me alone, you horrible Counter-Hons," she cried, and rushed upstairs to her bedroom.

Love had increased threefold in one short day.

ON SATURDAY THE blow fell.

"Linda and Fanny, Fa wants you in the business-room. And sooner you than me by the look of him," said Jassy, meeting us in the drive as we came in from riding. Our hearts plunged into our boots. We looked at each other with apprehension.

"Better get it over," said Linda, and we hurried to the business-room, where we saw at once that the worst had occurred.

Aunt Sadie, looking unhappy, and Uncle Matthew, grinding his teeth, confronted us with our crime. The room was full of blue lightning flashing from his eyes, and Jove's thunder was not more awful than what he now roared at us:

"Do you realize," he said, "that, if you were married women, your husbands could divorce you for doing this?"

Linda began to say no they couldn't. She knew the laws of divorce from having read the whole of the Russell case off newspapers with which the fires in the spare bed rooms were laid.

"Don't interrupt your father," said Aunt Sadie, with a warning look.

Uncle Matthew, however, did not even notice. He was in the full flood and violence of his storm.

"Now we know you can't be trusted to behave yourselves, we shall have to take certain steps. Fanny can go straight home tomorrow, and I never want you here again, do you understand? Emily will have to control you in future, if she can, but you'll go the same way as your mother, sure as eggs is eggs. As for you, miss, there's no more question of a London season now—we shall have to watch you in future every minute of the day—not very agreeable, to have a child one can't trust—and there would be too many opportunities in London for slipping off. You can stew in your own juice here. And no more hunting this year. You're damned lucky not to be thrashed; most fathers would give you a good hiding, do you hear? Now you can both go to bed, and you're not to speak to each other before Fanny leaves. I'm sending her over in the car tomorrow."

It was months before we knew how they found out. It seemed like magic, but the explanation was simple. Somebody had left a scarf in Tony Kroesig's rooms, and he had rung up to ask whether it belonged to either of us.

Chapter 8

As always, uncle Matthew's bark was worse than his bite, though, while it lasted, it was the most terrible row within living memory at Alconleigh. I was sent back to Aunt Emily the next day, Linda waving and crying out of her bedroom window: "Oh, you *are* lucky, not to be me," (most unlike her, her usual cry being, "Isn't it lovely to be lovely *one*.") and she was stopped from hunting once or twice. Then relaxation began, the thin end of the wedge, and gradually things returned to normal, though it was reckoned in the family that Uncle Matthew had got through a pair of dentures in record time.

Plans for the London season went on being made, and went on including me. I heard afterwards that both Davey and John Fort William took it upon themselves to tell Aunt Sadie and Uncle Matthew (especially Uncle Matthew) that, according to modern ideas, what we had done was absolutely normal, though, of course, they were obliged to own that it was very wrong of us to have told so many and such shameless lies.

We both said we were very sorry, and promised faithfully that we would never act in such an underhand way again, but always ask Aunt Sadie if there was something we specially wanted to do.

"Only then, of course, it will always be no," as Linda said, giving me a hopeless look.

Aunt Sadie took a furnished house for the summer near Belgrave Square. It was a house with so little character that I can remember absolutely nothing about it, except that my bedroom had a view over chimney-pots, and that on hot summer evenings I used to sit and watch the swallows, always in pairs, and wish sentimentally that I too could be a pair with somebody.

We really had great fun, although I don't think it was dancing that we enjoyed so much as the fact of being grown up and in London. At the dances the great bar to enjoyment was what Linda called the chaps. They were terribly dull, all on the lines of the ones Louisa had brought to Alconleigh; Linda, still in her dream of love for Tony, could not distinguish between them, and never even knew their names. I looked about hopefully for a possible life-partner, but, though I honestly tried to see the best in them, nothing remotely approximating my requirements turned up.

Tony was at Oxford for his last term, and did not come to London until quite the end of the season.

We were chaperoned, as was to be expected, with Victorian severity. Aunt Sadie or Uncle Matthew literally never let us out of the sight of one or the other; as Aunt Sadie liked to rest in the afternoon, Uncle Matthew would solemnly take us off to the House of Lords, park us in the Peeresses' Gallery, and take his own forty winks on a back bench opposite. When he was awake in the house, which was not often, he was a perfect nuisance to the Whips, never voting with the same party twice running; nor were the workings of his mind too easy to follow. He voted, for instance, in favour of steel traps, of blood sports and of steeplechasing, but against vivisection and the exporting of old horses to Belgium. No doubt he had his reasons, as Aunt Sadie would remark, with finality, when we commented on this inconsistency. I rather liked those drowsy afternoons in the dark Gothic chamber, fascinated by the mutterings and antics that went on the whole time, and besides, the occasional speech one was able to hear was generally rather interesting. Linda liked it too, she was far away, thinking her own thoughts. Uncle Matthew would wake up at tea-time, conduct us to the Peers' dining-room for tea and buttered buns, and then take us home to rest and dress for the dance.

Saturday to Monday was spent by the Radlett family at Alconleigh, they rolled down in their huge, rather sick-making Daimler, and by me at Shenley, where Aunt Emily and Davey were always longing to hear every detail of our week.

Clothes were probably our chief preoccupation at this time. Once Linda had been to a few dress shows, and got her eye in, she had all hers made by Mrs. Josh, and, somehow, they had a sort of originality and prettiness that I never achieved, although mine, which were bought at expensive shops, cost about five times as much. This showed, said Davey, who used to come and see us whenever he was in London, that either you get your clothes in Paris or it is a toss-up. Linda had one particularly ravishing ball-dress made of masses of pale grey tulle down to her feet. Most of the dresses were still short that summer, and Linda made a sensation whenever she appeared in her yards of tulle, very much disapproved of by Uncle Matthew, on the grounds that he had known three women burnt to death in tulle ball-dresses.

She was wearing this dress when Tony proposed to her in the Berkeley Square summer-house at six o'clock on a fine July morning. He had been down from Oxford about a fort-night, and it was soon obvious that he had eyes for nobody but her. He went to all the same dances, and, after stumping round with a few other girls, would take Linda to supper, and thereafter spend the evening glued to her side. Aunt Sadie seemed to notice nothing, but to the whole rest of the debutante world the outcome was a foregone conclusion, the only question being when and where Tony would propose.

The ball from which they had emerged (it was in a lovely old house on the east side of Berkeley Square, since demolished) was only just alive, the band sleepily thump-thumped its tunes through the nearly empty rooms; poor Aunt Sadie sat on a little gold chair trying to keep her eyes open and passionately longing for bed, with me beside her, dead tired and very cold, my partners all gone home. It was broad daylight. Linda had been away for hours, nobody seemed to have set eyes on her since supper-time, and Aunt Sadie, though dominated by her fearful sleepiness, was apprehensive, and rather angry. She was beginning to wonder whether Linda had not committed the unforgivable sin, and gone off to a night club.

Suddenly the band perked up and began to play "John Peel" as a prelude to "God Save the King"; Linda, in a grey cloud, was galloping up and down the room with Tony; one look at her face told all. We climbed into a taxi behind Aunt Sadie (she never would keep a chauffeur up at night), we splashed away past the great hoses that were washing the streets, we climbed the stairs to our rooms, without a word being spoken by any of us. A thin oblique sunlight was striking the chimney-pots as I opened my window. I was too tired to think, I just fell into bed.

WE WERE ALLOWED to be late after dances, though Aunt Sadie was always up and seeing to the household arrangements by nine o'clock. As Linda came sleepily downstairs the next morning, Uncle Matthew shouted furiously at her from the hall:

"That bloody Hun Kroesig has just telephoned, he wanted to speak to you. I told him to get to hell out of it. I don't want you mixed up with any Germans, do you understand?"

"Well, I am mixed up," said Linda, in an offhand, would-be casual voice, "as it happens I'm engaged to him."

At this point Aunt Sadie dashed out of her little morning-room on the ground floor, took Uncle Matthew by the arm, and led him away. Linda locked herself into her bedroom and cried for an hour, while Jassy, Matt, Robin, and I speculated upon future developments in the nursery.

There was a great deal of opposition to the engagement, not only from Uncle Matthew, who was beside himself with disappointment and disgust at Linda's choice, but also quite as much from Sir Leicester Kroesig. He did not want Tony to marry at all until he was well settled in his career in the City, and then he had hoped for an alliance with one of the other big banking families. He despised the landed gentry, whom he regarded as feckless, finished and done with in the modern world, he also knew that the vast, the enviable capital sums which such families undoubtedly still possessed, and of which they made so foolishly little use, were always entailed upon the eldest son, and that very small provision, if any, was made for the dowries of daughters. Sir Leicester and Uncle Matthew met, disliked each other on sight, and were at one in their determination to stop the marriage. Tony was sent off to America, to work in a bank house in New York, and poor Linda, the season now being at an end, was taken home to eat her heart out at Alconleigh.

"Oh, Jassy, darling Jassy, lend me your running-away money to go to New York with."

"No, Linda. I've saved and scraped for five years, ever since I was seven, I simply can't begin all over again now. Besides I shall want it for when I run away myself."

"But, darling, I'll give it you back, Tony will, when we're married."

"I know men," said Jassy, darkly.

She was adamant.

"If only Lord Merlin were here," Linda wailed. "He would help me." But Lord Merlin was still in Rome.

She had 15s. 6d. in the world, and was obliged to content herself with writing immense screeds to Tony every day. She carried about in her pocket a quantity of short, dull letters in an immature handwriting and with a New York postmark.

After a few months Tony came back, and told his father that he could not settle down to business or banking, or think about his future career at all, until the date for his marriage had been fixed. This was quite the proper line to take with Sir Leicester. Anything that interfered with making money must be regulated at once. If Tony, who was a sensible fellow, and had never given his father one moment's anxiety in his life, assured him that he could only be serious about banking after marriage, then married he must be, the sooner the better. Sir Leicester explained at length what he considered the disadvantages of the union. Tony agreed in principle, but said that Linda was young, intelligent, energetic, that he had great influence with her, and did not doubt that she could be made into a tremendous asset. Sir Leicester finally gave his consent.

"It might have been worse," he said, "after all, she is a lady."

Lady Kroesig opened negotiations with Aunt Sadie. As Linda had virtually worked herself into a decline, and was poisoning the lives of all around her by her intense disagreeableness, Aunt Sadie, secretly much relieved by the turn things had taken, persuaded Uncle Matthew that the marriage, though by no means ideal, was inevitable, and that, if he did not wish to alienate for ever his favourite child, he had better put a good face on it.

"I suppose it might have been worse," Uncle Matthew said doubtfully, "at least the fella's not a Roman Catholic."

Chapter 9

THE ENGAGEMENT WAS duly announced in *The Times*. The
Kroesigs now invited the Alconleighs to spend a Saturday to Monday at their house near Guildford. Lady Kroesig, in her letter to
Aunt Sadie, called it a week-end, and said it would be nice to get to
know each other better. Uncle Matthew flew into a furious temper.
It was one of his idiosyncrasies that, not only did he never stay in
other people's houses (except, very occasionally, with relations),
but he regarded it as a positive insult that he should be invited to do
so. He despised the expression "week-end," and gave a sarcastic
snort at the idea that it would be nice to know the Kroesigs better.
When Aunt Sadie had calmed him down a bit, she put forward
the suggestion that the Kroesig family, father, mother, daughter
Marjorie and Tony, should be asked instead if they would spend
Saturday to Monday at Alconleigh. Poor Uncle Matthew, having
swallowed the great evil of Linda's engagement, had, to do him justice, resolved to put the best face he could on it, and had no wish to
make trouble for her with her future in-laws. He had at heart a great
respect for family connections, and once, when Bob and Jassy
were slanging a cousin whom the whole family, including Uncle

Matthew himself, very much disliked, he had turned upon them, knocked their heads together sharply, and said:

"In the first place he's a relation, and in the second place he's a clergyman, so shut up."

It had become a classical saying with the Radletts.

So the Kroesigs were duly invited. They accepted, and the date was fixed. Aunt Sadie then got into a panic, and summoned Aunt Emily and Davey. (I was staying at Alconleigh anyhow, for a few weeks' hunting.) Louisa was feeding her second baby in Scotland, but hoped to come south for the wedding later on.

The arrival at Alconleigh of the four Kroesigs could not have been more inauspicious. As the car which had met them at the station was heard humming up the drive, every single light in the whole house fused—Davey had brought a new ultra-violet lamp with him, which had done the trick. The guests had to be led into the hall in pitch darkness, while Logan fumbled about in the pantry for a candle, and Uncle Matthew rushed off to the fuse box. Lady Kroesig and Aunt Sadie chatted politely about this and that, Linda and Tony giggled in the corner, and Sir Leicester hit his gouty foot on the edge of a refectory table, while the voice of an invisible Davey could be heard, apologizing in a high wail, from the top of the staircase. It was really very embarrassing.

At last the lights went up, and the Kroesigs were revealed. Sir Leicester was a tall fair man with grey hair, whose undeniable good looks were marred by a sort of silliness in his face; his wife and daughter were two dumpy little fluffy females. Tony evidently took after his father, and Marjorie after her mother. Aunt Sadie, thrown out of her stride by the sudden transformation of what had been mere voices in the dark into flesh and blood, and feeling herself unable to produce more topics of conversation, hurried them upstairs to rest, and dress for dinner. It was always considered at Alconleigh that the journey from London was an experience involving great exhaustion, and people were supposed to be in need of rest after it.

"What is this lamp?" Uncle Matthew asked Davey, who was still saying how sorry he was, still clad in the exiguous dressing-gown which he had put on for his sun-bath.

"Well, you know how one never can digest anything in the winter months."

"I can, damn you," said Uncle Matthew. This, addressed to Davey, could be interpreted as a term of endearment.

"You think you can, but you can't really. Now this lamp pours its rays into the system, your glands begin to work, and your food does you good again."

"Well, don't pour any more rays until we have had the voltage altered. When the house is full of bloody Huns one wants to be able to see what the hell they're up to."

For dinner, Linda wore a white chintz dress with an enormous skirt, and a black lace scarf. She looked entirely ravishing, and it was obvious that Sir Leicester was much taken with her appearance—Lady Kroesig and Miss Marjorie, in bits of georgette and lace, seemed not to notice it. Marjorie was an intensely dreary girl, a few years older than Tony, who had failed so far to marry, and seemed to have no biological reason for existing.

"Have you read *Brothers*?" Lady Kroesig asked Uncle Matthew, conversationally, as they settled down to their soup.

"What's that?"

"The new Ursula Langdok—*Brothers*—it's about two brothers. You ought to read it."

"My dear Lady Kroesig, I have only read one book in my life, and that is *White Fang*. It's so frightfully good I've never bothered to read another. But Davey here reads books—you've read *Brothers*, Davey, I bet."

"Indeed, I have not," said Davey petulantly.

"I'll lend it to you," said Lady Kroesig, "I have it with me, and I finished it in the train."

"You shouldn't," said Davey, "read in trains, ever. It's madly wearing to the optic nerve centres, it imposes a most fearful strain.

May I see the menu, please? I must explain that I'm on a new diet, one meal white, one meal red. It's doing me so much good. Oh, dear, what a pity. Sadie—oh, she's not listening—Logan, could I ask for an egg, very lightly boiled, you know. This is my white meal, and we are having saddle of mutton I see."

"Well, Davey, have your red meal now and your white meal for breakfast," said Uncle Matthew. "I've opened some Mouton Roths-child, and I know how much you like that—I opened it specially for you."

"Oh, it is too bad," said Davey, "because I happen to know that there are kippers for breakfast, and I do so love them. What a ghastly decision. No! it must be an egg now, with a little hock. I could never forgo the kippers, so delicious, so digestible, but, above all, so full of proteins."

"Kippers," said Bob, "are brown."

"Brown counts as red. Surely you can see that."

But when a chocolate cream, in generous supply, but never quite enough when the boys were at home, came round, it was seen to count as white. The Radletts often had cause to observe that you could never entirely rely upon Davey to refuse food, however unwholesome, if it was really delicious.

Aunt Sadie was making heavy weather with Sir Leicester. He was full of boring herbaceous enthusiasms, and took it for granted that she was too.

"What a lot you London people always know about gardens," she said. "You must talk to Davey, he is a great gardener."

"I am not really a London person," said Sir Leicester, reproach-fully. "I work in London, but my home is in Surrey."

"I count that," Aunt Sadie said, gently but firmly, "as the same."

The evening seemed endless. The Kroesigs obviously longed for bridge, and did not seem to care so much for racing demon when it was offered as a substitute. Sir Leicester said he had had a tiring week, and really should go to bed early.

"Don't know how you chaps can stand it," said Uncle Matthew, sympathetically. "I was saying to the bank manager at Merlinford only yesterday, it must be the hell of a life fussing about with other blokes' money all day, indoors."

Linda went to ring up Lord Merlin, who had just returned from abroad. Tony followed her, they were gone a long time, and came back looking flushed and rather self-conscious.

The next morning, as we were hanging about in the hall waiting for the kippers, which had already announced themselves with a heavenly smell, two breakfast trays were seen going upstairs, for Sir Leicester and Lady Kroesig.

"No, really, that beats everything, dammit," said Uncle Matthew. "I never heard of a *man* having breakfast in bed before." And he looked wistfully at his entrenching tool.

He was slightly mollified, however, when they came downstairs, just before eleven, all ready to go to church. Uncle Matthew was a great pillar of the church, read the lessons, chose the hymns, and took round the bag, and he liked his household to attend. Alas, the Kroesigs turned out to be blasted idolators, as was proved when they turned sharply to the east during the creed. In short, they were of the company of those who could do no right, and sighs of relief echoed through the house when they decided to catch an evening train back to London.

"TONY IS BOTTOM to Linda, isn't he?" I said, sadly.

Davey and I were walking together through Hen's Grove the next day. Davey always knew what you meant, it was one of the nice things about him.

"Bottom," he said sadly. He adored Linda.

"And nothing will wake her up?"

"Not before it's too late, I fear. Poor Linda, she has an intensely romantic character, which is fatal for a woman. Fortunately for them, and for all of us, most women are madly matter of fact, otherwise the world could hardly carry on."

Lord Merlin was braver than the rest of us, and said right out what he thought. Linda went over to see him and asked him.

"Are you pleased about my engagement?" to which he replied:

"No, of course not. Why are you doing it?"

"I'm in love," said Linda proudly.

"What makes you think so?"

"One doesn't think, one knows," she said.

"Fiddlesticks."

"Oh, you evidently don't understand about love, so what's the use of talking to you."

Lord Merlin got very cross, and said that neither did immature little girls understand about love.

"Love," he said, "is for grown-up people, as you will discover one day. You will also discover that it has nothing to do with marriage. I'm all in favour of you marrying soon, in a year or two, but for God's sake, and all of our sakes, don't go and marry a bore like Tony Kroesig."

"If he's such a bore, why did you ask him to stay?"

"I didn't ask him. Baby brought him, because Cecil had 'flu and couldn't come. Besides, I can't guess you'll go and marry every stopgap I have in my house."

"You ought to be more careful. Anyhow, I can't think why you say Tony's a bore, he knows everything."

"Yes, that's exactly it, he does. And what about Sir Leicester? And have you seen Lady Kroesig?"

But the Kroesig family was illuminated for Linda by the great glow of perfection which shone around Tony, and she would hear nothing against them. She parted rather coldly from Lord Merlin, came home, and abused him roundly. As for him, he waited to see what Sir Leicester was giving her for a wedding present. It was a pigskin dressing-case with dark tortoiseshell fittings and her initials on them in gold. Lord Merlin sent her a morocco one double the size, fitted with blonde tortoiseshells, and instead of initials, LINDA in diamonds.

He had embarked upon an elaborate series of Kroesig-teases of which this was to be the first.

The arrangements for the wedding did not go smoothly. There was trouble without end over settlements. Uncle Matthew, whose estate provided a certain sum of money for younger children, to be allocated by him as he thought best, very naturally did not wish to settle anything on Linda, at the expense of the others, in view of the fact that she was marrying the son of a millionaire. Sir Leicester, however, refused to settle a penny unless Uncle Matthew did—he had no great wish to make a settlement in any case, saying that it was against the policy of his family to tie up capital sums. In the end, by sheer persistence, Uncle Matthew got a beggarly amount for Linda. The whole thing worried and upset him very much, and confirmed him, if need be, in his hatred of the Teutonic race.

Tony and his parents wanted a London wedding, Uncle Matthew said he had never heard of anything so common and vulgar in his life. Women were married from their homes; he thought fashionable weddings the height of degradation, and refused to lead one of his daughters up the aisle of St. Margaret's through a crowd of gaping strangers. The Kroesigs explained to Linda that, if she had a country wedding, she would only get half the number of wedding presents, and also that the important, influential people, who would be of use, later, to Tony, would never come down to Gloucestershire in the depth of winter. All these arguments were lost on Linda. Since the days when she was planning to marry the Prince of Wales she had had a mental picture of what her wedding would be like, that is, as much like a wedding in a pantomime as possible, in a large church, with crowds both outside and in, with photographers, arum lilies, tulle, bridesmaids, and an enormous choir singing her favourite tune, "The Lost Chord." So she sided with the Kroesigs against poor Uncle Matthew, and, when fate tipped the scales in their favour by putting out of action the heating in Alconleigh church, Aunt Sadie took a London house, and the wedding was duly celebrated with every circumstance of publicized vulgarity at St. Margaret's.

What with one thing and another, by the time Linda was married, her parents and her parents-in-law were no longer on speaking terms. Uncle Matthew cried without restraint all through the ceremony; Sir Leicester seemed to be beyond tears.

Chapter 10

I THINK LINDA'S marriage was a failure almost from the beginning, but I really never knew much about it. Nobody did. She had married in the face of a good deal of opposition; the opposition proved to have been entirely well founded, and, Linda being what she was, maintained, for as long as possible, a perfect shopfront.

They were married in February, had a hunting honeymoon from a house they took at Melton, and settled down for good in Bryanston Square after Easter. Tony then started work in his father's old bank, and prepared to step into a safe Conservative seat in the House of Commons, an ambition which was very soon realized.

Closer acquaintance with their new in-laws did not make either the Radlett or the Kroesig families change their minds about each other. The Kroesigs thought Linda eccentric, affected, and extravagant. Worst of all, she was supposed not to be useful to Tony in his career. The Radletts considered that Tony was a first-class bore. He had a habit of choosing a subject, and then droning round and round it like an inaccurate bomb-aimer round his target, ever unable to hit; he knew vast quantities of utterly dreary facts, of which he did not hesitate to inform his companions, at great length and in great detail, whether they appeared to be interested or not.

He was infinitely serious, he no longer laughed at Linda's jokes, and the high spirits which, when she first knew him, he had seemed to possess, must have been due to youth, drink, and good health. Now that he was grown up and married he put all three resolutely behind him, spending his days in the bank house and his evenings at Westminster, never having any fun or breathing fresh air: his true self emerged, and he was revealed as a pompous, money-grubbing ass, more like his father every day.

He did not succeed in making an asset out of Linda. Poor Linda was incapable of understanding the Kroesig point of view; try as she might (and in the beginning she tried very hard, having an infinite desire to please) it remained mysterious to her. The fact is that, for the first time in her life, she found herself face to face with the bourgeois attitude of mind; and the fate often foreseen for me by Uncle Matthew as a result of my middle-class education had actually befallen her. The outward and visible signs which he so deprecated were all there—the Kroesigs said notepaper, perfume, mirror and mantelpiece, they even invited her to call them Father and Mother, which, in the first flush of love, she did, only to spend the rest of her married life trying to get out of it by addressing them to their faces as "you," and communicating with them by postcard or telegram. Inwardly their spirit was utterly commercial, everything was seen by them in terms of money. It was their barrier, their defence, their hope for the future, their support for the present, it raised them above their fellowmen, and with it they warded off evil. The only mental qualities that they respected were those which produced money in substantial quantities, it was their one criterion of success, it was power and it was glory. To say that a man was poor was to label him a rotter, bad at his job, idle, feckless, immoral. If it was somebody whom they really rather liked, in spite of this cancer, they could add that he had been unlucky. They had taken care to insure against this deadly evil in many ways. That it should not overwhelm them through such cataclysms beyond their control as war or revolution they had placed large sums of money in a dozen

different countries; they owned ranches, and estancias, and South
African farms, an hotel in Switzerland, a plantation in Malaya, and
they possessed many fine diamonds, not sparkling round Linda's
lovely neck to be sure, but lying in banks, stone by stone, easily
portable.

Linda's upbringing had made all this incomprehensible to her;
for money was a subject that was absolutely never mentioned at
Alconleigh. Uncle Matthew had no doubt a large income, but it
was derived from, tied up in, and a good percentage of it went back
into, his land. His land was to him something sacred, and, sacred
above that, was England. Should evil befall his country he would
stay and share it, or die, never would the notion have entered his
head that he might save himself, and leave old England in any sort
of lurch. He, his family and his estates were part of her and she was
part of him, for ever and ever. Later on, when war appeared to be
looming upon the horizon, Tony tried to persuade him to send
some money to America.

"What for?" said Uncle Matthew.

"You might be glad to go there yourself, or send the children. It's
always a good thing to have—"

"I may be old, but I can still shoot," said Uncle Matthew, furiously, "and I haven't got any children—for the purposes of fighting
they are all grown up."

"Victoria—"

"Victoria is thirteen. She would do her duty. I hope, if any
bloody foreigners ever got here, that every man, woman and child
would go on fighting them until one side or the other was wiped
out. Anyhow, I loathe abroad, nothing would induce me to live
there, I'd rather live in the gamekeeper's hut in Hen's Grove, and,
as for foreigners, they are all the same, and they all make me sick,"
he said, pointedly, glowering at Tony, who took no notice, but went
droning on about how clever he had been in transferring various
funds to various places. He had always remained perfectly unaware
of Uncle Matthew's dislike for him, and, indeed, such was my

uncle's eccentricity of behaviour, that it was not very easy for some-body as thick-skinned as Tony to differentiate between Uncle Matthew's behaviour towards those he loved and those he did not.

On the first birthday she had after her marriage, Sir Leicester gave Linda a cheque for £1,000. Linda was delighted and spent it that very day on a necklace of large half pearls surrounded by rubies, which she had been admiring for some time in a Bond Street shop. The Kroesigs had a small family dinner party for her, Tony was to meet her there, having been kept late at his office. Linda arrived, wearing a very plain white satin dress cut very low, and her necklace, went straight up to Sir Leicester, and said: "Oh, you were kind to give me such a wonderful present—look——"

Sir Leicester was stupefied.

"Did it cost all I sent you?" he said.

"Yes," said Linda. "I thought you would like me to buy one thing with it, and always remember it was you who gave it to me."

"No, dear. That wasn't at all what I intended. £1,000 is what you might call a capital sum, that means something on which you expect a return. You should not just spend it on a trinket which you wear three or four times a year, and which is most unlikely to appreciate in value. (And, by the way, if you buy jewels, let it always be diamonds—rubies and pearls are too easy to copy, they won't keep their price.) But, as I was saying, one hopes for a return. So you could either have asked Tony to invest it for you, or, which is what I really intended, you could have spent it on entertaining important people who would be of use to Tony in his career."

These important people were a continual thorn in poor Linda's side. She was always supposed by the Kroesigs to be a great hin-drance to Tony, both in politics and in the City, because, try as she might, she could not disguise how tedious they seemed to her. Like Aunt Sadie, she was apt to retire into a cloud of boredom on the smallest provocation, a vague look would come into her eyes, and her spirit would absent itself. Important people did not like this; they were not accustomed to it; they like to be listened and attended to by the young with concentrated deference when they were so kind as to bestow their company. What with Linda's yawns, and Tony informing them how many harbour-masters there were in the British Isles, important people were inclined to eschew the young Kroesigs. The old Kroesigs deeply deplored this state of affairs, for which they blamed Linda. They saw that she did not take the slightest interest in Tony's work. She tried to at first but it was beyond her; she simply could not understand how somebody who already had plenty of money could go and shut himself away from God's fresh air and blue skies, from the spring, the summer, the autumn, the winter, letting them merge into each other unaware that they were passing, simply in order to make more. She was far too young to be interested in politics, which were anyhow, in those days before Hitler came along to brighten them up, a very esoteric amusement.

"Your father was cross," she said to Tony, as they walked home after dinner. Sir Leicester lived in Hyde Park Gardens, it was a beautiful night, and they walked.

"I don't wonder," said Tony, shortly.

"But look, darling, how pretty it is. Don't you see how one couldn't resist it?"

"You are so affected. Do try and behave like an adult, won't you?"

THE AUTUMN AFTER Linda's marriage Aunt Emily took a little house in St. Leonard's Terrace, where she, Davey and I installed ourselves. She had been rather unwell, and Davey thought it would be a good thing to get her away from all her country duties and to make her rest, as no woman ever can at home. His novel, *The Abrasive Tube,* had just appeared, and was having a great success in intellectual circles. It was a psychological and physiological study of a South Polar explorer, snowed up in a hut where he knows he must eventually die, with enough rations to keep him going for a few months. In the end he dies. Davey was fascinated by Polar expeditions; he liked to observe, from a safe distance, how far the body can go when driven upon thoroughly indigestible foodstuffs deficient in vitamins.

"Pemmican," he would say, gleefully, falling upon the delicious food for which Aunt Emily's cook was renowned, "must have been so bad for them."

Aunt Emily, shaken out of the routine of her life at Shenley, took up with old friends again, entertained for us, and enjoyed herself so much that she talked of living half the year in London. As for me, I have never, before or since, been happier. The London season I had with Linda had been the greatest possible fun; it would be untrue and ungrateful to Aunt Sadie to deny that; I had even quite enjoyed the long dark hours we spent in the Peeresses' gallery; but there had been a curious unreality about it all, it was not related, one felt, to life. Now I had my feet firmly planted on the ground. I was allowed to do what I liked, see whom I chose, at any hour, peacefully, naturally, and without breaking rules, and it was wonderful to bring my friends home and have them greeted in a friendly, if somewhat detached manner, by Davey, instead of smuggling them up the back stairs for fear of a raging scene in the hall.

During this happy time I became happily engaged to Alfred Wincham, then a young don at, now Warden of, St. Peter's College, Oxford. With this kindly scholarly man I have been perfectly happy ever since, finding in our home at Oxford that refuge from the storms and puzzles of life which I had always wanted. I say no more about him here; this is Linda's story, not mine.

We saw a great deal of Linda just then; she would come and chat for hours on end. She did not seem to be unhappy, though I felt sure she was already waking from her Titania-trance, but was obviously lonely, as her husband was at his work all day and at the House in the evening. Lord Merlin was abroad, and she had, as yet, no other very intimate friends; she missed the comings and goings, the cheerful bustle and hours of pointless chatter which had made up the family life at Alconleigh. I reminded her how much, when she was there, she had longed to escape, and she agreed, rather doubtfully, that it was wonderful to be on one's own. She was much pleased by my engagement, and liked Alfred.

"He has such a serious, clever look," she said. "What pretty little black babies you'll have, both of you so dark."

He only quite liked her; he suspected that she was a tough nut, and rather, I must own, to my relief, she never exercised over him the spell in which she had entranced Davey and Lord Merlin.

One day, as we were busy with wedding invitations, she came in and announced:

"I am in pig, what d'you think of that?"

"A most hideous expression, Linda dear," said Aunt Emily, "but I suppose we must congratulate you."

"I suppose so," said Linda. She sank into a chair with an enormous sigh. "I feel awfully ill, I must say."

"But think how much good it will do you in the long run," said Davey, enviously, "such a wonderful clearout."

"I see just what you mean," said Linda. "Oh, we've got such a ghastly evening ahead of us. Some important Americans. It seems Tony wants to do a deal or something, and these Americans will only do the deal if they take a fancy to me. Now can you explain that? I know I shall be sick all over them, and my father-in-law will be so cross. Oh, the horror of important people—you are lucky not to know any."

LINDA'S CHILD, A girl, was born in May. She was ill for a long time before, and very ill indeed at her confinement. The doctors told her that she must never have another child, as it would almost certainly kill her if she did. This was a blow to the Kroesigs, as bankers, it seems, like kings, require many sons, but Linda did not appear to mind at all. She took no interest whatever in the baby she had got. I went to see her as soon as I was allowed to. She lay in a bower of blossom and pink roses, and looked like a corpse. I was expecting a baby myself, and naturally took a great interest in Linda's.

"What are you going to call her—where is she, anyway?"

"In Sister's room—it shrieks. Moira, I believe."

"Not Moira, darling, you can't. I never heard such an awful name."

"Tony likes it, he had a sister called Moira who died, and what d'you think I found out (not from him, but from their old nanny)? She died because Marjorie whacked her on the head with a hammer when she was four months old. Do you call that interesting? And then they say we are an uncontrolled family—why even Fa has never actually murdered anybody, or do you count that beater?"

"All the same, I don't see how you can saddle the poor little thing with a name like Moira, it's too unkind."

"Not really, if you think. It'll have to grow up a Moira if the Kroesigs are to like it (people always grow up to their names I've noticed) and they might as well like it because frankly, I don't."

"Linda, how can you be so naughty, and, anyway, you can't possibly tell whether you like her or not, yet," I ventured.

"Oh, yes I can. I can always tell if I like people from the start, and I don't like Moira, that's all. She's a fearful Counter-Hon, wait till you see her."

At this point the Sister came in, and Linda introduced us.

"Oh, you are the cousin I hear so much about," she said. "You'll want to see the baby."

She went away and presently returned carrying a Moses basket full of wails.

"Poor thing," said Linda indifferently. "It's really kinder not to look."

"Don't pay any attention to her," said the Sister. "She pretends to be a wicked woman, but it's all put on."

I did look, and, deep down among the frills and lace, there was the usual horrid sight of a howling orange in a fine black wig.

"Isn't she sweet," said the Sister. "Look at her little hands."

I shuddered slightly, and said:

"Well, I know it's dreadful of me, but I don't much like them as small as that; I'm sure she'll be divine in a year or two."

The wails now entered on a crescendo, and the whole room was filled with hideous noise.

"Poor soul," said Linda. "I think it must have caught sight of itself in a glass. Do take it away, Sister."

Davey now came into the room. He was meeting me there to drive me down to Shenley for the night. The Sister came back and shooed us both off, saying that Linda had had enough. Outside her room, which was in the largest and most expensive nursing home in London, I paused, looking for the lift.

"This way," said Davey, and then, with a slightly self-conscious giggle: "Brought up in the harem, I know my way around. Oh, how are you, Sister Thesiger? How very nice to see you."

"Captain Warbeck—I must tell Matron you are here."

And it was nearly an hour before I could drag Davey out of this home away from home. I hope I am not giving the impression that Davey's whole life was centred round his health. He was fully occupied with his work, writing, and editing a literary review, but his health was his hobby, and, as such, more in evidence during his spare time, the time when I saw most of him. How he enjoyed it! He seemed to regard his body with the affectionate preoccupation of a farmer towards a pig—not a good doer, the small one of the litter, which must somehow be made to be a credit to the farm. He weighed it, sunned it, aired it, exercised it, and gave it special diets, new kinds of patent food and medicine, but all in vain. It never put on so much as a single ounce of weight, it never became a credit to the farm, but, somehow it lived, enjoying good things, enjoying its life, though falling victim to the ills that flesh is heir to, and other imaginary ills as well, through which it was nursed with unfailing care, with concentrated attention, by the good farmer and his wife.

AUNT EMILY SAID at once, when I told her about Linda and poor Moira:

"She's too young. I don't believe very young mothers ever get wrapped up in their babies. It's when women are older that they so adore their children, and maybe it's better for the children to have young unadoring mothers and to lead more detached lives."

"But Linda seems to loathe her."

"That's so like Linda," said Davey. "She has to do things by extremes."

"But she seemed so gloomy. You must say that's not very like her."

"She's been terribly ill," said Aunt Emily. "Sadie was in despair. Twice they thought she would die."

"Don't talk of it," said Davey. "I can't imagine the world without Linda."

Chapter 11

LIVING IN OXFORD, engrossed with my husband and young family, I saw less of Linda during the next few years than at any time in her life. This, however, did not affect the intimacy of our relationship, which remained absolute, and, when we did meet, it was still as though we were seeing each other every day. I stayed with her in London from time to time, and she with me in Oxford, and we corresponded regularly. I may as well say here that the one thing she never discussed with me was the deterioration of her marriage; in any case it would not have been necessary, the whole thing being as plain as relations between married people ever can be. Tony was, quite obviously, not good enough as a lover to make up, even at first, for his shortcomings in other respects, the boredom of his company and the mediocrity of his character. Linda was out of love with him by the time the child was born, and, thereafter, could not care a rap for the one or the other. The young man she had fallen in love with, handsome, gay, intellectual and domineering, melted away upon closer acquaintance, and proved to have been a chimera, never to have existed outside her imagination. Linda did not commit the usual fault of blaming Tony for what was entirely her own mistake, she merely turned from him in absolute indifference. This was made easier by the fact that she saw so little of him.

Lord Merlin now launched a tremendous Kroesig-tease. The Kroesigs were always complaining that Linda never went out, would not entertain, unless absolutely forced to, and did not care for society. They told their friends that she was a country girl, entirely sporting, that if you went into her drawing-room she would be found training a retriever with dead rabbits hidden behind the sofa cushions. They pretended that she was an amiable, half-witted, beautiful rustic, incapable of helping poor Tony, who was obliged to battle his way through life alone. There was a grain of truth in all this, the fact being that the Kroesig circle of acquaintances was too ineffably boring; poor Linda, having been unable to make any headway at all in it, had given up the struggle, and retired to the more congenial company of retrievers and dormice.

Lord Merlin, in London for the first time since Linda's marriage, at once introduced her into his world, the world towards which she had always looked, that of smart bohemianism; and here she found her feet, was entirely happy, and had an immediate and great success. She became very gay and went everywhere. There is no more popular unit in London society than a young, beautiful, but perfectly respectable woman who can be asked to dinner without her husband, and Linda was soon well on the way to having her head turned. Photographers and gossip writers dogged her footsteps, and indeed one could not escape the impression, until half an hour of her company put one right again, that she was becoming a bit of a bore. Her house was full of people from morning till night, chatting. Linda, who loved to chat, found many congenial spirits in the carefree, pleasure-seeking London of those days, when unemployment was rife as much among the upper as the lower classes. Young men, pensioned off by their relations, who would sometimes suggest in a perfunctory manner that it might be a good thing if they found some work, but without seriously helping them to do so (and, anyhow, what work was there for such as they?) clustered round Linda like bees round honey, buzz, buzz, buzz, chat, chat, chat. In her bedroom, on her bed, sitting on the stairs outside while she had a bath, in the kitchen while she ordered the food, shopping, walking round the park, cinema, theatre, opera, ballet, dinner, supper, night clubs, parties, dances, all day, all night—endless, endless, chat.

"But what do you suppose they talk about?" Aunt Sadie, disapproving, used to wonder. What, indeed?

Tony went early to his bank, hurrying out of the house with an air of infinite importance, an attaché case in one hand and a sheaf of newspapers under his arm. His departure heralded the swarm of chatterers, almost as if they had been waiting round the street corner to see him leave, and thereafter the house was filled with them. They were very nice, very good-looking, and great fun—their manners were perfect. I never was able, during my short visits, to distinguish them much one from another, but I saw their attraction, the unfailing attraction of vitality and high spirits. By no stretch of the imagination, however, could they have been called "important," and the Kroesigs were beside themselves at this turn of affairs.

Tony did not seem to mind; he had long given up Linda as hopeless from the point of view of his career, and was rather pleased and flattered by the publicity which now launched her as a beauty. "The beautiful wife of a clever young M.P." Besides, he found that they were invited to large parties and balls, to which it suited him very well to go, coming late after the House, and where there were often to be found not only Linda's unimportant friends, with whom she would amuse herself, but also colleagues of his own, and by no means unimportant ones, whom he could buttonhole and bore at the bar. It would have been useless, however, to explain this to the old Kroesigs, who had a deeply rooted distrust of smart society, of dancing, and of any kind of fun, all of which led, in their opinion, to extravagance, without compensating material advantages. Fortunately for Linda, Tony at this time was not on good terms with his father, owing to a conflict of policies in the bank; they did not go to Hyde Park Gardens as much as when they were first married, and visits to Planes, the Kroesig house in Surrey, were, for the time being, off. When they did meet, however, the old Kroesigs made it clear to Linda that she was not proving a satisfactory daughter-in-law. Even Tony's divergence of views was put down to her, and Lady Kroesig told her friends, with a sad shake of the head, that Linda did not bring out the best in him.

LINDA NOW PROCEEDED to fritter away years of her youth, with nothing whatever to show for them. If she had had an intellectual upbringing the place of all this pointless chatter, jokes and parties might have been taken by a serious interest in the arts, or by reading; if she had been happy in her marriage that side of her nature which craved for company could have found its fulfilment by the nursery fender; things being as they were, however, all was frippery and silliness.

Alfred and I once had an argument with Davey about her, during which we said all this. Davey accused us of being prigs, though at heart he must have known that we were right.

"But Linda gives one so much pleasure," he kept saying, "she is like a bunch of flowers. You don't want people like that to bury themselves in serious reading; what would be the good?"

However, even he was forced to admit that her behaviour to poor little Moira was not what it should be. (The child was fat, fair, placid, dull and backward, and Linda still did not like her; the Kroesigs, on the other hand, adored her, and she spent more and more time, with her nanny, at Planes. They loved having her there, but that did not stop them from ceaseless criticism of Linda's behaviour. They now told everybody that she was a silly society butterfly, hard-hearted neglecter of her child.)

Alfred said, almost angrily:

"It's so odd that she doesn't even have love affairs. I don't see what she gets out of her life, it must be dreadfully empty."

Alfred likes people to be filed neatly away under some heading that he can understand; careerist, social climber, virtuous wife and mother, or adulteress.

Linda's social life was completely aimless; she simply collected around her an assortment of cosy people who had the leisure to chat all day; whether they were millionaires or paupers, princes or refugee Rumanians, was a matter of complete indifference to her. In spite of the fact that, except for me and her sisters, nearly all her friends were men, she had such a reputation for virtue that she was currently suspected of being in love with her husband.

"Linda believes in love," said Davey, "she is passionately romantic. At the moment I am sure she is, subconsciously, waiting for an irresistible temptation. Casual affairs would not interest her in the least. One must hope that when it comes it will not prove to be another Bottom."

"I suppose she is really rather like my mother," I said, "and all of hers have been Bottoms."

"Poor Bolter!" said Davey, "but she's happy now, isn't she, with her white hunter?"

TONY SOON BECAME, as was to be expected, a perfect mountain of pomposity, more like his father every day. He was full of large, clear-sighted ideas for bettering the condition of the capitalist classes, and made no bones of his hatred and distrust of the workers.

"I hate the lower classes," he said one day, when Linda and I were having tea with him on the terrace of the House of Commons. "Ravening beasts, trying to get my money. Let them try, that's all."

"Oh, shut up, Tony," said Linda, bringing a dormouse out of her pocket, and feeding it with crumbs. "I love them, anyway I was brought up with them. The trouble with you is you don't know the lower classes and you don't belong to the upper classes, you're just a rich foreigner who happens to live here. Nobody ought to be in Parliament who hasn't lived in the country, anyhow part of their life — why, my old Fa knows more what he's talking about, when he does talk in the House, than you do."

"I have lived in the country," said Tony. "Put that dormouse away, people are looking."

He never got cross, he was far too pompous.

"Surrey," said Linda, with infinite contempt.

"Anyhow, last time your Fa made a speech, about the Peeresses in their own right, his only argument for keeping them out of the House was that, if once they got in, they might use the Peers' lavatory."

"Isn't he a love?" said Linda. "It's what they all thought, you know, but he was the only one who dared to say it."

"That's the worst of the House of Lords," said Tony. "These back-woodsmen come along just when they think they will, and bring the whole place into disrepute with a few dotty remarks, which get an enormous amount of publicity and give people the impression that we are governed by a lot of lunatics. These old peers ought to realize that it's their duty to their class to stay at home and keep quiet. The amount of excellent, solid, necessary work done in the House of Lords is quite unknown to the man in the street."

Sir Leicester was expecting soon to become a peer, so this was a subject close to Tony's heart. His general attitude to what he called the man in the street was that he ought constantly to be covered by machine-guns; this having become impossible, owing to the weakness, in the past, of the great Whig families, he must be doped into submission with the fiction that huge reforms, to be engineered by the Conservative party, were always just round the next corner. Like this he could be kept quiet indefinitely, as long as there was no war. War brings people together and opens their eyes, it must be avoided at all costs, and especially war with Germany, where the Kroesigs had financial interests and many relations. (They were originally a Junkers family, and snobbed their Prussian connections as much as the latter looked down on them for being in trade.)

Both Sir Leicester and his son were great admirers of Herr Hitler: Sir Leicester had been to see him during a visit to Germany, and had been taken for a drive in a Mercedes-Benz by Dr. Schacht.

Linda took no interest in politics, but she was instinctively and unreasonably English. She knew that one Englishman was worth a hundred foreigners, whereas Tony thought that one capitalist was worth a hundred workers. Their outlook upon this, as upon most subjects, differed fundamentally.

Chapter 12

BY A CURIOUS irony of fate it was at her father-in-law's house in Surrey that Linda met Christian Talbot. The little Moira, aged six, now lived permanently at Planes; it seemed a good arrangement as it saved Linda, who disliked housekeeping, the trouble of running two establishments, while Moira was given the benefit of country air and food. Linda and Tony were supposed to spend a couple of nights there every week, and Tony generally did so. Linda, in fact, went down for Sunday about once a month.

Planes was a horrible house. It was an overgrown cottage, that is to say, the rooms were large with all the disadvantages of a cottage, low ceilings, small windows with diamond panes, uneven floorboards, and a great deal of naked knotted wood. It was furnished neither in good nor in bad taste, but simply with no attempt at taste at all, and was not even very comfortable. The garden which lay around it would be a lady water-colourist's heaven, herbaceous borders, rockeries and water-gardens were carried to a perfection of vulgarity, and flaunted a riot of huge and hideous flowers, each individual bloom appearing twice as large, three times as brilliant as it ought to have been and if possible of a different colour from that which nature intended. It would be hard to say whether it was more frightful, more like glorious technicolor, in spring, in summer, or in autumn. Only in the depth of winter, covered by the kindly snow, did it melt into the landscape and become tolerable.

One April Saturday morning, in 1937, Linda, with whom I had been staying in London, took me down there for the night, as she sometimes did. I think she liked to have a buffer between herself and the Kroesigs, perhaps especially between herself and Moira. The old Kroesigs were by way of being very fond of me, and Sir Leicester sometimes took me for walks and hinted how much he wished that it had been me, so serious, so well educated, such a good wife and mother, whom Tony had married.

We motored down past acres of blossom.

"The great difference," said Linda, "between Surrey and proper, real country, is that in Surrey, when you see blossom, you know there will be no fruit. Think of the Vale of Evesham, and then look at all this pointless pink stuff—it gives you quite a different feeling. The garden at Planes will be a riot of sterility, just you wait."

It was. You could hardly see any beautiful, pale, bright, yellow-green of spring, every tree appeared to be entirely covered with a waving mass of pink or mauve tissue-paper. The daffodils were so thick on the ground that they too obscured the green, they were new varieties of a terrifying size, either dead white or dark yellow, thick and fleshy; they did not look at all like the fragile friends of one's childhood. The whole effect was of a scene for musical comedy, and it exactly suited Sir Leicester, who, in the country, gave a surprisingly adequate performance of the old English squire. Picturesque. Delightful.

He was pottering in the garden as we drove up, in an old pair of corduroy trousers, so much designed as an old pair that it seemed improbable that they had ever been new, an old tweed coat on the same lines, secateurs in his hand, a depressed Corgi at his heels, and a mellow smile on his face.

"Here you are," he said, heartily. (One could almost see, as in the strip advertisements, a bubble coming out of his head—thinks—"You are a most unsatisfactory daughter-in-law, but nobody can say

it's our fault, we always have a welcome and a kind smile for you.")
"Car going well, I hope? Tony and Moira have gone out riding, I
thought you might have passed them. Isn't the garden looking
grand just now, I can hardly bear to go to London and leave all this
beauty with no one to see it. Come for a stroll before lunch — Foster
will see to your gear — just ring the front-door bell, Fanny, he may
not have heard the car."

He led us off into Madam Butterfly-land.

"I must warn you," he said, "that we have got rather a rough diamond coming to lunch. I don't know if you've ever met old Talbot
who lives in the village, the old professor? Well, his son, Christian.
He's by way of being rather a Communist, a clever chap gone all
wrong, and a journalist on some daily rag. Tony can't bear him, never
could as a child, and he's very cross with me for asking him today, but
I always think it's as well to see something of these Left-wing fellows.
If people like us are nice to them they can be tamed wonderfully."

He said this in the tone of one who might have saved the life of a
Communist in the war, and, by this act, turned him, through grati-
tude, into a true-blue Tory. But in the first world war Sir Leicester
had considered that, with his superior brain, he would have been
wasted as cannon fodder, and had fixed himself in an office in
Cairo. He neither saved nor took any lives, nor did he risk his own,
but built up many valuable business contacts, became a major and
got an O.B.E., thus making the best of all worlds.

So Christian came to luncheon, and behaved with the utmost
intransigence. He was an extraordinarily handsome young man,
tall and fair, in a completely different way from that of Tony, thin
and very English-looking. His clothes were outrageous — he wore a
really old pair of grey flannel trousers, full of little round moth-
holes in the most embarrassing places, no coat, and a flannel shirt,
one of the sleeves of which had a tattered tear from wrist to elbow.

"Has your father been writing anything lately?" Lady Kroesig
asked, as they sat down to luncheon.

"I suppose so," said Christian, "as it's his profession. I can't say

I've asked him, but one assumes he has, just as one assumes that Tony has been banking something lately."

He then planted his elbow, bare through the rent, onto the table between himself and Lady Kroesig and swivelling right round to Linda, who was on his other side, he told her, at length and in immense detail, of a production of *Hamlet* he had seen lately in Moscow. The cultured Kroesigs listened attentively, throwing off occasional comments calculated to show that they knew *Hamlet* well— "I don't think that quite fits in with my idea of Ophelia," or "But Polonius was a very old man," to all of which Christian turned an utterly deaf ear, gobbling his food with one hand, his elbow on the table, his eyes on Linda.

After luncheon he said to Linda:

"Come back and have tea with my father, you'd like him," and they went off together, leaving the Kroesigs to behave for the rest of the afternoon like a lot of hens who have seen a fox.

Sir Leicester took me to his water-garden, which was full of enormous pink forget-me-nots, and dark-brown irises, and said:

"It is really rather too bad of Linda, little Moira has been so much looking forward to showing her the ponies. That child idolizes her mother."

She didn't, actually, in the least. She was fond of Tony and quite indifferent to Linda, calm and stolid and not given to idolatry, but it was part of the Kroesigs' creed that children should idolize their mothers.

"Do you know Pixie Townsend?" he asked me, suddenly.

"No," I said, which was true, nor did I then know anything about her. "Who is she?"

"She's a very delightful person." He changed the subject.

Linda returned just in time to dress for dinner, looking extremely beautiful. She made me come and chat while she had her bath— Tony was reading to Moira upstairs in the night nursery. Linda was perfectly enchanted with her outing. Christian's father, she said, lived in the smallest house imaginable, an absolute contrast to what

Christian called the Kroesighof, because, although absolutely tiny, it had nothing whatever of a cottage about it—it was in the grand manner, and full of books. Every available wall space was covered with books, they lay stacked on tables and chairs and in heaps on the floor. Mr. Talbot was the exact opposite of Sir Leicester, there was nothing picturesque about him, or anything to indicate that he was a learned man, he was brisk and matter-of-fact, and had made some very funny jokes about Davey, whom he knew well.

"He's perfect heaven," Linda kept saying, her eyes shining. What she really meant, as I could see too clearly, was that Christian was perfect heaven. She was dazzled by him. It seemed that he had talked without cease, and his talk consisted of variations upon a single theme—the betterment of the world through political change. Linda, since her marriage, had heard no end of political shop talked by Tony and his friends, but this related politics entirely to personalities and jobs. As the persons all seemed to her infinitely old and dull, and as it was quite immaterial to her whether they got jobs or not, Linda had classed politics as a boring subject, and used to go off into a dream when they were discussed. But Christian's politics did not bore her. As they walked back from his father's house that evening he had taken her for a tour of the world. He showed her Fascism in Italy, Nazism in Germany, civil war in Spain, inadequate Socialism in France, tyranny in Africa, starvation in Asia, reaction in America and Right-wing blight in England. Only the U.S.S.R., Norway and Mexico came in for a modicum of praise.

Linda was a plum ripe for shaking. The tree was now shaken, and down she came. Intelligent and energetic, but with no outlet for her energies, unhappy in her marriage, uninterested in her child, and inwardly oppressed with a sense of futility, she was in the mood either to take up some cause, or to embark upon a love affair. That a cause should now be presented by an attractive young man made both it and him irresistible.

Chapter 13

THE POOR ALCONLEIGHS were now presented with crises in the lives of three of their children almost simultaneously. Linda ran away from Tony, Jassy ran away from home, and Matt ran away from Eton. The Alconleighs were obliged to face the fact, as parents must sooner or later, that their children had broken loose from control and had taken charge of their own lives. Distracted, disapproving, worried to death, there was nothing they could do; they had become mere spectators of a spectacle which did not please them in the least. This was the year when the parents of our contemporaries would console themselves, if things did not go quite as they hoped for their own children, by saying: "Never mind, just think of the poor Alconleighs!"

Linda threw discretion, and what worldly wisdom she may have picked up during her years in London society, to the winds; she became an out-and-out Communist, bored and embarrassed everybody to death by preaching her new-found doctrine, not only at the dinner-table, but also from a soap-box in Hyde Park, and other equally squalid rostra, and finally, to the infinite relief of the Kroesig family, she went off to live with Christian. Tony started proceedings for divorce. This was a great blow to my aunt and uncle. It is true that they had never liked Tony, but they were infinitely old-fashioned in their ideas; marriage, to their way of thinking, was marriage, and adultery was wrong. Aunt Sadie was, in particular, profoundly shocked by the light-hearted way in which Linda had abandoned the little Moira. I think it all reminded her too much of my mother, and that she envisaged Linda's future from now on as a series of uncontrollable bolts.

Linda came to see me in Oxford. She was on her way back to London after having broken the news at Alconleigh. I thought it was really very brave of her to do it in person, and indeed, the first thing she asked for (most unlike her) was a drink. She was quite unnerved.

"Goodness," she said. "I'd forgotten how terrifying Fa can be — even now, when he's got no power over one. It was just like after we lunched with Tony; in the businessroom just the same, and he simply roared, and poor Mummy looked miserable, but she was pretty furious too, and you know how sarcastic she can be. Oh, well, that's over. Darling, it's heaven to see you again."

I hadn't seen her since the Sunday at Planes when she met Christian, so I wanted to hear all about her life.

"Well," she said, "I'm living with Christian in his flat, but it's very small, I must say, but perhaps that is just as well, because I'm doing the housework, and I don't seem to be very good at it, but luckily he is."

"He'll need to be," I said.

Linda was notorious in the family for her unhandiness, she could never even tie her own stock, and on hunting days either Uncle Matthew or Josh always had to do it for her. I so well remember her standing in front of a looking-glass in the hall, with Uncle Matthew tying it from behind, both the very picture of concentration, Linda saying: "Oh, now I see. Next time I know I shall be able to manage." As she had never in her life done so much as make her own bed, I could not imagine that Christian's flat could be very tidy or comfortable if it was being run by her.

"You are horrid. But oh how dreadful it is, cooking, I mean. That oven—Christian puts things in and says: 'Now you take it out in about half an hour.' I don't dare tell him how terrified I am, and at the end of half an hour I summon up all my courage and open the oven, and there is that awful hot blast hitting one in the face. I don't wonder people sometimes put their heads in and leave them out of sheer misery. Oh, dear, and I wish you could have seen the Hoover running away with me, it suddenly took the bit between its teeth and made for the lift shaft. How I shrieked—Christian only just rescued me in time. I think housework is far more tiring and frightening than hunting is, no comparison, and yet after hunting we had eggs for tea and were made to rest for hours, but after housework people expect one to go on just as if nothing special had happened." She sighed.

"Christian is very strong," she said, "and very brave. He doesn't like it when I shriek."

She seemed tired I thought and rather worried, and I looked in vain for signs of great happiness or great love.

"So what about Tony—how has he taken it?"

"Oh, he's awfully pleased, actually, because he can now marry his mistress without having a scandal, or being divorced, or upsetting the Conservative Association."

It was so like Linda never to have hinted, even to me, that Tony had a mistress.

"Who is she?" I said.

"Called Pixie Townsend. You know the sort, young face, with white hair dyed blue. She adores Moira, lives near Planes, and takes her out riding every day. She's a terrific Counter-Hon, but I'm only too thankful now that she exists, because I needn't feel in the least bit guilty—they'll all get on so much better without me."

"Married?"

"Oh, yes, and divorced her husband years ago. She's frightfully good at all poor Tony's things, golf and business and Conservatism, just like I wasn't, and Sir Leicester thinks she's perfect. Goodness, they'll be happy."

"Now I want to hear more about Christian, please."

"Well, he's heaven. He's a frightfully serious man, you know, a Communist, and so am I now, and we are surrounded by comrades all day, and they are terrific Hons, and there's an anarchist. The comrades don't like anarchists, isn't it queer? I always thought they were the same thing, but Christian likes this one because he threw a bomb at the King of Spain; you must say it's romantic. He's called Ramon, and he sits about all day and broods over the miners at Oviedo because his brother is one."

"Yes, but, darling, tell about Christian."

"Oh, he's perfect heaven—you must come and stay—or perhaps that wouldn't be very comfortable—come and see us. You can't think what an extraordinary man he is, so detached from other human beings that he hardly notices whether they are there or not. He only cares for ideas."

"I hope he cares for you."

"Well, I think he does, but he is very strange and absent-minded. I must tell you, the evening before I ran away with him (I only moved down to Pimlico in a taxi, but running away sounds romantic) he dined with his brother, so naturally I thought they'd talk about me and discuss the whole thing, so I couldn't resist ringing him up at about midnight and saying: 'Hullo, darling, did you have a nice evening, and what did you talk about?' and he said: 'I can't remember—oh, guerrilla warfare, I think.'"

"Is his brother a Communist too?"

"Oh, no, he's in the Foreign Office. Fearfully grand, looks like a deep-sea monster—you know."

"Oh, that Talbot—yes, I see. I haven't connected them. So now what are your plans?"

"Well, he says he's going to marry me when I'm divorced. I think it's rather silly, I rather agree with Mummy that once is enough, for marriage, but he says I'm the kind of person one marries if one's living with them, and the thing is it would be bliss not to be called Kroesig any more. Anyway, we'll see."

"Then what's your life? I suppose you don't go to parties and things now, do you?"

"Darling, such killing parties, you can't think—he won't let us go to ordinary ones at all. Grandi had a dinner-dance last week, and he rang me up himself and asked me to bring Christian, which I thought was awfully nice of him actually—he always has been nice to me—but Christian got into quite a temper and said if I couldn't see any reason against going I'd better go, but nothing would induce him to. So in the end, of course, neither of us went, and I heard afterwards it was the greatest fun. And we mayn't go to the Ribs or to . . ." and she mentioned several families known as much for their hospitality as for their Right-wing convictions.

"The worst of being a Communist is that the parties you may go to are—well—awfully funny and touching, but not very gay, and they're always in such gloomy places. Next week, for instance, we've got three, some Czechs at the Sacco and Vanzetti Memorial Hall at Golders Green, Ethiopians at the Paddington Baths, and the Scotsboro boys at some boring old rooms or other. You know."

"The Scotsboro, boys," I said. "Are they really still going? They must be getting on."

"Yes, and they've gone downhill socially," said Linda, with a giggle. "I remember a perfectly divine party Brian gave for them—it was the first party Merlin ever took me to so I remember it well, oh, dear, it was fun. But next Thursday won't be the least like that. (Darling, I am being disloyal, but it is such heaven to have a chat after all these months. The comrades are sweet, but they never chat, they make speeches all the time.) But I'm always saying to Christian how much I wish his buddies would either brighten up their parties a bit or else stop giving them, because I don't see the point of sad parties, do you? And Left-wing people are always sad because they mind dreadfully about their causes, and the causes are always going so badly. You see, I bet the Scotsboro boys will be electrocuted in the end, if they don't die of old age first, that is. One does feel so much on their side, but it's no good, people like Sir

Leicester always come out on top, so what can one do? However, the comrades don't seem to realize that, and, luckily for them, they don't know Sir Leicester, so they feel they must go on giving these sad parties."

"What do you wear at them?" I asked, with some interest, thinking that Linda, in her expensive-looking clothes, must seem very much out of place at these baths and halls.

"You know, that was a great tease at first, it worried me dreadfully, but I've discovered that, so long as one wears wool or cotton, everything is all right. Silk and satin would be the blunder. But I only ever do wear wool and cotton, so I'm on a good wicket. No jewels, of course, but then I left them behind at Bryanston Square, it's the way I was brought up but I must say it gave me a pang. Christian doesn't know about jewellery—I told him, because I thought he'd be rather pleased I'd given them all up for him, but he only said: 'Well, there's always the Burma Jewel Company.' Oh, dear, he is such a funny man, you must meet him again soon. I must go, darling, it has so cheered me up to see you."

I don't quite know why, but I felt somehow that Linda had been once more deceived in her emotions, that this explorer in the sandy waste had only seen another mirage. The lake was there, the trees were there, the thirsty camels had gone down to have their evening drink; alas, a few steps forward would reveal nothing but dust and desert as before.

A FEW MINUTES only after Linda had left me to go back to London, Christian and the comrades, I had another caller. This time it was Lord Merlin. I liked Lord Merlin very much, I admired him, I was predisposed in his favour, but I was by no means on such intimate terms with him as Linda was. To tell the real truth he frightened me. I felt that, in my company, boredom was for him only just round the corner, and that, anyhow, I was merely regarded as pertaining to Linda, not existing on my own except as a dull little don's wife. I was nothing but the confidante in white linen.

"This is a bad business," he said, abruptly, and without preamble, though I had not seen him for several years. "I'm just back from Rome, and what do I find—Linda and Christian Talbot. It's an extraordinary thing that I can't ever leave England without Linda getting herself mixed up with some thoroughly undesirable character. This is a disaster—how far has it gone? Can nothing be done?"

I told him that he had just missed Linda, and said something about her marriage with Tony having been unhappy. Lord Merlin waved this remark aside—it was a disconcerting gesture and made me feel a fool.

"Naturally she never would have stayed with Tony—nobody expected that. The point is that she's out of the frying-pan into an empty grate. How long has it been going on?"

I said I thought it was partly the Communism that had attracted her.

"Linda has always felt the need of a cause."

"Cause," he said, scornfully. "My dear Fanny, I think you are mixing up cause with effect. No, Christian is an attractive fellow, and I quite see that he would provide a perfect reaction from Tony, but it is a disaster. If she is in love with him he will make her miserable, and, if not, it means she has embarked upon a career like your mother's, and that, for Linda, would be very bad indeed. I don't see a ray of comfort anywhere. No money either, of course, and she needs money, she ought to have it."

He went to the window, and looked across the street at Christ Church gilded by the westerly sun.

"I've known Christian," he said, "from a child—his father is a great friend of mine. Christian is a man who goes through the world attached to nobody—people are nothing in his life. The women who have been in love with him have suffered bitterly because he has not even noticed that they are there. I expect he is hardly aware that Linda has moved in on him—his head is in the clouds and he is always chasing after some new idea."

"This is rather what Linda has just been saying."

"Oh, she's noticed it already? Well, she is not stupid, and, of course, at first it adds to the attraction—when he comes out of the clouds he is irresistible, I quite see that. But how can they ever settle down? Christian has never had a home, or felt the need for one; he wouldn't know what to do with it—it would hamper him. He'll never sit and chat to Linda, or concentrate upon her in any way, and she is a woman who requires, above all things, a great deal of concentration. Really it is too provoking that I should have been away when this happened, I'm sure I could have stopped it. Now, of course, nobody can."

He turned from the window and looked at me so angrily that I felt it had all been my fault—actually I think he was unaware of my presence.

"What are they living on?" he said.

"Very little. Linda has a small allowance from Uncle Matthew, I believe, and I suppose Christian makes something from his journalism. I hear the Kroesigs go about saying that there is one good thing, she is sure to starve."

"Oh, they do, do they?" said Lord Merlin, taking out his notebook, "can I have Linda's address, please, I am on my way to London now."

Alfred came in, as usual unaware of exterior events and buried in some pamphlet he was writing.

"You don't happen to know," he said to Lord Merlin, "what the daily consumption of milk is in Vatican City?"

"No, of course not," said Lord Merlin, angrily. "Ask Tony Kroesig, he'll be sure to. Well, good-bye, Fanny. I'll have to see what I can do."

What he did was to present Linda with the freehold of a tiny house far down Cheyne Walk. It was the prettiest little dolls' house that ever was seen, on that great bend of the river where Whistler had lived. The rooms were full of reflections of water and full of south and west sunlight; it had a vine and a Trafalgar balcony. Linda adored it. The Bryanston Square house, with an easterly outlook, had been originally dark, cold and pompous. When Linda had had it done up by some decorating friend, it had become white, cold, and tomblike. The only thing of beauty that she had possessed was a picture, a fat tomato-colored bathing-woman, which had been given her by Lord Merlin to annoy the Kroesigs. It had annoyed them, very much. This picture looked wonderful in the Cheyne Walk house, you could hardly tell where the real water-reflections ended and the Renoir ones began. The pleasure which Linda derived from her new surroundings, the relief which she felt at having once and for all got rid of the Kroesigs, were, I think, laid by her at Christian's door, and seemed to come from him. Thus the discovery that real love and happiness had once more eluded her was delayed for quite a long time.

Chapter 14

THE ALCONLEIGHS WERE shocked and horrified over the whole Linda affair, but they had their other children to think of, and were, just now, making plans for the coming out of Jassy, who was as pretty as a peach. She, they hoped, would make up to them for their disappointment with Linda. It was most unfair, but very typical of them, that Louisa, who had married entirely in accordance with their wishes and had been a faithful wife and most prolific mother, having now some five children, hardly seemed to count any more. They were really rather bored by her.

Jassy went with Aunt Sadie to a few London dances at the end of the season, just after Linda had left Tony. She was thought to be rather delicate, and Aunt Sadie had an idea that it would be better for her to come out properly in the less strenuous autumn season, and, accordingly, in October, took a little house in London into which she prepared to move with a few servants, leaving Uncle Matthew in the country, to kill various birds and animals. Jassy complained very much that the young men she had met so far were dull and hideous, but Aunt Sadie took no notice. She said that all girls thought this at first, until they fell in love.

A few days before they were to have moved to London Jassy ran away. She was to have spent a fortnight with Louisa in Scotland, had put Louisa off without telling Aunt Sadie, had cashed her savings, and, before anybody even knew that she was missing, had arrived in America. Poor Aunt Sadie received, out of the blue, a cable saying: "On way Hollywood. Don't worry. Jassy."

At first the Alconleighs were completely mystified. Jassy had never shown the smallest interest in stage or cinema, they felt certain she had no wish to become a film star, and yet, why Hollywood? Then it occurred to them that Matt might know something, he and Jassy being the two inseparables of the family, and Aunt Sadie got into the Daimler and rolled over to Eton. Matt was able to explain everything. He told Aunt Sadie that Jassy was in love with a film star called Gary Coon (or Cary Goon, he could not remember which), and that she had written to Hollywood to ask him if he were married, telling Matt that if he proved not to be she was going straight out there to marry him herself. Matt said all this, in his wobbling half grown-up, half little-boy voice, as if it were the most ordinary situation imaginable.

"So I suppose," he ended up, "that she got a letter saying he's not married and just went off. Lucky she had her running-away money. What about some tea, Mum?"

Aunt Sadie, deeply preoccupied as she was, knew the rules of behaviour and what was expected of her, and stayed with Matt while he consumed sausages, lobsters, eggs, bacon, fried sole, banana mess and a chocolate sundae.

As always in times of crisis, the Alconleighs now sent for Davey, and, as always, Davey displayed a perfect competence to deal with the situation. He found out in no time that Cary Goon was a second-rate film actor whom Jassy must have seen when she was in London for the last parties of the summer. He had been in a film then showing called *One Splendid Hour*. Davey got hold of the film, and Lord Merlin put it on in his private cinema for the benefit of the family. It was about pirates, and Cary Goon was not even the hero, he was just a pirate and seemed to have nothing in particular to recommend him; no good looks, talent, or visible charm, though he did display a certain agility shinning up and down ropes. He also killed a man with a weapon not unlike the entrenching tool, and this, we felt, may have awakened some hereditary emotion in Jassy's bosom. The film itself was one of those of which it is very difficult for the ordinary English person, as opposed to the film fan, to make head or tail, and every time Cary Goon appeared the scene had to be played over again for Uncle Matthew, who had come determined that no detail should escape him. He absolutely identified the actor with his part, and kept saying:

"What does the fella want to do that for? Bloody fool, he might know there would be an ambush there. I can't hear a word the fella says—put that bit on again, Merlin."

At the end he said he didn't think much of the cove, he appeared to have no discipline and had been most impertinent to his commanding officer. "Needs a haircut and I shouldn't wonder if he drinks."

Uncle Matthew said how do you do good-bye quite civilly to Lord Merlin. He really seemed to be mellowing with age and misfortune.

After great consultations it was decided that some member of the family, not Aunt Sadie or Uncle Matthew, would have to go to Hollywood and bring Jassy home. But who? Linda, of course, would have been the obvious person, had she not been under a cloud and, furthermore, engrossed with her own life. But it would be of no use to send one bolter to fetch back another bolter, so somebody else must be found. In the end, after some persuasion ("madly inconvenient just now that I have started this course of inoculations") Davey consented to go with Louisa—the good, the sensible Louisa.

By the time this had been decided, Jassy had arrived in Hollywood, had broadcast her matrimonial intentions to all and sundry, and the whole thing appeared in the newspapers, which devoted pages of space to it, and (it was a silly season with nothing else to occupy their readers) turned it into a sort of serial story. Alconleigh now entered upon a state of siege. Journalists braved Uncle Matthew's stock-whips, his bloodhounds, his terrifying blue flashes, and hung around the village, penetrating even into the house itself in their search for local colour. Their stories were a daily delight. Uncle Matthew was made into something between Heathcliff, Dracula, and the Earl of Dorincourt, Alconleigh a sort of Nightmare Abbey or House of Usher, and Aunt Sadie a character not unlike David Copperfield's mother. Such courage, ingenuity and toughness was displayed by these correspondents that it came as no surprise to any of us when, later on, they did so well in the war. "War report by So-and-So——"

Uncle Matthew would then say:

"Isn't that the damned sewer I found hiding under my bed?"

He greatly enjoyed the whole affair. Here were opponents worthy of him, not jumpy housemaids, and lachrymose governesses with wounded feelings, but tough young men who did not care what methods they used so long as they could get inside his house and produce a story.

He also seemed greatly to enjoy reading about himself in the newspapers and we all began to suspect that Uncle Matthew had a hidden passion for publicity. Aunt Sadie, on the other hand, found the whole thing very distasteful indeed.

It was thought most vital to keep it from the press that Davey and Louisa were leaving on a voyage of rescue, as the sudden surprise of seeing them might prove an important element in influencing Jassy to return. Unfortunately, Davey could not embark on so long and so trying a journey without a medicine chest, specially designed. While this was being made they missed one boat, and, by the time it was ready, the sleuths were on their track—this unlucky medicine chest having played the same part that Marie Antoinette's *nécessaire* did in the escape to Varennes.

Several journalists accompanied them on the crossing, but did not reap much of a reward, as Louisa was prostrated with sea-sickness and Davey spent his whole time closeted with the ship's doctor, who asserted that his trouble was a cramped intestine, which could easily be cured by manipulation, rays, diet, exercises and injections, all of which, or resting after which, occupied every moment of his day.

On their arrival in New York, however, they were nearly torn to pieces, and we were able, in common with the whole of the two great English-speaking nations, to follow their every move. They even appeared on the newsreel, looking worried and hiding their faces behind books.

It proved to have been a useless trip. Two days after their arrival in Hollywood Jassy became Mrs. Cary Goon. Louisa telegraphed this news home, adding, "Cary is a terrific Hon."

There was one comfort, the marriage killed the story.

"He's a perfect dear," said Davey, on his return. "A little man like a nut. I'm sure Jassy will be madly happy with him."

Aunt Sadie, however, was neither reassured nor consoled. It seemed hard luck to have reared a pretty love of a daughter in order for her to marry a little man like a nut, and live with him thousands of miles away. The house in London was cancelled, and the Alconleighs lapsed into such a state of gloom that the next blow, when it fell, was received with fatalism.

Matt, aged sixteen, ran away from Eton, also in a blaze of newspaper publicity, to the Spanish war. Aunt Sadie minded this very much, but I don't think Uncle Matthew did. The desire to fight seemed to him entirely natural, though, of course, he deplored the fact that Matt was fighting for foreigners. He did not take a particular line against the Spanish reds, they were brave boys and had had the good sense to bump off a lot of idolatrous monks, nuns and priests, a proceeding of which he approved, but it was surely a pity to fight in a second-class war when there would so soon be a first-class one available. It was decided that no steps should be taken to retrieve Matt.

Christmas that year was a very sad one at Alconleigh. The children seemed to be melting away like the ten little Indians. Bob and

Louisa, neither of whom had given their parents one moment of disquiet in their lives, John Fort William, as dull as a man could be, Louisa's children, so good, so pretty, but lacking in any sort of originality, could not make up for the absence of Linda, Matt and Jassy, while Robin and Victoria, full as they were of jokes and fun, were swamped by the general atmosphere, and kept to themselves as much as possible in the Hons' cupboard.

LINDA WAS MARRIED in the Caxton Hall as soon as her divorce was through. The wedding was as different from her first as the Left-wing parties were different from the other kind. It was not exactly sad, but dismal, uncheerful, and with no feeling of happiness. Few of Linda's friends, and none of her relations except Davey and me were there; Lord Merlin sent two Aubusson rugs and some orchids but did not turn up himself. The pre-Christian chatters had faded out of Linda's life, discouraged, loudly bewailing the great loss she was in theirs.

Christian arrived late, and hurried in, followed by several comrades.

"I must say he is wonderful-looking," Davey hissed in my ear, "but oh, bother it all!"

There was no wedding breakfast, and, after a few moments of aimless and rather embarrassed hanging about in the street outside the hall, Linda and Christian went off home. Feeling provincial, up in London for the day and determined to see a little life, I made Davey give me luncheon at the Ritz. This had a still further depressing effect on my spirits. My clothes, so nice and suitable for the George, so much admired by the other dons' wives ("My dear, where did you get that lovely tweed?"), were, I now realized, almost bizarre in their dowdiness; it was the floating panels of taffeta all over again. I thought of those dear little black children, three of them now, in their nursery at home, and of dear Alfred in his study, but just for the moment this thought was no consolation. I passionately longed to have a tiny fur hat, or a tiny ostrich hat, like the two ladies at the next table. I longed for a neat black dress, diamond clips and a dark mink coat, shoes like surgical boots, long crinkly black suède gloves, and smooth polished hair. When I tried to explain all this to Davey, he remarked, absentmindedly:

"Oh, but it doesn't matter a bit for you, Fanny, and, after all, how can you have time to keep yourself well groomed with so many other, more important things to think of."

I suppose he thought this would cheer me up.

SOON AFTER HER marriage the Alconleighs took Linda back into the fold. They did not count second weddings of divorced people, and Victoria had been severely reprimanded for saying that Linda was engaged to Christian.

"You can't be engaged when you're married."

It was not the fact of the ceremony which had mollified them, in their eyes Linda would be living from now on in a state of adultery, but they felt the need of her too strongly to keep up a quarrel. The thin end of the wedge (luncheon with Aunt Sadie at Gunters) was inserted, and soon everything was all right again between them, Linda went quite often to Alconleigh, though she never took Christian there, feeling that it would benefit nobody were she to do so.

Linda and Christian lived in their house in Cheyne Walk, and, if Linda was not as happy as she had hoped to be, she exhibited, as usual, a wonderful shop-front. Christian was certainly very fond of her, and, in his way, he tried to be kind to her, but, as Lord Merlin had prophesied, he was much too detached to make any ordinary woman happy. He seemed, for weeks on end, hardly to be aware of her presence; at other times he would wander off and not reappear for days, too much engrossed in whatever he was doing to let her know where he was or when she might expect to see him again. He would eat and sleep where he happened to find himself—on a bench at St. Pancras' station, or just sitting on the doorstep of some empty house. Cheyne Walk was always full of comrades, not chatting to Linda, but making speeches to each other, restlessly rushing about, telephoning, typewriting, drinking, quite often sleeping in their clothes, but without their boots, on Linda's drawing-room sofa.

Money troubles accrued. Christian, though he never appeared to spend any money, had a disconcerting way of scattering it. He had few, but expensive amusements, one of his favourites being to ring up the Nazi leaders in Berlin, and other European politicians, and have long teasing talks with them, costing pounds a minute. "They never can resist a call from London," he would say, nor, unfortunately, could they. At last, greatly to Linda's relief, the telephone was cut off, as the bill could not be paid.

I must say that Alfred and I both liked Christian very much. We are intellectual pinks ourselves, enthusiastic agreers with the *New Statesman*, so that his views, while rather more advanced than ours, had the same foundation of civilized humanity, and he seemed to us a great improvement on Tony. All the same, he was a hopeless husband for Linda. Her craving was for love, personal and particular, centred upon herself; wider love, for the poor, the sad, and the unattractive, had no appeal for her, though she honestly tried to believe that it had. The more I saw of Linda at this time, the more certain I felt that another bolt could not be very far ahead.

Twice a week Linda worked in a Red bookshop. It was run by a huge, perfectly silent comrade, called Boris. Boris liked to get drunk from Thursday afternoon, which was closing day in that district, to Monday morning, so Linda said she would take it over on Friday and Saturday. An extraordinary transformation would then occur. The books and tracts which mouldered there month after month, getting damper and dustier until at last they had to be thrown away, were hurried into the background, and their place taken by Linda's own few but well-loved favourites. Thus for *Whither British Airways?* was substituted *Round the World in Forty Days, Karl Marx, the Formative Years* was replaced by *The Making of a Marchioness,* and *The Giant of the Kremlin* by *Diary of a Nobody,* while *A Challenge to Coal-Owners* made way for *King Solomon's Mines.*

Hardly would Linda have arrived in the morning on her days there, and taken down the shutters, than the slummy little street would fill with motor-cars, headed by Lord Merlin's electric brougham. Lord Merlin did great propaganda for the shop, saying that Linda was the only person who had ever succeeded in finding him *Froggie's Little Brother* and *Le Père Goriot.* The chatters came back in force, delighted to find Linda so easily accessible again, and without Christian, but sometimes there were embarrassing moments when they came face to face with comrades. Then they would buy a book and beat a hasty retreat, all except Lord Merlin, who had never felt disconcerted in his life. He took a perfectly firm line with the comrades.

"How are you today?" he would say with great emphasis, and then glower furiously at them until they left the shop.

All this had an excellent effect upon the financial side of the business. Instead of showing, week by week, an enormous loss, to be refunded from one could guess where, it now became the only Red bookshop in England to make a profit. Boris was greatly praised by his employers, the shop received a medal, which was stuck upon the sign, and the comrades all said that Linda was a good girl and a credit to the Party.

The rest of her time was spent in keeping house for Christian and the comrades, an occupation which entailed trying to induce a series of maids to stay with them, and making sincere, but sadly futile, efforts to take their place when they had left, which they usually did at the end of the first week. The comrades were not very nice or very thoughtful to maids.

"You know, being a Conservative is much more restful," Linda said to me once in a moment of confidence, when she was being unusually frank about her life, "though one must remember that it is bad, not good. But it does take place within certain hours, and then finish, whereas Communism seems to eat up all one's life and energy. And the comrades are such Hons, but sometimes they make me awfully cross, just as Tony used to make one furious when he talked about the workers. I often feel rather the same when they talk about us—you see, just like Tony, they've got it all wrong. I'm all for them stringing up Sir Leicester, but if they started on Aunt Emily and Davey, or even on Fa, I don't think I could stand by and watch. I suppose one is neither fish, flesh, nor good red herring, that's the worst of it."

"But there is a difference," I said, "between Sir Leicester and Uncle Matthew."

"Well, that's what I'm always trying to explain. Sir Leicester grubs up his money in London, goodness knows how, but Fa gets it from his land, and he puts a great deal back into the land, not only money, but work. Look at all the things he does for no pay—all those boring meetings, County Council, J.P., and so on. And he's a good landlord, he takes trouble. You see, the comrades don't know the country—they didn't know you could get a lovely cottage with a huge garden for 2s. 6d. a week until I told them, and then they hardly believed it. Christian knows, but he says the system is wrong, and I expect it is."

"What exactly does Christian do?" I said.

"Oh, everything you can think of. Just at the moment he's writing a book on famine—goodness! it's sad—and there's a dear little Chinese comrade who comes and tells him what famine is like, you never saw such a fat man in your life."

I laughed.

Linda said, hurriedly and guiltily:

"Well, I may seem to laugh at the comrades, but at least one does know they are doing good not harm, and not living on other people's slavery like Sir Leicester, and really you know I do simply love them, though I sometimes wish they were a little more fond of chatting, and not quite so sad and earnest and down on everybody."

Chapter 15

Early in 1939, the population of Catalonia streamed over the Pyrenees into the Roussillon, a poor and little-known province of France, which now, in a few days, found itself inhabited by more Spaniards than Frenchmen. Just as the lemmings suddenly pour themselves in mass suicide off the coast of Norway, knowing neither whence they come nor whither bound, so great is the compulsion that hurls them into the Atlantic, thus half a million men, women and children suddenly took flight into the bitter mountain weather, without pausing for thought. It was the greatest movement of population, in the time it took, that had ever hitherto been seen. Over the mountains they found no promised land; the French government, vacillating in its policy, neither turned them back with machine-guns at the frontier, nor welcomed them as brothers-in-arms against Fascism. It drove them like a herd of beasts down to the cruel salty marshes of that coast, enclosed them, like a herd of beasts, behind barbed-wire fences, and forgot all about them.

Christian, who had always, I think, had a half-guilty feeling about not having fought in Spain, immediately rushed off to Perpignan to see what was happening, and what, if anything, could be done. He wrote an endless series of reports, memoranda, articles and private letters about the conditions he had found in the camps, and then settled down to work in an office financed by various English humanitarians with the object of improving the camps, putting refugee families in touch again, and getting as many as possible out of France. This office was run by a young man who had lived many years in Spain called Robert Parker. As soon as it became clear that there would not be, as at first was expected, an outbreak of typhus, Christian sent for Linda to join him in Perpignan.

It so happened that Linda had never before been abroad in her life. Tony had found all his pleasures, hunting, shooting, and golf, in England, and had grudged the extra days out of his holiday which would have been spent in travelling; while it would never have occurred to the Alconleighs to visit the Continent for any other purpose than that of fighting. Uncle Matthew's four years in France and Italy between 1914 and 1918 had given him no great opinion of foreigners.

"Frogs," he would say, "are slightly better than Huns or Wops, but abroad is unutterably bloody and foreigners are fiends."

The bloodiness of abroad, the fiendishness of foreigners, had, in fact, become such a tenet of the Radlett family creed that Linda set forth on her journey with no little trepidation. I went to see her off at Victoria, she was looking intensely English in her long blond mink coat, the *Tatler* under her arm, and Lord Merlin's morocco dressing-case, with a canvas cover, in her hand.

"I hope you have sent your jewels to the bank," I said.

"Oh, darling, don't tease, you know how I haven't got any now. But my money," she said with a self-conscious giggle, "is sewn into my stays. Fa rang up and begged me to, and I must say it did seem quite an idea. Oh, why aren't you coming? I do feel so terrified— think of sleeping in the train, all alone."

"Perhaps you won't be alone," I said. "Foreigners are greatly given, I believe, to rape."

"Yes, that would be nice, so long as they didn't find my stays. Oh, we are off—good-bye, darling, do think of me," she said, and, clenching her suède-covered fist, she shook it out of the window in a Communist salute.

I must explain that I know everything that now happened to Linda, although I did not see her for another year, because afterwards, as will be shown, we spent a long quiet time together, during which she told it all to me, over and over again. It was her way of reliving happiness.

Of course the journey was an enchantment to her. The porters in their blue overalls, the loud, high conversations, of which, although she thought she knew French quite well, she did not understand a single word, the steamy, garlic-smelling heat of the French train, the delicious food, to which she was summoned by a little hurried bell, it was all from another world, like a dream.

She looked out of the window and saw chateaux, lime avenues, ponds and villages exactly like those in the Pink Library of her childhood—she thought she must, at any moment, see Sophie in her white dress and unnaturally small black pumps cutting up goldfish, gorging herself on new bread and cream, or scratching the face of good, uncomplaining Paul. Her very stilted, very English French, got her across Paris and into the train for Perpignan without a hitch. Paris. She looked out of the window at the lighted dusky streets, and thought that never could any town have been so hauntingly beautiful. A strange stray thought came into her head that, one day, she would come back here and be very happy, but she knew that it was not likely, Christian would never want to live in Paris. Happiness and Christian were still linked together in her mind at this time.

At Perpignan she found him in a whirl of business. Funds had been raised, a ship had been chartered, and plans were on foot for sending six thousand Spaniards out of the camps to Mexico. This entailed an enormous amount of staff work, as families (no Spaniard would think of moving without his entire family) had to be reunited from camps all over the place, assembled in a camp in Perpignan, and taken by train to the port of Cette, whence they finally embarked. The work was greatly complicated by the fact that Spanish husbands and wives do not share a surname. Christian explained all this to Linda almost before she was out of the train; he gave her an absent-minded peck on the forehead and rushed her to his office, hardly giving her time to deposit her luggage at an hotel on the way and scouting the idea that she might like a bath. He did not ask how she was or whether she had had a good journey — Christian always assumed that people were all right unless they told him to the contrary, when, except in the case of destitute, coloured, oppressed, leprous, or otherwise unattractive strangers, he would take absolutely no notice. He was really only interested in mass wretchedness, and never much cared for individual cases, however genuine their misery, while the idea that it is possible to have three square meals a day and a roof and yet be unhappy or unwell, seemed to him intolerable nonsense.

The office was a large shed with a yard round it. This yard was permanently full of refugees with mountains of luggage and quantities of children, dogs, donkeys, goats, and other appurtenances, who had just struggled over the mountains in their flight from Fascism, and were hoping that the English would be able to prevent them being put into camps. In certain cases they could be lent money, or given railway tickets enabling them to join relations in France and French Morocco, but the vast majority waited hours for an interview, only to be told that there was no hope for them. They would then, with great and heartbreaking politeness, apologize for having been a nuisance and withdraw. Spaniards have a highly developed sense of human dignity.

Linda was now introduced to Robert Parker and to Randolph Pine, a young writer who, having led a more or less playboy existence in the South of France, had gone to fight in Spain, and was now working in Perpignan from a certain feeling of responsibility towards those who had once been fellow soldiers. They seemed pleased that Linda had arrived, and were most friendly and welcoming, saying that it was nice to see a new face.

"You must give me some work to do," said Linda.

"Yes, now what can we think of for you?" said Robert. "There's masses of work, never fear, it's just a question of finding the right kind. Can you speak Spanish?"

"No."

"Oh, well, you'll soon pick it up."

"I'm quite sure I shan't," said Linda doubtfully.

"What do you know about welfare work?"

"Oh, dear, how hopeless I seem to be. Nothing, I'm afraid."

"Lavender will find her a job," said Christian, who had settled down at his table and was flapping over a card index.

"Lavender?"

"A girl called Lavender Davis."

"No! I know her quite well, she used to live near us in the country. In fact she was one of my bridesmaids."

"That's it," said Robert, "she said she knew you, I'd forgotten. She's wonderful, she really works with the Quakers in the camps, but she helps us a great deal too. There's absolutely nothing she doesn't know about calories and babies' nappies, and expectant mummies, and so on, and she's the hardest worker I've ever come across."

"I'll tell you," said Randolph Pine, "what you can do. There's a job simply waiting for you, and that is to arrange the accommodation on this ship that's going off next week."

"Oh, yes, of course," said Robert, "the very thing. She can have this table and start at once."

"Now look," said Randolph. "I'll show you. (What delicious scent you have, Après l'Ondée? I thought so.) Now here is a map of the ship—see—best cabins, not such good cabins, lousy cabins, and battened down under the hatches. And here is a list of the families who are going. All you have to do is to allocate each family its cabin—when you have decided which they are to have, you put the number of the cabin against the family—here—you see? And the number of the family on the cabin here, like that. Quite easy, but it takes time, and must be done so that when they arrive on the boat they will know exactly where to go with their things."

"But how do I decide who gets the good ones and who is battened? Awfully tricky, isn't it?"

"Not really. The point is it's a strictly democratic ship run on republican principles, class doesn't enter into it. I should give decent cabins to families where there are small children or babies. Apart from that do it any way you like. Take a pin if you like. The only thing that matters is that it should be done, otherwise there'll be a wild scramble for the best places when they get on board."

Linda looked at the list of families. It took the form of a card index, the head of each family having a card on which was written the number and names of his dependents.

"It doesn't give their ages," said Linda. "How am I to know if there are young babies?"

"That's a point," said Robert. "How is she to?"

"Quite easy," said Christian. "With Spaniards you can always tell. Before the war they were called either after saints or after episodes in the sex life of the Virgin—Annunciata, Asuncion, Purificacion, Concepcion, Consalacion, etc. Since the Civil War they are all called Carlos after Charlie Marx, Federico after Freddie Engels or Estalina (very popular until the Russians let them down with a wallop), or else nice slogans like Solidaridad-Obreara, Libertad, and so on. Then you know the children are under three. Couldn't be simpler, really."

Lavender Davis now appeared. She was indeed the same Lavender, dowdy, healthy and plain, wearing an English country tweed and brogues. Her short brown hair curled over her head, and she had no make-up. She greeted Linda with enthusiasm, indeed, it had always been a fiction in the Davis family that Lavender and Linda were each other's greatest friends. Linda was delighted to see her, as one always is delighted to see a familiar face, abroad.

"Come on," said Randolph, "now we're all here let's go and have a drink at the Palmarium."

For the next weeks, until her private life began to occupy Linda's attention, she lived in an atmosphere of alternate fascination and horror. She grew to love Perpignan, a strange little old town, so different from anything she had ever known, with its river and broad quays, its network of narrow streets, its huge wild-looking plane trees, and all around it the bleak vine-growing country of the Roussillon bursting into summery green under her very eyes. Spring came late, but when it came it was hand-in-hand with summer, and almost at once everything was baking and warm, and in the villages the people danced every night on concrete dancing floors under the plane trees. At weekends the English, unable to eradicate such a national habit, shut up the office and made for Collioure on the coast, where they bathed and sunbathed and went for Pyrenean picnics.

But all this had nothing to do with the reason for their presence in these charming surroundings—the camps. Linda went to the camps nearly every day, and they filled her soul with despair. As she could not help very much in the office owing to her lack of Spanish, nor with the children, since she knew nothing about calories, she was employed as a driver, and was always on the road in a Ford van full of supplies, or of refugees, or just taking messages to and from the camps. Often she had to sit and wait for hours on end while a certain man was found and his case dealt with; she would quickly be surrounded by a perfect concourse of men talking to her in their heavy guttural French. By this time the camps were quite decently organized; there were rows of orderly, though depressing huts, and the men were getting regular meals, which, if not very appetizing, did at least keep body and soul together. But the sight of these thousands of human beings, young and healthy, herded behind wire away from their womenfolk, with nothing on earth to do day after dismal day, was a recurring torture to Linda. She began to think that Uncle Matthew had been right—that abroad, where such things could happen, was indeed unutterably bloody, and that foreigners, who could inflict them upon each other, must be fiends.

One day as she sat in her van, the centre, as usual, of a crowd of Spaniards, a voice said:

"Linda, what on earth are you doing here?"

And it was Matt.

He looked ten years older than when she had last seen him, grown up, in fact, and extremely handsome, his Radlett eyes infinitely blue in a dark-brown face.

"I've seen you several times," he said, "and I thought you had been sent to fetch me away so I made off, but then I found out you are married to that Christian fellow. Was he the one you ran away from Tony with?"

"Yes," said Linda. "I'd no idea, Matt. I thought you'd have been sure to go back to England."

"Well, no," said Matt. "I'm an officer you see—must stay with the boys."

"Does Mummy know you're all right?"

"Yes, I told her—at least if Christian posted a letter I gave him."

"I don't suppose so—he's never been known to post a letter in his life. He is funny, he might have told me."

"He didn't know—I sent it under cover to a friend of mine to forward. Didn't want any of the English to find out I was here, or they would start trying to get me home. I know."

"Christian wouldn't," said Linda. "He's all for people doing what they want to in life. You're very thin, Matt, is there anything you'd like?"

"Yes," said Matt, "some cigarettes and a couple of thrillers."

After this Linda saw him most days. She told Christian, who merely grunted and said: "He'll have to be got out before the world war begins. I'll see to that," and she wrote and told her parents. The result was a parcel of clothes from Aunt Sadie, which Matt refused to accept, and a packing-case full of vitamin pills from Davey, which Linda did not even dare to show him. He was cheerful and full of jokes and high spirits, but then there is a difference, as Christian said, between staying in a place because you are obliged to, and staying there because you think it right. But in any case, with the Radlett family, cheerfulness was never far below the surface.

The only other cheerful prospect was the ship. It was only going to rescue from hell a few thousand of the refugees, a mere fraction of the total amount, but, at any rate, they would be rescued, and taken to a better world, with happy and useful future prospects.

When she was not driving the van Linda worked hard over the cabin arrangements, and finally got the whole thing fixed and finished in time for the embarkation.

All the English except Linda went to Cette for the great day, taking with them two M.P.s and a duchess, who had helped the enterprise in London and had come out to see the fruit of their work. Linda went over by bus to Argelès to see Matt.

"How odd the Spanish upper classes must be," she said, "they don't raise a finger to help their own people, but leave it all to strangers like us."

"You don't know Fascists," Matt said, gloomily.

"I was thinking yesterday when I was taking the Duchess round Barcarès—yes, but why an English duchess, aren't there any Spanish ones, and, come to that, why is it nothing but English working in Perpignan? I knew several Spaniards in London, why don't they come and help a bit? They'd be awfully useful. I suppose they speak Spanish."

"Fa was quite right about foreigners being fiends," said Matt, "upper-class ones are, at least. All these boys are terrific Hons, I must say."

"Well, I can't see the English leaving each other in the lurch like this, even if they did belong to different parties. I think it's shameful."

Christian and Robert came back from Cette in a cheerful mood. The arrangements had gone like clockwork, and a baby which had been born during the first half-hour on the ship was named Embarcacion. It was the kind of joke Christian very much enjoyed. Robert said to Linda:

"Did you work on any special plan when you were arranging the cabins, or how did you do it?"

"Why? Wasn't it all right?"

"Perfect. Everybody had a place, and made for it. But I just wondered what you went by when you allocated the good cabins, that's all."

"Well, I simply," said Linda, "gave the best cabins to the people who had *Labrador* on their card, because I used to have one when I was little and he was such a terrific—so sweet, you know."

"Ah," said Robert, gravely, "all is now explained. *Labrador* in Spanish happens to mean labourer. So you see under your scheme (excellent by the way, most democratic) the farm hands all found themselves in luxury while the intellectuals were battened. That'll teach them not to be so clever. You did very well, Linda, we were all most grateful."

"He was such a sweet Labrador," said Linda dreamily, "I wish you could have seen him. I do miss not having pets."

"Can't think why you don't make an offer for the leech," said Robert.

One of the features of Perpignan was a leech in a bottle in the window of a chemist's shop, with a typewritten notice saying: IF THE LEECH GOES UP IN THE BOTTLE, THE WEATHER WILL BE FAIR IF THE LEECH GOES DOWN—STORMY.

"It might be nice," said Linda, "but I can't somehow imagine her getting very fond of one—too busy fussing about the weather all day, up and down, up and down—no time for human relationships."

Chapter 16

LINDA NEVER COULD remember afterwards whether she had really minded when she discovered that Christian was in love with Lavender Davis, and, if so, how much. She could not at all remember her emotions at that time. Certainly wounded pride must have played a part, though perhaps less so with Linda than it would have with many women, as she did not suffer from much inferiority feeling. She must have seen that the past two years, her running away from Tony, all now went for nothing—but was she stricken at the heart, was she still in love with Christian, did she suffer the ordinary pangs of jealousy? I think not.

All the same, it was not a flattering choice. Lavender had seemed, for years and years, stretching back into childhood, to epitomize everything that the Radletts considered most unromantic: a keen girl guide, hockey player, tree climber, head girl at her school, rider astride. She had never lived in a dream of love; the sentiment was, quite obviously, far removed from her thoughts, although Louisa and Linda, unable to imagine that anybody could exist without some tiny spark of it, used to invent romances for Lavender—the games mistress at her school or Dr. Simpson of Merlinford (of whom Louisa had made up one of her nonsense rhymes— "He's doctor and king's proctor too, and she's in love with him but he's in love with you"). Since those days she had trained as a nurse and as a welfare worker, had taken a course of law and political economy, and, indeed, might have done it all, Linda saw only too well, with the express intention of fitting herself to be a mate for Christian. The result was that in their present surroundings, with her calm assured confidence in her own ability, she easily outshone poor Linda. There was no competition, it was a walk-over.

Linda did not discover their love in any vulgar way—surprising a kiss, or finding them in bed together. It was all far more subtle, more dangerous than that, being quite simply borne in upon her week after week that they found perfect happiness in each other, and that Christian depended entirely on Lavender for comfort and encouragement in his work. As this work now absorbed him heart and soul, as he thought of nothing else and never relaxed for a moment, dependence upon Lavender involved the absolute exclusion of Linda. She felt uncertain what to do. She could not have it out with Christian; there was nothing tangible to have out, and, in any case, such a proceeding would have been absolutely foreign to Linda's character. She dreaded scenes and rows more than anything else in the world, and she had no illusions about what Christian thought of her. She felt that he really rather despised her for having left Tony and her child so easily, and that, in his opinion, she took a silly, lighthearted and superficial view of life. He liked serious, educated women, especially those who had made a study of welfare, especially Lavender. She had no desire to hear all this said. On the other hand she began to think that it would be as well for her to get away from Perpignan herself before Christian and Lavender went off together, as it seemed to her most probable that they would, wandering off hand in hand to search for and relieve other forms of human misery. Already she felt embarrassed when she was with Robert and Randolph, who were obviously very sorry for her and were always making little manœuvres to prevent her noticing that Christian was spending every minute of the day with Lavender.

One afternoon, looking idly out of the window of her hotel bedroom, she saw them walking up the Quai Sadi Carnot together, completely absorbed, utterly contented in each other's company, radiating happiness. Linda was seized by an impulse and acted on it. She packed her things, wrote a hasty letter to Christian saying that she was leaving him for good, as she realized that their marriage had been a failure. She asked him to look after Matt. She then burnt her boats by adding a postscript (a fatal feminine practice), "I think you had much better marry Lavender." She bundled herself and her luggage into a taxi and took the night train for Paris.

The journey this time was horrible. She was, after all, very fond of Christian, and as soon as the train had left the station, she began to ask herself whether she had not in fact behaved stupidly and badly. He probably had a passing fancy for Lavender, based on common interests, which would fade away as soon as he got back to London. Possibly it was not even that, but simply that he was obliged, for his work, to be with Lavender all the time. His absent-minded treatment of Linda was, after all, nothing new, it had begun almost as soon as he had got her under his roof. She began to feel that she had done wrong to write that letter.

She had her return ticket, but very little money indeed, just enough, she reckoned, for dinner on the train and some food the next day. Linda always had to translate French money into pounds, shillings and pence before she knew where she was with it. She seemed to have about 18s. 6d. with her, so there could be no question of a sleeper. She had never before sat up all night in a train, and the experience appalled her; it was like some dreadful feverish illness, when the painful hours drag by, each one longer than a week. Her thoughts brought her no comfort. She had torn up her life of the past two years, all that she had tried to put into her relationship with Christian, and thrown it away like so much waste-paper. If this was to be the outcome why had she ever left Tony, her real husband for better or for worse, and her child? That was where her duty had lain, and well she knew it. She thought of my mother and shuddered. Could it be that she, Linda, was from now on doomed to a life that she utterly despised, that of a bolter?

And in London what would she find? A little empty, dusty house. Perhaps, she thought, Christian would pursue her, come and insist that she belonged to him. But in her heart she knew that he would not, and that she did not, and that this was the end. Christian believed too sincerely that people must be allowed to do as they wish in life, without interference. He was fond of Linda, she knew, but disappointed in her, she also knew; he would not himself have made the first move to separate, but would not much regret the fact that she had done so. Soon he would have some new scheme in his head, some new plan for suffering mortals, any mortals, anywhere, so long as there were enough of them and their misery was great. Then he would forget Linda, and possibly also Lavender, as if they had never been. Christian was not in passionate quest of love, he had other interests, other aims, and it mattered very little to him what woman happened to be in his life at a given moment. But in his nature, she knew, there was a certain ruthlessness. She felt that he would not forgive what she had done, or try to persuade her to go back on it, nor, indeed, was there any reason why he should do so.

It could not be said, thought Linda, as the train pursued its way through the blackness, that her life so far had been a marked success. She had found neither great love nor great happiness, and she had not inspired them in others. Parting with her would have been no death blow to either of her husbands, on the contrary, they would both have turned with relief to a much-preferred mistress, who was more suited to them in every way. Whatever quality it is that can hold indefinitely the love and affection of a man she plainly did not possess, and now she was doomed to the lonely, hunted life of a beautiful but unattached woman. Where now was love that would last to the grave and far beyond? What had she done with her youth? Tears for her lost hopes and ideals, tears of self-pity in fact, began to pour down her cheeks. The three fat Frenchmen who shared the carriage with her were in a snoring sleep, she wept alone.

Sad and tired as Linda was, she could not but perceive the beauty of Paris that summer morning as she drove across it to the Gare du Nord. Paris in the early morning has a cheerful, bustling aspect, a promise of delicious things to come, a positive smell of coffee and croissants, quite peculiar to itself.

The people welcome a new day as if they were certain of liking it, the shopkeepers pull up their blinds serene in the expectation of good trade, the workers go happily to their work, the people who have sat up all night in night-clubs go happily to their rest, the orchestra of motor-car horns, of clanking trams, of whistling police-men tunes up for the daily symphony, and everywhere is joy. This joy, this life, this beauty did but underline poor Linda's fatigue and sadness, she felt it but was not of it. She turned her thoughts to old familiar London, she longed above all for her own bed, feeling as does a wounded beast when it crawls home to its lair. She only wanted to sleep undisturbed in her own bedroom.

But when she presented her return ticket at the Gare du Nord she was told, furiously, loudly and unsympathetically, that it had expired.

"See, Madame — May 29th. Today's the 30th, isn't it? So — !" Tremendous shruggings.

Linda was paralysed with horror. Her 18s. 6d. was by now down to 6s. 3d. hardly enough for a meal. She knew nobody in Paris, she had absolutely no idea what she ought to do, she was too tired and too hungry to think clearly. She stood like a statue of despair. Her porter, tired of waiting beside a statue of despair, deposited the luggage at its feet and went grumbling off. Linda sank onto her suit-case and began to cry; nothing so dreadful had ever happened to her before. She cried bitterly, she could not stop. People passed to and fro as if weeping ladies were the most ordinary phenomenon at the Gare du Nord. "Fiends! fiends!" she sobbed. Why had she not listened to her father, why had she ever come to this bloody abroad? Who would help her? In London there was a society, she knew, which looked after ladies stranded at railway stations; here, more likely, there would be one for shipping them off to South America. At any moment now somebody, some genial-looking old woman might come up and give her an injection, after which she would disappear for ever.

She became aware that somebody was standing beside her, not an old lady, but a short, stocky, very dark Frenchman in a black Homburg hat. He was laughing. Linda took no notice, but went on crying. The more she cried the more he laughed. Her tears were tears of rage now, no longer of self-pity.

At last she said, in a voice which was meant to be angrily impressive, but which squeaked and shook through her handkerchief:

"Leave me alone."

For answer he took her hand and pulled her to her feet.

"Hello, hello," he said.

"Will you please leave me alone?" said Linda, rather more doubtfully, here at least was a human being who showed signs of taking some interest in her. Then she thought of South America.

"I should like to point out that I am not," she said, "a white slave. I am the daughter of a very important British nobleman."

The Frenchman gave a great bellow of laughter.

"One does not," he said in the nearly perfect English of somebody who has spoken it from a child, "have to be Sherlock Holmes to guess that."

Linda was rather annoyed. An Englishwoman abroad may be proud of her nationality and her virtue without wishing them to jump so conclusively to the eye.

"French ladies," he went on, "covered with the outward signs of wealth never sit crying on their suitcases at the Gare du Nord in the very early morning, while white slaves always have protectors, and it is only too clear that you are unprotected just now."

This sounded all right, and Linda was mollified.

"Now," he said, "I invite you to luncheon with me, but first you must have a bath and rest and a cold compress on your face."

He picked up her luggage and walked to a taxi.

"Get in, please."

Linda got in. She was far from certain that this was not the road to Buenos Aires, but something made her do as he said. Her powers of resistance were at an end, and she really saw no alternative.

"Hotel Montalembert," he told the taxi man. "Rue du Bac. I apologize, madame, for not taking you to the Ritz, but I have a feeling for the Hotel Montalembert just now, that it will suit your mood this morning."

Linda sat upright in her corner of the taxi, looking, she hoped, very prim. As she could not think of anything pertinent to say she remained silent. Her companion hummed a little tune, and seemed vastly amused. When they arrived at the hotel, he took a room for her, told the liftman to show her to it, told the *concierge* to send her up a *café complet*, kissed her hand, and said:

"Good-bye for the present—I will fetch you a little before one o'clock and we will go out to luncheon."

Linda had her bath and breakfast and got into bed. When the telephone bell rang she was so sound asleep that it was a struggle to wake up.

"A gentleman is waiting for you, Madame."

"Say I will be right down," said Linda, but it took her quite half an hour to get ready.

Chapter 17

A H! YOU KEEP me waiting," he said, kissing her hand, or at least making a gesture of raising her hand towards his lips and then dropping it rather suddenly. "That is a very good sign."

"Sign of what?" said Linda. He had a two-seater outside the hotel and she got into it. She was feeling more like herself again.

"Oh, of this and that," he said, letting in the clutch, "a good augury for our affair, that it will be happy and last long."

Linda became intensely stiff, English and embarrassed, and said, self-consciously:

"We are not having an affair."

"My name is Fabrice — may one ask yours?"

"Linda."

"Linda. What a pretty name! With me, it usually lasts five years."

He drove to a restaurant where they were shown, with some deference, to a table in a red plush corner. He ordered the luncheon and the wine in rapid French, the sort of French that Linda frankly could not follow, then, putting his hands on his knees, he turned to her and said:

"Now tell me, madame."

"Tell you what?"

"Well, but of course, the story. Who was it that left you to cry on that suitcase?"

"He didn't. I left him. It was my second husband and I have left him for ever because he has fallen in love with another woman—a welfare worker, not that you'd know what that is, because I'm sure they don't exist in France. It just makes it worse, that's all."

"What a very curious reason for leaving one's second husband. Surely with your experience of husbands you must have noticed that falling in love with other women is one of the things they do? However, it's an ill wind, and I don't complain. But why the suitcase? Why didn't you put yourself in the train and go back to Monsieur the important lord, your father?"

"That's what I was doing until they told me that my return ticket had expired. I only had 6s. 3d., and I don't know anybody in Paris, and I was awfully tired, so I cried."

"The second husband—why not borrow some money from him? Or had you left a note on his pillow—women never can resist these little essays in literature, and they do make it rather embarrassing to go back, I know."

"Well, anyhow he's in Perpignan, so I couldn't have."

"Ah, you come from Perpignan. And what were you doing there, in the name of heaven?"

"In the name of heaven we were trying to stop you frogs from teasing the poor Epagnards," said Linda with some spirit.

"E-spa-gnols! So we are teasing them, are we?"

"Not so badly now—terribly at the beginning."

"What were we supposed to do with them? We never invited them to come, you know."

"You drove them into camps in that cruel wind, and gave them no shelter for weeks. Hundreds died."

"It is quite a job to provide shelter, at a moment's notice, for half a million people. We did what we could—we fed them—the fact is that most of them are still alive."

"Still herded in camps."

"My dear Linda, you could hardly expect us to turn them loose on the countryside with no money—what would be the result? Do use your common sense."

"You should mobilize them to fight in the war against Fascism that's coming any day now."

"Talk about what you know and you won't get so angry. We haven't enough equipment for our own soldiers in the war against Germany that's coming—not any day, but after the harvest, probably in August. Now go on telling me about your husbands. It's so very much more interesting."

"Only two. My first was a Conservative, and my second is a Communist."

"Just as I guessed, your first is rich, your second is poor. I could see you once had a rich husband, the dressing-case and the fur coat, though it is a hideous colour, and no doubt, as far as one could see, with it bundled over your arm, a hideous shape. Still, mink usually betokens a rich husband somewhere. Then this dreadful linen suit you are wearing has ready-made written all over it."

"You are rude, it's a very pretty suit."

"And last year's. Jackets are getting longer you will find. I'll get you some clothes—if you were well dressed you would be quite good-looking, though it's true your eyes are small. Blue, a good colour, but small."

"In England," said Linda, "I am considered a beauty."

"Well, you have points."

So this silly conversation went on and on, but it was only froth on the surface. Linda was feeling, what she had never so far felt for any man, an overwhelming physical attraction. It made her quite giddy, it terrified her. She could see that Fabrice was perfectly certain of the outcome, so was she perfectly certain, and that was what frightened her. How could one, how could she, Linda, with the horror and contempt she had always felt for casual affairs, allow herself to be picked up by any stray foreigner, and, having seen him only for an hour, long and long to be in bed with him? He was not even good-looking, he was exactly like dozens of other dark men in Homburgs that can be seen in the streets of any French town. But there was something about the way he looked at her which seemed to be depriving her of all balance. She was profoundly shocked, and, at the same time, intensely excited.

After luncheon they strolled out of the restaurant into brilliant sunshine.

"Come and see my flat," said Fabrice.

"I would rather see Paris," said Linda.

"Do you know Paris well?"

"I've never been here before in my life."

Fabrice was really startled.

"Never been here before?" He could not believe it. "What a pleasure for me, to show it all to you. There is so much to show, it will take weeks."

"Unfortunately," said Linda, "I leave for England tomorrow."

"Yes, of course. Then we must see it all this afternoon."

They drove slowly round a few streets and squares, and then went for a stroll in the Bois. Linda could not believe that she had only just arrived there, that this was still the very day which she had seen unfolding itself, so full of promise, through her mist of morning tears.

"How fortunate you are to live in such a town," she said to Fabrice. "It would be impossible to be very unhappy here."

"Not impossible," he said. "One's emotions are intensified in Paris—one can be more happy and also more unhappy here than in any other place. But it is always a positive source of joy to live here, and there is nobody so miserable as a Parisian in exile from his town. The rest of the world seems unbearably cold and bleak to us, hardly worth living in." He spoke with great feeling.

After tea, which they had out of doors in the Bois, he drove slowly back into Paris. He stopped the car outside an old house in the Rue Bonaparte, and said, again:

"Come and see my flat."

"No, no," said Linda. "The time has now come for me to point out that I am *une femme sérieuse*."

Fabrice gave his great bellow of laughter.

"Oh," he said, shaking helplessly, "how funny you are. What a phrase, *femme sérieuse*, where did you find it? And if so serious, how do you explain the second husband?"

"Yes, I admit that I did wrong, very wrong indeed, and made a great mistake. But that is no reason for losing control, for sliding down the hill altogether, for being picked up by strange gentlemen at the Gare du Nord and then immediately going with them to see their flat. And please, if you will be so kind as to lend me some money, I want to catch the London train tomorrow morning."

"Of course, by all means," said Fabrice.

He thrust a roll of banknotes into her hand, and drove her to the Hotel Montalembert. He seemed quite unmoved by her speech, and announced he would come back at eight o'clock to take her out to dinner.

Linda's bedroom was full of roses, it reminded her of when Moira was born.

"Really," she thought with a giggle, "this is a very penny-novelettish seduction, how can I be taken in by it?"

But she was filled with a strange, wild, unfamiliar happiness, and knew that this was love. Twice in her life she had mistaken something else for it; it was like seeing somebody in the street who you think is a friend, you whistle and wave and run after him, and it is not only not the friend, but not even very like him. A few minutes later the real friend appears in view, and then you can't imagine how you ever mistook that other person for him. Linda was now looking upon the authentic face of love, and she knew it, but it frightened her. That it should come so casually, so much by a series of accidents, was frightening. She tried to remember how she had felt when she had first loved her two husbands. There must have been strong and impelling emotion; in both cases she had disrupted her own life, upset her parents and friends remorselessly, in order to marry them, but she could not recall it. Only she knew that never before, not even in dreams, and she was a great dreamer of love, had she felt anything remotely like this. She told herself, over and over again, that tomorrow she must go back to London, but she had no intention of going back, and she knew it.

Fabrice took her out to dinner and then to a night club, where they did not dance, but chatted endlessly. She told him about Uncle Matthew, Aunt Sadie and Louisa and Jassy and Matt, and he could not hear enough, and egged her on to excesses of exaggeration about her family and all their various idiosyncrasies.

"And Jassy—and Matt—go on, tell me."

And she recounted, for hours.

In the taxi on their way home she refused again to go back with him or to let him come into the hotel with her. He did not insist, he did not try to hold her hand, or touch her at all. He merely said:

"You are putting up a magnificent fight, madame, and I offer you my heartfelt felicitations."

Outside the hotel she gave him her hand to say good night. He took it in both of his and really kissed it.

"Till tomorrow," he said, and got back into the taxi.

"ALLÔ—ALLÔ."

"Hullo."

"Good morning. Are you having your breakfast?"

"Yes."

"I thought I heard a coffee-cup clattering. It is good?"

"It's so delicious that I have to keep stopping, for fear of finishing it too quickly. Are you having yours?"

"Had it. I must tell you that I like very long conversations in the morning, and I shall expect you to tell me some stories."

"Like Scheherazade?"

"Yes, just like. And you're not to get that note in your voice of 'now I'm going to ring off,' as English people always do."

"What English people do you know?"

"I know some. I was at school in England, and at Oxford."

"No! When?"

"1920."

"When I was nine. Fancy, perhaps I saw you in the street—we used to do all our shopping in Oxford."

"Elliston & Cavell?"

"Oh, yes, and Webber's."

There was a silence.

"Go on," he said.

"Go on, what?"

"I mean don't ring off. Go on telling."

"I shan't ring off. As a matter of fact I adore chatting. It's my favourite thing, and I expect you will want to ring off ages before I do."

They had a long and very silly conversation, and, at the end of it, Fabrice said:

"Now get up, and in an hour I will fetch you and we will go to Versailles."

At Versailles, which was an enchantment to Linda, she was reminded of a story she had once read about two English ladies who had seen the ghost of Marie Antoinette sitting in her garden at the Little Trianon. Fabrice found this intensely boring, and said so.

"Stories," he said, "are only of interest when they are true, or when you have made them up specially to amuse me. Ghost stories, made up by some dim old English virgins, are neither true nor interesting. So no more ghost stories, please, Madame."

"All right," said Linda, crossly. "I'm doing my best to please— you tell me a story."

"Yes, I will—and this story is true. My grandmother was very beautiful and had many lovers all her life, even when she was quite old. A short time before she died she was in Venice with my mother, her daughter, and one day, floating up some canal in their gondola, they saw a little palazzo of pink marble, very exquisite. They stopped the gondola to look at it, and my mother said: 'I don't believe anybody lives there, what about trying to see the inside?'

"So they rang the bell, and an old servant came and said that nobody had lived there for many, many years, and he would show it to them if they liked. So they went in and upstairs to the *salone*, which had three windows looking over the canal and was decorated with fifteenth-century plaster work, white on a pale blue background. It was a perfect room. My grandmother seemed strangely moved, and stood for a long time in silence. At last she said to my mother:

"'If, in the third drawer of that bureau there is a filigree box containing a small gold key on a black velvet ribbon, this house belongs to me.'

"And my mother looked, and there was, and it did. One of my grandmother's lovers had given it to her years and years before, when she was quite young, and she had forgotten all about it."

"Goodness," said Linda, "what fascinating lives you foreigners do lead."

"And it belongs to me now."

He put his hand up to Linda's forehead and stroked back a strand of hair which was loose:

"And I would take you there tomorrow if—"

"If what?"

"One must wait here now, you see, for the war."

"Oh, I keep forgetting the war," said Linda.

"Yes, let's forget it. How badly your hair is done, my dear."

"If you don't like my clothes and don't like my hair and think my eyes are so small, I don't know what you see in me."

"Nevertheless I admit there is something," said Fabrice.

Again they dined together.

Linda said: "Haven't you any other engagements?"

"Yes, of course. I have cancelled them."

"Who are your friends?"

"Society people. And yours?"

"When I was married to Tony, that is, my first husband, I used to go out in society, it was my life. In those days I loved it. But then

Christian didn't approve of it, he stopped me going to parties and frightened away my friends, whom he considered frivolous and idiotic, and we saw nothing but serious people trying to put the world right. I used to laugh at them, and rather long for my other friends, but now I don't know. Since I was at Perpignan perhaps I have become more serious myself."

"Everybody is getting more serious, that's the way things are going. But, whatever one may be in politics, right, left, Fascist, Communist, society people are the only possible ones for friends. You see, they have made a fine art of personal relationships and of all that pertains to them—manners, clothes, beautiful houses, good food, everything that makes life agreeable. It would be silly not to take advantage of that. Friendship is something to be built up carefully, by people with leisure, it is an art, nature does not enter into it. You should never despise social life—that of high society—I mean, it can be a very satisfying one, entirely artificial of course, but absorbing. Apart from the life of the intellect and the contemplative religious life, which few people are qualified to enjoy, what else is there to distinguish man from the animals but his social life? And who understands it so well and who can make it so smooth and so amusing as society people? But one cannot have it at the same time as a love affair, one must be whole-hearted to enjoy it, so I have cancelled all my engagements."

"What a pity," said Linda, "because I'm going back to London tomorrow morning."

"Ah yes, I had forgotten. What a pity."

"ALLÔ—ALLÔ."

"Hullo."

"Were you asleep?"

"Yes, of course. What's the time?"

"About two. Shall I come round and see you?"

"Do you mean now?"

"Yes."

"I must say it would be very nice, but the only thing is, what would the night porter think?"

"My dear, how English you are. Well, I shall tell you—he will be in no doubt whatsoever."

"No, I suppose not."

"But I don't imagine he's under any illusion as it is. After all, I come here for you three times every day—you've seen nobody else, and French people are quite quick at noticing these things, you know."

"Yes—I see——"

"All right then—I'll be over directly."

THE NEXT DAY Fabrice installed her in a flat, he said it was more convenient. He said, "When I was young I liked to be very romantic and run all kinds of risks. I used to hide in wardrobes, be brought into the house in a trunk, disguise myself as a footman, and climb in at windows. How I used to climb! I remember once, halfway up a creeper there was a wasps' nest—oh the agony—I wore a Kestos *soutien-gorge* for a week afterwards. But now I prefer to be comfortable, to follow a certain routine, and have my own key."

Indeed, Linda thought, nobody could be less romantic and more practical than Fabrice, no nonsense about him. A little nonsense, she thought, would have been rather nice.

It was a beautiful flat, large and sunny, and decorated in the most expensive kind of modern taste. It faced south and west over the Bois de Boulogne, and was on a level with the tree-tops. Tree-tops and sky made up the view. The enormous windows worked like windows of a motor-car, the whole of the glass disappearing into the wall. This was a great joy to Linda, who loved the open air and loved to sunbathe for hours with no clothes on, until she was hot and brown and sleepy and happy. Belonging to the flat, belonging, it was evident, to Fabrice, was a charming elderly housekeeper called Germaine. She was assisted by various other elderly women who came and went in a bewildering succession. She was obviously most efficient, she had all Linda's things out of her suitcase, ironed and folded away, in a moment, and then went off to the kitchen, where she began to prepare dinner. Linda could not help wondering how many other people Fabrice had kept in this flat; however, as she was unlikely to find out, and, indeed, had no wish to know, she put the thought from her. There was no trace of any former occupant, not so much as a scribbled telephone number or the mark of a lipstick anywhere to be seen; the flat might have been done up yesterday.

In her bath, before dinner, Linda thought rather wistfully of Aunt Sadie. She, Linda, was now a kept woman and an adulteress, and Aunt Sadie, she knew, wouldn't like that. She hadn't liked it when Linda had committed adultery with Christian, but he, at least, was English, and Linda had been properly introduced to him and knew his surname. Also, Christian had all along intended to marry her. But how much less would Aunt Sadie like her daughter to pick up an unknown, nameless foreigner and go off to live with him in luxury. It was a long step from lunching in Oxford to this, though Uncle Matthew would, no doubt, have considered it a step down the same road if he knew her situation, and he would disown her for ever, throw her out into the snow, shoot Fabrice, or take any other violent action which might occur to him. Then something would happen to make him laugh, and all would be well again. Aunt Sadie was a different matter. She would not say very much, but she would brood over it and take it to heart, and wonder if there had not been something wrong about her method of bringing up Linda which had led to this; Linda most profoundly hoped that she would never find out.

In the middle of this reverie the telephone bell rang. Germaine answered it, tapped on the bathroom door, and said:

"The duke will be a bit late, madame."

"All right—thank you," said Linda.

At dinner she said:

"Could one know your name?"

"Oh," said Fabrice. "Haven't you discovered that? What an extraordinary lack of curiosity. My name is Sauveterre. In short, *madame*, I am happy to tell you that I am a very rich duke, a most agreeable thing to be, even in these days."

"How lovely for you. And, while we are on the subject of your private life, are you married?"

"No."

"Why not?"

"My fiancée died."

"Oh, how sad—what was she like?"

"Very pretty."

"Prettier than me?"

"Much prettier. Very correct."

"More correct than me?"

"You—you are mad, madame, not correct at all. And she was kind—really kind."

For the first time since she knew him, Fabrice had become infinitely sentimental, and Linda was suddenly shaken by the pangs of a terrible jealousy, so terrible that she felt quite faint. If she had not already recognized the fact, she would have known now, for certain and always, that this was to be the great love of her life.

"Five years," she said, "is quite a long time when it's all in front of you."

But Fabrice was still thinking of the fiancée.

"She died much more than five years ago—fifteen years in the autumn. I always go and put late roses on her grave, those little tight roses with very dark green leaves that never open properly—they remind me of her. God, how sad it was."

"And what was her name?" said Linda.

"Louise. The only daughter of the last Duke de Rancé. I often go and see her mother, who is still alive, a remarkable old woman. She was brought up in England at the court of the Empress Eugénie, and Rancé married her in spite of that, for love. You can imagine how strange everybody found it."

A deep melancholy settled on them both. Linda saw too clearly that she could not hope to compete with a fiancée who was not only prettier and more correct than she was, but also dead. It seemed most unfair. Had she remained alive her prettiness would surely, after fifteen years of marriage, have faded away, her correctness have become a bore; dead, she was embalmed for ever in her youth, her beauty, and her *gentillesse*.

After dinner, however, Linda was restored to happiness. Being made love to by Fabrice was an intoxication, quite different from anything she had hitherto experienced.

("I was forced to the conclusion," she said, when telling me about this time, "that neither Tony nor Christian had an inkling of what we used to call the facts of life. But I suppose all Englishmen are hopeless as lovers."

"Not all," I said, "the trouble with most of them is that their minds are not on it, and it happens to require a very great deal of application. Alfred," I told her, "is wonderful."

"Oh, good," she said, but she sounded unconvinced I thought.)

They sat until late looking out of the open window. It was a hot evening, and, when the sun had gone, a green light lingered behind the black bunches of the trees until complete darkness fell.

"Do you always laugh when you make love?" said Fabrice.

"I hadn't thought about it, but I suppose I do. I generally laugh when I'm happy and cry when I'm not, I am a simple character, you know. Do you find it odd?"

"Very disconcerting at first, I must say."

"But why—don't most women laugh?"

"Indeed, they do not. More often they cry."

"How extraordinary—don't they enjoy it?"

"It has nothing to do with enjoyment. If they are young they call on their mothers, if they are religious they call on the Virgin to forgive them. But I have never known one who laughed except you. But I suppose it's to be expected; you're mad."

Linda was fascinated.

"What else do they do?"

"What they all do, except you, is to say; 'How you must despise me.'"

"But why should you despise them?"

"Oh, really, my dear, one does, that's all."

"Well, I call that most unfair. First you seduce them, then you despise them, poor things. What a monster you are."

"They like it. They like grovelling about and saying 'What have I done. Good heavens, Fabrice, what must you think of me? Oh, I am ashamed.' It's all part of the thing to them. But you, you seem unaware of your shame, you just roar with laughter. It is very strange. And not unpleasant, I must admit."

"Then what about the fiancée," said Linda, "didn't you despise her?"

"Of course not. She was a virtuous woman."

"Do you mean to say you never went to bed with her?"

"Never. Never would such a thing have crossed my mind in a thousand thousand years."

"Goodness," said Linda. "In England we always do."

"My dear, the animal side of the English is well known. The English are a drunken and an incontinent race, it is well known."

"They don't know it. They think it's foreigners who are all those things."

"French women are the most virtuous in the world," said Fabrice, in the tones of exaggerated pride with which Frenchmen always talk about their women.

"Oh, dear," said Linda, sadly. "I was so virtuous once. I wonder what happened to me. I went wrong when I married my first husband, but how was I to know? I thought he was a god and that I should love him for ever. Then I went wrong again when I ran away with Christian, but I thought I loved him, and I did too, much more than Tony, but he never really loved me, and very soon I bored him, I wasn't serious enough, I suppose. Anyhow, if I hadn't done these things, I shouldn't have ended up on a suitcase at the

Gare du Nord and I would never have met you, so, really, I'm glad. And in my next life, wherever I happen to be born, I must remember to fly to the boulevards as soon as I'm of marriageable age, and find a husband there."

"How nice," said Fabrice, "and, as a matter of fact, French marriages are generally very very happy you know. My father and mother had a cloudless life together, they loved each other so much that they hardly went out in society at all. My mother still lives in a sort of afterglow of happiness from it. What a good woman she is!"

"I must tell you," Linda went on, "that my mother and one of my aunts, one of my sisters and my cousin, are virtuous women, so virtue is not unknown in my family. And anyway, Fabrice, what about your grandmother?"

"Yes," said Fabrice, with a sigh. "I admit that she was a great sinner. But she was also a very great lady, and she died fully redeemed by the rites of the Church."

Chapter 18

THEIR LIFE NOW began to acquire a routine. Fabrice dined with her every night in the flat—he never took her out to a restaurant again—and stayed with her until seven o'clock the following morning. "I hate sleeping alone," he said. At seven he would get up, dress, and go home, in time to be in his bed at eight o'clock, when his breakfast was brought in. He would have his breakfast, read the newspapers, and at nine, ring up Linda and talk nonsense for half an hour, as though he had not seen her for days.

"Go on," he would say, if she showed any signs of flagging. "Go on, tell me some more."

During the day she hardly ever saw him. He always lunched with his mother, who had the first-floor flat in the house where he lived on the ground floor. Sometimes he took Linda sightseeing in the afternoon, but generally he did not appear until about half-past seven, soon after which they dined.

Linda occupied her days buying clothes, which she paid for with great wads of banknotes given her by Fabrice.

"I might as well be hanged for a sheep as a lamb," she thought. "And as he despises me anyway it can't make very much difference."

Fabrice was delighted. He took an intense interest in her clothes, looked them up and down, made her parade round her drawing-room in them, forced her to take them back to the shops for alterations which seemed to her quite unnecessary, but which proved in the end to have made all the difference. Linda had never before fully realized the superiority of French clothes to English. In London she had been considered exceptionally well dressed, when she was married to Tony; she now realized that never could she have had, by French standards, the smallest pretensions to *chic*. The things she had with her seemed to her so appallingly dowdy, so skimpy and miserable and without line, that she went to the Galeries Lafayette and bought herself a ready-made dress there before she dared to venture into the big houses. When she did finally emerge from them with a few clothes, Fabrice advised her to get a great many more. Her taste, he said, was not at all bad, for an Englishwoman, though he doubted whether she would really become *élégante* in the true sense of the word.

"Only by trial and error," he said, "can you find out your type, can you see where you are going. So keep on, my dear, work at it. You're not doing at all badly."

The weather now became hot and sultry, holiday, seaside weather. But this was 1939, and men's thoughts were not of relaxation, but of death, not of bathing-suits but of uniforms, not of dance music but of trumpets, while beaches for the next few years were to be battle and not pleasure grounds. Fabrice said every day how much he longed to take Linda to the Rivièra, to Venice and to his beautiful chateau in the Dauphiné. But he was a reservist, and would be called up any day now. Linda did not mind staying in Paris at all. She could sunbathe in her flat as much as she wanted to. She felt no particular apprehensions about the coming war, she was essentially a person who lived in the present.

"I couldn't sunbathe naked like this anywhere else," she said, "and it's the only holiday thing I enjoy. I don't like swimming, or tennis, or dancing, or gambling, so you see I'm just as well off here sunbathing and shopping, two perfect occupations for the day, and you, my darling love, at night. I should think I'm the happiest woman in the world."

ONE BOILING HOT afternoon in July she arrived home wearing a new and particularly ravishing straw hat. It was large and simple, with a wreath of flowers and two blue bows. Her right arm was full of roses and carnations, and in her left hand was a striped bandbox, containing another exquisite hat. She let herself in with her latchkey, and stumped, on the high cork soles of her sandals, to the drawing-room.

The green venetian blinds were down, and the room was full of warm shadows, two of which suddenly resolved themselves into a thin man and a not so thin man—Davey and Lord Merlin.

"Good heavens," said Linda, and she flopped down onto a sofa, scattering the roses at her feet.

"Well," said Davey, "you do look pretty."

Linda felt really frightened, like a child caught out in some misdeed, like a child whose new toy is going to be taken away. She looked from one to the other. Lord Merlin was wearing black spectacles.

"Are you in disguise?" said Linda.

"No, what do you mean? Oh, the spectacles—I have to wear them when I go abroad, I have such kind eyes you see, beggars and things cluster round and annoy me."

He took them off and blinked.

"What have you come for?"

"You don't seem very pleased to see us," said Davey. "We came, actually, to see if you were all right. As it's only too obvious that you are, we may as well go away again."

"How did you find out? Do Mummy and Fa know?" she added, faintly.

"No, absolutely nothing. They think you're still with Christian. We haven't come in the spirit of two Victorian uncles, my dear Linda, if that's what you're thinking. I happened to see a man I know who had been to Perpignan, and he mentioned that Christian was living with Lavender Davis——"

"Oh good," said Linda.

"What? And that you had left six weeks ago. I went round to Cheyne Walk and there you obviously weren't, and then Mer and I got faintly worried to think of you wandering about the Continent, so ill suited (we thought, how wrong we were) to look after yourself, and at the same time madly curious to know your whereabouts and present circumstances, so we put in motion a little discreet detective work, which revealed your whereabouts—your circumstances are now as clear as daylight, and I, for one, feel most relieved."

"You gave us a fright," said Lord Merlin, crossly. "Another time, when you are putting on this Cléo de Mérode act, you might send a postcard. For one thing, it is a great pleasure to see you in the part, I wouldn't have missed it for worlds. I hadn't realized, Linda, that you were such a beautiful woman."

Davey was laughing quietly to himself.

"Oh, goodness, how funny it all is—so wonderfully old-fashioned. The shopping! The parcels! The flowers! So tremendously Victorian. People have been delivering cardboard boxes every five minutes since we arrived. What an interest you are in one's life, Linda dear. Have you told him he must give you up and marry a pure young girl yet?"

Linda said disarmingly: "Don't tease, Davey. I'm *so* happy you can't think."

"Yes, you look happy I must say. Oh, this flat is such a joke."

"I was just thinking," said Lord Merlin, "that, however much taste may change, it always follows a stereotyped plan. Frenchmen used to keep their mistresses in *appartements*, each exactly like the other, in which the dominant note, you might say, was lace and velvet. The walls, the bed, the dressing-table, the very bath itself were hung with lace, and everything else was velvet. Nowadays for lace you substitute glass, and everything else is satin. I bet you've got a glass bed, Linda?"

"Yes—but——"

"And a glass dressing-table, and bathroom, and I wouldn't be surprised if your bath were made of glass, with goldfish swimming about in the sides of it. Goldfish are a prevailing motif all down the ages."

"You've looked," said Linda sulkily. "Very clever."

"Oh, what heaven," said Davey. "So it's true! He hasn't looked, I swear, but you see it's not beyond the bounds of human ingenuity to guess."

"But there are some things here," said Lord Merlin, "which do raise the level, all the same. A Gauguin, those two Matisses (chintzy, but accomplished) and this Savonnerie carpet. Your protector must be very rich."

"He is," said Linda.

"Then, Linda dear, could one ask for a cup of tea?"

She rang the bell, and soon Davey was falling upon *éclairs* and *mille feuilles* with all the abandon of a schoolboy.

"I shall pay for this," he said, with a devil-may-care smile, "but never mind, one's not in Paris every day."

Lord Merlin wandered round with his tea-cup. He picked up a book which Fabrice had given Linda the day before, of romantic nineteenth-century poetry.

"Is this what you're reading now?" he said. "'*Dieu, que le son du cor est triste au fond des bois.*' I had a friend, when I lived in Paris, who had a boa constrictor as a pet, and this boa constrictor got itself inside a French horn. My friend rang me up in a fearful state, saying: '*Dieu, que le son du boa est triste au fond du cor.*' I've never forgotten it."

"What time does your lover generally arrive?" said Davey, taking out his watch.

"Not till about seven. Do stay and see him, he's such a terrific Hon."

"No, thank you, not for the world."

"Who is he?" said Lord Merlin.

"He's called the Duke of Sauveterre."

A look of great surprise, mingled with horrified amusement, passed between Davey and Lord Merlin.

"Fabrice de Sauveterre?"

"Yes. Do you know him?"

"Darling Linda, one always forgets, under that look of great sophistication, what a little provincial you really are. Of course we know him, and all about him, and, what's more, so does everyone except you."

"Well, don't you think he's a terrific Hon?"

"Fabrice," said Lord Merlin with emphasis, "is undoubtedly one of the wickedest men in Europe, as far as women are concerned. But I must admit that he's an extremely agreeable companion."

"Do you remember in Venice," said Davey, "one used to see him at work in that gondola, one after another, bowling them over like rabbits, poor dears?"

"Please remember," said Linda, "that you are eating his tea at this moment."

"Yes, indeed, and so delicious. Another *éclair*, please, Linda. That summer," he went on, "when he made off with Ciano's girl friend, what a fuss there was, I never shall forget, and then, a week later, he dumped her in Cannes and went to Salzburg with Martha Birmingham, and poor old Claud shot at him four times, and always missed him."

"Fabrice has a charmed life," said Lord Merlin. "I suppose he has been shot at more than anybody, and, as far as I know, he's never had a scratch."

Linda was unmoved by these revelations, which had been forestalled by Fabrice himself. Anyhow, no woman really minds hearing of the past affairs of her lover, it is the future alone that has the power to terrify.

"Come on, Mer," said Davey. "Time the little lady got herself into a *négligée*. Goodness, what a scene there'll be when he smells Mer's cigar, there'll be a *crime passionel*, I shouldn't wonder. Good-bye, Linda darling, we're off to dine with our intellectual friends, you know, shall you be lunching with us at the Ritz tomorrow? About one, then. Good-bye—give our love to Fabrice."

When Fabrice came in he sniffed about, and asked whose cigar. Linda explained.

"They say they know you."

"Surely—Merlin, such a nice chap, and poor Warbeck, always so ill. I knew them in Venice. What did they think of all this?"

"Well, they roared at the flat."

"Yes, I can imagine. It is quite unsuitable for you, this flat, but it's convenient, and with the war coming——"

"Oh, but I love it, I wouldn't like anything else half so much. Wasn't it clever of them, though, to find me?"

"Do you mean to say you never told anybody where you were?"

"I really didn't think of it—the days go by, you know—one simply doesn't remember these things."

"And it was six weeks before they thought of looking for you? As a family you seem to me strangely disorganized."

Linda suddenly threw herself into his arms, and said, with great passion:

"Never, never let me go back to them."

"My darling—but you love them. Mummy and Fa, Matt and Robin and Victoria and Fanny. What is all this?"

"I never want to leave you again as long as I live."

"Aha! But you know you will probably have to, soon. The war is going to begin, you know."

"Why can't I stay here? I could work—I could become a nurse— well, perhaps not a nurse, actually, but something."

"If you promise to do what I tell you, you may stay here for a time. At the beginning we shall sit and look at the Germans across the Maginot Line, then I shall be a great deal in Paris, between Paris and the front, but mostly here. At that time I shall want you here. Then somebody, we or the Germans, but I am very much afraid the Germans, will pour across the line, and a war of movement will begin. I shall have notice of that stage, and what you must promise me is that the very minute I tell you to leave for London you will leave, even if you can see no reason for doing so. I should be hampered beyond words in my duties if you were still here. So will you solemnly promise, now?"

"All right," said Linda. "Solemnly. I don't believe anything so dreadful could happen to me, but I promise to do as you say. Now will you promise that you will come to London as soon as it's all over and find me again? Promise?"

"Yes," said Fabrice. "I will do that."

LUNCHEON WITH DAVEY and Lord Merlin was a gloomy meal. Preoccupation reigned. The two men had stayed up late and merrily with their literary friends, and showed every sign of having done so. Davey was beginning to be aware of the cruel pangs of dyspepsia, Lord Merlin was suffering badly from an ordinary straightforward hangover, and, when he removed his spectacles, his eyes were seen to be not kind at all. But Linda was far the most wretched of the three, she was, in fact, perfectly distracted by having overheard two French ladies in the foyer talking about Fabrice. She had arrived, as, from old habits of punctuality drummed into her by Uncle Matthew she always did, rather early. Fabrice had never taken her to the Ritz, she thought it delightful, she knew she was looking quite as pretty, and nearly as well dressed, as anybody there, and settled herself happily to await the others. Suddenly she heard, with that pang which the heart receives when the loved one's name is mentioned by strangers:

"And have you seen Fabrice at all?"

"Well, I have, because I quite often see him at Mme. de Sauveterre's, but he never goes out anywhere, as you know."

"Then what about Jacqueline?"

"Still in England. He is utterly lost without her, poor Fabrice, he is like a dog looking for its master. He sits sadly at home, never goes to parties, never goes to the club, sees nobody. His mother is really worried about him."

"Who would ever have expected Fabrice to be so faithful. How long is it?"

"Five years, I believe. A wonderfully happy *ménage.*"

"Surely Jacqueline will come back soon."

"Not until the old aunt has died. It seems she changes her will incessantly, and Jacqueline feels she must be there all the time— after all, she has her husband and children to consider."

"Rather hard on Fabrice?"

"What else could one expect? His mother says he rings her up every morning and talks for an hour—"

It was at this point that Davey and Lord Merlin, looking tired and cross, arrived, and took Linda off to luncheon with them. She was longing to stay and hear more of this torturing conversation, but, eschewing cocktails with a shudder, they hurried her off to the dining-room, where they were only fairly nice to her, and frankly disagreeable to each other.

She thought the meal would never come to an end, and, when at last it did, she threw herself into a taxi and drove to Fabrice's house. She must find out about Jacqueline, she must know his intentions. When Jacqueline returned would that be the moment for her, Linda, to leave as she had promised? War of movement indeed!

The servant said that M. le Duc had just gone out with Madame la Duchesse, but that he would be back in about an hour. Linda said she would wait, and he showed her into Fabrice's sitting-room. She took off her hat, and wandered restlessly about. She had been here several times before, with Fabrice, and it had seemed, after her brilliantly sunny flat, a little dismal. Now that she was alone in it she began to be aware of the extreme beauty of the room, a grave and solemn beauty which penetrated her. It was very high, rectangular in shape, with grey boiseries and cherry-coloured brocade curtains. It looked into a courtyard and never could get a ray of sunshine, that was not the plan. This was a civilized interior, it had nothing to do with out of doors. Every object in it was perfect. The furniture had the severe lines and excellent proportions of 1780, there was a portrait by Lancret of a lady with a parrot on her wrist, a bust of the same lady by Bouchardon, a carpet like the one in Linda's flat, but larger and grander, with a huge coat of arms in the middle. A high carved bookcase contained nothing but French classics bound in contemporary morocco, with the Sauveterre crest, and, open on a map table, lay a copy of Redouté's roses.

Linda began to feel much more calm, but, at the same time, very sad. She saw that this room indicated a side of Fabrice's character which she had hardly been allowed to apprehend, and which had its roots in old civilized French grandeur. It was the essential Fabrice, something in which she could never have a share — she would always be outside in her sunny modern flat, kept away from all this, kept rigidly away even if their liaison were to go on for ever. The origins of the Radlett family were lost in the mists of antiquity, but the origins of Fabrice's family were not lost at all, there they were, each generation clutching at the next. The English, she thought, throw off their ancestors. It is the great strength of our aristocracy, but Fabrice has his round his neck, and he will never get away from them.

She began to realize that here were her competitors, her enemies, and that Jacqueline was nothing in comparison. Here, and in the grave of Louise. To come here and make a scene about a rival mistress would be utterly meaningless, she would be one unreality complaining about another. Fabrice would be annoyed, as men always are annoyed on these occasions, and she would get no satisfaction. She could hear his voice, dry and sarcastic:

"Ah! You amaze me, madame."

Better go, better ignore the whole affair. Her only hope was to keep things on their present footing, to keep the happiness which she was enjoying day by day, hour by hour, and not to think about the future at all. It held nothing for her, leave it alone. Besides, everybody's future was in jeopardy now the war was coming, this war which she always forgot about.

She was reminded of it, however, when, that evening, Fabrice appeared in uniform.

"Another month I should think," he said. "As soon as they have got the harvest in."

"If it depended on the English," said Linda, "they would wait until after the Christmas shopping. Oh, Fabrice, it won't last very long, will it?"

"It will be very disagreeable while it does last," said Fabrice. "Did you come to my flat today?"

"Yes, after lunching with those two old cross-patches I suddenly felt I wanted to see you very much."

"How nice!" He looked at her quizzically, as though something had occurred to him, "But why didn't you wait?"

"Your ancestors frightened me off."

"Oh, they did? But you have ancestors yourself I believe, *madame?*"

"Yes, but they don't hang about in the same way as yours do."

"You should have waited," said Fabrice, "it is always a very great pleasure to see you, both for me and for my ancestors. It cheers us all up."

Germaine now came into the room with huge armfuls of flowers and a note from Lord Merlin, saying:

"Here are some coals for Newcastle. We are tottering home by the ferry-boat. Do you think I shall get Davey back alive? I enclose something which might, one day, be useful."

It was a note for 20,000 francs.

"I must say," said Linda, "considering what cruel eyes he has, he does think of everything."

She felt sentimental after the occurrences of the day.

"Tell me, Fabrice," she said, "what did you think the first moment you ever saw me?"

"If you really want to know, I thought: 'Why, she looks like the little Bosquet girl.'"

"Who is that?"

"There are two Bosquet sisters, the elder, who is a beauty, and a little one who looks like you."

"Thanks so much," said Linda, "I would prefer to look like the other one."

Fabrice laughed. "Then, I said to myself, how funny, how old-fashioned all this seems——"

When the war, which had for so long been pending, did actually break out some six weeks later, Linda was strangely unmoved by the fact. She was enveloped in the present, in her own detached and futureless life, which, anyhow, seemed so precarious, so much from one hour to another: exterior events hardly impinged on her consciousness. When she thought about the war it seemed to her almost a relief that it had actually begun, in so far as a beginning is the first step towards an end. That it had only begun in name and not in fact did not occur to her. Of course, had Fabrice been taken away by it her attitude would have been very different, but his job, an intelligence one, kept him mostly in Paris, and, indeed, she now saw rather more of him than formerly, as he moved into her flat, shutting up his own and sending his mother to the country. He would appear and disappear at all sorts of odd moments of the night and day, and, as the sight of him was a constant joy to Linda, as she could imagine no greater happiness than she always felt when the empty space in front of her eyes became filled by his form, these sudden apparitions kept her in a state of happy suspense and their relationship at fever point.

Since Davey's visit Linda had been getting letters from her family. He had given Aunt Sadie her address and told her that Linda was doing war work in Paris, providing comforts for the French army, he said vaguely, and with some degree of truth. Aunt Sadie was pleased about this, she thought it very good of Linda to work so hard (all night sometimes, Davey said), and was glad to hear that she earned her keep. Voluntary work was often unsatisfactory and expensive. Uncle Matthew thought it a pity to work for foreigners, and deplored the fact that his children were so fond of crossing oceans, but he also was very much in favour of war work. He was himself utterly disgusted that the War Office were not able to offer him the opportunity of repeating his exploit with the entrenching tool, or, indeed, any job at all, and he went about like a bear with a sore head, full of unsatisfied desire to fight for his King and country.

I wrote to Linda and told her about Christian, who was back in London, had left the Communist party and had joined up. Lavender had also returned: she was now an A.T.S.

Christian did not show the slightest curiosity about what had happened to Linda, he did not seem to want to divorce her or to marry Lavender, he had thrown himself heart and soul into army life and thought of nothing but the war.

Before leaving Perpignan he had extricated Matt, who, after a good deal of persuasion, had consented to leave his Spanish comrades in order to join the battle against Fascism on another front. He went into Uncle Matthew's old regiment, and was said to bore his brother officers in the mess very much by arguing that they were training the men all wrong, and that, during the battle of the Ebro, things had been done thus and thus. In the end his colonel, who was rather brighter in the head than some of the others hit upon the obvious reply, which was, "Well anyway, your side lost!" This shut Matt up on tactics, but got him going on statistics — "30,000 Germans and Italians, 500 German 'planes," and so forth — which were almost equally dull and boring.

Linda heard no more about Jacqueline, and the wretchedness into which she had been thrown by those few chance words overheard at the Ritz was gradually forgotten. She reminded herself that nobody ever really knew the state of a man's heart, not even, perhaps specially not, his mother, and that in love it is actions that count. Fabrice had no time now for two women, he spent every spare moment with her and that in itself reassured her. Besides, just as her marriages with Tony and Christian had been necessary in order to lead up to her meeting with Fabrice, so this affair had led up to his meeting with her: undoubtedly he must have been seeing Jacqueline off at the Gare du Nord when he found Linda crying on her suitcase. Putting herself in Jacqueline's shoes, she realized how much preferable it was to be in her own: in any case it was not Jacqueline who was her dangerous rival, but that dim, virtuous figure from the past, Louise. Whenever Fabrice showed signs of becoming a little less practical, a little more nonsensical and romantic, it was of his fiancée that he would speak, dwelling with a gentle sadness upon her beauty, her noble birth, her vast estates and her religious mania. Linda once suggested that, had the fiancée lived to become a wife, she might not have been a very happy one.

"All that climbing," she said, "in at other people's bedroom windows, might it not have upset her?"

Fabrice looked intensely shocked and reproachful and said that there never would have been any climbing, that, where marriage was concerned, he had the very highest ideals, and that his whole life would have been devoted to making Louise happy. Linda felt herself rebuked, but was not entirely convinced.

All this time Linda watched the tree-tops from her window. They had changed, since she had been in the flat, from bright green against a bright blue sky, to dark green against a lavender sky, to yellow against a cerulean sky, until now they were black skeletons against a sky of moleskin, and it was Christmas Day. The windows could no longer be opened until they disappeared, but, whenever the sun did come out, it shone into her rooms, and the flat was always as warm as toast. On this Christmas morning Fabrice arrived, quite unexpectedly, before she was up, his arms full of parcels, and soon the floor of her bedroom was covered with waves of tissue paper through which, like wrecks and monsters half submerged beneath a shallow sea, appeared fur coats, hats, real mimosa, artificial flowers, feathers, scent, gloves, stockings, underclothes and a bulldog puppy.

Linda had spent Lord Merlin's 20,000 francs on a tiny Renoir for Fabrice: six inches of seascape, a little patch of brilliant blue, which she thought would look just right in his room in the Rue Bonaparte. Fabrice was the most difficult person to buy presents for, he possessed a larger assortment of jewels, knick-knacks and rare objects of all kinds than anybody she had ever known. He was delighted with the Renoir, nothing, he said, could have pleased him more, and Linda felt that he really meant it.

"Oh, such a cold day," he said. "I've just been to church."

"Fabrice, how can you go to church when there's me?"

"Well, why not?"

"You're a Roman Catholic, aren't you?"

"Of course I am. What do you suppose? Do you think I look like a Calvinist?"

"But then aren't you living in mortal sin? So what about when you confess?"

"One doesn't go into detail," said Fabrice, carelessly, "and, in any case, these little sins of the body are quite unimportant."

Linda would have liked to think that she was more in Fabrice's life than a little sin of the body, but she was used to coming up against these closed doors in her relationship with him, and had learnt to be philosophical about it and thankful for the happiness that she did receive.

"In England," she said, "people are always renouncing each other on account of being Roman Catholics. It's sometimes very sad for them. A lot of English books are about this, you know."

"The English are madmen, I have always said it. You almost sound as if you want to be given up. What has happened since Saturday? Not tired of your war work, I hope?"

"No, no, Fabrice. I just wondered, that's all."

"But you look so sad, *ma chérie*, what is it?"

"I was thinking of Christmas Day at home. I always feel sentimental at Christmas."

"If what I said might happen does happen and I have to send you back to England, shall you go home to your father?"

"Oh, no," said Linda, "anyway, it won't happen. All the English papers say we are killing Germany with our blockade."

"Blockade," said Fabrice, impatiently. "What nonsense! Let me tell you, *madame*, they don't give a damn about your blockade. So where would you go?"

"To my own house in Chelsea, and wait for you to come."

"It might be months, or years."

"I shall wait," she said.

THE SKELETON TREE-TOPS began to fill out, they acquired a pinkish tinge, which gradually changed to golden-green. The sky was often blue, and, on some days, Linda could once more open her windows and lie naked in the sun, whose rays by now had a certain strength. She always loved the spring, she loved the sudden changes of temperature, the dips backward into winter and forward into summer, and, this year, living in beautiful Paris, her perceptions heightened by great emotion, she was profoundly affected by it. There was now a curious feeling in the air, very different from and much more nervous than that which had been current before Christmas, and the town was full of rumours. Linda often thought of the expression *"fin de siècle."* There was a certain analogy, she thought, between the state of mind which it denoted and that prevailing now, only now it was more like *"fin de vie."* It was as though everybody around her, and she herself, were living out the last few days of their lives, but this curious feeling did not disturb her, she was possessed by a calm and happy fatalism. She occupied the hours of waiting between Fabrice's visits by lying in the sun, when there was any, and playing with her puppy. On Fabrice's advice she even began to order some new clothes for the summer. He seemed to regard the acquisition of clothes as one of the chief duties of woman, to be pursued through war and revolution, through sickness, and up to death. It was as one who might say, "whatever happens the fields must be tilled, the cattle tended, life must go on." He was so essentially urban that to him the slow roll of the seasons was marked by the spring tailored suits, the summer prints, the autumn *ensembles*, and the winter furs of his mistress.

On a beautiful windy blue and white day in April the blow fell.

Fabrice, whom Linda had not seen for nearly a week, arrived from the front looking grave and worried, and told her that she must go back to England at once.

"I've got a place for you in the aeroplane," he said, "for this afternoon. You must pack a small suitcase, and the rest of your things must go after you by train. Germaine will see to them. I have to go to the Ministère de la Guerre, I'll be back as soon as possible, and anyhow in time to take you to Le Bourget. Come on," he added, "just time for a little war work." He was in his most practical and least romantic mood.

When he returned he looked more preoccupied than ever. Linda was waiting for him, her box was packed, she was wearing the blue suit in which he had first seen her, and had her old mink coat over her arm.

"Well," said Fabrice, who always at once noticed what she had on, "what is this? A fancy-dress party?"

"Fabrice, you must understand that I can't take away the things you have given me. I loved having them while I was here, and while they gave you pleasure seeing me in them, but, after all, I have some pride. After all, I wasn't brought up in a bordello."

"*Ma chère*, try not to be so middle-class, it doesn't suit you at all. There's no time for you to change—wait, though—" He went into her bedroom, and came out again with a long sable coat, one of his Christmas presents. He took her mink coat, rolled it up, threw it into the waste-paper basket, and put the other over her arm in its place.

"Germaine will send your things after you," he said. "Come now, we must go."

Linda said good-bye to Germaine, picked up the bulldog puppy, and followed Fabrice into the lift, out into the street. She did not fully understand that she was leaving that happy life behind her for ever.

Chapter 19

AT FIRST, BACK in Cheyne Walk, she still did not understand. The world was grey and cold certainly, the sun had gone behind a cloud, but only for a time: it would come out again, she would soon once more be enveloped in that heat and light which had left her in so warm a glow, there was still much blue in the sky, this little cloud would pass. Then, as sometimes happens, the cloud, which had seemed at first such a little one, grew and grew, until it became a thick grey blanket smothering the horizon. The bad news began, the terrible days, the unforgettable weeks. A great horror of steel was rolling over France, was rolling towards England, swallowing on its way the puny beings who tried to stop it, swallowing Fabrice, Germaine, the flat, and the past months of Linda's life, swallowing Alfred, Bob, Matt, and little Robin, coming to swallow us all. London people cried openly in the buses, in the streets, for the English army which was lost.

Then, suddenly one day, the English army turned up again. There was a feeling of such intense relief, it was as if the war were over and won. Alfred and Bob and Matt and little Robin all reappeared, and, as a lot of French soldiers also arrived, Linda had a wild hope that Fabrice might be with them. She sat all day by the

telephone, and when it rang and it was not Fabrice she was furious
with the unlucky telephoner—I know, because it happened to me.
She was so furious that I dropped the receiver and went straight
round to Cheyne Walk.

I found her unpacking a huge trunk, which had just arrived from
France. I had never seen her looking so beautiful. It made me gasp,
and I remembered how Davey had said, when he got back from
Paris, that at last Linda was fulfilling the promise of her childhood,
and had become a beauty.

"How do you imagine this got here?" she said, between tears and
laughter. "What an extraordinary war. The Southern Railway
people brought it just now and I signed for it, all as though nothing
peculiar were happening—I don't understand a word of it. What
are you doing in London, darling?"

She seemed unaware of the fact that half an hour ago she had
spoken to me, and indeed bitten my head off, on the telephone.

"I'm with Alfred. He's got to get a lot of new equipment and see
all sorts of people. I believe he's going abroad again very soon."

"Awfully good of him," said Linda, "when he needn't have
joined up at all, I imagine. What does he say about Dunkirk?"

"He says it was like something out of the *Boy's Own*—he seems
to have had a most fascinating time."

"They all did, the boys were here yesterday and you never heard
anything like their stories. Of course they never quite realized how
desperate it all was until they got to the coast. Oh, isn't it wonderful
to have them back? If only—if only one knew what had happened
to one's French buddies—" She looked at me under her eyelashes,
and I thought she was going to tell me about her life, but, if so, she
changed her mind and went on unpacking.

"I shall have to put these winter things back in their boxes really,"
she said. "I simply haven't any cupboards that will hold them all,
but it's something to do, and I like to see them again."

"You should shake them," I said, "and put them in the sun. They
may be damp."

"Darling, you are wonderful, you always know."

"Where did you get that puppy?" I said enviously. I had wanted a bulldog for years, but Alfred never would let me have one because of the snoring.

"Brought him back with me. He's the nicest puppy I ever had, so anxious to oblige, you can't think."

"What about quarantine then?"

"Under my coat," said Linda, laconically. "You should have heard him grunting and snuffling, it shook the whole place, I was terrified, but he was so good. He never budged. And talking of puppies, those ghastly Kroesigs are sending Moira to America, isn't it typical of them? I've made a great thing with Tony about seeing her before she goes, after all I am her mother."

"That's what I can't ever understand about you, Linda."

"What?"

"How you could have been so dreadful to Moira."

"Dull," said Linda. "Uninteresting."

"I know, but the point is that children are like puppies, and if you never see puppies, if you give them to the groom or the game-keeper to bring up, look how dull and uninteresting they always are. Children are just the same—you must give them much more than their life if they are to be any good. Poor Little Moira—all you gave her was that awful name."

"Oh, Fanny, I do know. To tell you the truth I believe it was always in the back of my mind that, sooner or later, I should have to run away from Tony, and I didn't want to get too fond of Moira, or make her too fond of me. She might have become an anchor, and I simply didn't dare let myself be anchored to the Kroesigs."

"Poor Linda."

"Oh, don't pity me. I've had eleven months of perfect and unalloyed happiness, very few people can say that, in the course of long long lives, I imagine."

I imagined so too. Alfred and I are happy, as happy as married people can be. We are in love, we are intellectually and physically suited in every possible way, we rejoice in each other's company, we have no money troubles and three delightful children. And yet, when I consider my life, day by day, hour by hour, it seems to be composed of a series of pinpricks. Nannies, cooks, the endless drudgery of housekeeping, the nerve-racking noise and boring repetitive conversation of small children (boring in the sense that it bores into one's very brain), their absolute incapacity to amuse themselves, their sudden and terrifying illnesses, Alfred's not infrequent bouts of moodiness, his invariable complaints at meals about the pudding, the way he will always use my tooth-paste and will always squeeze the tube in the middle. These are the components of marriage, the wholemeal bread of life, rough, ordinary, but sustaining; Linda had been feeding upon honey-dew, and that is an incomparable diet.

The old woman who had opened the door to me came in and said was that everything, because, if so, she would be going home.

"Everything," said Linda. "Mrs. Hunt," she said to me, when she had gone. "A terrific Hon—she comes daily."

"Why don't you go to Alconleigh?" I said, "or to Shenley? Aunt Emily and Davey would love to have you, and I'm going there with the children as soon as Alfred is off again."

"I'd like to come for a visit some time, when I know a little more what is happening, but at the moment I must stop here. Give them my love though. I've got such masses to tell you, Fanny, what we really need is hours and hours in the Hons' cupboard."

AFTER A GOOD deal of hesitation Tony Kroesig and his wife, Pixie, allowed Moira to go and see her mother before leaving England. She arrived at Cheyne Walk in Tony's car, still driven by a chauffeur in uniform not the King's. She was a plain, stodgy, shy little girl, with no echo of the Radletts about her; not to put too fine a point on it she was a real little Gretchen.

"What a sweet puppy," she said, awkwardly, when Linda had kissed her. She was clearly very much embarrassed.

"What's his name?"

"Plon-plon."

"Oh. Is that a French name?"

"Yes, it is. He's a French dog, you see."

"Daddy says the French are terrible."

"I expect he does."

"He says they have let us down, and what can we expect if we have anything to do with such people."

"Yes, he would."

"Daddy thinks we ought to fight with the Germans and not against them."

"M'm. But Daddy doesn't seem to be fighting very much with anybody, or against anybody, or at all, as far as I can see. Now, Moira, before you go I have got two things for you, one is a present and the other is a little talk. The talk is very dull, so we'll get that over first, shall we?"

"Yes," said Moira, apathetically. She lugged the puppy onto the sofa beside her.

"I want you to know," said Linda, "and to remember, please, Moira (stop playing with the puppy a minute and listen carefully to what I am saying) that I don't at all approve of you running away like this, I think it most dreadfully wrong. When you have a country which has given you as much as England has given all of us, you ought to stick to it, and not go wandering off as soon as it looks like being in trouble."

"But it's not my fault," said Moira, her forehead puckering. "I'm only a child and Pixie is taking me. I have to do what I'm told, don't I?"

"Yes, of course, I know that's true. But you'd much rather stay, wouldn't you?" said Linda, hopefully.

"Oh no, I don't think so. There might be air-raids."

At this Linda gave up. Children might or might not enjoy air-raids actually in progress, but a child who was not thrilled by the idea of them was incomprehensible to her, and she could not imag-

ine having conceived such a being. Useless to waste any more time
and breath on this unnatural little girl. She sighed and said:

"Now wait a moment and I'll get your present."

She had in her pocket, in a velvet box, a coral hand holding a diamond arrow, which Fabrice had given her, but she could not bear to
waste anything so pretty on this besotted little coward. She went to
her bedroom and found a sports wristwatch, one of her wedding
presents when she had married Tony and which she had never
worn, and gave this to Moira, who seemed quite pleased by it, and
left the house as politely and unenthusiastically as she had arrived.

Linda rang me up at Shenley and told me about this interview.

"I'm in such a temper," she said, "I must talk to somebody. To
think I ruined nine months of my life in order to have that. What
do your children think about air-raids, Fanny?"

"I must say they simply long for them, and I am sorry to say they
also long for the Germans to arrive. They spend the whole day
making booby-traps for them in the orchard."

"Well that's a relief anyhow—I thought perhaps it was the generation. Actually of course, it's not Moira's fault, it's all that bloody
Pixie—I can see the form only too clearly, can't you? Pixie is frightened to death and she has found out that going to America is like
the children's concert, you can only make it if you have a child in
tow. So she's using Moira—well, it does serve one right for doing
wrong." Linda was evidently very much put out. "And I hear Tony
is going too, some Parliamentary mission or something. All I can
say is what a set."

All through those terrible months of May, June and July, Linda
waited for a sign from Fabrice, but no sign came. She did not doubt
that he was still alive, it was not in Linda's nature to imagine that
anyone might be dead. She knew that thousands of Frenchmen
were in German hands, but felt certain that, had Fabrice been
taken prisoner (a thing which she did not at all approve of, inciden-
tally, taking the old-fashioned view that, unless in exceptional cir-

cumstances, it is a disgrace), he would undoubtedly manage to escape. She would hear from him before long, and, meanwhile, there was nothing to be done, she must simply wait. All the same, as the days went by with no news, and as all the news there was from France was bad, she did become exceedingly restless. She was really more concerned with his attitude than with his safety—his attitude towards events and his attitude towards her. She felt sure that he would never be associated with the armistice, she felt sure that he would want to communicate with her, but she had no proof, and, in moments of great loneliness and depression, she allowed herself to lose faith. She realized how little she really knew of Fabrice, he had seldom talked seriously to her, their relationship having been primarily physical while their conversations and chats had all been based on jokes.

They had laughed and made love and laughed again, and the months had slipped by with no time for anything but laughter and love. Enough to satisfy her, but what about him? Now that life had become so serious, and, for a Frenchman, so tragic, would he not have forgotten that meal of whipped cream as something so utterly unimportant that it might never have existed? She began to think, more and more, to tell herself over and over again, to force herself to realize, that it was probably all finished, that Fabrice might never be anything for her now but a memory.

At the same time the few people she saw never failed when talking, everybody talked then, about France to emphasize that the French "one knew," the families who were "*bien*," were all behaving very badly, convinced Pétainists. Fabrice was not one of them, she thought, she felt, but she wished she knew, she longed for evidence.

In fact, she alternated between hope and despair, but as the months went by without a word, a word that she was sure he could have sent if he had really wanted to, despair began to prevail.

Then, on a sunny Sunday morning in August, very early, her telephone bell rang. She woke up with a start, aware that it had been ringing already for several moments, and she knew with absolute certainty that this was Fabrice.

"Are you Flaxman 2815?"

"Yes."

"I've got a call for you. You're through."

"*Allô—allô?*"

"Fabrice?"

"*Oui.*"

"Oh! Fabrice—I've been waiting for you for so long."

"How nice! Then I may come right away?"

"Oh, wait—yes, you can come at once, but don't go for a minute, go on talking, I want to hear the sound of your voice."

"No, no, I have a taxi outside, I shall be with you in five minutes. There's too much one can't do on the telephone, my dear, so look——" Click.

She lay back, and all was light and warmth. Life, she thought, is sometimes sad and often dull, but there are currants in the cake and here is one of them. The early morning sun shone past her window onto the river, her ceiling danced with water-reflections. The Sunday silence was broken by two swans winging slowly upstream, and then by the chugging of a little barge, while she waited for that other sound, a sound more intimately connected with the urban love affair than any except the telephone bell, that of a stopping taxicab. Sun, silence, and happiness. Presently she heard it in the street, slowly, slower, it stopped, the flag went up with a ring, the door slammed, voices, clinking coins, footsteps. She rushed downstairs.

Hours later Linda made some coffee.

"So lucky," she said, "that it happens to be Sunday, and Mrs. Hunt isn't here. What would she have thought?"

"Just about the same as the night porter at the Hotel Montalembert, I expect," said Fabrice.

"Why did you come, Fabrice? To join General de Gaulle?"

"No, that was not necessary, because I have joined him already. I was with him in Bordeaux. My work has to be in France, but we have ways of communicating when we want to. I shall go and see him, of course, he expects me at midday, but actually I came on a private mission."

He looked at her for a long time.

"I came to tell you that I love you," he said, at last.

Linda felt giddy.

"You never said that to me in Paris."

"No."

"You always seemed so practical."

"Yes, I suppose so. I had said it so often and often before in my life, I had been so romantic with so many women, that when I felt this to be different I really could not bring out all those stale old phrases again, I couldn't utter them. I never said I loved you, I never tutoyé'd you, on purpose. Because from the first moment I knew that this was as real as all the others were false, it was like recognizing somebody—there, I can't explain."

"But that is exactly how I felt too," said Linda, "don't try to explain, you needn't, I know."

"Then, when you had gone, I felt I had to tell you, and it became an obsession with me to tell you. All those dreadful weeks were made more dreadful because I was being prevented from telling you."

"How ever did you get here?"

"One moves about," said Fabrice, vaguely. "I must leave again tomorrow morning, very early, and I shan't come back until the war is over, but you'll wait for me, Linda, and nothing matters so much now that you know. I was tormented, I couldn't concentrate on anything, I was becoming useless in my work. In future I may have much to bear, but I shan't have to bear you going away without knowing what a great great love I have for you."

"Oh, Fabrice, I feel—well, I suppose religious people sometimes feel like this."

She put her head on his shoulder, and they sat for a long time in silence.

WHEN HE HAD paid his visit to Carlton Gardens they lunched at the Ritz. It was full of people Linda knew, all very smart, very gay, and talking with the greatest flippancy about the imminent arrival of the Germans. Had it not been for the fact that all the young men there had fought bravely in Flanders, and would, no doubt, soon be fighting bravely again, and this time with more experience, on other fields of battle, the general tone might have been considered shocking. Even Fabrice looked grave, and said they did not seem to realize——

Davey and Lord Merlin appeared. Their eyebrows went up when they saw Fabrice.

"Poor Merlin has the wrong kind," Davey said to Linda.

"The wrong kind of what?"

"Pill to take when the Germans come. He's just got the sort you give to dogs."

Davey brought out a jewelled box containing two pills, one white and one black.

"You take the white one first and then the black one—he really must go to my doctor."

"I think one should let the Germans do the killing," said Linda. "Make them add to their own crimes and use up a bullet. Why should one smooth their path in any way? Besides, I back myself to do in at least two before they get me."

"Oh, you're so tough, Linda, but I'm afraid it wouldn't be a bullet for me, they would torture me, look at the things I've said about them in the *Gazette*."

"No worse than you've said about all of us," Lord Merlin remarked.

Davey was known to be a most savage reviewer, a perfect butcher, never sparing even his dearest friends. He wrote under several pseudonyms, which in no way disguised his unmistakable style, his cruellest essays appearing over the name Little Nell.

"Are you here for long, Sauveterre?"

"No, not for long."

Linda and Fabrice went in to luncheon. They talked of this and that, mostly jokes. Fabrice told her scandalous stories about some of the other lunchers known to him of old, with a wealth of unlikely detail. He spoke only once about France, only to say that the struggle must be carried on, everything would be all right in the end. Linda thought how different it would have been with Tony or Christian. Tony would have held forth about his experiences and made boring arrangements for his own future, Christian would have launched a monologue on world conditions subsequent to the recent fall of France, its probable repercussions in Araby and far Cashmere, the inadequacy of Pétain to deal with such a wealth of displaced persons, the steps that he, Christian, would have taken had he found himself in his, the Marshal's, shoes. Both would have spoken to her exactly, in every respect, as if she had been some chap in their club. Fabrice talked to her, at her, and for only her, it was absolutely personal talk, scattered with jokes and allusions private to them both. She had a feeling that he would not allow himself to be serious, that if he did he would have to embark on tragedy, and that he wanted her to carry away a happy memory of his visit. But he also gave an impression of boundless optimism and faith, very cheering at that dark time.

Early the next morning, another beautiful, hot, sunny morning, Linda lay back on her pillows and watched Fabrice while he dressed, as she had so often watched him in Paris. He made a certain kind of face when he was pulling his tie into a knot, she had quite forgotten it in the months between, and it brought back their Paris life to her suddenly and vividly.

"Fabrice," she said. "Do you think we shall ever live together again?"

"But of course we shall, for years and years and years, until I am ninety. I have a very faithful nature."

"You weren't very faithful to Jacqueline."

"Aha—so you know about Jacqueline, do you? She was so lovely, poor thing—lovely, elegant, but aggravating, my God! Anyway, I was immensely faithful to her and it lasted five years, it always does with me (either five days or five years). But as I love you ten times more than the others that brings it to when I am ninety, and, by then, it will have become such a habit with me——"

"And how soon shall I see you again?"

"I'll be back and forth." He went to the window. "I thought I heard a car—oh yes, it is turning round. There, I must go. *Au revoir, madame.*"

He kissed her hand politely, almost absentmindedly, it was as if he had already gone, and walked quickly from the room. Linda went to the open window and leaned out. He was getting into a large motor-car with two French soldiers on the box and a Free French flag waving from the bonnet. As it moved away he looked up.

"Back and forth—back and forth——" cried Linda with a brilliant smile. Then she got back into bed and cried very much. She felt utterly in despair at this second parting.

Chapter 20

THE AIR-RAIDS ON London now began. Early in September, just as I had moved there with my family, a bomb fell in the garden of Aunt Emily's little house in Kent. It was a small bomb compared with what one saw later, and none of us were hurt, but the house was more or less wrecked. Aunt Emily, Davey, my children and I, then took refuge at Alconleigh, where Aunt Sadie welcomed us with open arms, begging us to make it our home for the war. Louisa had already arrived there with her children, John Fort William had gone back to his regiment and their Scotch home had been taken over by the Navy.

"The more the merrier," said Aunt Sadie. "I should like to fill the house, and, besides, it's better for rations. Nice, too, for your children to be brought up all together, just like old times. With the boys away and Victoria in the Wrens Matthew and I would be a very dreary old couple here all alone."

The big rooms at Alconleigh were filled with the contents of some science museum and no evacuees had been billeted there, I think it was felt that nobody who had not been brought up to such rigours could stand the cold of that house.

Soon the party received a very unexpected addition. I was

upstairs in the nursery bathroom doing some washing for Nanny, measuring out the soap-flakes with wartime parsimony and wishing that the water at Alconleigh were not so dreadfully hard, when Louisa burst in.

"You'll never guess," she said, "in a thousand thousand years who has arrived."

"Hitler," I said, stupidly.

"Your mother, Auntie Bolter. She just walked up the drive and walked in."

"Alone?"

"No, with a man."

"The Major?"

"He doesn't look like a major. He's got a musical instrument with him and he's very dirty. Come on, Fanny, leave those to soak——"

And so it was. My mother sat in the hall drinking a whisky-and-soda and recounting in her birdlike voice with what incredible adventures she had escaped from the Riviera. The major with whom she had been living for some years, always having greatly preferred the Germans to the French, had remained behind to collaborate, and the man who now accompanied my mother was a ruffianly looking Spaniard called Juan, whom she had picked up during her travels, and without whom, she said, she could never have got away from a ghastly prison camp in Spain. She spoke of him exactly as though he were not there at all, which produced rather a curious effect, and indeed seemed most embarrassing until we realized that Juan understood no word of any language except Spanish. He sat staring blankly into space, clutching a guitar and gulping down great draughts of whisky. Their relationship was only too obvious, Juan was undoubtedly (nobody doubted for a moment, not even Aunt Sadie), the Bolter's lover, but they were quite incapable of verbal exchange, my mother being no linguist.

Presently Uncle Matthew appeared, and the Bolter told her adventures all over again to him. He said he was delighted to see her, and hoped she would stay as long as she liked, he then turned his blue eyes upon Juan in a most terrifying and uncompromising stare. Aunt Sadie led him off to the business-room, whispering, and we heard him say:

"All right then, but only for a few days."

One person who was off his head with joy at the sight of her was dear old Josh.

"We must get her ladyship up onto a horse," he said, hissing with pleasure.

My mother had not been her ladyship since three husbands (four, if one were to include the Major), but Josh took no account of this, she would always be her ladyship to him. He found a horse, not worthy of her, in his eyes, but not an absolute dud either, and had her out cub-hunting within a week of her arrival.

As for me it was the first time in my life that I had really found myself face to face with my mother. When a small child I had been obsessed by her and the few appearances she had made had absolutely dazzled me, though, as I have said, I never had any wish to emulate her career. Davey and Aunt Emily had been very clever in their approach to her, they, and especially Davey, had gradually and gently and without in any way hurting my feelings, turned her into a sort of joke. Since I was grown up I had seen her a few times, and had taken Alfred to visit her on our honeymoon, but the fact that, in spite of our intimate relationship, we had no past life in common put a great strain upon us and these meetings were not a success. At Alconleigh, in contact with her morning, noon and night, I studied her with the greatest curiosity; apart from anything else she was, after all, the grandmother of my children. I couldn't help rather liking her. Though she was silliness personified there was something engaging about her frankness and high spirits and endless good nature. The children adored her, Louisa's as well as mine, and she soon became an extra unofficial nurserymaid, and was very useful to us in that capacity.

She was curiously dated in her manner, and seemed still to be living in the 1920's. It was as though, at the age of thirty-five, having refused to grow any older, she had pickled herself, both mentally and physically, ignoring the fact that the world was changing and that she was withering fast. She had a short canary-coloured shingle (windswept) and wore trousers with the air of one still flouting the conventions, ignorant that every suburban shopgirl was doing the same. Her conversation, her point of view, the very slang she used, all belonged to the late 'twenties, that period now deader than the dodo. She was intensely unpractical, foolish, and apparently fragile, and yet she must have been quite a tough little person really, to have walked over the Pyrenees, to have escaped from a Spanish camp, and to have arrived at Alconleigh looking as if she had stepped out of the chorus of *No, No, Nanette.*

Some confusion was caused in the household at first by the fact that none of us could remember whether she had, in the end, actually married the Major (a married man himself and father of six) or not, and, in consequence, nobody knew whether her name was now Mrs. Rawl or Mrs. Plugge. Rawl had been a white hunter, the only husband she had ever lost respectably through death, having shot him by accident in the head during a safari. The question of names was soon solved, however, by her ration book, which proclaimed her to be Mrs. Plugge.

"This Gewan," said Uncle Matthew, when they had been at Alconleigh a week or so, "what's going to be done about him?"

"Well, Matthew dulling," she larded her phrases with the word darling, and that is how she pronounced it. "Hoo-arn saved my life, you know, over and over again, and I can't very well tear him up and throw him away, now can I, my sweet?"

"I can't keep a lot of dagoes here, you know." Uncle Matthew said this in the same voice with which he used to tell Linda that she couldn't have any more pets, or if she did they must be kept in the stables. "You'll have to make some other arrangements for him, Bolter, I'm afraid."

"Oh, dulling, keep him a little longer, please, just a few more days, Matthew dulling," she sounded just like Linda, pleading for some smelly old dog, "and then I promise I'll find some place for him and tiny me to go to. You can't think what a lousy time we had together, I must stick to him now, I really must."

"Well, another week if you like, but it's not to be the thin end of the wedge, Bolter, and after that he must go. You can stay as long as you want to, of course, but I do draw the line at Gewan."

Louisa said to me, her eyes as big as saucers: "He rushes into her room before tea and lives with her." Louisa always describes the act of love as living with. "Before tea, Fanny, can you imagine it?"

"SADIE, DEAR," SAID Davey. "I am going to do an unpardonable thing. It is for the general good, for your own good too, but it is unpardonable. If you feel you can't forgive me when I've said my say, Emily and I will have to leave, that's all."

"Davey," said Aunt Sadie in astonishment, "what can be coming?"

"The food, Sadie, it's the food. I know how difficult it is for you in wartime, but we are all, in turns, being poisoned. I was sick for hours last night, the day before Emily had diarrhea, Fanny has that great spot on her nose, and I'm sure the children aren't putting on the weight they should. The fact is, dear, that if Mrs. Beecher were a Borgia she could hardly be more successful—all that sausage mince is poison, Sadie. I wouldn't complain if it were merely nasty, or insufficient, or too starchy, one expects that in the war, but actual poison does, I feel, call for comment. Look at the menus this week—Monday, poison pie; Tuesday, poison burger steak; Wednesday, Cornish poison——"

Aunt Sadie looked intensely worried.

"Oh, dear, yes, she is an awful cook, I know, but Davey, what can one do? The meat ration only lasts about two meals, and there are fourteen meals in a week, you must remember. If she minces it up with a little sausage meat—poison meat (I do so agree with you really)—it goes much further, you see."

"But in the country surely one can supplement the ration with game and farm produce? Yes, I know the home farm is let, but surely you could keep a pig and some hens? And what about game? There always used to be such a lot here."

"The trouble is Matthew thinks they'll be needing all their ammunition for the Germans, and he refuses to waste a single shot on hares or partridges. Then you see Mrs. Beecher (oh, what a dreadful woman she is, though of course, we are lucky to have her) is the kind of cook who is quite good at a cut off the joint and two veg., but she simply hasn't an idea of how to make up delicious foreign oddments out of little bits of nothing at all. But you are quite, absolutely right, Davey, it's not wholesome. I really will make an effort to see what can be done."

"You always used to be such a wonderful housekeeper, Sadie dear, it used to do one so much good, coming here. I remember one Christmas I put on four and a half ounces. But now I am losing steadily, my wretched frame is hardly more than a skeleton and I fear that, if I were to catch anything, I might peter out altogether. I take every precaution against that, everything is drenched in T.C.P., I gargle at least six times a day, but I can't disguise from you that my resistance is very low, very."

Aunt Sadie said: "It's quite easy to be a wonderful housekeeper when there is a first-rate cook, two kitchen-maids, a scullerymaid, and when you can get all the food you want. I'm afraid I am dreadfully stupid at managing on rations, but I really will try and take a pull. I'm very glad indeed that you mentioned it, Davey, it was absolutely right of you, and of course, I don't mind at all."

But no real improvement resulted. Mrs. Beecher said "yes, yes" to all suggestions, and continued to send up Hamburger steaks, Cornish pasty and shepherd pie, which continued to be full of poison sausage. It was very nasty and very unwholesome, and, for once, we all felt that Davey had not gone a bit too far. Meals were no pleasure to anybody and a positive ordeal to Davey, who sat, a pinched expression on his face, refusing food and resorting more and more often to the vitamin pills with which his place at the table was surrounded—too many by far even for his collection of jewelled boxes—a little forest of bottles, vitamin A, vitamin B, vitamins A and C, vitamins B_3 and D, one tablet equals two pounds of summer butter—ten times the strength of a gallon of cod-liver oil—for the blood—for the brain—for muscle—for energy—anti this and protection against that—all but one bore a pretty legend.

"And what's in this, Davey?"

"Oh, that's what the panzer troops have before going into action."

Davey gave a series of little sniffs. This usually denoted that his nose was about to bleed, pints of valuable red and white corpuscles so assiduously filled with vitamins would be wasted, his resistance still further lowered.

Aunt Emily and I looked up in some anxiety from the rissoles we were sadly pushing round our plates.

"Bolter," he said, severely, "you've been at my Mary Chess again."

"Oh, Davey dulling, such a tiny droppie."

"A tiny drop doesn't stink out the whole room. I'm sure you have been pouring it into the bath with the stopper out. It is a shame. That bottle is my quota for a month, it is too bad of you, Bolter."

"Dulling, I swear I'll get you some more—I've got to go to London next week, to have my wiggie washed, and I'll bring back a bottle, I swear."

"And I very much hope you'll take Gewan with you and leave him there," growled Uncle Matthew. "Because I won't have him in this house much longer, you know. I've warned you, Bolter."

Uncle Matthew was busy from morning to night with his Home Guard. He was happy and interested and in a particularly mellow mood, for it looked as if his favourite hobby, that of clocking Germans, might be available again at any moment. So he only noticed Juan from time to time, and, whereas in the old days he would have had him out of the house in the twinkling of an eye, Juan had now been an inmate of Alconleigh for nearly a month. However, it was beginning to be obvious that my uncle had no intention of putting up with his presence for ever and things were clearly coming to a head where Juan was concerned. As for the Spaniard himself, I never saw a man so wretched. He wandered about miserably, with nothing whatever to do all day, unable to talk to anybody, while at mealtimes the disgust on his face fully equalled that of Davey. He hadn't even the spirit to play his guitar.

"Davey, you must talk to him," said Aunt Sadie.

My mother had gone to London to have her hair dyed, and a family council was gathered in her absence to decide upon the fate of Juan.

"We obviously can't turn him out to starve, as the Bolter says he saved her life, and, anyhow, one has human feelings."

"Not towards Dagoes," said Uncle Matthew, grinding his dentures.

"But what we can do is to get him a job, only first we must find out what his profession is. Now, Davey, you're good at languages, and you're so clever, I'm sure if you had a look at the Spanish dictionary in the library you could just manage to ask him what he used to do before the war. Do try, Davey."

"Yes, darling, do," said Aunt Emily. "The poor fellow looks too miserable for words at present, I expect he'd love to have some work."

Uncle Matthew snorted.

"Just give me the Spanish dictionary," he muttered. "I'll soon find the word for 'get out.'"

"I'll try," said Davey, "but I can guess what it will be I'm afraid. G for gigolo."

"Or something equally useless, like M for matador or H for hidalgo," said Louisa.

"Yes. Then what?"

"Then B for be off," said Uncle Matthew, "and the Bolter will have to support him, but not anywhere near me, I beg. It must be made perfectly clear to both of them that I can't stand the sight of the sewer lounging about here any longer."

When Davey takes on a job he does it thoroughly. He shut himself up for several hours with the Spanish dictionary, and wrote down a great many words and phrases on a piece of paper. Then he beckoned Juan into Uncle Matthew's business-room and shut the door.

They were only there a short time, and, when they emerged, both were wreathed in happy smiles.

"You've sacked him, I hope?" Uncle Matthew said, suspiciously.

"No, indeed, I've not sacked him," said Davey, "on the contrary, I've engaged him. My dears, you'll never guess, it's too absolutely glamorous for words, Juan is a cook, he was the cook, I gather, of some cardinal before the Civil War. You don't mind I hope, Sadie. I look upon this as an absolute lifeline—Spanish food, so delicious, so unconstipating, so digestible, so full of glorious garlic. Oh, the joy, no more poison-burger—how soon can we get rid of Mrs. Beecher?"

Davey's enthusiasm was fully justified, and Juan in the kitchen was the very greatest possible success. He was more than a first-class cook, he had an extraordinary talent for organization, and soon, I suspect, became king of the local black market. There was no nonsense about foreign dishes made out of little bits of nothing at all; succulent birds, beasts, and crustaceans appeared at every meal, the vegetables ran with extravagant sauces, the puddings were obviously based upon real ice-cream.

"Juan is wonderful," Aunt Sadie would remark in her vague manner, "at making the rations go round. When I think of Mrs. Beecher—really, Davey, you were so clever."

One day she said: "I hope the food isn't too rich for you now, Davey?"

"Oh no," said Davey. "I never mind rich food, it's poor food that does one such an infinity of harm."

Juan also pickled and bottled and preserved from morning till night, until the store cupboard, which he had found bare except for a few tins of soup, began to look like a pre-war grocer's shop. Davey called it Aladdin's Cave, or Aladdin for short, and spent a lot of his time there, gloating. Months of tasty vitamins stood there in neat rows, a barrier between him and that starvation which had seemed, under Mrs. Beecher's regime, only just round the corner.

Juan himself was now a very different fellow from the dirty and disgruntled refugee who had sat about so miserably. He was clean, he wore a white coat and hat, he seemed to have grown in stature, and he soon acquired a manner of great authority in his kitchen. Even Uncle Matthew acknowledged the change.

"If I were the Bolter," he suggested, "I should marry him."

"Knowing the Bolter," said Davey, "I've no doubt at all that she will."

Early in November I had to go to London for the day, on business for Alfred, who was now in the Middle East, and to see my doctor. I went by the eight o'clock train, and, having heard nothing of Linda for some weeks, I took a taxi and drove straight to Cheyne Walk. There had been a heavy raid the night before, and I passed through streets which glistened with broken glass. Many fires still smouldered, and fire engines, ambulances, and rescue men hurried to and fro, streets were blocked, and several times we had to drive quite a long way round. There seemed to be a great deal of excitement in the air. Little groups of people were gathered outside shops and houses, as if to compare notes; my taxi-driver talked incessantly to me over his shoulder. He had been up all night, he said, helping the rescue workers. He described what he had found.

"It was a spongy mass of red," he said, ghoulishly, "covered with feathers."

"Feathers?" I said, horrified.

"Yes. A feather bed, you see. It was still breathing, so I takes it to the hospital, but they says that's no good to us, take it to the mortuary. So I sews it in a sack and takes it to the mortuary."

"Goodness," I said.

"Oh, that's nothing to what I have seen."

Linda's nice daily woman, Mrs. Hunt, opened the door to me at Cheyne Walk.

"She's very poorly, ma'am, can't you take her back to the country with you? It's not right for her to be here, in her condition. I hate to see her like this."

Linda was in her bathroom, being sick. When she came out she said:

"Don't think it's the raid that's upset me. I like them. I'm in the family way, that's what it is."

"Darling, I thought you weren't supposed to have another baby."

"Oh, doctors! They don't know anything, they are such fearful idiots. Of course I can, and I'm simply longing for it, this baby won't be the least bit like Moira, you'll see."

"I'm going to have one too."

"No—how lovely—when?"

"About the end of May."

"Oh, just the same as me.

"And Louisa, in March."

"Haven't we been busy? I do call that nice, they can all be Hons together."

"Now, Linda, why don't you come back with me to Alconleigh? Whatever is the sense of stopping here in all this? It can't be good for you or the baby."

"I like it," said Linda. "It's my home, and I like to be in it. And besides, somebody might turn up, just for a few hours you know, and want to see me, and he knows where to find me here."

"You'll be killed," I said, "and then he won't know where to find you."

"Darling Fanny, don't be so silly. There are seven million people living in London, do you really imagine they are all killed every night? Nobody is killed in air-raids, there is a great deal of noise and a great deal of mess, but people really don't seem to get killed much."

"Don't—don't——" I said. "Touch wood. Apart from being killed or not it doesn't suit you. You look awful, Linda."

"Not so bad when I'm made up. I'm so fearfully sick, that's the trouble, but it's nothing to do with the raids, and that part will soon be over now and I shall be quite all right again."

"Well, think about it," I said, "it's very nice at Alconleigh, wonderful food——"

"Yes, so I hear. Merlin came to see me, and his stories of caramelized carrots swimming in cream made my mouth water.

He said he was preparing to throw morality to the winds and bribe this Juan to go to Merlinford, but he found out it would mean having the Bolter too and he couldn't quite face that."

"I must go," I said uncertainly. "I don't like to leave you, darling, I do wish you'd come back with me."

"Perhaps I will later on, we'll see."

I went down to the kitchen and found Mrs. Hunt. I gave her some money in case of emergency, and the Alconleigh telephone number, and begged her to ring me up if she thought there was anything I could do.

"She won't budge," I said. "I've done all I can to make her, but it doesn't seem to be any good, she's as obstinate as a donkey."

"I know, ma'am. She won't even leave the house for a breath of air, sits by that telephone day in day out playing cards with herself. It ain't hardly right she should sleep here all alone in my opinion, either, but you can't get her to listen to sense. Last night, ma'am, whew! it was terrible, walloping down all night, and those wretched guns never got a single one, whatever they may tell you in the papers. It's my opinion they must have got women on those guns, and, if so, no wonder. Women!"

A week later Mrs. Hunt rang me up at Alconleigh. Linda's house had received a direct hit and they were still digging for her.

Aunt Sadie had gone on an early bus to Cheltenham to do some shopping, Uncle Matthew was nowhere to be found, so Davey and I simply took his car, full of Home Guard petrol, and drove to London, hell for leather. The little house was an absolute ruin, but Linda and her bulldog were unhurt, they had just been got out and put to bed in the house of a neighbour. Linda was flushed and excited, and couldn't stop talking.

"You see," she said. "What did I tell you, Fanny, about air-raids not killing people. Here we are, right as rain. My bed simply went through the floor, Plon-plon and I went on it, most comfortable."

Presently a doctor arrived and gave her a sedative. He told us she would probably go to sleep and that when she woke up we could drive her down to Alconleigh. I telephoned to Aunt Sadie and told her to have a room ready.

The rest of the day was spent by Davey in salvaging what he could of Linda's things. Her house and furniture, her beautiful Renoir, and everything in her bedroom was completely wrecked, but he was able to rescue a few oddments from the splintered, twisted remains of her cupboards, and in the basement he found, untouched, the two trunks full of clothes which Fabrice had sent after her from Paris. He came out looking like a miller, covered with white dust from head to foot, and Mrs. Hunt took us round to her own little house and gave us some food.

"I suppose Linda may miscarry," I said to Davey, "and I'm sure it's to be hoped she will. It's most dangerous for her to have this child—my doctor is horrified."

However, she did not, in fact she said that the experience had done her a great deal of good, and had quite stopped her from feeling sick. She demurred again at leaving London, but without much conviction. I pointed out that if anybody was looking for her and found the Cheyne Walk house a total wreck they would be certain at once to get into touch with Alconleigh. She saw that this was so, and agreed to come with us.

Chapter 21

WINTER NOW SET in with its usual severity on those Cotswold uplands. The air was sharp and bracing, like cold water; most agreeable if one only goes out for short brisk walks or rides, and if there is a warm house to go back to. But the central-heating apparatus at Alconleigh had never been really satisfactory and I suppose that by now the pipes, through old age, had become thoroughly furred up—in any case they were hardly more than tepid. On coming into the hall from the bitter outside air one did feel a momentary glow of warmth; this soon lessened, and gradually, as circulation died down, one's body became pervaded by a cruel numbness. The men on the estate, the old ones that is, who were not in the army, had no time to chop up logs for the fires; they were occupied from morning till night, under the leadership of Uncle Matthew, in drilling, constructing barricades and blockhouses, and otherwise preparing to make themselves a nuisance to the German army before ending up as cannon-fodder.

"I reckon," Uncle Matthew would say proudly, "that we shall be able to stop them for two hours—possibly three—before we are all killed. Not bad for such a little place."

We made our children go out and collect wood, Davey became

an assiduous and surprisingly efficient woodman (he had refused to join the Home Guard, he said he always fought better out of uniform), but, somehow, they only produced enough to keep the nursery fire going, and the one in the brown sitting-room, if it was lit after tea, and, as the wood was pretty wet, this only really got warm just when it was time to tear oneself away and go up the freezing stairs to bed. After dinner the two armchairs on each side of the fire were always occupied by Davey and my mother. Davey pointed out that it would be more trouble for everybody in the end if he got one of his chills; the Bolter just dumped herself down. The rest of us sat in a semicircle well beyond the limits of any real warmth, and looked longingly at the little flickering yellow flames, which often subsided into sulky smoke. Linda had an evening coat, a sort of robe from head to foot, of white fox lined with white ermine. She wrapped herself in this for dinner, and suffered less than we others did. In the daytime she either wore her sable coat and a pair of black velvet boots lined with sable to match, or lay on the sofa tucked up in an enormous mink bedspread lined with white velvet quilting.

"It used to make me so laugh when Fabrice said he was getting me all these things because they would be useful in the war, the war would be fearfully cold he always said, but I see now how right he was."

Linda's possessions filled the other females in the house with a sort of furious admiration.

"It does seem rather unfair," Louisa said to me one afternoon when we were pushing our two youngest children out in their prams together. We were both dressed in stiff Scotch tweeds, so different from supple flattering French ones, in woollen stockings, brogues, and jerseys, knitted by ourselves, of shades carefully chosen to "go with" though not "to match" our coats and skirts. "Linda goes off and has this glorious time in Paris, and comes back covered with rich furs, while you and I — what do we get for sticking all our lives to the same dreary old husbands? Three-quarter-length shorn lamb."

"Alfred isn't a dreary old husband," I said loyally. But of course I knew exactly what she meant.

Aunt Sadie thought Linda's clothes too pretty.

"What lovely taste, darling," she would say when another ravishing garment was brought out. "Did that come from Paris too? It's really wonderful what you can get there, on no money, if you're clever."

At this my mother would give tremendous winks in the direction of anybody whose eye she might happen to catch, including Linda herself. Linda's face would then become absolutely stony. She could not bear my mother; she felt that, before she met Fabrice, she had been heading down the same road herself, and she was appalled to see what lay at the end of it. My mother started off by trying a "let's face it, dear, we are nothing but two fallen women" method of approach to Linda, which was most unsuccessful. Linda became not only stiff and cold, but positively rude to the poor Bolter, who, unable to see what she could have done to offend, was at first very much hurt. Then she began to be on her dignity, and said it was great nonsense for Linda to go on like this; in fact, considering she was nothing but a high-class tart, it was most pretentious and hypocritical of her. I tried to explain Linda's intensely romantic attitude towards Fabrice and the months she had spent with him, but the Bolter's own feelings had been dulled by time, and she either could not or would not understand.

"It was Sauveterre she was living with, wasn't it?" my mother said to me, soon after Linda arrived at Alconleigh.

"How do you know?"

"Everybody knew on the Riviera. One always knew about Sauveterre somehow. And it was rather a thing, because he seemed to have settled down for life with that boring Lamballe woman; then she had to go to England on business and clever little Linda nabbed him. A very good cop for her, dulling, but I don't see why she has to be so high-hat about it. Sadie doesn't know, I quite realize that, and of course wild horses wouldn't make me tell her, I'm not that kind of a girl, but I do think, when we're all together, Linda might be a tiny bit more jolly."

The Alconleighs still believed that Linda was the devoted wife of Christian, who was now in Cairo, and, of course, it had never occurred to them for a moment that the child might not be his. They had quite forgiven her for leaving Tony, though they thought themselves distinctly broad-minded for having done so. They would ask her from time to time what Christian was doing, not because they were interested, but so that Linda shouldn't feel out of it when Louisa and I talked about our husbands. She would then be obliged to invent bits of news out of imaginary letters from Christian.

"He doesn't like his Brigadier very much," or,

"He says Cairo is great fun, but one can have enough of it."

In point of fact Linda never got any letters at all. She had not seen her English friends now for so long, they were scattered in the war to the ends of the earth, and, though they might not have forgotten about Linda, she was no longer in their lives. But, of course, there was only one thing she wanted, a letter, a line even, from Fabrice. Just after Christmas it came. It was forwarded in a type-written envelope from Carlton Gardens with General de Gaulle's stamp on it. Linda, when she saw it lying on the hall table, became perfectly white. She seized it and rushed up to her bedroom.

About an hour later she came to find me.

"Oh, darling," she said, her eyes full of tears. "I've been all this time and I can't read one word. Isn't it torture? Could you have a look?"

She gave me a sheet of the thinnest paper I ever saw, on which were scratched, apparently with a rusty pin, a series of perfectly incomprehensible hieroglyphics. I could not make out one single word either, it seemed to bear no relation to handwriting, the marks in no way resembled letters.

"What can I do?" said poor Linda. "Oh, Fanny."

"Let's ask Davey," I said.

She hesitated a little over this, but feeling that it would be better, however intimate the message, to share it with Davey than not to have it at all, she finally agreed.

Davey said she was quite right to ask him.

"I am very good at French handwriting."

"Only you wouldn't laugh at it?" Linda said, in a breathless voice like a child.

"No, Linda, I don't regard it as a laughing matter any longer," Davey replied, looking with love and anxiety at her face, which had become very drawn of late. But when he had studied the paper for some time, he too was obliged to confess himself absolutely stumped by it.

"I've seen a lot of difficult French writings in my life," he said, "and this beats them all."

In the end Linda had to give up. She went about with the piece of paper, like a talisman, in her pocket, but never knew what Fabrice had written to her on it. It was cruelly tantalizing. She wrote to him at Carlton Gardens, but this letter came back with a note regretting that it could not be forwarded.

"Never mind," she said. "One day the telephone bell will ring again and he'll be there."

LOUISA AND I were busy from morning to night. We now had one Nanny (mine) among eight children. Fortunately they were not at home all the time. Louisa's two eldest were at a private school, and two of hers and two of mine went for lessons to a convent Lord Merlin had most providentially found for us at Merlinford. Louisa got a little petrol for this, and she or I or Davey drove them there in Aunt Sadie's car every day. It can be imagined what Uncle Matthew thought of this arrangement. He ground his teeth, flashed his eyes, and always referred to the poor good nuns as "those damned parachutists." He was absolutely convinced that whatever time they could spare from making machine-gun nests for other nuns, who would presently descend from the skies, like birds, to occupy the nests, was given to the seduction of the souls of his grandchildren and great-nieces.

"They get a prize you know for anybody they can catch — of course you can see they are men, you've only got to look at their boots."

Every Sunday he watched the children like a lynx for genuflections, making the sign of the Cross, and other Papist antics, or even for undue interest in the service, and when none of these symptoms was to be observed he was hardly reassured.

"These Romans are so damned artful."

He thought it most subversive of Lord Merlin to harbour such an establishment on his property, but only really what one might expect of a man who brought Germans to one's ball and was known to admire foreign music. Uncle Matthew had most conveniently forgotten all about "Une voce poco fa," and now played, from morning to night, a record called "The Turkish Patrol," which started piano, became forte, and ended up pianissimo.

"You see," he would say, "they come out of a wood, and then you can hear them go back into the wood. Don't know why it's called Turkish, you can't imagine Turks playing a tune like that, and of course there aren't any woods in Turkey. It's just the name, that's all."

I think it reminded him of his Home Guard, who were always going into woods and coming out of them again, poor dears, often covering themselves with branches as when Birnam Wood came to Dunsinane.

So we worked hard, mending and making and washing, doing any chores for Nanny rather than actually look after the children ourselves. I have seen too many children brought up without Nannies to think this at all desirable. In Oxford, the wives of progressive dons did it often as a matter of principle; they would gradually become morons themselves, while the children looked like slum children and behaved like barbarians.

As well as looking after the clothes of our existing families we also had to make for the babies we were expecting, though they did inherit a good deal from brothers and sisters. Linda, who naturally had no store of baby clothes, did nothing of all this. She arranged one of the slatted shelves in the Hons' cupboard as a sort of bunk, with pillows and quilts from spare bedrooms, and here, wrapped in her mink bedspread, she would lie all day with Plon-plon beside her, reading fairy stories. The Hons' cupboard, as of old, was the warmest, the one really warm place in the house. Whenever I could I brought my sewing and sat with her there, and then she would put down the blue or the green fairy book, Anderson or Grimm, and tell me at length about Fabrice and her happy life with him in Paris. Louisa sometimes joined us there, and then Linda would break off and we would talk about John Fort William and the children. But Louisa was a restless busy creature, not much of a chatter, and, besides, she was irritated to see how Linda did absolutely nothing, day after day.

"Whatever is the baby going to wear, poor thing," she would say crossly to me, "and who is going to look after it, Fanny? It's quite plain already that you and I will have to, and really, you know, we've got enough to do as it is. And another thing, Linda lies there covered in sables or whatever they are, but she's got no money at all, she's a pauper—I don't believe she realizes that in the least. And what is Christian going to say when he hears about the baby, after all, legally his, he'll have to bring a suit to illegitimize it, and then there'll be such a scandal. None of these things seems to have occurred to Linda. She ought to be beside herself with worry, instead of which she is behaving like the wife of a millionaire in peacetime. I've no patience with her."

All the same, Louisa was a good soul. In the end it was she who went to London and bought a layette for the baby. Linda sold Tony's engagement ring, at a horribly low price, to pay for it.

"Do you never think about your husbands?" I asked her one day, after she had been talking for hours about Fabrice.

"Well, funnily enough, I do quite often think of Tony. Christian, you see, was such an interlude, he hardly counts in my life at all, because, for one thing, our marriage lasted a very short time, and then it was quite overshadowed by what came after. I don't know, I find these things hard to remember, but I think that my feelings for him were only really intense for a few weeks, just at the very beginning. He's a noble character, a man you can respect, I don't blame myself for marrying him, but he has no talent for love.

"But Tony was my husband for so long, more than a quarter of my life, if you come to think of it. He certainly made an impression. And I see now that the thing going wrong was hardly his fault, poor Tony, I don't believe it would have gone right with anybody (unless I had happened to meet Fabrice) because in those days I was so extremely nasty. The really important thing, if a marriage is to go well, without much love, is very very great niceness—*gentillesse*—and wonderful good manners. I was never *gentille* with Tony, and often I was hardly polite to him, and, very soon after our honeymoon, I became exceedingly disagreeable. I'm ashamed now to think what I was like. And poor old Tony was so good-natured, he never snapped back, he put up with it all for years and then just ambled off to Pixie. I can't blame him. It was my fault from beginning to end."

"Well, he wasn't very nice really, darling, you shouldn't worry yourself about it too much, and look how he's behaving now."

"Oh, he's the weakest character in the world, it's Pixie and his parents who made him do that. If he'd still been married to me he would have been a Guards officer by now, I bet you."

One thing Linda never thought about, I'm quite sure, was the future. Some day the telephone bell would ring and it would be Fabrice, and that was as far as she got. Whether he would marry her, and what would happen about the child, were questions which not only did not preoccupy her, but which never seemed to enter her head. Her mind was entirely on the past.

"It's rather sad," she said one day, "to belong, as we do, to a lost generation. I'm sure in history the two wars will count as one war and that we shall be squashed out of it altogether, and people will forget that we ever existed. We might just as well never have lived at all, I do think it's a shame."

"It may become a sort of literary curiosity," Davey said. He sometimes crept, shivering, into the Hons' cupboard to get up a little circulation before he went back to his writing. "People will be interested in it for all the wrong reasons, and collect Lalique dressing-table sets and shagreen boxes and cocktail cabinets lined with looking-glass and find them very amusing. Oh good," he said, peering out of the window, "that wonderful Juan is bringing in another pheasant."

(Juan had an invaluable talent, he was expert with a catapult. He spent all his odd moments—how he had odd moments was a mystery, but he had—creeping about the woods or down by the river armed with this weapon. As he was an infallible shot, and moreover, held back by no sporting inhibitions, that a pheasant or a hare should be sitting or a swan the property of the King being immaterial to Juan, the results of these sallies were excellent from the point of view of larder and stock-pot. When Davey really wanted to relish his food to the full he would recite, half to himself, a sort of little grace, which began: "Remember Mrs. Beecher's tinned tomato soup."

The unfortunate Craven was, of course, tortured by these goings on, which he regarded as little better than poaching. But his nose, poor man, was kept well to the grindstone by Uncle Matthew, and, when he was not on sentry-go, or fastening the trunks of trees to bicycle-wheels across the lanes to make barricades against tanks, he was on parade. Uncle Matthew was a byword in the county for the smartness of his parades. Juan, as an alien, was luckily excluded from these activities, and was able to devote all his time to making us comfortable and happy, in which he very notably succeeded.)

"I don't want to be a literary curiosity," said Linda. "I should like to have been a living part of a really great generation. I think it's too dismal to have been born in 1911."

"Never mind, Linda, you will be a wonderful old lady."

"You will be a wonderful old gentleman, Davey," said Linda.

"Oh, me? I fear I shall never make old bones," replied Davey, in accents of the greatest satisfaction.

And, indeed, there was a quality of agelessness about him. Although he was quite twenty years older than we and only about five years younger than Aunt Emily, he had always seemed much nearer to our generation than to hers, nor had he altered in any respect since the day when he had stood by the hall fire looking unlike a captain and unlike a husband.

"Come on, dears, tea, and I happen to know that Juan has made a layer-cake, so let's go down before the Bolter gets it all."

Davey carried on a great meal-time feud with the Bolter. Her table manners had always been casual, but certain of her habits, such as eating jam with a spoon which she put back into the jam-pot, and stubbing out her cigarette in the sugar-basin, drove poor Davey, who was very ration-conscious, to a frenzy of irritation, and he would speak sharply to her, like a governess to a maddening child.

He might have spared himself the trouble. The Bolter took absolutely no notice whatever, and went on spoiling food with insouciance.

"Dulling," she would say, "whatever does it matter, my perfectly divine Hoo-arn has got plenty more up his tiny sleeve, I promise you."

AT THIS TIME there was a particularly alarming invasion scare. The arrival of the Germans, with full paraphernalia of airborne troops dressed as priests, ballet dancers, or what you will, was expected from one day to the next. Some unkind person put it about that they would all be the doubles of Mrs. Davis, in W.V.S. uniform. She had such a knack of being in several places at once that it already seemed as if there were a dozen Mrs. Davises para-chuting about the countryside. Uncle Matthew took the invasion very seriously indeed, and one day he gathered us all together, in the business-room and told us in detail the part that we were expected to play.

"You women, with the children, must go to the cellar while the battle is on," he said, "there is an excellent tap, and I have provisioned you with bully-beef for a week. Yes, you may be there several days, I warn you."

"Nanny won't like that," Louisa began, but was quelled by a furious look.

"While we are on the subject of Nanny," Uncle Matthew said, "I warn you, there's to be no question of cluttering up the roads with your prams, mind, no evacuation under any circumstances at all. Now, there is one very important job to be done, and that I am entrusting to you, Davey. You won't mind it I know, old boy, if I say that you are a very poor shot—as you know, we are short of ammunition, and what there is must, under no circumstances, be wasted—every bullet must tell. So I don't intend to give you a gun, at first, anyhow. But I've got a fuse and a charge of dynamite (I will show you, in a moment), and I shall want you to blow up the store-cupboard for me."

"Blow up Aladdin," said Davey. He turned quite pale. "Matthew, you must be mad."

"I would let Gewan do it, but the fact is, though I rather like old Gewan now, I don't altogether trust the fella. Once a foreigner always a foreigner in my opinion. Now I must explain to you why I regard this as a most vital part of the operations. When Josh and Craven and I and all the rest of us have been killed there is only one way in which you civilians can help, and that is by becoming a charge on the German army. You must make it their business to feed you—never fear, they'll do so, they don't want typhus along their lines of communication—but you must see that it's as difficult as possible for them. Now that store cupboard would keep you going for weeks, I've just had a look at it; why, it would feed the entire village. All wrong. Make them bring in the food and muck up their transport, that's what we want, to be a perfect nuisance to them. It's all you'll be able to do, by then, just be a nuisance, so the store cupboard will have to go, and Davey must blow it up."

Davey opened his mouth to make another observation, but Uncle Matthew was in a very frightening mood and he thought better of it.

"Very well, dear Matthew," he said, sadly, "you must show me what to do."

But as soon as Uncle Matthew's back was turned he gave utterance to loud complaints.

"No, really, it is too bad of Matthew to insist on blowing up Aladdin," he said. "It's all right for him, he'll be dead, but he really should consider us a little more."

"But I thought you were going to take those black and white pills," said Linda.

"Emily doesn't like the idea, and I had decided only to take them if I were arrested, but now I don't know. Matthew says the German army will have to feed us, but he must know as well as I do that if they feed us at all, which is extremely problematical, it will be on nothing but starch—it will be Mrs. Beecher again, only worse, and I can't digest starch especially in the winter months. It is such a shame. Horrid old Matthew, he's so thoughtless."

"Well, but Davey," said Linda, "how about us? We're all in the same boat, but we don't grumble."

"Nanny will," said Louisa with a sniff, which plainly said, "and I wish to associate myself with Nanny."

"Nanny! She lives in a world of her own," said Linda. "But we're all supposed to know why we're fighting, and, speaking for myself, I think Fa is absolutely right. And if I think that, in my condition——"

"Oh, you'll be looked after," said Davey, bitterly, "pregnant women always are. They'll send you vitamins and things from America, you'll see. But nobody will bother about me, and I am so delicate, it simply won't do for me to be fed by the German army, and I shall never be able to make them understand about my inside. I know Germans."

"You always said nobody understood as much about your inside as Dr. Meyerstein."

"Use your common sense, Linda. Are they likely to drop Dr. Meyerstein over Alconleigh? You know perfectly well he's been in a camp for years. No, I must make up my mind to a lingering death — not a very pleasant prospect, I must say."

Linda took Uncle Matthew aside after that, and made him show her how to blow up Aladdin.

"Davey's spirit is not so frightfully willing," she said, "and his flesh is definitely weak."

There was a certain coldness between Linda and Davey for a little while after this, each thought the other had been quite unreasonable. It did not last, however. They were much too fond of each other (in fact, I am sure that Davey really loved Linda most in the world) and, as Aunt Sadie said, "Who knows, perhaps the necessity for these dreadful decisions will not arise."

SO THE WINTER slowly passed. The spring came with extraordinary beauty, as always at Alconleigh, with a brilliance of colouring, a richness of life, that one had forgotten to expect during the cold grey winter months. All the animals were giving birth, there were young creatures everywhere, and we now waited with longing and impatience for our babies to be born. The days, the very hours, dragged slowly by, and Linda began to say "better than that" when asked the time.

"What's the time, darling?"

"Guess."

"Half-past twelve?"

"Better than that, a quarter to one."

We three pregnant women had all become enormous, we dragged ourselves about the house like great figures of fertility, heaving tremendous sighs, and feeling the heat of the first warm days with exaggerated discomfort.

Useless to her now were Linda's beautiful Paris clothes, she was down to the level of Louisa and me in a cotton smock, maternity skirt and sandals. She abandoned the Hons' cupboard, and spent her days, when it was fine weather, sitting by the edge of the wood, while Plon-plon, who had become an enthusiastic, though unsuccessful, rabbiter, plunged panting to and fro in the green mists of the undergrowth.

"If anything happens to me, darling, you will look after Plon-plon," she said. "He has been such a comfort to me all this time."

But she spoke idly, as one who knows, in fact, that she will live for ever, and she mentioned neither Fabrice nor the child, as surely she would have done had she been touched by any premonition.

Louisa's baby, Angus, was born at the beginning of April. It was her sixth child and third boy, and we envied her from the bottom of our hearts for having got it over.

On the 28th May both our babies were born—both boys. The doctors who said that Linda ought never to have another child were not such idiots after all. It killed her. She died, I think, completely happy, and without having suffered very much, but for us at Alconleigh, for her father and mother, brothers and sisters, for Davey and for Lord Merlin a light went out, a great deal of joy that never could be replaced.

At about the same time as Linda's death Fabrice was caught by the Gestapo and subsequently shot. He was a hero of the Resistance, and his name has become a legend in France.

I have adopted the little Fabrice, with the consent of Christian, his legal father. He has black eyes, the same shape as Linda's blue ones, and is a most beautiful and enchanting child. I love him quite as much as, and perhaps more than, I do my own.

THE BOLTER CAME to see me while I was still in the Oxford nursing home where my baby had been born and where Linda had died.

"Poor Linda," she said, with feeling, "poor little thing. But Fanny, don't you think perhaps it's just as well? The lives of women like Linda and me are not so much fun when one begins to grow older."

I didn't want to hurt my mother's feelings by protesting that Linda was not that sort of woman.

"But I think she would have been happy with Fabrice," I said. "He was the great love of her life, you know."

"Oh, dulling," said my mother, sadly. "One always thinks that. Every, every time."

ALSO BY NANCY MITFORD

THE BLESSING

When Grace Allingham, a naïve young Englishwoman, goes to live in France with her dashingly aristocratic husband Charles-Edouard, she finds herself overwhelmed by the bewilderingly foreign cuisine and the shockingly decadent manners and mores of the French. But it is the discovery of her husband's French notion of marriage—which includes a permanent mistress and a string of casual affairs—that sends Grace packing back to London with their "blessing," young Sigismond, in tow. While others urge the couple to reconcile, little Sigi—convinced that it will improve his chances of being spoiled—applies all his juvenile cunning to keeping his parents apart. Drawing on her own years in Paris and her long affair with a Frenchman, Mitford elevates cultural and romantic misunderstandings to the heights of comedy.

Fiction/978-0-307-74083-0

DON'T TELL ALFRED

Fanny Wincham—last seen as a young woman in *The Pursuit of Love* and *Love in a Cold Climate*—has lived contentedly for years as housewife to an absent-minded Oxford don, Alfred. But her life changes overnight when her beloved Alfred is appointed English Ambassador to Paris. Soon she finds herself mixing with royalty and Rothschilds while battling her hysterical predecessor, Lady Leone, who refuses to leave the premises. When Fanny's tenderhearted secretary begins filling the embassy with rescued animals and her teenage sons run away from Eton and show up with a rock star in tow, things get entirely out of hand.

Fiction/978-0-307-74084-7

ALSO AVAILABLE:
Love in a Cold Climate, 978-0-307-74082-3
Wigs on the Green, 978-0-307-74085-4

VINTAGE BOOKS
Available at your local bookstore, or visit
www.randomhouse.com

ISBN-10: 1502512955
ISBN-13: 978-1502512956

DEDICATION

For Sabine

police officer
partner
unsurpassed
friend
colleague
love of my life

"Our nation's critics make our country a better place to live tomorrow. It is precisely those who stand up and define an existing social problem or condition who pave the way to the ultimate solution of a problem or condition."

Police Chief David Couper
West High School Graduation
Madison, Wisc.
June, 1973

Contents

A: Major Recommendations: National Commission on Law Enforcement and the Administration of Justice (1967)

B: Madison's Improvement Plan

C: Madison's Improvement Timeline

D: The Twelve Principles of Quality Leadership

Preface

The author in his office with pictures of Dr. Martin Luther King, Jr. and Mahatma Gandhi in the background. These pictures hung in his office for over 20 years. (Photo credit: Glenn Trudel, Madison, Wisconsin).

REFLECTING BACK, I NEVER thought I would be a chief of police. I was born in Minnesota in 1938; the eldest of two children. I was raised in the Minneapolis-St. Paul metro area. My father was a car salesman who worked only on commission. My mother, like most mothers at that time, was a stay-at-home mom. I would say that given the swings in our family finances, we were lower than middle class. I remember things like refrigerators and cars being

repossessed, late rent payments, and my parents
being hounded by bill collectors. We never owned a
home.

When I was a kid, I had a drive to organize things
and work to improve them. This drive never left me.
In middle school, I organized an animal hospital and
set up a system for feeding neighborhood stray dogs
and cats. Then there was my neighborhood football
team. I got local merchants to sponsor us, had
numbered jerseys made, and set up a schedule to play
other teams. It sounds strange today, but we didn't
have a coach and no parent ever came to one of our
games.

I was more a jock than a scholar when I attended
University High School in Minneapolis. I played
football as a defensive end and wrestled as a light
heavyweight. In my senior year, I joined the 4th
Infantry Battalion, a local Marine Corps reserve unit.
It happened after I saw the 1943 film "Gung Ho." It
was about the 2nd Marine Raider Battalion in World
War II.

The battalion was led by Lt. Col. Evans Carlson
(played by Randolph Scott). I'll never forget the
speech he gave to his men. It was about the concept
of "gung ho." Carlson saw the idea work when he
served in China during the 1930s. The Chinese
characters "gung" and "ho" mean *work together-work in
harmony*.[1]

---

[1] Carlson explained in a 1943 interview: "I was trying to
build up the same sort of working spirit I had in China
where all the soldiers dedicated themselves to one idea and
worked together to put that idea over. I told the boys about
it again and again. I told them of the motto of the Chinese
Cooperatives, Gung Ho. It means Work Together-Work in
Harmony." See the 1943 *Life Magazine* article at:
http://books.google.com/books
December 7, 2011; 0758 hrs.).

After graduation in 1956, I went on active duty for four years. I spent two years as a member of the Marine detachment aboard the aircraft carrier U.S.S. Boxer in the South Pacific during the hydrogen bomb tests. What I remember most about my sea duty was leading my first amphibious landing. Our sailors on the Boxer had been given liberty ashore on nearby Kwajalein Island. I was aboard the carrier as sergeant of the guard when I was called out to break-up a fight between our sailors and those from another ship from our battle group. I assembled my guard detachment, outfitted them with batons, and headed to shore in a landing craft.

Landing on the beach, we found most of the fighting over. The only police action was giving first aid to a few of the remaining combatants. It was this amphibious landing that gave me my first taste of police work.

I loved the Marines and wanted more responsibility. I wanted to be an officer, but to be an officer in the Marines, you needed to have a college degree. So I went back home and enrolled in the University of Minnesota.

By this time I was married with a child and needed a job. It was obvious to me that with my military background policing was the answer. What other skills could I possibly need?

That's how I became a cop. I went to school during the day and worked on the beat at night. Like many of my colleagues who joined the police, I had also stumbled into the job.

When I began as a patrol officer in Edina, Minn., a suburb of Minneapolis, I wasn't planning on

staying. I simply needed a job. But I soon got hooked. Policing was exciting. It was teamwork and it was making things right – doing justice. Just like in "Gung Ho;" *work together-work in harmony*. My studies in sociology and deviant behavior intermingled with what I was learning as a brand new cop.

After two years in Edina, I joined the Minneapolis department. I spent seven years there patrolling a beat, training recruit officers, and investigating crimes. I made arrests, got involved in high-speed chases, gave emergency aid at accidents, was shot at (never seriously injured) and helped people—yes, helped them. For the first time I realized that policing was all about protecting people and their rights.

In 1968, I applied for my first chief's job in Burnsville, Minn., another Minneapolis suburb, population 15,000. I had a master's degree in sociology, time in the ranks, and I was eager to be in charge. This time I would be working with a forward-thinking city manager that would let me try out some radical ideas I was developing about police.

First, they could be much better; second, police should always obey the law while enforcing it; third, police should treat everyone they encounter with dignity and respect; fourth, the ranks of police should be more diversified to reflect the communities they serve; fifth (in these times of civil protest), police should always first attempt to handle demonstrators in a soft, persuasive, and gentle manner; and sixth, police officers deserve to work for leaders who treat them as adults, with respect, and listen to them and their ideas.

I didn't encounter civil unrest and protest in Burnsville, but it didn't prevent me from thinking during this time about what I would do if I were a chief in such a situation.

Two opportunities were presented to me in the late 60s. First, would I be interested in leading the campus police at my alma mater, the University of Minnesota? Or, would I be interested in applying for the chief's position in Madison, Wisconsin – a city well acquainted with student protest?

The student-faculty selection committee at the University of Minnesota chose me to be their new chief. I had been selected out of a field of candidates that included a chief and captain from the Minneapolis Police Department. As it turned out, politics were at play and I never received the appointment.

This left me with the opportunity to apply at Madison. It would be in Madison that I would put my vision for policing into operation over the next 20 years. Changing police takes a long time. I grew to understand that more fully as the years went by.

The Madison police commission wanted peace brought back to their city and to improve police relations with citizens in the community and students on the campus of the University of Wisconsin. They wanted racial minorities and women hired, and improvements in police department operations. Madison was the city that had, since the late 1940s, consistently ranked one of the best cities in America, and the commission expected a police department that reflected that.

It wasn't easy coming to Madison as an outsider at the end of 1972. Soon after I took over command of the department, my assistant chief, Herman Thomas, who created dissention in the ranks, challenged my authority, and ran a covert intelligence operation, actively undermined me. I soon found I had a local version of J. Edgar Hoover to contend

with.

My vision for police is that they can be fair, effective and humanitarian. They can protect our civil rights, work with a variety of people, and take arrested persons into custody with a minimum amount of force. This may differ quite radically from what you may think police should do.

So, what kind of police officer am I talking about? This is what I told citizens who sat on our police selection boards when they asked me that question. Most people don't have a clue about police other than what they have seen on television and in the movies.

I asked them to imagine this scenario: it's after midnight. You are at home waiting for your teenage daughter to return from a date. It's now well past her curfew time. You are thinking about calling the police to report her missing when suddenly she bursts through the front door. She is crying and looks terrible. You notice her blouse has been torn and she has red marks on her face. Your worst fears now have been realized. She has been raped! Now think about the kind of police officer you would like to come into your home and talk with you and your daughter about what happened. That's also the kind of man or woman I would like on the police department.

Five years ago, when I started writing this book, there wasn't much progress going on in policing. It seemed that police were once again in a rut left by that fateful day on September 11, 2001. That day changed just about everything in policing. It changed our nation's police for the worst as they lost their essential role to protect their citizens and their rights. Rather, they became caught up in "homeland security," outfitted themselves in robot-like body

armor, and procured the latest chemical agents and military equipment.

These technological advancements were not only to have been used to control violent people who resist arrest but also those who were not. Often they are used to punish those who are merely voicing what they think was wrong about our government and its policies—a right guaranteed by our Constitution. What many of us see is a slow but steady shift of our nation's police toward militarization. In 2011, it was most evident in how many police departments responded to the Occupy Wall Street Movement.

Today, I can look back over a half-century of experience working closely with people. I see police continuing to struggle with four recurring and major obstacles that have literally "arrested" their development:

- Anti-intellectualism.
- Violence.
- Corruption.
- Discourtesy.

Quite frankly, if these obstacles aren't overcome, we are going to experience serious trouble controlling our police. In this book, I specifically identify what's wrong with police today. I also provide an overview of police history and my time in Madison. I believe police can change and I provide seven absolutely necessary steps that they need to take in order to improve. And then I'll tell you about one of the most critical things police do in a free society and how police can do it better – the handling of public protest.

Chapter 1
Stuck in the Rut Again

SOME THINGS PREVENT ordinary citizens from even thinking about their police unless they themselves or a loved one has an encounter with them. For most of us who attempt to abide by society's norms, these occurrences are few and far between. But every once in a while, we have an event or incident that causes us to ask, what in the world were the police thinking?

Back in the 60s, it was police dogs, water cannons, and lots of tear gas. More recently, we have seen a variety of police responses to the Occupy Movement in various American cities. Some police responses have been measured and restrained, while others have not.

Once in a while we find an iconic incident as that which happened in November, 2011: a police leader casually walking along a line of students sitting down and linking their arms on the sidewalk on the campus of the University of California at Davis and then spraying them in the face with pepper spray. What was he thinking? And, more importantly, how did he and his officers that day understand their job as police officers? Who was being protected and served and who wasn't? Other events have caught our eyes and ears -- widespread law- breaking by police officers involving ticket-fixing, theft, illegal drugs, and trafficking in stolen guns. In other instances, reporters in New York City have been prevented by police from covering public events and demonstrations and police have actively resisted open records laws requiring them to release information to the public. And a city newspaper in Milwaukee

revealed that a number of police officers continued to work and enforce laws in their city after they had committed crimes that would have resulted in others, who were not police officers, spending time in jail or, at least, being fired from their jobs. Upon my retirement from police, I had imagined our nation's police departments would continue to improve. I especially expected that my own department in Madison, with whom I had worked for over two decades, would continue the path I set of ongoing improvement and continue to serve as a model police department for others.

In fact, many of the innovative policies and practices I put in place—like decentralizing police services, including union representation on the department management team, hiring well-educated and experienced men and women, diversifying the department, and maintaining a sturdy commitment to developing leadership—did carry on.

But other critical practices and approaches didn't. The department didn't continue to randomly survey its customers (those who had used police services or been subject to an encounter with police, including people police had arrested and jailed). Nor did a commitment to systems improvement as taught by Dr. W. Edwards Deming, the renowned professor from the Massachusetts Institute of Technology, remain a part of daily police work; or having both leaders and employees give each other evaluative feedback, so that leaders as well as rank-and-file officers know how they are doing.

When I was chief of police, I made a commitment to share what I was doing in Madison with other police agencies around the country, even internationally. At the time, two professional organizations—the International Association of Chiefs of Police (IACP) and the Police Executive

Research Forum (PERF) in Washington, D.C.—
helped me by encouraging me to teach three-day
seminars on Quality Leadership and the Madison
Experience. During this time, in the mid-1980s, I
taught many emerging police leaders throughout the
country about what we in Madison were doing.
PERF also went on to publish two of my books, in
which I presented the characteristics of a good police
department for citizens and elected officials, and
shared what we were doing in Madison.[2]

At the same time, an associate, Herman Goldstein,
developer of the problem-oriented policing method,
remained a close colleague of mine during the years
he taught at the University of Wisconsin Law School
in Madison. In 1990, he wrote *Problem-Oriented
Policing*,[3] which offered one of the most significant
concepts in both American and international policing.
Madison, I'm proud to say, was the first department
in the country to implement his ideas. For over 20
years there has been an international conference
highlighting work police have done using this
method. And in 2003, a national center for problem-
oriented policing was established in Madison, and its
popular website receives over 10,000 inquiries every
month. In addition, the center has distributed over
900,000 guides and publications about the method.
The guidebooks they publish are peer-reviewed and
cover solutions to hundreds of police problems, from
handling aggressive panhandlers to preventing armed
robberies.

Despite this decades-long effort to train and
provide resources for police officers and their
agencies, the method has yet to be standardized

---

[2] *How to Rate Your Local Police* (1983) and *Quality Policing: The
Madison Experience*
(1991).
[3] Herman Goldstein. *Problem-Oriented Policing. Philadelphia:
Temple University Press. 1990.*

among American police. Links between practitioners and academics in the police field are few and far between. The police field has yet to identify a standard body of knowledge on which both practitioners and academics can build. This has been the primary motivator for me in writing this book. Unless police have these links and learn from and document their experiences, we won't see them rise above the level they are today. And that will be tragic for our nation.

Years ago as a young police officer, I remember finding myself being profoundly enmeshed in the life of being a cop. I soon realized that my identity, social life, and even family life revolved around me being a cop. I worked every day with police and socialized with them when I was off-duty. My preferred company was other police. I also realized I was closer to the man I was paired with at work—my partner—than I was to the woman to whom I was married. I shared more of my thoughts, feelings, hopes, and dreams with him than I did with her. Each day at work, I trusted my partner with my life. And then I realized that if he did something wrong, I would no more give him up than I would my own mother.

This is the power of a subculture. At the same time, I also felt that being a police officer was a very special, critical, and necessary function within our society. Yet, I had become a fully-fledged member of what sociologists call subculture; a distinct group of people who have patterns of behavior and beliefs that set them apart from society as a whole.

Subcultures can emerge because of the age, ethnicity, class, employment, geographical location, gender, or sexual orientation of their members.

Members may wear a particular style of clothing, display certain symbols, or use particular mannerisms,

language, or patterns of speech to signal their belonging to a subculture. Police work is a subculture.

I came to see that joining the police was more than a job. It's a life-changing event; an event that finds one initiated into a very distinct group in which certain expectations exist. For example, you have the right to use coercive and even deadly force in your work. You use certain distinct words to describe the work you do and different groups of people you encounter. Police officers have intimate knowledge about the behavior of others, and elements of both danger and secrecy exist in their work. All of this easily sets the police apart from normal society. And when you add to it irregular working hours, a lengthy selection and training process, taking of an oath of office, and wearing a badge, a uniform, and a gun, police are distinguished from most any other occupation in our society.

I came to realize the uniqueness of this subculture one night standing outside our patrol shift briefing room in downtown Minneapolis when one of the officers on my shift made a derogatory remark about my partner. It was 1965, and I had been on the Minneapolis department for three years. The speaker was one of those officers who would show up late on a call, after we had gotten things settled down, and then proceed to agitate the citizens with whom we were working. He was a troublemaker. Often, he would get a conflict going again and then have to make a physical arrest. In such situations, my partner and I could do little but help him out, even though we knew it was a bad arrest—not an illegal one, but a cheap one, because he had caused the problem. He was wrong, but we never criticized him in front of the public or to any of our supervisors.

One time this guy was verbally poking me outside of roll call and trying to agitate me like I was some

guy he ran into on the street. He was getting to me. I could sense my fellow officers looking to see what I was going to do. But I calmed down and slowly turned to him. "Look, asshole. See this badge on my chest? It's just like your badge. And if you keep provoking me, I'm not going to act like some poor mope on the street you can push around. I'm going to rip your badge off and shove it up your ass. Understand? And stop butting in on our calls."

It was quiet. Our sergeant came out, looked at the two of us and called us in to the briefing. Later, many of my colleagues thanked me for doing what they should have done. *Doing what they should have done*— one or more of us should have dealt with this bad apple much sooner.

Somebody should have told him to quit jumping calls and irritating people. But we didn't. We didn't because he was a fellow officer. So, for the first time, I began to see not only the positive camaraderie of policing, but also the dark side of it—what this subculture could do to any one of us, how it could change us, and keep us from doing the right thing.

Police work is seductive. Even outsiders fall prey to it. During the years of federal funding in the late 1960s, there appeared a lot of researchers and academics at the police station wanting to study us and what we did. Almost every outside academic or researcher who wanted to study us quickly became co-opted – became a supporter. On ride-alongs, such a person might say, "If I were you, I wouldn't have taken that from that guy—I'd have punched him in the face and arrested him!" This kind of seductiveness is especially dangerous in police work.

Egon Bittner, a prominent sociologist who had studied police for many years, observed that the core

of the police role is the non-negotiable use of force.[4] He was right. No one else besides police in our society has the authority to place their hands on us, restrain or arrest us, without our permission. That makes police unique in our society. There are few people who can legally touch us without our consent and force us to comply with their orders. Police can. They can stop us, ask us questions, put their hands on us, search us, arrest us and put us in jail. The force they use doesn't have to be physical (though the threat of physical force is always there); police can ask questions of us that no one else has the right to ask. And if we refuse to answer them we could be arrested, handcuffed, put in the back seat of a patrol car, and taken to jail, where we are strip-searched, photographed, fingerprinted, and placed in a cell until we can bail out. If we can't bail out because we don't have the money, we will stay in jail overnight until we appear before a judge in the morning.

This authority to use both physical and psychological force necessitates that police have adequate training and that the training continue throughout their career. Socializing police trainees into the work of policing is a lengthy process that begins even during the application process. And that socialization can work to ensure either good or bad policing.

Because the selection and training processes for police are so intense and, after graduation, the work schedule so unique (with shifts on nights, weekends, and often holidays), new police officers soon find they have few people to socialize with outside of their colleagues. This too makes the job of a police officer quite unique, along with the emotional and physical intensity of the work. Most officers even see their

---

[4] Egon Bittner. *The Functions of Police in Modern Society.* New York: Routledge. 1970.

relationships with old friends and acquaintances severed once they become police. Their friends and family begin to see them as different – even spouses.

For example, on weekend nights, when most people socialize, police are often working. And if police officers are invited to friends' social events, they may be confronted with violations of the law—which, before they were hired and trained as police, they had no responsibility to intervene in. They may be confronted with excessive alcohol consumption, underage drinkers present, or their friends' recreational use of marijuana or other illegal drugs.

Police recruits are told early on in the academy that they will most likely not be able to keep their old friends, and that their old friends will even steer clear of them, now that they are cops. Recruits are also reminded that department regulations require them to be on-duty 24 hours a day, to report any criminal activity they see, even when off-duty. Failure to do so could result in their termination.

This puts police officers in an uncomfortable position: they have to leave the party. And even if they do leave, once having known what went on there, they risk being reported for overlooking criminal activity. It soon becomes apparent to new officers that it is a lot easier and safer to socialize with fellow police than with their old friends and acquaintances. It just avoids potential conflicts. And, besides, their old friends really can't understand what being a cop is really like.

In a partnered assignment, such as in a two-officer patrol car, an officer begins to realize that he (or she) not only spends most of his waking life with his partner, but also depends upon that partner for his personal safety and even for his job retention in the case of junior officers on probation. When one

depends so much on another person for their economic and personal safety, it is easy to see why police misconduct is tolerated within the ranks. As long as a partner's behavior doesn't negatively impact another officer's safety, it is often tolerated and not reported.

While new police officers often think putting on a badge and carrying a firearm won't change them, their friends, or their lifestyles, they are sadly mistaken. New police officers quickly find out that, to a large degree, the only other people who can understand their lot in life are other police officers. Becoming a police officer is a robust, indelible socialization process.

But of course, what is taught in the police academy regarding proper norms for police behavior may not be what police recruits experience once they are assigned to the station house. The first major incidence of police corruption that caught my attention was in the very early months of my police career. It was early in 1960 and the Edina police had just hired me. I still vividly recall that situation to this day.[5]

It was disgraceful. It was reported in the national news that a burglary ring was discovered inside the Denver Police Department. Off- and on-duty officers operated it. When the investigation was finished, 35 officers were arrested. Over a seven-year period, these rogue cops had committed more than 100 thefts from citizens they swore to protect and serve. One of their crimes was (at the time) the largest burglary take in the city's history. They broke in and cracked the safe in a local supermarket and pocketed $40,000. When Denver citizens found out their police officers were the same people perpetrating this crime

---

[5] *Time Magazine*, October 13, 1961

wave, they were outraged and remained so for some time.

When the investigation by the police department finally got under way, investigators uncovered a well-organized and staffed burglary ring. The officers involved looked for burglary opportunities while on duty.

When they decided to break into a business, they posted lookout officers and carefully monitored the police radio for any indication that they had been spotted. Once their crimes were discovered and reported, many times the same officers returned to investigate it. If any evidence was inadvertently left behind, they simply destroyed it.

Over the years, these crooked cops experienced few failures in their well-planned crimes. That's hardly surprising: they had become the crime experts. They committed crimes based on what they knew. But one night, it all changed. They got caught. It wasn't a citizen, but a fellow officer.

Unfortunately for them, they ran into an honest cop. After spotting a business being burglarized, he spotted the perpetrators and gave chase.

During the chase, the safe they had stolen fell out of the trunk of the fleeing vehicle. The officer was eluded, and when he circled back he saw a man about to retrieve the safe. When the officer moved to arrest him, the man identified himself as a fellow Denver police officer. This was the time the subculture kicked in for this officer. What was he to do? He pondered the matter. But in the morning he reported what he had witnessed to his chief.

Upon listening to the officer, the chief (not believing him) sent him to see a psychiatrist instead

of launching an investigation. The chief wasn't suspicious of the facts reported to him, but of the officer's mental stability. The psychiatrist, however, reported back to the chief that he believed the officer. He wasn't lying nor was he mentally ill. It was then, and only then, that the Denver Police Department began an investigation.

The investigation, nevertheless, took almost a year. During that time, the department found that not only was corruption rampant, but it also had spread to other police departments in the area. After the Denver officers were arrested, an elected sheriff and five county deputies joined them in jail.

There was a tremendous public outcry. And after being severely criticized for his laxity, the chief resigned. The greatest loss, however, wasn't the events themselves as much as the loss of trust that the citizens of Denver had in their police.

For many years afterwards, every Denver police officer has had to live with this shameful blemish. When two officers answered a call at a construction site a few weeks after the arrests were made public, it was reported that workers on the site shouted, "Hey, guys, lock up your cars, cops in the neighborhood."

At the same time, a thousand miles away in Edina, I also heard these kinds of comments from some people I arrested—was I one of those cop burglars? At the time, I felt the shame those Denver officers caused all of us who wore a badge. Denver wasn't as far away as I thought—bad cops impact all cops.

Throughout my career I learned that without effective oversight, adequate salaries, and high public expectations, police will slide backwards—because left alone, isolated, underpaid, and with low public expectations, these police won't be the kind of people

we want to protect us and our way of life.

Thankfully, an honest man in Denver, who happened to be a police officer, had the integrity and courage to ignore the subculture he was part of, and blow the whistle on his corrupt colleagues. Yet we must realize that even in the case of a police burglary ring, it is difficult for any other officer to complain and break the code of silence that informally exists within most police departments.

For some months, before all this was uncovered, Denver officers, it was speculated, had talked about the rumors they heard, maybe even joked about them. But who took the next step and looked into whether or not they were true? If the police are to be kept free from corruption, honesty and integrity must be among their fiercest internal values. If integrity had been a prime value among Denver police at the time, then it wouldn't have been so difficult for a good cop to turn in a bad one. For police to be seen as above reproach in their conduct, they themselves must be willing to turn in a colleague who is dishonest. Unless honesty is a prime working value held by police, honest police departments cannot exist.

I don't remember having many ethical challenges when I first began policing at Edina. But one occasion comes to mind. It was one night, when a car roared by my marked squad car. It obviously was exceeding the speed limit. I was new on the job, only a few weeks, but I knew what to do. I pursued the vehicle, turned on my red lights and siren, and notified the dispatcher I was in pursuit. The driver would not stop. I called into the dispatcher again that I was in a chase and I requested backup.

After a mile or two, the car finally stopped. When I cautiously approached the vehicle, I heard

laughing and found the three occupants having a good chuckle. I was wondering where my backup was when I recognized the occupants – colleagues from the afternoon shift I had just relieved.

I don't remember having had to think about my response. Sure, I could ignore this and have a good laugh, be one of the boys—no harm, no foul, ha-ha. Or I could report their illegal behavior to the chief. Looking back, maybe I should have. I chose to do something else. I told them I was highly pissed-off and that what they had done was dangerous and not so funny. I let them know in no uncertain terms that if they *ever* did something like that to me again, I would arrest them.

I don't know what they were expecting from me. Maybe it was a test. If it was, I didn't pass. Or did I? Afterward, we never talked about the incident again, and we continued to have a good working relationship. What those officers did was both illegal and improper. I decided to use my discretion. I gave them a warning. If I had gone along with their antics, they would have continued to play their little jokes on me and perhaps other officers. If I had turned them into the chief, I would have been ostracized as a guy who couldn't take a joke and would have lost their support at work—and maybe even their backup protection if I needed help. It was a difficult decision. I think I made the right one. They didn't screw around with me again.

When I was an officer in Minneapolis, it was a little different. If we encountered off-duty officers who were drunk, we parked their cars and took them home. The stakes were much higher in a big-city department. Police work was far more dangerous there. I do, however, distinctly remember one incursion into the blue subculture. While working on the tactical squad (dubbed "Flying Squad"), my

partner and I took down an after-hours tippling house—an unlicensed establishment that illegally served alcohol after hours. When I entered and asked for the person in charge, a man came forward, looked at me, and asked who I was and what unit I came from. Then he said something strange: "Does Captain Heilen know you are doing this?"

Now, I knew this captain wasn't in charge of this precinct. He worked downtown. I told the owner that, no, the captain didn't know about this, and that if he did, so what? Then he told me I had should call the captain. I ignored his request.

As we were processing the arrests, I noticed Captain Heilen driving up to the establishment we had taken down. Instead of arriving in a department vehicle, he was in his personal car. It was after 3 a.m. and well outside of his normal work hours. He called me over and said, "Do you know what you are doing?" I said yes, I did, and told him what we had found and that I was surprised to see him out so early in the morning. He paused, stared, and then, without a word, drove away.

My colleagues looked at me, wondering what was going to happen. Nothing ever did. No one at headquarters or my supervisor ever discussed the arrests with me. Even today, I have a deep-seated feeling that those of us on the tactical squad that early morning so long ago made the blue subculture a little less threatening.

That's because we were the new breed, the different ones, college cops. That night those of us on that new tactical squad defined ourselves as to who we were. I'd like to think that night made a difference in Minneapolis. I always wondered how much of a payoff the captain got for what appeared to be a police protection racket. I hope the proprietor

thought he was a bad investment and quit paying him.

Minneapolis was different for me. In Minneapolis, I had to work with drunks and sadists on my shift. I also had colleagues who took things that weren't theirs to take. They used their badges to get free meals from restaurants, free drinks, and free admission to movies. Some of them were even so bold as to bring their families into a restaurant when they were off- duty and expect the owner to pick up the tab. And the waitresses never saw a tip on the table.

Interestingly, they were also the guys who were pretty fast with their fists, not the tough guys you'd like to see show up on a tense call. No, they were the guys who were quick to punch a mouthy drunk, or a bad guy in handcuffs. I came to see that they were actually cowards. They needed to be watched because they would start trouble on the street, particularly with people of color—like that colleague of mine I had to confront outside of roll call.

When I started studying the sociology of police at the University of Minnesota, I came to understand the subtle nature of corruption and the police culture. I read studies about "honest cops" who were on the take.

Usually, the unit or precinct in which they worked had been historically crooked, and the officers who had to work there found that to be accepted, they were expected to receive their part of the take. Within the culture of corruption, taking money means that the person receiving it is just as guilty as the others. Some cops took the money, but gave their share to their church or a charity as a way to stay clean and still be accepted by their peers. While this might have been good for their

consciences, they were still crooked cops.

What I have just stated may be quite foreign to people who don't carefully read daily news or scan the Internet. If you do, however, you will see a steady stream of reports throughout the country regarding police corruption, abuse of force, and other illegal behavior. In each of these instances, plaintiffs receive large cash settlements and some police officers go to jail. Corruption isn't something that happened in the 1930s—it goes on today in many of our nation's cities and police departments. But, remember, when police officers have to depend on their fellow officers to help them when they are in danger, taking their share of the take, going along with petty thievery, and overlooking a few protection schemes often becomes an acceptable trade-off for one's personal safety.

In Minneapolis, coffee was always free to police—my colleagues told me the owners of these businesses wanted police to stop by and be seen; it was cheap protection. But when I was on the street and a restaurant owner picked up my tab, my policy was to leave a tip for the server equal to the cost of the meal rather than cause a scene. I did tell them that if they wanted me to return, they needed to let me pay for my meal.

The question I had about these freebies was perhaps quite different from that of my colleagues. It was: what does it do to the police to be put in such a situation? To be considered such a low-caste member of the community that they are thought to be too poor to pay for their own food— or, worse yet, considered moochers?

Occasionally in Minneapolis, I showed up at burglaries, and the owner of the victimized business or home hadn't yet arrived, I noticed some cops taking things. If it was my call, I put a stop to it

because I had to write the report – I was in charge here until detectives arrived. But if it wasn't my call, I simply turned away and left. Unfortunately, some business owners, when they did arrive at the scene of a break-in, encouraged police to take things. "Take something," they'd say, "I'll just claim it on my insurance." Partners in crime. When I refused to stop by liquor stores on my beat and pick up my Christmas present (one or more bottles of liquor), my colleagues griped that I was ruining it for them.

One of the more difficult areas of improving police is dealing with corruption when it is imbedded in the police subculture. I use the term corruption broadly to include acts such as: stealing things, receiving regular payoffs—enforcing or not enforcing the law, accepting gifts and favors not afforded the general public, disregarding departmental rules and orders, lying, issuing false reports, giving false testimony or committing other acts a person knows are dishonest or morally wrong. Corruption exists when police break the law, whether in pursuit of enforcing it or to enhance their own lives by accepting special favors like free food, liquor, or other things of value.

On the other hand, proper professional police work involves scrupulous adherence to the law while enforcing it. It is being honest to a fault. Because of the disparity in power between police and citizens, the lack of transparency in most police organizations, and few public mechanisms to effectively regulate or control police behavior, the problem still exists as to how to effectively reduce and eliminate police corruption.

I have mentioned some ways an individual officer—myself—dealt with corrupt practices he encountered. Ultimately, though, the goal shouldn't be to learn how an officer might effectively deal with

a corrupt police culture, but rather to figure out how that culture can be eliminated through the introduction of new professional ethical expectations in the police department.

This, of course, goes back to the way these ethical practices are taught to entry-level police and reinforced within the station house. But the primary failure of most efforts to reduce or eliminate corruption and other misconduct in a police department is that they usually fail to acknowledge the power of the police subculture I have described. When dishonesty is a matter of common practice, and when it significantly supplements the income and lifestyle of those who practice it, it is very difficult to eliminate.

However, an article in the July, 2009 issue of the *Harvard Business Review* gives me encouragement that honest organizations can be developed.[6] The authors, James O'Toole and Warren Bennis, addressed the problem of trust in our nation's corporations— specifically, our financial institutions. (The situation that inspired it was, of course, the meltdown of our nation's financial system in 2008, which plunged us into the most significant period of economic downturn since the Great Depression of the 1930s.)

The authors noted that our culture has tended to evaluate executive performance based on one criterion: the extent to which an executive created wealth for their investors. But today, they said, all that is changing. Thanks to the new forces of globalization, executive performance should now be evaluated by the extent to which they create organizations that are economically, ethically, and socially sustainable.

[6] James O'Toole and Warren Bennis. "What's Needed Next: A Culture of Candor." *Harvard Business Review,* July 2009.

This is a radical change, and a new definition, brought about by a very new way of looking at leadership in our society. According to O'Toole and Bennis, the way out of the mind-set that drove us into economic crisis is the way of organizational transparency—as they call it, a culture of candor:

No organization can be honest with the public if it is not honest with itself…leaders need to make a conscious decision to support transparency and create a culture of candor… Organizations that fail to achieve transparency will have it forced upon them. There's no way to keep a lot of secrets in the age of the Internet.7

So how can this apply to the police? Well, like Wall Street, police organizations are bastions of secrecy and opaqueness. Some secrecy, of course, is necessary for police, such as in the ongoing investigation of a crime. But for much of what police do, it isn't. Police would benefit ethically by opening their practices up to public view.

And if we are serious about transparency and a developing a culture of candor within the police, it has to begin from the top. Police leaders must start telling the truth and being truthful. They must desist from keeping organizational secrets long after they could be shared with the community.

This especially includes secrets about mistakes. Leaders who can admit mistakes will tend to encourage others in their organization to own up to their own mistakes. The objective here isn't some kind of organizational or personal catharsis, but rather that mistakes be acknowledged and identified with the purpose of improving the process or system that caused them, admitting mistakes so that they aren't made again.

It's not that bad people try to get into police departments or financial organizations, and then do bad things. In fact, the opposite is true: good people with good intentions are hired to work in organizations that unfortunately have poor systems in operation, or organizations in which the existing culture is harmful.

And it is simply not enough to talk to new police officers about values, ethics, and guidelines or have them swear to and sign the *Law Enforcement Code of Ethics*.[7] It is more, much more. Those are significant, but courses or discussions about ethical problems can't eliminate deep-rooted issues and corrupt organizational practices. Instead, more must be done to create police organizations that encourage good people to continue to be good. And it starts when police seriously begin to police themselves.

While there may not exist an empirical police personality, there are a number of qualitative studies existing which further describe the socialization process new police officers undergo which contribute to the development of a specific police subculture.[8] This socialization encourages a worldview that can override an individual's upbringing, prior experience in life, and education. In many instances, police attitudes are very similar to those of white, blue-collar workers: experience, not education, is the finest teacher, racial and ethnic minorities are to be avoided, and the highest personal achievement is to be *respected* by those with whom you work.

But police officers additionally see themselves as being up against a world that is hostile, and this affects how they behave toward others in that world. Understandably, along with being respected, bravery

[7] *Ibid.*
[8] International Association of Chiefs of Police, 1957.

and courage are critical personal attributes to them as well. If an officer isn't considered brave and courageous, how can other police depend on him or her?

Combine this aggregate of personal attributes of police with the danger and secrecy of their work, their isolation, scarcity of their numbers, and the carrying of a firearm during and after working hours, and it is easy to see why police perceive themselves as the thin blue line.

Christopher Cooper, an African-American, and former Washington, D.C. police officer, offers some glaring examples of the police subculture in operation. The article from which the following editorial appeared in *The Philadelphia Inquirer* in 2000 appears below. His remarks pertain to the arrest by Philadelphia police of a citizen named Thomas Jones.[9] The arrest was documented on video by a number of other citizens and posted on the Internet.[10]

Regardless of the severity of Jones' alleged actions, his having been set upon by a mob composed of law enforcement

---

[9] One of the first to write about the working personality of police was Jerome Skolnick, "A Sketch of a Policeman's Working Personality." A copy of this manuscript can be found at:
http://cw.marianuniversity.edu/tpluzinski/SelectedR/Police%20Personality.pdf January 1, 2011, 1138 hrs. See also Jonathan Rubinstein's chapter, "Cops Rules" in *City Police*. New York: Farrar, Strauss, Giroux, 1973. I would also suggest the reader be aware of the classic work by John Van Mannen on "The Asshole" in *Policing: A View from the Street*. Peter Manning and John Van Maanen, eds. New York: Random House. 1978.
[10] You can see the two-minute video at:
http://www.break.com/usercontent/2008/5/Police-Beating-Caught-By-News-Helicopter-505411. December 28, 2010; 1212 hrs.

agents indicates cowardice and a lack of professionalism by the officers involved...

Sadly, in our early tenure as cops, we are instructed on the "code" of the police subculture. These are norms that are almost always perverse... The first is that if a citizen runs from one of us, we are to beat him severely... And if that citizen has killed a cop, he shouldn't make it to the station alive...

Some police officers, fortunately, decide to resist such norms...

A different perspective is held by people and academicians of color, as well as some whites. We recognize that American policing suffers from a perverse subculture, and that all too often, individual officers lack the courage to stand up to that code. The result is a too-frequent lack of integrity and respect for human life, a lack of respect that all too often exacerbates the racial tensions that still exist in our society.

John Van Maanen is a sociologist who has written extensively on the police subculture. He incisively describes the view many police officers have of those they call "assholes" and the importance of getting them off the street. Who or what in police jargon is an asshole? Generally speaking, this term isn't just for a regular crook, but a person who pushes other people around and who doesn't submit to the police definition of the situation—that is, what's *really* going on.

In my experience, the term has meant someone who is both a troublemaker and challenges police authority. To Van Maanen, however, the label, as used by police, is a distinct and formal label; a tri-party typology consisting of 1) suspicious persons, 2) know-nothings, and 3) assholes. That is, a person may be one of three types in an encounter with police: a suspicious person, a person who knows

nothing about police work or what's going on, or, worst of all, someone who refuses to submit to police authority; a person who disrespects police and/or pushes other people around. How does this happen? Van Maanen writes:

> *By virtue of [police] independence from superiors, their carefully guarded autonomy in the field, their deeply felt notions about real police work and those who would interfere with it, and their increasing isolation from the public they serve... police view their critics as threatening and as persons who generally should be taught or castigated, [in such a situation] one could argue that the explosive potential of citizen-police encounters will grow.*[11]

Attitudes like these on the part of police can lead to or cover up the continual problem police have—corruption. Wrongdoing by police, therefore, is both aided and abetted by a distinct, separate, and impenetrable police subculture -- one that does not hold honesty and impeccable professional behavior as working values and, instead, sees critics as threatening and needing to be taught a lesson.[12]

One particular experiment I encountered during my studies at the University of Minnesota impacted

---

[11] John Van Maanen. "The Asshole." Policing: A View from the Street. Peter K. Manning and John Van Maanen, eds. New York: Random House. 1978.

[12] For a deeper exploration into police subculture see: Elizabeth Reuss-Ianni and Francis A.J. Ianni. "Street Cops and Management Cops: The Two Cultures of Policing." *Control in the Police Organization*, Maurice Punch, ed. Cambridge, MA: MIT Press. 1983, Peter K.Manning. *Police Work: The Social Organization of Policing*. Cambridge, MA: MIT Press. 1977, Maurice Punch. *Policing the Inner City*. London: McMillan. 1979, and John Van Maanen. "Working the Street: A Development View of Police Behavior." *The Potential for Reform in Criminal Justice*. Herbert Jacob, ed. Beverley Hills, CA: Sage Press. 1974.

me about the power of subculture. It was called the Stanford Prison Experiment.[13] In 1971, social psychologist Philip Zimbardo conducted an experiment having to do with power and authority. Every police officer should be well aware of it because it applies so much to police work.

As part of the experiment, Zimbardo and his staff put together a prison-like structure in the basement of a Stanford University building. Then they randomly selected college students who were paid to play the role of either a guard or a prisoner.

Within a few days, the scheduled two-week experiment had to be called off because the randomly selected student-guards had begun to mentally, and even physically, abuse fellow students who had been randomly chosen to serve as the inmates.

Zimbardo concluded that most all of us are susceptible to acting in such a way, because our behavior is determined more by the situation in which we find ourselves—its various group dynamics, organizational cultures, and our own need to be accepted—than by our inherent nature or professed values.

This finding makes sense and can easily be applied to Nazi concentration camps, My Lai, Rwanda, Abu Ghraib, and Darfur. It is far too easy to create systems and situations in which good people simply acquiesce and find themselves unable to resist what they know is wrong or unable to do what they know is right because of the perceived power of the group or the need to be accepted.

I had a similar experience early in my Marine

---

[13] A complete discussion of the experiment can be found at http://www.prisonexp.org.

career when I was assigned as a brig guard on the U.S.S. Boxer. I was 19 at the time. I soon experienced the same pressures that Zimbardo mentioned. I found myself being hardened toward the prisoners and a willing participant in maintaining the harsh and inmate-harassing climate of a ship's brig. I was becoming a person I didn't want to be. Luckily, an opportunity arose for me work as an orderly to the ship's captain. I was glad I got out of there when I did.

What is needed is to develop policing systems that are essentially ethical in nature—systems that will lead to virtuous and transparent conduct, and reinforce the good most people try to accomplish in their lives; the culture of candor noted earlier.

While it may be difficult to imagine a secretive, hierarchical organization like a police department being transparent and speaking openly with its community, it isn't an impossibility. But to make it happen, police leaders, especially a department's chief, must cultivate a culture in which it is permissible to speak truth to power, and an organizational culture that supports honest behaviors that are consistent with the *Law Enforcement Code of Ethics*.

While codes of ethics are nice to post on the walls of a police station, it is far more crucial for them to be practiced on the street. For it is only within this kind of transparent and democratic organization that police will be able to reach their highest level of performance. It is only within this kind of organization that police will find the freedom to innovate, effectively solve problems, meet tomorrow's challenges, and enjoy the respect and trust of the communities they serve.

If a police department publicly articulates,

supports, and practices such aims, willful misconduct will become few and far between. But if the department does not—its culture continues to be closed and secretive, and cannot learn to police itself—its community will one day suffer the negative effects, if it hasn't already.

Misconduct, of course, can occur both inside and outside the police department. It isn't just that some bad police officers in the organization may have problems or difficulty carrying out their duties, but that how they conduct their work may be predicated on how they feel about a certain person or group of people.

When citizens feel they have been subjected to improper behavior by the police, it takes a lot of courage and effort to do something about it. More often than not, police departments close ranks against complainants. The presumption such a department holds is that it couldn't have done anything wrong, and so there must be something wrong with the complainant. Just like when the Denver chief sent the officer who complained about the burglary ring within his department to a psychiatrist.

In responding to complaining citizens, police often check whether or not the complainant has a police record. Meaning, essentially, that the person then can be labeled unreliable. Further questioning is along the line of whether or not the person is trying to get out of an arrest charge or is one of those cop haters. As a result, the first part of an investigation into a complaint against police is often an examination of the complainant's possible motives.

Citizens quickly pick up on this and then come to the conclusion that they are no longer so much a victim of police misconduct as someone who has offended the police. It takes a very professional

internal affairs investigator not to act in such a way
that a complainant feels like they have done
something wrong.

It is true that some people bring false charges
against police, and that some people try to fabricate
cases against police in order to receive monetary
settlements or to get charges against them reduced.
Regardless, it is extremely important that police
departments always operate from the assumption that
a complaint is worthy of a prompt and thorough
investigation.

Unfortunately, the traditional police subculture
has its ways of deciding which police behaviors are
serious cause for concern and not the police
administration. For example, the police officer who
shoplifts $100 in merchandise from a clothing store
while off-duty is often perceived differently from an
officer who, while on-duty, accepts $100 in cash or
goods from a merchant for not enforcing the parking
regulations in front of his business. The former
usually will find little support among fellow officers;
while the latter, because the offense occurred while
he was on- duty, may in fact be supported by
colleagues who are also engaged in similar
misconduct.

Another example is that officers who assault
their spouses or children in a domestic quarrel that
occurs off-duty won't get as much support from
peers as officers who use excessive force during the
arrest of a known troublemaker. The former is
understandable, but the latter is excusable, if not
expected.

Whether fellow officers will come to the
defense of colleagues accused of misconduct is often
determined by the unwritten but widely- known
behavioral norms of the police organization. If rank-

and-file officers view a merchant's cash payment of $100 to an officer for ignoring parking violators in front of his business as inappropriate and wrong, the practice of accepting such payments most likely will be rare or nonexistent.

The same goes with regard to using extra force when a person resists an arrest, runs from police, or fights with them. Many departments have problems with officers using excessive force in these situations to punish offenders. When this is a department-wide problem and not just one particular officer's, it will usually be found that it is an accepted practice among the rank and file, and that officers *expect* their colleagues to use extra force in such situations.[14] Of course, many departments look the other way when bad behavior happens, simply calling it understandable in a particular situation. But with the advent of new technology, complaints are no longer simply the assertions of bad guys who ran from police. Now, thanks to not only department-mounted video cameras on squad cars but also the video-recording capability citizen bystanders have on their cell phones, it is easy to make records of such events.[15]

---

[14] For a good illustration, go to YouTube on the internet and search "police brutality." Within seconds, you'll see a huge number of videos showing officers after a high-speed chase running up to the vehicle they've pursued and pummeling the driver. This wasn't what they were taught to do and no doubt department rules prohibit such behavior—yet it happens because it's simply what many police, as a subculture, do when a chase ends (or even when a person verbally abuses police). In all but the finest police departments there will be some kind of summary beating for those who disregard police authority – that is, "assholes."

[15] As a response, many police departments have put video cameras in their patrol cars that record not only outside activity but also behavior that occurs within the police vehicle.

In cases in which an officer exhibited bad behavior while following the unwritten norms of doing real police work, a department often closes ranks to protect the officers. We may even hear the chief saying something like, "We have a tough job to do out there. That guy chose to run away and resist arrest from my officers, and he simply got what was coming. If you don't understand this, I'm sorry, but *you* try and go out on patrol at night and deal with the people we do."

And if it was just one or two officers making an arrest, perhaps their use of extra force won't be an issue. But if there were a number of officers at the scene, all doing the beating—and especially if the person being beaten belongs to a racial minority group—the incident could go public and create widespread disorder in the community.

This happened in 1991 after a videotape of the beating of Rodney King by Los Angeles police was publicly released and, as I mentioned earlier, after the public beating of Thomas Jones by police in Philadelphia. Often these situations lead to a public inquiry and law suits that result in million-dollar settlements.[16] Afterward, police and city leaders may be required to sign consent decrees promising they'll make changes in their police departments. Over the years, cities throughout the nation have been forced by a court of law to make specific improvements to

---

[16] Nearly $1 billion has been paid over the past decade to resolve claims against the New York City Police Department according to an investigation by the Associated Press. The total spending outstrips that of other U.S. cities, though some smaller cities and departments also shell out tens of millions of dollars a year in payouts. http://www.huffingtonpost.com/2010/10/14/ap-investigation-nearly-1_n_763008.html, December 30, 2010; 1008 hrs

their police departments. In almost every instance, these court-ordered efforts to try to change police behavior on the street have been ineffective.

The way to improve police behavior is for leaders to always practice the behavior expected of officers. Eliminating existing inappropriate and illegal practices on the street will require that all supervisors and officers be informed that such practices are no longer condoned or protected. Once the rank and file understands their supervisors won't overlook these kinds of behaviors, there will be fewer cases of misconduct than when these behaviors are protected or overlooked by senior officers.

But getting to that point can be arduous and will take solid commitment and personal modeling on the part of police leaders. What must be crystal-clear is that command and supervisory officers support ethical behavior at all times. They all must know that the department has specific rules and that those who don't follow them will be disciplined.

Never must mean never, and a gratuity must be understood to be anything of value—even a cup of coffee—not afforded the general public. When officers see themselves as moral agents, formally educated, uniquely trained, prepared to withstand the temptations that will be presented to them, and are adequately compensated for their work misconduct will no longer be the problem it is today, but rather an occasional stumble on the part of an individual officer. Officers will make mistakes. When they do, police leaders need to be able to assure them they will be dealt with fairly.

For too long, both police departments and their communities have looked the other way when confronted with so-called petty police misconduct: free coffee and meals, special discounts, and favors.

Misconduct and endemic corruption are close bedfellows. One precedes the other, and the difference between them is a matter of degree. If a little bit is tolerated by department leadership or by the community, it soon will grow into a larger problem. Those we select to be our police cannot bend the truth just a little, throw one extra punch at a suspect, or only take small things. Preventing these things from occurring in the first place is much, much easier than weeding out such practices in an historically corrupt police department.

Shortly after I left the Minneapolis Police Department and went to Burnsville, I raised some concerns in the city's newspapers about how the police were using force to suppress dissent on the University of Minnesota campus. A few weeks later, a spaghetti dinner benefit was held for Walt Dziedzic, an officer I had served with who was running for the Minneapolis City Council. It was one of those legendary police get- togethers—lots of storytelling and beer drinking. I was reminiscing with some of my old buddies on the tactical squad when the discussion got around to some of the things I had recently written and the changes I was making in Burnsville.

One officer, after listening to our conversation, turned to me and said with a puzzled look on his face, "Couper, I thought youse was one of us—a 'stone copper.'"

At first I didn't understand what he was saying. What on earth was a stone copper? My friend Dave Gorski, with whom I had worked on the tactical squad and who now was with me in Burnsville, explained, "You were known as a tough street cop— a 'stone copper.' And now he doesn't understand how you could have changed, how you turned your back on them." Now I understood. "I used to kick

ass and now I don't," I said with a smile, "What's the matter with me?" Later, I was to hear the term *dinosaurs* when police officers were describing other officers who were having trouble with, or refusing to, change.

If police are going to evolve and grow—that is, improve—they will have to replace the public's image of them as stone coppers. This isn't an impossible task; other occupational fields have, over the course of the years, continually improved not only their public images but also their capabilities. For instance, ambulance drivers are now well-trained, tested, and licensed emergency medical technicians. In the past, almost anyone could practice medicine, with barbers performing minor surgical procedures, until professionally minded physicians called for education, training and the licensing of those who wish to practice their art.

Don't get me wrong—things have progressed in the police field since I entered it in the 1960s. In those days, I went to injury accidents, applied first aid, and then rushed the victim to the hospital in my police car with little or no training. Today, this would be ground for legal action.

The year I joined the police, a street officer was quoted in *The New York Times* complaining about the passing of the good old days; the time when police handled most things with a nightstick and administered curbstone justice. He complained:

The only time [a police officer] took anything to court was when he couldn't handle it with his nightstick. But today the commissioner says it's not the job of a policeman to adjudicate anything. All we are here for is to make an arrest and take the case to court. The more arrests we make, the better he thinks we are doing our job. In the old days, if some bum came in here and told me that he was robbed of a

thousand dollars, I'd toss him out on his ear. Not today.
Today if he comes in and tells me someone stole his purple
Pekinese, I got to make out a complaint and go looking for
it.[17]

In the 1950s through the 70s, few governmental leaders made the case that control of police could be accomplished internally by developing, training, reinforcing a set of professional ethics, and hiring more capable police officers, and that this ethic could be continuously reinforced by supervisors and managers committed to coaching, developing, and leading their officers. Instead, most police leaders created more ways to impose control over their officers, such as centralization and patrol cars with radios. This is consistent with the way we have tended to do things in America—bosses exist to control their workers.

Much of this thinking comes from Frederick Winslow Taylor at the dawn of the Industrial Age in the early 20th century. Taylor was a mechanical engineer who sought to improve the efficiency of work, primarily in the industrial setting, through what he called scientific management. Even though his ideas seem crude today, he was one of the first to examine work as a phenomenon worthy of systematic observation and study, and his studies influenced our nation's thinking about work.

Taylor's philosophy of scientific management is driven by four major principles: 1) Work can be scientifically studied and methods of work developed, 2) it is wiser to select and train employees rather than leave them to train themselves, 3) workers should be given detailed instruction on how to perform their assigned work, and 4) work should be divided between managers and workers – managers plan the

---

[17] *New York Times.* December 5, 1960.

work and workers do it.[18]

Even in today's light, Taylor's concepts seem reasonable in that workers should be both trained and their work planned and directed. However, in its application, Taylor's work translated primarily into *control* and did not anticipate the emergence today of an educated workforce. Educated and trained workers today can play a critical role in improving the quality of their work. Taylor's ideas about work still dominate the thinking of many leaders in industry, business, the military, and, yes, the police. We can still see Taylor's ideas at work in police departments when we hear that it is management's job to supervise and direct officers because they are incapable of understanding the nature of their work.

Taylor wrote:

I can say without the slightest hesitation that the science of handling pig-iron is so great that the man who is…physically able to handle pig-iron and is sufficiently phlegmatic and stupid to choose this for his occupation— is rarely able to comprehend the science of handling pig- iron.[19]

Now, although these comments sound extreme, there initially was some reason for Taylor to develop the ideas he did. At the turn of the 20th century, many workers were illiterate—unable to read or write or even speak English. Consequently, they needed close supervision and direction. Leaders were smart, workers were not. But we can no longer say this about today's highly skilled and educated workforce, and we most certainly cannot say it with regard to today's police.

---

[18] Frederick Winslow Taylor. *The Principles of Scientific Management.* New York: Harper & Brothers. 1911.
[19] *Ibid.* p. 59.

Even in Taylor's day, workers and their unions viewed scientific management with suspicion. While Taylor truly believed that the worker was worthy of his hire and that a worker's pay should be linked to his productivity, he never thought they had anything to offer with regard to improving things or the systems in which they work.

We can see Taylor's influence in response to police corruption during the time of Prohibition. Police reformers began to centralize operations, removed officers from foot beats, put them into radio- controlled patrol vehicles, and instituted military-style rank and command systems. We see vestiges of Taylor's influence when some police departments have their rank-and-file officers wear blue shirts and their supervisors wear white, or when police departments require officers to punch a time clock before work, or adopt other workplace practices that more resemble those of a factory. If police supervisors wear white shirts, it is implied that they are not expected to get them dirty doing the work of policing. And if police officers punch time clocks when they show up for work it will be very difficult to get them to think of themselves as professionals.

Controlling police officers by such external measures—namely, unnecessary rules and regulations, and class distinctions, continues to be the way many police chiefs respond to two of the major behavioral problems that have always challenged police: corruption and inefficiency.

No matter how effective police may appear to their citizens, if they are on the take, they aren't good. No matter how busy police may appear, if they are not concerned about continuously improving the services they deliver, they are not as effective as they

could be. This is something citizens should be aware of.

Historically, rather than improve the quality of officers in the ranks, reformers have often tried to implement more rules and regulations, more supervisory control, and the demeaning of officers on the street for their inability to control crime. But all that external control eventually backfires on police administrators and supervisors. How rank-and-file officers are treated by their leaders impacts those whom police encounter on the street. It is simply a fact of human nature.

So, how do the police move from being that kind of cop who used his nightstick as a primary tool and meted out curbstone justice? How do we move into today's world which demands well-educated and trained police officers who are, in fact, professionals; who are committed to the rule of law and preserving and maintaining the values articulated in our nation's Constitution and especially the Bill of Rights?

In most professional organizations, training and education is central to who they are. This is accomplished by closely working with academic institutions and training academies, and maintaining high standards for recognition and accreditation in a particular field. A profession's key values are also usually highly publicized and known by those whom they serve; e.g. a physician's commitment to do no harm.[20] This can be accomplished through something as simple as a short statement about the way the work should be practiced, how people ought to be treated, and how new ideas and challenges should be approached and responded to.

---

[20] The physician's Hippocratic Oath, while it does not assure correct ethical behavior or competency on the part of the practitioner, it does set forward a basic moral construct for the practice of medicine

When I first joined the police, the talk in the field was about bringing professionalism into law enforcement. At that time, a professional was an educated person who practiced from an empirically based body of knowledge, and was licensed by a state board to practice. A professional could also be disciplined by that board for acts of malpractice or violating the public's trust. Other occupations, like medicine and law—occupations that *served* people—historically fell into this category. Police didn't seem to fit in.

Professionals perform necessary social functions in our society, they help people. Police, on the other hand, were seen more as controlling people and not necessarily helping them. Worse yet, they hurt them— using threats, fines, physical force, and arrest to carry out their work.

In the wake of Lyndon Johnson's presidential commission, federal money in the 1970s and 80s enabled the development of thousands of police academic programs in our nation's colleges and universities that assisted in the education of tens of thousands of police officers. While we have seen a rise in the educational level of our American police officers during the past 40 years, there is a troubling side to it as well.

With the availability of college tuition assistance, many police officers demanded special courses. They were not interested in a general liberal arts education, but rather in hands-on police science courses. Only a few were interested in literature, languages, or social sciences. And even fewer law enforcement officers stood up and stressed the significant role a general liberal arts education could have in preparing men and women to function as police officers in a complex and diverse society such

as ours. (Perhaps this was because many police leaders themselves didn't have a college education or an appreciation of higher education, and as such couldn't speak to its importance.) To me, it was another aspect of the blue subculture to keep itself isolated and not having to confront the impact of education that, at the university level, was liberal in scope and nature.

While many universities and colleges established a four-year degree program in criminal justice, such as the University of Minnesota did, it wasn't the case nationally, as the two-year college system agreed to develop special curricula for police officers and granted college credits for police experience and training academy courses. Many of these courses had the intellectual rigor of a commercial trade school and were designed and taught by active-duty police officers rather than college professors.

That isn't to say some of these classes were not essential for police to attend, just that they would have been more appropriately taught in the police academy, rather than a college classroom.

One of the fallouts of this emphasis on police science was the demand from police to drop the requirement of a foreign language, otherwise a key component in most liberal arts curricula. Police argued that they didn't want a language requirement, and that there was no reason to mandate one. Looking back, though, what could be more critical in our nation's cities now than having multilingual police officers on patrol?

Thankfully, some urban departments, like New York with 138 languages spoken in the borough of Queens alone, are willing to pay a premium for bilingual officers.

So while it is true that many police officers attended local colleges and universities over the past 40 years, relatively few received a rigorous education. To make a long story short, the tail wagged the dog, as many of our academic institutions capitulated to the lure of federal dollars and complaints from police officers, and offered the classes police demanded. What was often missing, however, was an education.

I'm not saying that police have not improved over the years, but rather their improvement has been slow, too slow, in a fast-changing, 21st century environment. As an example I would like to offer the following comparison: football and policing.

From time to time in the past I have used a sports illustration to make my point about the need for continuous improvement. I use professional football as an example because a good part of my early life prior to becoming a police officer was spent playing football and the game has mushroomed in popularity in the United States. I played football throughout high school, college, and in the Marines. I also played a season of semi-professional football in California.

If we compare the top football team in 1960, the Philadelphia Eagles, who beat my home-state Green Bay Packers 17–13 that year in the National Football League (NFL) championship game, with the top team in 2011, the Green Bay Packers, we can see some major performance differences in both size, speed, and technique between these two teams a half-century apart.

If we could somehow resurrect the 1960 Philadelphia Eagles and put them on the same field with today's Packer team, who do you think would win and by how large a score? If you were to make a wager, which team would you put your money on? I

don't think many of us would choose to bet against the Packers. In just about every statistical area, the Packers substantially outperform the Eagles. I would maintain that all of today's NFL teams are bigger, stronger, and faster, not just the Packers.

They pass and kick farther and more accurately. They have more training, better play strategies, and more financial resources than their predecessors in 1960. Therefore, one can safely say that the game of football has significantly improved during the course of the past half-century and the Packers would, therefore, be expected to trounce the Eagles.

Now let's go back again to 1960. It was the year I entered policing. Would it be fair to make comparisons between police departments of then and now? Are the police departments on which I first began serving in the 60s of higher quality, fairer and more effective today than they were then?

To be fair, police departments don't have to compete against one another each week, nor do their reported statistics easily measure their effectiveness. If we were to measure reported crime rates between the two eras it would probably not be fair. But if we could compare today's and yesterday's police departments, we would see much *less* difference between police than we would between the Eagles and the Packers.

Whether or not it is fair to compare police departments from decade to decade might be arguable. But the amount of improvement that has or has not occurred within police departments during this time period maybe worth thinking about. Should police departments be judged on how well they maintain the *status quo* or by how much they have improved?

Comparing police to football players is, of course, somewhat like comparing apples and oranges. The skills required to be a successful professional football player, I would argue, are much fewer and more narrowly focused than the many skills required of a competent police officer. During my football career as an offensive tackle and defensive end, I didn't have to pass or kick the ball; my job was to keep the player in front of me from tackling our ball carrier, or, on defense, to tackle the person with the ball. I was expected to play both offense and defense, to be on the kickoff or return teams, and to line up to either defend or try to score an extra point. Today, most college and professional football teams have special teams to perform those functions and have clearly defined units that usually don't consist of the same players.

When I came into the police, on the other hand, I couldn't just be good at a couple of functions. I had to play both offense and defense. I had to be able to drive a police vehicle, talk on a radio, investigate crimes, write reports, give chase to suspects, defend myself, and make arrests without seriously injuring others. I also had to be able to provide first aid to injured persons, convey them to a hospital, know state laws, city ordinances, and rules of arrest, search and seizure, be a referee during neighborhood squabbles and marital disputes, and be able to settle a host of messes that people get themselves into.

In comparison, the job competencies required of me as a football player seemed rather narrow compared with those that citizens expected and required of me when I became a police officer. Three other job functions stand out with regard to excelling at the game of football or policing: tenure, leadership, and training.

As to tenure, there are no, if any, professional

coaches who will take a head coaching job without a contract. They know that building a good team takes time and that any coaching job has its ups and downs.

As to leadership, I'm sure that all managing directors, owners, and/or presidents of professional sports teams and their shareholders believe that the leadership skills of the coach and his staff are one of the most significant factors in the team's success. Shareholders and fans know that it's not just what the coach says but how the coach leads that determines performance.

As to training, I often wonder how many hours of practice (both on- and off-season) it takes to be a successful professional athlete. We can probably agree that most likely, thousands and thousands of hours of both intensive play and practice are involved. Many Olympic athletes have written about their single-mindedness in preparing for the games— swimmers who spent six hours a day in the pool, runners who trained mile after mile, and cyclists who rode hundreds of intense training miles every week. Some successful players began playing football about the time they entered elementary school and have played the sport for most of their life.

Brett Favre retired from football and then rejoined another team, and was again one of the top NFL quarterbacks as he approached 40 years of age. He went on to "un-retire" two more times until he quit for good at age 42.

If we compare the training of football players with that of police officers (or compare police with physicians, lawyers, or other professionals), we will find there is a tremendous difference in both their training and preparation. It is such a difference that it would be difficult to argue that, given all their public responsibilities, police are well trained.

How many hours of training are required for a person to practice the art of policing? In some places the answer is none. The average length of initial police training in the United States is less than five months. When compared to other professionals in today's society, the current length of police training is highly insufficient.

Given the numerous responsibilities assigned to police, the high expectations the public has of them, and the many situations they can face requiring life-or-death decisions, how should police be trained? What level of formal education should they reach? How long should their initial academy training last? And what provisions should be made for periodic in-service training throughout their career?

In each of the areas I mentioned above—tenure, leadership, and training—it would appear that everything that seemed right and reasonable to expect from a high-performance sports team or corporation ought to also be expected of a critical public agency like the police. If you thoroughly studied what police are expected to do in our society and then devised education and training to meet those expectations, I'm confident that the standards you set would significantly exceed the current standards for our nation's police.

Perhaps an argument could be made that high expectations regarding police are not reasonable—that policing is, by its nature, an elementary task not suited to people with educations and career aspirations.

I can tell you that from my review of police misconduct around the country, to continue to think this way is both unfortunate and costly. Cities around the country have had to respond to police

misconduct cases that often cost them tens of millions of dollars. In Minneapolis, a department in which I served for a number of years, the city has paid out over $13 million during the past seven years to victims of police misconduct. Larger cities, like New York, Los Angles, Philadelphia, and Washington, D.C., often pay out millions of dollars each year to settle mistakes made by police.[21]

I don't recommend that we lower our expectations of police, but rather that we raise them. We should expect first class behavior from police officers because they ultimately represent who we are as a people and as a society. At a minimum, we should expect police to accurately identify and apprehend criminals with a minimal amount of physical force. They should be able to write full and truthful reports of their activities, and give honest testimony in court. We also should expect them to possess skills that help in the prevention of crime, to be able to aid individuals who are   in danger of harm, and to assist people who cannot care for themselves.   We should further expect police to know the laws they are to enforce, protect our civil rights, and also to be able to do a number of other tasks such as directing and controlling traffic, resolving inter-personal conflicts, identifying community problems, and preserving order. But overall, we should expect our police officers to be educated, honest, competent, and courteous— respectful in every way to everyone they encounter. They should do so because police are often the most visible representatives of our system of government—of America itself.

These skill sets and functions are so complex and difficult to perform in today's society that only

---

[21]http://www.startribune.com/local/minneapolis/1264949 38.html. January 3, 2012; 0645 hrs.

those who are academically prepared, intensely trained, and properly directed should be given such responsibilities.

In turn, citizens should demand that only the kind of people I outlined above are hired as police officers and are given both the necessary training and leadership to meet community expectations. We should also make sure that police officers have the kind of internal leadership that treats them with respect, listens to them, helps them grow professionally, and permits them to participate in workplace decisions. These are the qualities that will get police moving forward and out of the ruts they continue to be stuck in—subculture, corruption, and low expectations.

Chapter 2
The Circle Goes Round and Round

YOU CANNOT WRITE about the development of police in America without knowing about Robert Peel and the London Metropolitan Police. The development of uniformed, public police took place much   more slowly in England than in the rest of Europe. Public police were already established in Paris by the time the English did so. Before this time, a system of privately funded rewards was created to apprehend thieves and burglars. This private model continued well into the 19th century. There were privately funded police organizations in no fewer than 45 governmental units or parishes within a 10-mile radius of London. As one can imagine, there was little coordination, information-sharing, or discipline among or in these jurisdictions.

However, in 1829, a Metropolitan Police Act was passed by Parliament, which enabled the Home Secretary to establish a unified public police force in London. This significantly reduced the function of private police and brought the modern governmental function of policing a democracy into existence. Robert Peel was the Home Secretary.

Peel's Principles of Policing

1. *The basic mission for which the police exist is to prevent crime and disorder.*

2. *The ability of the police to perform their duties is dependent upon the public approval of police actions.*

3. *Police must secure the willing co-operation of the public in voluntary observation of the law to be able to secure and maintain the respect of the public.*

4. *The degree of co-operation of the public that can be secured diminishes proportionately to the necessity of the use of physical force.*

5. *Police seek and preserve public favor not by catering to public opinion, but by constantly demonstrating absolute impartial service to the law.*

6. *Police use physical force to the extent necessary to secure observance of the law or to restore order only when the exercise of persuasion, advice, and warning is found to be insufficient.*

7. *Police, at all times, should maintain a relationship with the public that gives reality to the historic tradition that the police are the public and the public are the police; the police being only members of the public who are paid to give full-time attention to duties which are incumbent upon every citizen in the interests of community welfare and existence.*

8. *Police should always direct their action strictly towards their functions, and never appear to usurp the powers of the judiciary.*

9. *The test of police efficiency is the absence of crime and disorder, not the visible evidence of police action in dealing with it.*

As time went on, the London Metropolitan Police essentially became the model for police forces in most democracies around the world, including ours. Our system of policing and Great Britain's

differ significantly from many other countries', in that our police exist to protect a citizen's rights just as much as those of the state. This is what makes policing a democracy unique among the world's police—the function isn't just about order but also about rights.

It is what makes it a challenging enterprise.

Peel's nine principles laid out the framework for police conduct in any society in which it is necessary for the police to work closely with citizens and have their respect. Remarkably, these principles are as valid today as they were when they were first developed over 150 years ago.[22]

The first principle is a powerful statement regarding the role of police; they are to *prevent* crime and disorder, as well as apprehend offenders. They don't serve primarily to control and arrest criminals. Instead, they have a responsibility to prevent crime from ever happening in the first place, which means police must be willing and able to work upstream in society regarding the causes of crime and create and maintain an effective system of preventing it.

The second and third principles state that police cannot function effectively in society unless they have the approval of the public. Good relationships, cooperation, trust, and confidence between the community and the police are paramount to having an effective police. Ultimately, the greatest way

[22] Lentz, Susan A. and Robert H. Chaires, The invention of Peel's principles: A study of policing 'textbook' history. *Journal of Criminal Justice* 35: 69–79. 2007. doi:10.1016/j.jcrimjus.2006.11.016. *Note: While Robert Peel has received the lion's share of citations down through the years, the Principles were actually a collaborative effort of Peel, Richard Mayne, and Charles Rowan.*

to foster adherence to the rule of law isn't through threats, but by creating a social climate wherein people *voluntarily* observe the law because they can see that it benefits themselves as well as the society of which they consider themselves to be members.

The fourth and sixth principles are the result of a wise observation about human behavior and the use of force. The public's cooperation with the police diminishes as increased force is used by the police. How police make arrests and take offenders into custody is often an area of contention and conflict between police and the community. The fourth principle states that if police want cooperation from the community, they need to use coercive force carefully and judiciously. The sixth notes that when physical force must be used, it should only be when persuasion, advice, and warning are found to be insufficient—that is, as a last resort.

The fifth principle is one of the primary ethical principles of democratic policing. Images of Lady Justice can be seen in many of our nation's courtrooms, with the scales of justice in her hands, but her eyes blindfolded, so she cannot see whether those who come before her seeking justice are young or old, rich or poor. She also cannot see the color of their skin. So too, police must be like Lady Justice, blind to an individual's race, gender, or socioeconomic class. They must be absolutely impartial when operating as agents of government, and not be influenced by illegal or improper public pressure or prejudicial attitudes.

The seventh principle reminds us that *everyone* is responsible for the peace, welfare, and harmony of our society, not just the police. As representatives of that society, police must be recruited from the community to serve the community. Police are those who are paid to give full-time attention to the public's

responsibility of maintaining a safe, peaceful, and orderly society. The police are the public and the public are the police.

The eighth principle identifies the necessary checks and balances that need to exist between the police and those of the judiciary. This necessary separation helps balance the power that each possesses; one to arrest, the other to judge. In America, we intentionally created a separation of the three powers of government: executive, legislative, and judicial.

Each balances the other's unique power. The executive power of the police is balanced by that of the legislature and the judiciary. The legislature creates the law, the police enforce, and the judiciary reviews.

The ninth principle reiterates what the first principle says about the primary role of police. Police should be judged by the absence of crime and disorder in their community and not by their activity or how many arrests they make. Although it is necessary and essential for police to apprehend criminals, an ideal community isn't one in which police focus on apprehension. An ideal community exists when police and citizens work together to prevent crime from ever occurring in the first place.

These are the kind of principles that are needed to guide police in a democracy—they seem reasonable and clear. Why, then, do police often fall short of them?

In a totalitarian system of government, the harsh treatment by police of perceived offenders is the way business is done. In a democracy, however, social control must be accomplished by government while individual rights are protected and police are

expected to be fair and just. Therefore, people who live in democracies have a different set of expectations than those living under other forms of government.

In a democracy, police have a very complex role compared to what is expected of the police in other systems. The power of the state must be balanced with the rights of an individual; other systems have no balance requirement—only to use the power given them by the state.

Uniquely, police in a democracy don't exist solely to maintain order on behalf of the state, but also to assure that the fundamental rights guaranteed to every citizen are protected in the process.

This is never more evident as when a totalitarian state responds to public protest. In this instance, the goal of the police is to prevent or repress, not facilitate, protest. We see that in today in Syria, China, and other less-than-democratic governments. In these instances, the very act of disagreeing with the government is illegal and subject to police action.

A democratic state and its police ensure its citizens the right of speech, public assembly, and the airing of grievances. This is essential in a democracy because citizens are ultimately in charge through their elected representatives and must have the right to speak out and organize to make their desires known. While the state itself has the monopoly on the use of force, that monopoly must be used sparingly in a democracy and only in accordance with the rule of law—there are no sovereign rights except those held by the people. In fact, as President Lincoln noted in his Gettysburg Address, ours is a government of the people, by the people, and for the people. How police in a democracy respond to public protest is a key

indicator of their competency.

In our nation's history, more often than not, our police leaders seem to have been unaware of Peel's guiding principles. The legacy of American police during the past 150 years has not been one of civility, honesty, and maintaining the respect of those whom they serve. Bad policing by some police departments and their officers has significantly tainted how citizens throughout our country view police today.

Nicholas Peart, a young college student in New York, reported to the *New York Times* in December, 2011, that he has been stopped and frisked by police officers at least five times. He is one of more than 600,000 citizens of color stopped by police in New York last year; 84 percent of those stops involved blacks or Latinos. He wrote about his experience:

The police use the excuse that they're fighting crime to continue the practice, but no one has ever actually proved that it reduces crime or makes the city safer. Those of us who live in the neighborhoods where stop-and-frisks are a basic fact of daily life don't feel safer as a result.

We need change. When I was young I thought cops were cool. They had a respectable and honorable job to keep people safe and fight crime. Now, I think their tactics are unfair and they abuse their authority. The police should consider the consequences of a generation of young people who want nothing to do with them — distrust, alienation and more crime.[23]

To illustrate this problem further, a recent study at Columbia Law School and reported in *The New York Times*, found that tens of thousands of times over a six year period, the police stopped and

---

[23] Peart, Nicholas K. "Why is the N.Y.P.D After Me?" *The New York Times*, December 17, 2011

questioned people on New York City streets without the legal justification for doing so. And residents in an area of Brooklyn's 73rd Precinct, an area in which the residents are predominately poor and black, were most likely in the city to be stopped and frisked by police officers.[24]

If, over the years, our nation's police leaders had internalized Peel's nine principles, trained on those principles, and made operational decisions based on them, I believe we would have a system of policing in America today that would be noted for its wisdom, skill in peacekeeping, courtesy, and respect from the communities it serves.

When we look at the system of American policing today, we find a wide range of organizational functions, structures, and sizes operated by multiple layers of government and a wide variation in organizational competencies and capabilities. Supplementing American policing today is the growing area of private security. In many cities, private guards sit comfortably in climate-controlled buildings behind secure doors aided by electronic monitoring systems while city police patrol the streets outside in all kinds of weather, without advanced technologies, and responsible primarily for those who will never be able to work in climate-controlled offices.

Policing in America is local and difficult to either control or coordinate. While consolidated or regional police forces can be found in Great Britain and other European countries, they are virtually nonexistent in our nation. Instead, we are a nation of small, fragmented, localized police organizations. Almost every city, village, and township has its own

---

[24] Study Finds Street Stops by N.Y. Police Unjustified. *New York Times*, October 26, 2010.

police department. There are 2,000 police departments in this country that have only *one* police officer in their employment. This balkanization of small and uncoordinated police departments results in a police function that has difficulty with coordination, conducting training, sharing information, reducing redundancy, and being as effective as it could be.

This is true whether we are talking about jurisdictions that share borders or that operate at different levels of government.

To get a grasp on this fragmentation of law enforcement jurisdictions in the United States consider this: there are more than 18,000 police departments staffed by more than 600,000 officers. The overwhelming majority (87 percent) of these departments are local and small—that is, they employ 25 or fewer police.

In contrast, only one percent of the nation's police departments employ 1,000 or more officers. The very largest of these departments is in New York City. The police department there employs around 35,000 officers. Compared with most police departments in the country, the departments in our nation's largest cities are virtual armies in size and scope, and have little in common with the overwhelming majority of American police departments. But, thanks to television and the movies, these departments have tended to exert a distorted impact on the rest of the country (including police themselves), who get their impressions about policing from them. There are also millions of Americans who live in these large cities, and those who live in low-income neighborhoods are inordinately impacted by the police who patrol these areas and, therefore, are more likely to come into contact with police.

One way to ensure more effective coordination and efficiency of the police function would be to require police to consolidate into regional area departments of not less than, say, 100-500 officers. I'm not the first person to suggest this; many independent studies of our nation's police have recommended it.26

I must also highlight that the local nature of our nation's police can also be an asset. There are small police departments that are close and responsive to the people they serve. Unfortunately, those police departments most often serve the wealthier neighborhoods of suburban America.

I don't expect that what I have to say will significantly alter the day-to-day functioning of our large, army-size police departments in our major cities. It would be nice if it were so. But my focus here is primarily on those smaller departments in American cities—departments of 500 or fewer officers who have concern for, understanding of, and connection with their communities. It is to the police officers in those ranks and their leaders that my remarks are primarily intended; those men and women who, day in and day out, deliver direct services to the majority of us who live in America.

This was a major recommendation in the report of the President's Crime Commission in 1967. Since that time, there have been few regional consolidations of police services.

While these police work primarily in our smaller, medium-size cities, they could also be in rural areas serving as police officers, deputy sheriffs, as well as state highway patrol officers who are assigned locally. There are also police functions that could be localized by federal, state, and county police, from

special jurisdictions like parks, ports, transportation systems, and native police on reservations. Each one of those specialized tasks can focus on the needs of those whom they serve.

Nevertheless, the style of American policing as we know it today has been intensely influenced by police in our large cities. At the beginning of the 20th century, our nation experienced large-scale immigration of workers into those cities, the expansion of urban areas, and also the rise, correspondingly, of political bosses. Work in those cities as a police officer frequently came about as a result of patronage—police jobs were handed out by a city's political bosses. These jobs were not sought out by educated men or those who wished to rise in American society. As might be expected, there were major scandals involving the police during this time, and often an entire police department would be dismissed and new officers appointed after a city election. The purpose of this wasn't to reform the department, but rather to hand out political favors and install officers in a police department sympathetic to a new mayor's agenda— good or bad. Policing at this time wasn't about protecting the rights of individual citizens. It was more about what violations should be overlooked and what laws should be enforced according to the wishes and benefit of local ward bosses.

In the mid-1850s, New York and Boston became our nation's first organized police departments. In each instance public police officers replaced private night watchmen just like that which occurred in London. These watchmen were either volunteers or partially paid by business owners. They didn't carry firearms; indeed, for many years, the only weapon American police had at their disposal was a nightstick. Arming police with guns came much later in our history—usually after an unarmed officer was

slain while making an arrest.

The New York Police Department was closely modeled after the consolidated Metropolitan Police Force in London. Similar to London, New York consolidated separate police jurisdictions in New York, like Brooklyn, Staten Island, and others into one department. This consolidation was exactly what the British had done in bringing together the numerous police agencies that surrounded London. What seemed to be missing, however, were a set of overriding ethical principles, or a Robert Peel, that could overcome petty partisanship and the abuses of local political bosses, and, particularly, the troubles the Prohibition Era brought on in the 1930s.

While we would hope that police leaders of this era would have been aware of Peel's principles of policing, it is necessary to remember they were not educated men. They didn't have a good grasp of European history, the Enlightenment, or the legal thinking that would have identified the dangers inherent in a police controlled more by political whim than by the rule of law.

Since that time, few large metropolitan areas in our nation have been able to consolidate the scores of police departments that surround almost every one of them. The 1967 President's Commission's report on the police tried to address this situation by recommending consolidation of police in major metropolitan areas. The report cited not only cost savings but also operational efficiencies in effectiveness as benefits of consolidation. The commission described, as an example, the police departments in and around the metropolitan area of Detroit. At the time, this area contained 85 separate police jurisdictions, 40 of which employed fewer than 20 police officers. Detroit wasn't unusual. The same situation exists today in almost every large

metropolitan area in the United States. We have a penchant for small, localized government. While police consolidation seems to make sense, we avoid doing it.

Looking back, American policing has had—and missed—a number of opportunities to advance. One came in the 1930s during Prohibition, after a presidential commission found most police had been corrupted by criminal syndicates that had moved in to provide now-illegal alcoholic beverages to a thirsty population. In addition, it found that police were often using torture to extract confessions from suspects. Reforms were demanded, but few of them survived.

Another opportunity came along in the late 1960s, while the nation was being torn apart by urban racial violence and an unpopular war in Southeast Asia. Another presidential commission was convened, which recommended a series of changes police should undertake. Few of their 23 recommendations were ever implemented, but these recommendations still remain current issues in policing. A spin-off of the 1967 report came to light again in the 1980s when it was realized that police needed to be more community-oriented and work towards solving problems. Even today, it remains to be seen whether those recommendations will be tried, let alone sustained.

I feel we are still in the rippling effect of the major forces that drove the presidential commission in 1967. The question is whether or not our nation's police will be able to effectively work in a diverse, multi- cultural society, keep the peace during times of civil protest, vigorously protect citizen's civil rights, have close relationships with immigrant communities and recruit their sons and daughters to serve proudly as police.

Over the years, and since the '60s, some police practices have become more effective. Police forces, as a case in point, in most of our major cities are now more integrated with regard to race and gender. They have also begun to use technology more effectively; especially communications, as in the case of enhanced 911 emergency systems and personal radios. Police also use modern day methods of identification and scientific methods of investigation.

One of the most notable changes came about through a federal allocation in the 1960s—grants for rank-and-file police officers who wanted to obtain a college education. I was one of those who took advantage of this program. It changed my life. As I mentioned earlier, serving as a student by day and a cop by night, I came to see police work in a new light. I began to see and understand that big changes were needed in not only American police departments but throughout our entire criminal justice system.

If our nation's police don't work on improving themselves before there is another major problem like Prohibition or a surge of massive protests in our streets, they will continue to repeat the cycle, the circle going round again, just as they have done in the past. Yet another opportunity will have been missed. Now let's get to that first missed opportunity -- the Wickersham Commission in the 1930s. To investigate the problems with enforcing prohibition laws, President Herbert Hoover appointed a commission—the National Commission of Law Observance and Enforcement—headed by former U.S. Attorney General George Wickersham.[25]

---

[25] 27*National Commission on Law Observance and Enforcement* (Wickersham Commission). 1931.

It was the problem of police corruption that came to a head during those years, 1920–1933. A constitutional amendment was our country's response to the problem of alcohol abuse. Though the law was well-intentioned, it ultimately had unanticipated consequences. Prohibition resulted in blatant disregard for the law in many sectors of our society and widespread corruption on the part of the police who were expected to enforce it.

The commission's report was written by August Vollmer,[26] a police chief himself, and highlighted not only the nation's disregard for the law but also, for the first time, documented the illegal use of torture by our nation's police in extracting confessions from suspects. This practice, called the third degree—the infliction of physical or mental pain to extract confessions—was identified by the commission as being widespread throughout the country.

In the desperate effort to compel obedience to law, experience has shown that those charged with the high function of enforcing the law sometimes stoop to attain their ends by means as illegal as the acts they seek to punish or suppress.[27]

The best-known argument isn't unfamiliar to police leaders: "Chief, if you knew for sure the person you have arrested was the person who had kidnapped and buried a little girl underground, and time is a factor because she will soon suffocate,

---

[26] August Vollmer served as chief of the Berkeley (CA) police department in the early 1900s and taught at the University of California School of Criminology. He went to Wichita (KS) in the early 1930s and established the four-year college degree as an entrance requirement. He was one of the first major police reformers in this country and consulted with many cities in regard to improving their police departments.

[27] *National Commission on Law Observance and Enforcement*, 1931.

wouldn't you use any means necessary to find that little girl and save her?"

But both international law and common moral decency prohibit the use of torture in any circumstance—even in the circumstance of an endangered child. The following is the definition of torture that comes from the United Nations' convention on the subject:

Torture means any act by which severe pain or suffering, whether physical or mental, is intentionally inflicted on a person for such purposes as obtaining from him or a third person information or a confession.[28]

There are some horrendous incidents that have ended up in civil actions against police that might question whether torture totally left the police station in the 1930s. Surveying the media during the last few years will show that torture continues to be a problem today in police ranks.

While the Wickersham Commission documented widespread evasion of the Prohibition laws and the counterproductive effect this was having on society, it surprisingly didn't recommend that the law be repealed. Instead, it recommended a more aggressive and extensive law enforcement effort to force the public's compliance. There are certainly some parallels here with regard to how our nation continues to respond to illegal drugs. With regard to marijuana, we could say today that there is similar widespread evasion of the law, and that this, too, has resulted in widespread corruption of those charged with enforcing these laws. We could also document that enforcement is both ineffective and counterproductive.

---

[28] *Convention Against Torture and Other Cruel, Inhuman or Degrading Treatment or Punishment.* United Nations. Part 1, Article 1. 1987

The work of the Wickersham Commission, however, still remains one of the most significant steps in our nation's history toward improving our nation's police. It was the first systematic investigation and documentation of police misconduct in the United States. It brought to light the illegal use of torture by police to extract confessions and information from suspects. And the work of the commission became a catalyst for later reform efforts, which called for police to be more accountable to their communities.

Four decades later another opportunity arose. This time it wasn't about police corruption but about a growing rate of crime in America fueled by civil rights and war protesters. In the 1960s and 70s, a number of major events occurred that caused our nation to snap out of its doldrums. It became a major opportunity for police reform. The events were related to the growing movement to end institutionalized racism and racial segregation in our nation, and a growing discontent with the course of the war in Vietnam. These two movements taxed and challenged the centralized police model that was a response to the charges leveled against the nation's police by the Wickersham Commission.

During this period police found themselves having poor relations with minority communities. Their hiring and promotional practices were criticized. Their crowd control tactics left much to be desired. It was also revealed that many police departments had gathered a large amount of illegal intelligence regarding protest leaders who had not committed any criminal acts.

Those of us who lived through that period can remember that to many, protest was first viewed as un-American, even equivalent to being a communist.

Leaders of national protest movements, such as Dr. Martin Luther King Jr. and Malcolm X, were seen as being influenced by outside agitators or foreign governments; therefore, American police (who were predominately white and working class) had little sympathy for protesters, and this lack of tolerance caused numerous hostile and brutal encounters.

President John F. Kennedy and his brother and attorney general, Robert Kennedy, witnessed the civil rights movement in the South, the unacceptable and violent response by police in those cities, and the slow progress of racial integration within our nation. The U.S. Supreme Court had ruled in 1954 that separate schools for black and white children were, themselves, unequal and unconstitutional. Robert Kennedy struggled continually with the nation's top police officer, Director J. Edgar Hoover, over these issues and the role of the Federal Bureau of Investigation (FBI) in helping the nation uphold its civil rights laws.

After John F. Kennedy was assassinated, President Lyndon Johnson's new administration wished to go further in seeing that civil rights, especially equality and justice, were guaranteed to every American, regardless of the color of their skin, national origin, or economic condition. It was Johnson's dream that our nation could come together and build what he called a Great Society.

This era was also the first time in our nation's history that fear of crime became the No. 1 concern of Americans. Responding to that concern, Johnson established the commission I mentioned earlier, which ultimately presented him with a report. A major part of the commission's work was to examine the state of our nation's criminal justice system, including police, and make recommendations for changes, in order to reduce the threat of crime and

social disorder.

The commission's recommendations for the police were developed after a thorough and broad inquiry into existing practices. The commission sought input from academics in the field of crime and criminology, as well as from police administrators. They boldly recommended that police—at this point, years removed from close contact with the people they serve, re-connect with their communities, meet regularly, listen to residents, and work out problems together. There was a specific recommendation for special community relations units to engage the community with its police. It was especially targeted at police departments in cities with large minority populations.

The message to our nation's police from the commission was to get back to their communities and hire minority officers. A year later in 1968, the National Commission on Civil Disorder called the Kerner Commission after its chairperson, was formed. In their report they remarked that our nation's police have come to view their community through the windshield of their patrol car and hear about its activities over a radio. This is a good description of police in America in the 1960s.[29]

Along with the commission's focus on improving relations with communities came some

---

[29] The commission came to be called the Kerner Commission after its chairman, Otto Kerner, the former governor of Illinois. President Lyndon Johnson appointed the commission in the midst of major civil disorder, much of it racially driven. There were major racial riots in the Watts section of Los Angeles (1965), Chicago's Division Street (1966), and in Detroit and Newark (1967). Johnson asked the commission three questions: "What happened? Why did it happen? What can be done to prevent it from happening again and again?"

specific recommendations to hire and promote minority officers, fully and fairly process citizen complaints, and develop operational policies that would guide police in the use of what is called police discretion—including the understanding of when to arrest and when not to arrest, as well as the appropriate use of force, both deadly and non-deadly.

An analysis of street riots during that time found that the event that frequently triggered the violence was a questionable arrest made by police or the shooting of a youthful offender. Eventually this resulted in police departments issuing written policies to help direct the actions of their officers in these potentially incendiary circumstances. Prior to this time, most police agencies didn't have written directives regarding when and when not to use force, make an arrest, write a citation, or chase a fleeing vehicle.

The commission also made tough recommendations to raise the educational requirement for police officers to that of a four-year college degree. It recommended three levels of entry into police service: community service officer, police officer, and police agent. Community service officers were to be police trainees and wouldn't carry a weapon or have the power to make an arrest, but would work closely with the community. And police officers would function much as they function today.

But the role and function of police agents would be very different. Agents would be given the most complicated, sensitive, and demanding assignments. As an example, agents would serve as juvenile officers, investigatory specialists, and community relations officers. Agents could also work in uniform in high-crime areas of the city. They would possess four-year college degrees, be highly

compensated, and encouraged to develop innovative police techniques and procedures. It was also expected that they would require a minimum amount of supervision.

The commission hoped this three-tiered structure would increase the attractiveness of police work by enabling a college graduate, after a short internship, and without prior police experience, to move into the position of police agent. The commission's recommendation also encouraged existing police officers to pursue college educations and work to become police agents. It further recommended that supervisory and command officers be required to possess a bachelor's degree. On top of all this, the commission recommended federal and state tuition assistance programs for current police officers and those seeking to serve as police.

Standards Relating to the Urban Police Function

- Identify criminal offenders and criminal activity, apprehend, participate in court proceedings
- Reduce the opportunities for the commission of crime
- Aid individuals who are in danger
- Protect constitutional guarantees
- Help with the flow of traffic
- Assist those in need of care
- Resolve conflict
- Identify problems
- Maintain a feeling of security
- Promote and preserve civil order
- Provide emergency services

These recommendations shook up the police of my day. There were not only compelling recommendations for college educations throughout the ranks, but also for enhanced hiring practices and intensive training programs. There also was a recommendation for legislation that would permit police officers to carry their seniority and pension plans between cities, as do many other professional employees. For me and many other officers, the opportunity for college tuition, increased pay, and that our promotions be based on ability over seniority were all music to our ears. It was the realization of a

dream—that a professional, competent, legally grounded police officer would be the norm in our society and not the exception.

With regard to the issue of police discretion and the use of force, the commission specifically recommended that deadly force be used by police only in life-threatening situations. This was a time when most state laws permitted police to use deadly force against any fleeing felon; even those who were fleeing from a property crime and were unarmed.

Additionally, it recommended the use of a new method of organization called team policing, designed to be more collaborative and community-based. The team-policing concept assigned officers to a team with a geographical responsibility, rather than one based on time of day. That is, rather than assigning police to an area for a period of time (a shift), their overall responsibility should be to a specific area of the city—a neighborhood.

There were also recommendations to establish state or regional crime labs and statewide police standards commissions, which would be formed to provide financial aid to governmental units that wished to implement the recommendations of the commission. The latter, unfortunately, didn't occur. But what did happen was significant. The nation's police started to go back to college and carry degrees from those institutions back to their police departments, and citizens now had a source to refer to in regard to what police should be doing—particularly, that they should be working more closely with and listening to their communities.

When the President's Commission released its report in 1967, it recommended that funds be provided to establish police standards boards in each state. These boards would then direct funds they

received to police departments for the purpose of implementing the commission's recommendations. This was to provide the financial assistance necessary to create the new professional police model they had recommended.[30]

The strategy, however, didn't pass political muster. Few national police leaders were in favor of the commission's recommendations. The response of Congress was to form a Law Enforcement Assistance Administration (LEAA). It turned out to be an unwieldy and administratively doomed organization.

Between 1969 and 1980, nearly $8 billion was appropriated by Congress to improve police. What happened during those years is now history—an unfortunate history. The law enforcement funding effort was changed from implementing the commission's recommendations to one of distributing block grants to the states. It does not take much to figure out what happened here. I heard grumbling about the federal government stepping in to tell local and state police what they should be doing. By going the route of block grants, states would be able to exercise discretion as to how the money would be spent—there were no specific requirements that the money be spent on implementing recommendations of the commission.

What happened was LEAA became a closet revenue-sharing program that did little to help the nation's police, with the exception of providing them more gadgets and hardware such as personal radios, computers, patrol boats, and weaponry. To be fair, one part of the program was of significant help to our nation's police and to me personally: the funding of formal education for police. Yet overall, most citizens

---

[30] *President's Commission on Law Enforcement and the Administration of Justice.* Task Force Report: The Police. Washington: U.S. Government Printing Office. 1967

witnessed little improvement in the quality of their local police services as a result of a national expenditure of $8 billion dollars.

Following the work of President Johnson's commission, the American Bar Association (ABA) looked into the various functions expected of police, something Johnson's commission had not done. The ABA's report, *Standards Relating to the Urban Police Function*, was made public in 1971.[31]

The ABA project was the collaborative work of both scholars and practitioners. This was the first deep inquiry into the nature and expectations of urban policing—what the public should expect city police to be able to do. It went on to identify the primary functions of policing in cities. Professor Frank Remington of the University of Wisconsin Law School chaired the project.

Two eras have now gone by our nation's police: Wickersham and the 1967 President's Commission. Wickersham addressed the police corruption brought about by Prohibition. The 1967 commission addressed the growing problem of police-community relations in our nation's cities.

We now are in the third era of policing—an era that, so far, is still evolving. It is the era I call community policing. Community policing emphasizes closer relationships between the police, their communities and a response to community-identified problems.[32] It may become another missed

---

[31] *Standards Relating to the Urban Police Function.* American Bar Association. 1971

[32] Herman Goldstein. *Problem-Oriented Policing. Philadelphia:* Temple University Press. 1990. I need to emphasize the critical connection between Goldstein's problem-oriented policing and community (or neighborhood) policing. The community looks to police to solve problems; Goldstein's

opportunity by our nation's police.

Yet it remains to be seen whether or not police will take advantage of this opportunity or go to something entirely different. Currently, police have spent over three decades ostensibly doing community-oriented policing; however, there are limited data available to measure the success of their effort. A new development could overshadow the work that has been done to implement a style of policing that has been in progress since the early 1980s. That development is the overwhelming dependence upon technology to conduct police work.

Many people, myself included, believe that this development was triggered by that day in September 2001, when terrorists attacked our nation. After the attacks, and even into the present day, our nation has been in a constant state of fear that, sadly, has been exploited by some of our nation's political leaders. While the attacks were certainly of a very low- tech nature—commandeering commercial airliners and flying them into buildings—our nation's response was to unleash the power of our technology: electronic surveillance, video cameras, security checkpoints, preventative detention and, massive military retaliation in the Middle East. A large amount of this technology surge filtered down to the nation's police in the form of new weaponry and methods of intelligence-gathering and surveillance.

---

method most effectively and in the long-run focuses on those community problems. Community, or neighborhood policing, decentralizes police to work in small geographical areas of the city—movement from doing work based on time of day to geographical area. I strongly supported the neighborhood policing concept in my article, "The Delivery of Neighborhood Police Services: A Challenge for Today's Professional," in the March 1972 issue of *The Police Chief* magazine

Yet in community policing, police officers' dependence isn't on technology but on people. The theory is that respectful working relations between police and citizens lead to safer communities, because safety and order are everyone's goals. When police and citizens work together on community-identified problems, they get resolved. The problem with dependence upon technology, on the other hand, is that it tends to draw police away from their community and essentially distances them from those whom they are to serve.

One of the top examples to enhance community-oriented policing is the problem-oriented method established by Herman Goldstein in the late 1970s.[33] It was then that many police, researchers, and policymakers became interested in improving the effectiveness of police. Research during this period pointed out the limitations of some very sacred assumptions police held—assumptions about random patrol, rapid response to calls, and follow-up investigations. These sacred cows of policing had been the basis for police practices for many years.

Instead, there was a new recognition that:

- *Police deal with a range of community problems, many of which are not strictly criminal in nature. Arrest and prosecution alone—the traditional functions of the criminal justice system—do not always effectively resolve problems.*
- *Giving police officers, who have great insight into community problems, the discretion to design solutions is extremely valuable for solving the problems.*
- *Police can use a variety of methods to redress recurrent problems.*

[33] Herman Goldstein. Problem-Oriented Policing. New York: McGraw-Hill, 1990.

- *The community values police involvement in noncriminal problems and recognizes the contribution police can make to solve these problems.*[34]

Early experiments in problem-oriented policing occurred while I was chief in Madison, as well as in Baltimore County, Maryland, and the United Kingdom. My favorite story about the problem-oriented method   was about an officer who found himself responding to a noise disturbance call at the same address night after night. Responding to noise complaints is part and parcel of urban policing. Noise complaints had become so routine that every night shift officer knew they would get one or more calls about noise to that address before the night was over.

In each instance, the complainants came from an elderly woman who lived above a tavern. Just about every night, she would call the police to complain about the loud noise from the tavern's jukebox. And night after night, officers would respond to the call, talk to her, and then, routinely, go downstairs and tell the bartender to turn down the music. The bartender would often wonder why he was turning down the jukebox, because it didn't seem to be very loud. Nevertheless, the jukebox would be turned down and the police officer would write a report. In fact, both the police officer and bartender knew that no matter how much the volume on the jukebox was lowered, another call would soon be forthcoming.

Finally, in exasperation, one of the officers decided to tally all the noise calls related to that

---

[34] http://www.popcenter.org/about/?p=history. December 27, 2010; 2205 hrs. Also the work of James Skolnick and David Bayley in 1986: *The New Blue Line: Police Innovation in Six American Cities.* New York: The Free Press

address. When he added them all up, he was astounded—during the past three months, there had been scores of multiple calls to this address. When he reviewed the reports as to what officers had done in response to the calls, he found that most of them did as he did: they told the bartender to turn down the jukebox and went back on patrol.

So the officer decided to go farther, to begin to work upstream to determine what was really causing this problem that was excessively taxing police resources. He talked to the woman and even listened from her apartment before and after he asked the bartender to turn the jukebox down. Then he talked to the owner of the tavern. The owner defended himself and his employees by saying that no matter how low they turned the jukebox down, the lady upstairs would continue to complain and call police.

Now the officer had some data. He began investigating and checking the noise level of the jukebox in the tavern and in the woman's apartment. It really didn't seem to be very loud in the tavern, but in the apartment it truly was a problem.

At this point, some police officers might have just advised the lady to buy some earplugs or to find another residence. But that, of course, would only forestall the problem until the next resident moved in and the unrelenting cycle of noise complaints continued.

Instead, this officer used the problem-solving method to address the situation. He began by looking at the nature of the problem, talking again with the bartenders and the patrons, as well as the woman upstairs. Then, after going over what he had learned from tallying the complaints and talking to the people involved, he began to look for causes.

At first, he thought the cause was the jukebox. But it turned out he was wrong. No matter how low it was turned down, it still resulted in a noise level that was too high on the second floor. Further investigation, which involved working with the tavern owner, revealed the problem to be the location of the jukebox: heating ducts next to the wall by the jukebox functioned as a noise amplifier on their way to the second floor.

The officer made some suggestions to the owner about moving the jukebox and placing a rubber pad under it. The owner agreed. The next night, there was no noise complaint from that address, and none in the following months. The officer's problem-oriented investigation reduced hundreds of police calls to that address. And the solution was simple.

This is a small illustration of how one officer worked upstream and did some very basic problem-solving that reduced frustration for a citizen, a business owner, and his employees, and freed officers for other calls.[35]

As problem-oriented policing has evolved over the last two decades, it has emphasized evaluation of problems and the importance of solid analysis, development of pragmatic responses to the problem, and the need to strategically engage other resources such as members of the community and other city departments as well as local businesses and service organizations, as partners.

---

[35] Over the years, one's memory often blends. I at first thought this situation involved one of my officers in Madison. However, Herman Goldstein reminded me of a similar story from Philadelphia he noted in his book, *Problem-Oriented Policing*.

While many other new policing orientations have emerged over the years (such as values-based policing, intelligence-based policing, and COMPSTAT[36]), none has the potential of improving policing more than the problem-oriented approach. So why is it not standard operating procedure for our nation's police?

There are many reasons new ideas in policing don't thrive, not the least of which is the American political penchant for throwing out everything your predecessor did, effective or not. But I suggest that the failure of this method to become standard practice among our nation's police is the fact that it directly challenges the police organization itself by empowering rank-and-file police officers—not just command officers—to develop effective and successful responses to problems in collaboration with community members. It also challenges one of those four obstacles to improving policing – anti-intellectualism.

I say this because I don't believe the lower ranks of officers are the basis of the problem. Whenever I have watched rank-and-file police officers being introduced to the concept of problem-oriented policing (either by reading articles on the subject or visiting their website[37], attending the national conference on problem- oriented policing, or being specifically trained in it, they become excited and invigorated about their work. A national problem-oriented policing conference has been held annually since 1990.

During the conference, attendees who listen to

---

[36] COMPSTAT: Computer Statistics; a method developed at the NYPD to hold officers and commanders responsible for crime increases and quality of life issues in their precincts.
[37] www.popcenter.org

success stories told by other rank-and-file officers who practice the method come to believe in its effectiveness. When police officers come to see their work as solving problems, and criminal behavior as not the problem but simply part of it, they start to work more effectively to find causes, and work to prevent the problems from happening in the first place. But it appears that when these officers return to their departments, they often don't find open minds or understanding leaders willing to make the necessary organizational changes so that they can practice the method.

Nevertheless, something is happening in the police field with regard to this method, as the national Problem-Oriented Policing Center demonstrates. In spite of the failure of our nation's police to shift from responding to incidents to becoming more problem-oriented, officers around the country have continued to show tremendous interest in this method.

Since the publication in 2001 of the first problem-oriented policing guide, nearly *one million* copies of the guides and other publications offered by the center have been sent out to individual officers and police agencies. These materials are now widely used in police training and college courses. Two years later, the center launched its website which provides curriculum guides, teaching aids, problem analysis tools, innovative learning experiences, and an immense range of information. Today, the site receives an average of 1.5 million visits each month, offers more than 3,000 full text PDF files for download, and more than 2,000 files are downloaded daily.[38]

---

[38] http://popcenter.org and my conversations with Michael Scott, director of the Problem- Oriented Policing Center.

With all this interest and activity, one would think this method would begin to take hold and modify the traditional police response to incidents. But doing problem-oriented policing means that police officers, supervisors, and commanders have to change their ways. And change in policing isn't something that begins easily or is able to sustain itself without considerable long-term commitment and persistence.

Problem-oriented policing can thus help police to build that critical body of knowledge that will improve their effectiveness in most of the things they do, something vitally necessary for the future.

According to Goldstein, there are four major impediments to problem-oriented policing.

- *The absence of a long-term commitment on the part of police leaders.*
- *The lack of analytical skills within a police agency.*
- *The lack of a clear academic connection.*
- *The current police subculture.*[39]

So why has the problem-oriented method not become the standard method of policing? Goldstein goes on:

Improvements in policing... will not come about by simply increasing the numbers of police and by augmenting and modernizing the equipment they use. We need to invest proportionately and more heavily in thinking—in an organized, systematic, and sustained way—about what it is that the police are called on to do—and how they should do it.[40]

---

[39] *Ibid.* On Further Developing Problem-Oriented Policing: The Most Critical Need, The Major Impediments, and a Proposal. *Crime Prevention Studies*, vol. 15. 2003.
[40] Herman Goldstein: On Further Developing Problem-Oriented Policing: The Most Critical Need, the Major Impediments, and a Proposal in *Mainstreaming Problem-*

What he is saying is that these things have, so far, proved insurmountable: the commitment of police leadership, the failure to train the necessary skills for problem-solving (primarily analysis and evaluation), the lack of a formal relationship with academia, and the oppressive nature of the police culture. Fortunately, the problems he cites can be resolved through sustained leadership, training, and public education – subjects that will be addressed in the chapters that follow along with the seven steps necessary to improve our nation's police.

A vast body of research has demonstrated that the problem- oriented policing method works, that it is effective in managing and controlling a wide range of crime and disorder. This isn't a new method anymore—it has been around for three decades. Departments that have never attempted to implement it should; and departments that have tried to implement it should now do it again—and, this time, do it correctly – with leadership.

These are a few of the prominent historical legacies that have prevented our nation's police from improving. In some instances, it has been the political system in which they have had to work. In others, it has been the police themselves and their leaders. There is really nothing— other than a lack of will, discipline, and persistence—that prevents our nation's police from moving forward.

For too long, there has existed a more effective way of implanting community-oriented policing. It is now a major part of our history. Police have now, through practice and academic research, developed a

Oriented Policing, Crime Prevention Studies, Volume 15, edited by Johannes Knutsson, Criminal Justice Press, Monsey, New York, U.S.A. 2002.

92

significant and established body of knowledge about community-oriented policing. It won't supplant the critical emergency or tactical functions of police, such as responding to crimes in progress, accidents, and other civic needs.

Instead, it will broaden the number of effective strategies and responses police can use to effectively solve problems.

Problem-oriented policing changes the way police do their daily work—their work becomes more creative, effective, collaborative with community members, and, ultimately, personally and professionally rewarding. The problem is that this body of knowledge is essentially unknown to most of the police field. Now is the time to change that, to make that knowledge more accessible, to put it into practice and, thereby, get our nation's police off the circular merry-go-round and moving forward.

Chapter 3
Growing a Leader

EVEN AS A youngster, I was a defender of the underdog. I remember being emotionally impacted when, as a boy traveling in the South with my parents, I was confronted by two drinking fountains: one signed white and the other colored. I had to ask my father what they were. Why were there two drinking fountains? After my father told me, I wondered what kind of country was I living in; a land of free men and women?

By the time I got out of the Marines in 1960 and enrolled at the University of Minnesota it seemed as though everything was changing around me. I felt I was in a time of promise. Yet, it was also a time of chaos. There was a struggle for civil-rights, a youth revolution, and a war that soon became unbearable. All those contemporary forces affected me. I became more and more interested in policing and less interested in returning to the Marines. I had to, nevertheless, confront the historical legacy of the job I was doing, the rules I was enforcing.

Looking back over those turbulent decades of American history in which I carried a badge and a gun, I'm still amazed at everything that happened. They were times of uncertainty, yet tremendous opportunity. I felt I was in the center of these movements. I would feel at times more aligned with those who participated in them than the police with whom I worked.

Edina, Minn., was a very good place to start. In 1960, it was a very progressive police department. It had an excellent reputation in the Minneapolis-St.

Paul metropolitan area. It was a wealthy suburb and paid a good monthly salary for that time: $450. The department had a professional air to it, an educated chief—Wayne Bennett—and was academically tied to the programs and certification offered by the Northwestern Traffic Institute in Illinois. Nonetheless, I wasn't sent to any formal training before I went out on patrol. My recruit training consisted of riding with a sergeant for a week. The next day back at work, I was out on my own, keys to a squad car, street map, and ticket book in hand.

What I did carry away with me from my Edina experience was a good set of ethics—they instilled in me the deep belief that police were to obey the law while they enforced it and treat everyone with courtesy. This was to help me immensely two years later when I joined the police department in Minneapolis.

There had been a successful citywide referendum in nearby Minneapolis to increase the size of the police department by 100 officers. I was a member of the second class hired. In our ranks was Ray Presley, the second African-American police officer hired by the Minneapolis Police Department. All those who took the police examination who were veterans of World War II or the Korean War, and made a passing score of 70 or more, went to the top of the list. They had what was called absolute veteran's preference. My class came right behind them. Many of us were veterans, too, but we were too young for either World War II or the Korean War. We were not eligible for veteran's preference. Looking back, my class was a wave that turned into a tsunami.

We were quite different from the rest of the police hired that year. Our class had the highest scores on the civil service examination, we were

younger, and many of us had some college experience (although few of us had degrees). Of the 400 members of the department, fewer than five officers held a college degree. Only two came from a racial minority group, and women could serve only in the youth bureau or as jailers in the women's section— never as patrol officers. That was the environment in which I worked and began to think more profoundly about policing.

In Minneapolis, I did have a formal, four-week recruit school. The director was Deputy Inspector Ed Farrell, a college graduate. While a few of us attended classes at the nearby campus of the University of Minnesota, we never thought of staying on the police department after receiving our college degree. A college degree was considered a ticket out of the police department.

I continued to take classes at the university, but soon ran out of money. Paying tuition with a growing family at that time on a patrolman's salary was getting to be too much of a financial burden. At first, I have to admit I was more interested in being a tough street cop than one with a degree. If I did get my degree, I thought, I was going to join a federal law enforcement agency—certainly not remain on the street.

My original plan to return to the Marines soon faded away in the excitement of city police work. While I didn't see myself remaining as a patrol officer for my career. Police work had gotten into my blood.

Then President Lyndon Johnson's proposal for a Great Society changed all that. With the passage of the Omnibus Crime Control and Safe Streets Acts in 1968, grant monies became available for me and other front-line cops to attend college. Now, I could afford to finish my education and support my family.

After reading the report from President Johnson's commission,[41] taking classes at the university in sociology, crime and deviant behavior, and personally supporting our nation's civil-rights movement, I came to view the potential of my job in a new and very different way. It is safe to say that all these events coming together triggered an epiphany for me. It transformed my view of what police could be in our society, especially the critical role they could play in protecting the rights of citizens and ensuring justice.

Like everyone else, I saw the troubling behavior of Southern police each night on national television—how they fought to uphold local and state racial segregation laws and how they worked to demean and disfranchise black citizens, despite the fact that the highest court of our nation had clearly stated that separate wasn't equal and that everyone had a right to vote and be treated equally. I soon came to see that other police officers (especially those from my recruit class) were beginning to think the same way I did. We were different—a new breed. We didn't think like most of the other senior officers with whom we worked.

As one of this new breed of college cops, I worked nights on the tactical squad and went to school during the day. These were busy days of adrenaline-pumping night patrol, being challenged by new ideas in the classroom, learning new ways of thinking, and finding new friends. Many of those new friends were members of the Students for a Democratic Society (SDS) and active in campus antiwar groups. They were my classmates, and we had engaging conversations at lunchtime. From me, I think they gained a different perspective of the police.

---

[41] *President's Commission on Law Enforcement and the Administration of Justice.* Task Force Report: The Police. Washington: U.S. Government Printing Office. 1967.

From them, I came to understand the anger and frustration they were feeling about police and their role in repressing protest and the gap they perceived between what our nation said and what it was doing. Today, I sense a similar attitude from those who are participating in our nation's Occupy Movement.

All these experiences started to broaden my perspective and views about dissent, freedom, and the role of police. What we Americans said we were (and what we valued) seemed to be terribly out of sync with how we, the police, were conducting business.

While finishing my degree, I left the tactical squad to try out some ideas I had about foot patrol—especially a foot patrol on Plymouth Avenue on the north side of Minneapolis. Plymouth Avenue was an area of the city that was predominantly black and earlier was the location of the frequent civil rights disturbances that culminated in a night of arson that took place after Dr. Martin Luther King Jr. was slain in Memphis.

I was able to try out my ideas because of an unusual leader at the north side precinct, Captain Ken Moore. He was a stand-up guy and agreed to my request to walk a beat on Plymouth Avenue, which was in his precinct. To anyone's recollection, it was the first foot beat in an all-black area of the city. This neighborhood resented police, and only a year or so earlier had torched a number of white-owned businesses in the district.

This was a good place to try and put my new ideas about neighborhood policing into practice.

The central location on my beat was a newly established neighborhood center called The Way. When I started walking the beat on Plymouth

Avenue, I went around and introduced myself. That was my first encounter with community policing. I remember that I didn't want to wear my uniform hat because I wanted people on my beat to know who I was— that I wasn't a faceless member of an occupation force. I wanted them to know I wasn't going to act like other cops they had encountered. I wanted to be there to help and to work with this community. So I went about establishing relationships (like any good community organizer) and tried to listen, meet community needs and work to solve the problems in the neighborhood.

One day a sergeant drove by and saw me walking my beat. I wasn't wearing my hat. Now this sergeant wasn't well-liked by the community in which I worked. His attitude and conduct in the community left much to be desired. He stopped and ordered me to go back to the station, get my hat, and put it on. I respectfully told him I thought it was better that I not wear my hat while walking this beat. He asked why. I replied that I didn't want to wear my hat because I was afraid people in the neighborhood might not recognize me and accidentally shoot me, "They might think I was you." He glared at me and quietly drove away. He knew what I was talking about. He also knew that the captain needed me on this beat, and that I was the only one in the precinct who would volunteer to walk in this part of the city.

My experience on that foot beat, working intimately with people in the neighborhood, caused me to think about police-community relations in a real sense. I knew that without officers who forged good relationships with the people they served and who could gain their trust, the police could do little to solve neighborhood problems, control crime, or keep peace in those neighborhoods.

Walking my beat alone one day, I thought of a

book I had recently read for one of my classes. It was James Baldwin's, *Nobody Knows My Name*.[42] Baldwin gave a stunning account of being black in America.

There is a statement he makes about Harlem swinging-hipsters and the police; I remember it even to this day. According to Baldwin, the white police officers he knew had to walk in twos and threes in his neighborhood. They had to do so for safety reasons. They couldn't walk alone because, Baldwin said, the only thing police knew to swing in Harlem was a nightstick. I didn't want that to be me.

It was also during this time that I was formulating some ideas about the proper police response to protest. I was beginning to see that proximity mattered, being close was safe—just like on the beat. Get close, talk, and stay in contact. The further the police positioned themselves from people in the crowd, the greater the chance the crowd would depersonalize them; to see them as objects and not people. Therefore, getting closer to the people, whether in managing crowds or patrolling neighborhoods on foot, seemed to be a good basic strategy that needed to be experimented with.

When I was promoted to detective, I moved from my foot beat on Plymouth Avenue to the detective bureau. Knowing that I now was, in their terms, a college boy, my fellow detectives, all of them, my father's age, would ask me when I was planning to leave.

Evidently, there had been a number of situations in the past when men joined the police department, attended the university, got a degree, and then immediately left for a better job that paid more.

---

[42] James Baldwin. *Nobody Knows My Name.* New York: Dial Press. 1961.

Internally, no one expected a college boy to remain working in the police department. I informed my co-workers that I was never leaving. That I love police work. There was stunned silence. They looked at each other, and I knew what they were thinking—now, they had to compete with guys like me for promotions. They wanted me to take my degree and leave. All guys like me will do is to cause trouble for them, to try and change things. They were right.

After seven years with the Minneapolis department and with my baccalaureate degree in hand, I was awarded a graduate fellowship from the National Institute for Mental Health (NIMH). This grant would support me through a master's degree and on to a Ph.D. in sociology.

My professors wrote convincing letters of recommendation to the police department in support of me taking a leave of absence for academic studies. Unexpectedly, the department granted me a leave for a year, permitting me to devote full time to my studies, doing research, and writing my thesis.

Being a NIMH fellow at the university and working with other students in the program made another lasting impression on me. Even more so than before, I began to see police with a new understanding of their potential role in making America a fairer, and more equal society. Cops with degrees could make a difference.

During my years as an undergraduate and graduate student, I had the opportunity not only to work with and learn from some outstanding academics like David Ward and John Clark, but also world-renowned criminologists like Donald Cressey, Tom Murton, and Ula Bondeson from Sweden. I became the graduate student representative to the faculty committee. I had friends who were faculty

members—friends I introduced to my colleagues still working the streets of Minneapolis. I still had not left the police department. But then, that was before I met Patrick McInnis.

I soon had a chance to put my ideas into practice. I had written some commentaries in the *Minneapolis Tribune* about my thoughts concerning the pressing need for improved police-community relations with the black community. It caught the eye of the new city manager of Burnsville, Patrick McInnis. McInnis asked to meet with me. After lunch, and before he offered me the job, we discussed leadership, operational policy, training, and police use of force. I remember him writing my job offer on a napkin. It was about 40 percent more than I was making as a detective. I accepted.

McInnis was in his mid-30s, only a few years older than I was, smart, and a forward thinker. And Burnsville was a growing city. From that group of 100 new police officers hired in Minneapolis, I was the first to serve as a chief. Many others, in later years, however, would go on to head up police departments in other cities.[43]

Other things were happening in the Minneapolis-St. Paul metropolitan area as police officers started to get their college degrees. Change was in the air. The first wave of college cops, so evident in the civil service scores of the Minneapolis hiring process in 1962, was now being positioned to make a difference.

---

[43] Fellow Marine and tactical squad officer David Gorski joined me in Burnsville and then went on to serve as chief of police in Golden Valley, MN; at Harvard University in Cambridge, Mass; and finally in Appleton, Wisc. Jim Mossey, also a fellow tactical squad officer, served as chief of police in Crystal, Minn., a suburb of Minneapolis, for many years.

Burnsville gave me my first opportunity in 1969 to walk my talk; ideas that were formed by seven years as a street cop in the high-crime and multiracial areas of Minneapolis and five years as an undergraduate and graduate student. These experiences gave me the opportunity to study police work not only from the position of a practitioner, but also a sociologist. I was able to test both my experience and my education. I repeatedly asked myself, is this true to my experience, and, if not, why not?

If it isn't, do I have data to support this new learning which may be a major change in the way I have always done things?

Even in Burnsville, I was feeling the emotional effects of the civil rights and antiwar protests that I directly experienced in Minneapolis and when I was on campus. I knew I was in a time of major social upheaval and this was, perhaps, the only chance I would get.

The kind of police we needed were police with formal educations—they would be the most likely to be open to what I was trying to do; they would be the most flexible. A higher educational requirement seemed to be the first and finest step toward getting my department to where I wanted it. In Burnsville, police were to be highly-educated before they started to practice. With the support of McInnis and the city council, I established a four-year college degree requirement. Today, Burnsville still maintains the four-year degree entrance requirement we established in early1969. They are one of the few departments in the nation to do so.

Right away, any person could tell the police in Burnsville were different. We did away with

traditional military-style uniforms. Instead, we wore navy-blue blazers, French-blue trousers, and nametags declaring: Public Safety Officer. Our patrol vehicles were white with gold reflective tape along the sides. Our unique approach received national attention in *Newsweek* magazine that noted:

> *From Clancy Cop, circa 1890, to gray jumpsuits in Menlo Park and blue blazers in Burnsville: Policemen are becoming respectable, just like doctors, schoolteachers and the corner druggist.*

It was a sign of things to come. A preferred future, I thought, for police. In that same article, I was quoted:

> *If we change our dress and titles, maybe we'll get some changes in behavior from both the officers and the community.*

It turned out to be true. Burnsville officers immediately noticed a change in attitude from the people they contacted while wearing their blue blazers. The city was proud of their officers.

In Burnsville, I was able to draw many students and college graduates to our department. The students worked as community service officers (CSOs) while they were in school; they didn't carry a firearm or have the arrest power. Still, they were able to handle minor traffic accidents and other incidents. When CSOs received their four-year degrees, they were appointed as sworn officers. We were able to attract applicants from racial minority groups and from broad and diverse backgrounds—everyone I hired who carried a gun and had arrest power had a four-year college degree.

I was looking for applicants who had a broad liberal arts education. I wasn't especially looking for graduates in police science. One of my recruiting posters called college graduates to "Join the other

Peace Corps." I was looking for the same kind of educated, sensitive person who might also be attracted to join that organization.

We are looking for college graduates who want to make a significant contribution to our society by helping build a model of police professionalism… if you are one of our "new breed," the kind of man [sic] that can handle responsibility and authority, make important decisions, and (most important), the kind that likes people, we will accept your application as a public safety officer in our management training program.

These were heady days for those of us who considered ourselves to be a new breed of police. We were convinced that police in our generation, and in the generations to come, would be very different from the past; they would be educated, they would protect the rights of all people, and they would work smarter. I would use that recruiting theme again in Madison.

I thought about recruiting women into the department, but I couldn't convince McInnis that it was a good idea. At this same time, the final report of the 1967 President's Commission made it clear that they also didn't think women police were a good idea. The use of women as patrol officers was never mentioned in their report. As it was, uniformed women patrol officers would break the gender barrier a few years later.

One thing McInnis and I did agree upon with conviction was that our department must be racially inclusive. He and I were able to make that happen, even in mostly all-white Burnsville. The racial and gender integration of our nation's police may seem rather passé today, but I can tell you that this was a long and often agonizing goal to accomplish.

Sexism and racism were alive and well during those days, and the unsung heroes of this story are the women, minorities, and gays who stepped into policing and those in the department who stood up for them. Without this integration of our nation's police, the prospect of improving them would be far more difficult, if not impossible.

Burnsville turned out to be my first experimental police department. In 1971, I put into practice the idea of neighborhood-oriented police services. I called it the neighborhood safety officer program and divided the city into sections that were policed not by time of day, but by turf. An officer would be responsible for handling all incidents and providing more efficient person-to-person contact with the residents, business owners, and school principals in their district without regard to time of day– turf over time.[44]

A year later, I was a speaker at a seminar during a meeting of United States Conference of Mayors (USCM) in Kansas City. The topic? Changing police.

Looking back at the publication that came out of that meeting, I realized that I had already begun to identify the tension between fighting crime and serving people:

Cops are strange people. We are the dilemma of a free society. We are a dilemma because we should not be needed… But here we are… The issues are glaring and frightening—we struggle between the roles of crime fighter and social worker and we struggle with unionization, professionalization, civilianization, standards, career development, mobility, community relations, and delivery of people-oriented services, conflict management, and change.[45]

---

[44] Neighborhood Safety Program Inaugurated in Burnsville. *Dakota County Tribune*, July 8, 1971.
[45] "Neighborhood Safety Program Inaugurated in

While at Burnsville, I also tried to open up the minds of my fellow police chiefs. I was now a member of the Minnesota Chiefs of Police Association. In that capacity, I was asked to chair the program committee for their annual meeting in the Twin Cities. This was during the late 1960s, when problems between various protest and civil rights groups were heating up and coming to the forefront.

As in most major cities, police in our area were clashing with protesters almost on a daily basis. It was expected that antiwar activists at the University of Minnesota would soon call for a strike and shut down the university. When this happened at other universities, the state governor would activate the National Guard and send them in to restore order. Soon this occurred on the campus of my own university.

I convinced my committee of chiefs that we should offer a number of low-key listening opportunities for our colleagues so that they could hear what various community leaders were saying about the issues of the day.

The theme I suggested was "Let's talk to them now, rather than on the street." I contacted various community activists I had come to know over the years. They included leaders of the American Indian Movement, gay rights organizations, and campus antiwar groups. When I asked them to participate, every one of them agreed.

When the president of the chiefs' association found out about the training program my committee was offering, he wasn't happy. A few others were also upset. Why would you do something like this? This is crazy and will only lead to trouble. I calmly explained

Burnsville. *Dakota County Tribune*, July 8, 1971.

both my thinking and the fact that my committee had approved this program. I further told them that this was an opportunity. It would help chiefs do their jobs more effectively by understanding what is going on today. They remained unconvinced, "We hope you're right, Couper," they warned. "If not, you may have one of the shortest memberships on record in our organization."

This caused me some concern, and I started second-guessing myself. Would my colleagues boycott these discussion sessions? Would they not show up? Would they argue with the discussion leaders? Would some of them walk out? I hoped not.

As the start of the day's program drew near, I went around and checked the discussion rooms. As I glanced into the first room, I relaxed. Many of the chiefs had already arrived and had taken their seats. Some had even begun conversations with the presenters. Later on, as I moved from room to room, I saw that they were packed, the chiefs were attentive, and very good questions were being asked. The atmosphere was cordial and respectful. When the time came to rotate to another discussion room, the chiefs moved to other rooms and listened to another community activist.

It was probably the first time many of them had talked face-to-face with an antiwar activist, an American Indian leader, or a person who championed rights for gay, lesbian, bisexual, and transgendered people.

The chiefs came through for me, and it gave me hope for the future. I said to myself, yes, this was something police leaders need to do—to talk with people who don't share their views or opinions— even those who even oppose them and what they do. I was encouraged that my vision for police may one

day happen.

The most noteworthy part of this day was that the discussion took place in a respectful atmosphere, something that couldn't happen at the scene of a protest. It is too easy for police leaders to become isolated, to see the world as consisting of two groups: them and us. On that training day, many years ago, I learned that structured community dialogue could happen. It was one way to break down barriers between people. That lesson would also serve me well later.

While I enjoyed the opportunity I had to lead the Burnsville department, I longed for a bigger challenge—a larger, more urban police department to test my ideas about crowd control, conflict management, breaking down racial and gender barriers, and neighborhood policing. My first opportunity came when the chief of the University of Minnesota police department retired. I thought this was a job that was tailor-made for me. Many of my friends, faculty members, and fellow students at the university thought so too, and urged me to apply. It made sense. If I was interested in trying out my ideas on handling protest, the university was certainly the place to be.

What could be better? The university was my *alma mater*. I not only knew the campus, but the cities and culture that surrounded it. And at this time in our nation's history, since the first days of the free speech movement in Berkeley, Calif., colleges and universities were hotbeds of protest and conflict. What could be more challenging at this point in my career? At the time, I had just completed my master's degree in sociology.

I was also working for the university on a part-time basis; counseling students interested in a police

career and helping establish the newly created Criminal Justice Studies Department with my former graduate professor and friend, David A. Ward. The establishment of a criminal justice studies department on campus wasn't without its opponents. At one time, we had a sit-in protest in our office by the SDS, who were actively opposing the department's presence on campus. I saw some familiar faces among the protesters.

It was during my oral interview for the university police chief's position that I first met Frank Remington, who had also chaired the ABA project on standards relating to the urban police function. Remington was a member of the student-faculty committee appointed to select a new chief and make its recommendation to the president of the university, Malcolm Moos. Remington was serving as a visiting professor at the time, but his academic home was the law school of the University of Wisconsin in Madison.

After interviews and various background investigations were conducted, my name was forwarded to the president as the committee's choice. In the meantime, I met with the university director of personnel concerning salary, benefits, and a starting date. Everything seemed to be going well. I was told President Moos would call me for a meeting and announce my appointment. I went back to Burnsville and waited.

As often happens, information concerning a pending appointment was released to the campus newspaper and then to Twin Cities media.

Within a day or two, my photo was in the campus and city newspapers indicating I was to be the new campus police chief. Soon after, I received a hard lesson in politics.

An old adversary from my days in Minneapolis had left his position as detective on the police department, run for the office of mayor in Minneapolis, and gotten elected. Detective Chuck Stenvig had headed the city's police union for years. He and I had frequently clashed over issues like the necessity for police higher education and relations with the black community. One of the things Stenvig vehemently disagreed with was my forming a local chapter of the national law enforcement fraternity, Lambda Alpha Epsilon, which intensely supported higher education and professionalization of police. To him, it was another union. To me, it was a national academic fraternity. Soon, the fraternity had members from all over the metropolitan area, not just from Minneapolis police. We not only championed higher education for police, but also sincere relations with the citizens—particularly those in the minority community.

As president of the fraternity, I had written an op-ed article that appeared in the *Minneapolis Tribune*. It addressed the need for police change in a number of areas. I also had an article in the publication of the International Association of Chiefs of Police concerning new ways to police our college campuses. Basically, Stenvig was opposed to any reform of police. As union head, his position was that the police were doing just fine—leave us alone.

Now, as mayor of the city, Stenvig used his new political muscle to go after me with a vengeance. When he found out about my candidacy at the university, he immediately contacted the media and told them that if I was appointed police chief at the university they would get no help from the Minneapolis police in the event of trouble on campus; meaning that in the event the university needed help, he, as mayor, would prohibit them from coming on campus. Other universities around the

country were experiencing strikes and most everyone assumed there would soon be one at the University of Minnesota.

While the possibility of a strike was real, Stenvig's threat wasn't. I knew it was a bluff because all metropolitan area police departments, including the university department, had signed mutual aid contracts to help one another in the event of an emergency such as a student strike.

Stenvig really couldn't pull off what he threated to do. But his bluff grabbed the headlines that week. It also grabbed the attention of Malcolm Moos, who now was reconsidering the recommendation of his student-faculty committee.

When the students heard Stenvig's threat, they were elated. What better endorsement of me than this? By all means, they said, keep the Minneapolis police off campus. At the time, there was increasing tension and some clashes between the Minneapolis police and university students over the war and racism in areas surrounding the campus.

I didn't think Stenvig's threat would sway Moos. Through all this, the university personnel director advised me to sit tight. I would receive the call from Moos. I never did. [46]

---

[46] Charles Stenvig went on to be elected to a second mayoral term in 1971. He began with little political experience beyond police union politics or party affiliation. He lost a third bid for office in 1973, came back to win again in 1975, then lost again in 1979. For a decade, Stenvig used public concern about crime and social unrest as a major part of his candidacy. He retired to Arizona and died in January 2010.
http://www.startribune.com/local/85040487.html.

During this waiting time, I came under pressure from McInnis. He said I should make up my mind as to what I was going to do—now. I had talked with him before I applied and had thought I had his support, but now I felt the situation had dramatically shifted.

I was sensing my position at Burnsville might be in jeopardy if I continued in the university process. I worked solely at McInnis' pleasure. So, with a large family (now consisting of six children), I withdrew my name from consideration. I got back to work in Burnsville until I received a call two years later from Madison. It was in early 1972.

The call was from Frank Remington. As I mentioned earlier, I had met him when I interviewed with the campus committee he chaired to select the university police chief. Remington had returned to the University of Wisconsin and told me that the city of Madison was about to begin the process of hiring a new chief of police. Would I be interested in applying? I said yes.

When I told McInnis I was going to apply for the chief's job in Madison he was not happy. In fact, he told me I had better get that job. This put some stress into my life and I now resolved that I had better put all my efforts into Madison.

When I looked into Madison, I found a report on the department that the city had commissioned a few years earlier. It was a general analysis of structure and rules of the department. Things looked okay, but the report didn't look deep into the organization. Nor did it mention any of its problems. Little did I know there was deep trouble brewing inside the department. Trouble that had been brewing for some time. I didn't know at the time that I was going to be the one to have to deal with it.

Chapter 4
The Madison Story

BEFORE I LEFT Burnsville, McInnis finally gave me his blessing. I remember him telling me that I was going to "have my hands full" there. He was right.

It wasn't long afterward that I had a chance to observe what I might be getting into. In the late spring of 1972, I flew to Madison from Minneapolis for my first interview with the Board of Police and Fire Commissioners (PFC). According to Wisconsin state law, commission members are appointed for five-year terms by mayors in cities over 5,000 in population. They serve as the hiring authority for the police and fire departments in those cities. Also according to state law, chiefs in these cities have tenure and cannot be removed except for cause. A tenured police chief was an unusual finding in an American city. At the time, I didn't think much of it. Whoever thinks he won't be successful? Not me. Later, tenure, for me, would make all the difference in the world.

It was an early Friday evening when I arrived. I was staying at a hotel just off State Street, the main avenue between the university and the Capitol. My interview was to be the following morning. It was a warm night and before I settled in for the evening, I walked along State Street to see the sights and have a beer. The sidewalks were packed with students and other young people; it reminded me of my trip to the Berkeley campus a few years earlier when I was sent there by my chief in Minneapolis to observe and take notes on crowd control tactics we could use. I noticed a very familiar sight—two students sitting on

the sidewalk with their backs against a building conversing. It was a wide sidewalk, and there was plenty of room for others to pass by. Two large Madison police officers walking down the sidewalk stopped and looked at the two college-age people.

"Get off the sidewalk!" one of them barked. The two jumped up and quickly retreated without a word.

Interesting, I thought. What if they had refused? What if instead, they had said, "But officer, we are simply sitting here, talking, not bothering anyone, and not blocking the sidewalk. We don't think what we are doing is illegal." What would the officers have done? I think I knew. If the students had challenged their authority, someone would have gone to jail or worse.

From my first observation of Madison police in action, I started to think about what I might be getting into. When I reviewed department reports and documents the PFC sent me, the department appeared traditional, but well organized. While it may have had problems controlling its use of force in handling student protests, the department apparently had a clean record with regard to corruption. The recent evaluation of the department a year or two earlier by the Public Administration Service, a nonprofit organization in Chicago, gave the department good marks. But what I witnessed that first night in Madison left me somewhat uneasy.

When the biographies of the top candidates were printed in the newspaper, I certainly appeared different from the others who had applied. I was the youngest and had less police and supervisory experience. But what I did have was more education, a national and worldview of policing, and some new ideas about managing conflict and working closely

with the community. They were the cards I was going to play during my interviews. In any other city, these kinds of credentials could be the kiss of death. But in Madison, they became assets.

What I saw on the street my first night in Madison was more consistent with the department's practices with the community than not. I later found out that, over the years, the department had lost the trust and confidence of a good portion of the community because of the rough tactics they used in handling public demonstrations and protests and the way they related to young people. There was also low-level racism in the city, and it was most obvious in the face of the police department. At the time I applied, the police department had only one black officer in its ranks, and persons of color were virtually absent among those employed by the city or county governments. Geographically, there appeared to be some racial segregation.

Quite often in the past, the department had overreacted when trying to control protests. The first major incident was the response of the department to the Oct. 18, 1967 demonstration against Dow Chemical Company. On that day, Dow was recruiting on the campus of the University of Wisconsin. This was at the height of the Vietnam War. Dow was the primary manufacturer of napalm, a jellied gasoline our forces used in Vietnam. Although it wasn't designed to be an antipersonnel weapon, it often was used that way. And when it was, it inflicted horrendous burns on whoever was in the general vicinity—enemy soldiers or civilians.

After I was appointed chief, I was able to bring out and review the television coverage of what happened that day. It was brutal for me to witness. It magnified the department's lack of preparation, planning, training, options regarding the use of force,

and leadership. It seemed so obvious to me that we, the police, had to change our tactics in response to situations like this. Unfortunately, I later found out that not everyone in the police department agreed with my thoughts on how the department handled Dow. While the incident had happened five years ago, for many officers on the department it was more like yesterday.

At this time in history, there wasn't only a war in Southeast Asia, but also a growing, sometimes violent public reaction against racial segregation and racism in our society. I wasn't shy in articulating to the police commission how I believed the police needed to improve in both areas. I said that if I were appointed chief, I would work to make a good police department better and bring racial minorities and women into the department. I saw my role in Madison as not only a change agent committed to justice but also that of a peacekeeper—I would work to bring peace to the city.

While some in the community and in the department considered me to be soft on policing— that is, being more liberal than conservative in my worldviews—there was also a hard side to me: tactical squad officer, martial arts and firearms expert, commendations for bravery and meritorious service. I had also authored a training manual on crowd control and trained others in its methods. This permitted me to, as Teddy Roosevelt had suggested, speak softly while carrying a big stick.

Through my conversations with Tom Stephens, president of the PFC, I felt I had his support. He agreed with what I was maintaining needed to be done with the department. Later, I came to understand Stephens was very much in tune with what citizens in Madison wanted. He knew Madison residents were tired of the continuing conflict and

animosity between students and police. Earlier public hearings the commission had held made that clear to him. But the current mayor, William Dyke, as well as most of the command staff of the police department, was still in battle mode.[47] Madison, after almost five years of continuous conflict, wanted peace, but didn't know how to disengage. I presented a way out.

The police commission was a diverse group of citizens. Stephens was the director of transportation for Oscar Mayer Foods, a local, nationally-known meatpacking business that had a long-term economic and historical relationship with the community. Other members of the five- person commission were Stuart Becker and Andy Somers, both attorneys; Lois Liddicoat, an insurance salesperson, and Ellsworth Swenson, a man with an organized-labor background. This was the traditional composition of the commission: lawyer, business owner, woman, and labor representative. For the most part, this balance, with the later addition of a minority representative, continued throughout my years in Madison.

The three final candidates for the chief's job were Herman Thomas, the acting chief of the department (William Emery had retired after 15 years

---

[47] On the day of my swearing-in, the evening newspaper reported: "Absent from the swearing-in-ceremony was Mayor William Dyke, who according to reliable sources was furious over the choice of Couper. Dyke, who wanted the commission to name his assistant, Robert Heck, tried unsuccessfully to downgrade Couper, apparently because he feels the young chief is too liberal. What particularly angers the mayor is that four out of the five commissioners are his own appointees… Dyke, in his vehement opposition to Couper, appeared to be in a very small minority in the city." (*The Capital Times* newspaper, December 20, 1972.) Dyke was beaten by Alderman Paul Soglin four months later in the spring election. He currently serves as a county judge in Iowa County, just west of Madison.

as chief because of medical problems). Many people in Madison were of the opinion that the antiwar years, the infamous bombing of Sterling Hall, and continuing street battles with the students had severely impacted his health); Assistant Chief Edward Daley; and William Heck, a former out-of-state police officer who was now an aide to Mayor Dyke.

Stephens later confided to me that on the first round of voting, I had only one vote—his. Later, during a second round of voting, I found out I'd received Stuart Becker's vote. The three remaining votes were distributed among Thomas, Daley, and Heck. None of the candidates had the three votes necessary to be appointed. Stephens and Becker then played a waiting game. I was the only candidate with two votes; the others only had one. Stephens and Becker needed one more commissioner to come on board with them for the third, winning vote.

During the waiting game, the wild card in the selection process came to be held by the police union, the Madison Professional Police Officers Association (MPPOA). When I learned about this, I remembered my losing battle with Stenvig back in Minneapolis. Were my disagreements with him again going to thwart my goal to lead a larger police department? Was a police union again going to be able to keep me out?

A very bright and charismatic detective headed the police union by the name of Roth "Buzz" Watson. He made it publicly clear that the MPPOA was dead set against Herman Thomas becoming chief. Thomas was known for his hard-handed, uncompromising management style, both inside and outside the department. The union wanted no more of that. But the union also was unsure of mayoral aide Bob Heck, in spite of their close relationship with Dyke. Heck's police experience seemed to be

limited to that of being a police dog handler for a state highway patrol on the East Coast.

I wasn't privy to the discussions between Watson and commission members, but gradually, the police union began to consider me as a possibility. Perhaps with me, they would have a chance at a new start; someone from outside the department and not aligned with anyone.

I learned later that Lois Liddicoat approached Stephens with the MPPOA proposal. She would be willing to support me under two conditions: that Watson would get a private meeting with me before I met anyone else in the department, and second, that I would be hired on a six- month probationary basis. When these two requests were first forwarded to me, I thought they were unusual, but reasonable. They didn't, at the time, appear to be harmful—or so I thought.

I'm speculating here, but I think the union thought having first contact with me would be in their best interest, that I would be more open to working with them than the other two candidates would be—especially if Watson could claim to have control of the swing vote during my probationary period. If all this was true, Watson had the potential power to get me to do what he wanted or see me go.

I agreed to the conditions the commission presented, and they publicly announced my appointment on Dec. 20, 1972. The vote was 3–2. As often happens in these matters, there wasn't a coming-together vote, a second, unanimous vote for purposes of solidarity. At the time this occurred, I had a lot of self-confidence and, quite frankly, the fact that I had two votes against me on the commission didn't faze me. I would get to work and win the opposition over just like I had done in

Burnsville. They were cops and so was I—cops stick together. I thought this would be the situation in Madison. I was dead wrong.

I never thought any of my officers would actively oppose me to the lengths they did. Moreover, I never imagined a situation in which a group of police officers would turn against their chief. I knew there were regulations against that. And wasn't that like mutiny? But this was Madison. And in Madison, some people were about to play hardball with me. I was to learn another hard lesson or two in politics.

Within a few weeks after taking over the department, I went about the task of interviewing all the department leaders. It was an eye-opening experience. While the top leaders of the department were bright and above-average in intelligence, most all had a very narrow view of the police function and very few of them could articulate what needed to be done to reduce the acrimony between the police department and the student and racial minority communities. Most of them clearly defended the past and simply couldn't see doing anything different than they had. But I knew the department had to change if we were going to be able to keep peace in the city. I also came to see that peacekeeping was as needed inside the department as much as it was in the community.

This was the time in America that has since been described as the "War at Home." The apogee of this war in Madison was the bombing of Sterling Hall, the home of the Army Math Research Center, on the nearby campus of the University of Wisconsin. The bombing happened two years before I arrived. The bombing resulted in the accidental death of Robert Fassnacht, a researcher who was unfortunately working late that night. The bombers, directed by a local activist by the name of Karleton

Armstrong, thought the building was empty. The bombing and Fassnacht's death was a shock to the city and to its image.

Since the late 1960s, the Madison department had been responding to student protests on campus and in the city. I sensed distinct feelings of both resentment and revenge among a significant number of officers who were assigned to police these events. At the same time, among the more junior officers, there was a growing discomfort concerning the way they were ordered to respond. Thankfully, one of my three top assistants, Ed Daley, was one who did question the department's protest strategies. Daley was a breath of fresh air. Without his support and the support of a core of other forward-thinking officers like Sergeants Jim Scrivner and Tom Hischke, Detective Jack Heibel, and Policewoman Morlynn Frankey, I might not have survived long enough to make the necessary changes that I did. During my watch, all of them rose to the rank of captain or higher.

I did a lot of work inside and outside the department during those first months. Apparently, Mayor Dyke had a problem with me. He didn't appear at my swearing-in ceremony and then avoided meeting with me. Stuart Becker, commission member and friend of the mayor, unsuccessfully tried to arrange a *rapprochement* between us. At the last minute, the mayor would always cancel.

Another problem was Herman Thomas, who was acting chief until my appointment. Now he became my second-in-command—a civil service position; he didn't serve at my pleasure. During the selection process I was promised that Thomas would retire as soon as I came aboard. He didn't.

And it was quite obvious he wasn't going to. He

wasn't supportive and wouldn't tell me when he was going to retire.

Regardless of Thomas, I continued on, talking to both department and community members about the future of the department. I confidently believed both Dyke and Thomas would come around. The mayor faced re- election in only a few months, and I figured Thomas would eventually support me. Isn't that what subordinates are supposed to do?

Soon, things began to heat up. Early one afternoon, Liddicoat asked to meet with me. She awkwardly requested that the two of us have a meeting alone with no staff members present. When she came into my office, she quickly came to the point. She asked me to promote Detective Roth Watson to the rank of captain, a position I was in the process of filling. It also was a position that needed approval from her and other commission members. I quickly understood where she was going with this. I listened to her request and told her why I thought it wasn't a good idea.

She left my office disappointed. I would soon learn how disappointed she was.

When I brought my first promotional requests to the commission a few days later for their approval, they were rejected—I couldn't get the three votes I needed. Stephens and Becker voted for my recommendations but Liddicoat didn't. She had jumped ship and joined Somers and Swenson. I no longer had the support of the majority of the commission.

When Liddicoat cast her vote against my promotions, I knew there was going to be a new game in town. The promotions' rejection was front-page news in the *Wisconsin State Journal*, the city's

morning paper, and local radio stations, pro and con, reported on the conflict throughout the day.

Still, I was able to advance after I found I had the authority to make acting promotions in the interim, so that I could carry on the work of the department. But only the commission could make a promotion permanent. I then withdrew my recommendations and offered to work with commission members to clear up any misunderstandings or concerns they might have regarding my choices and the process I used.

My appointees now had to serve in an acting capacity until I could work this through. Still, this was an unusual event—no one could ever remember the last time a police commission had rejected a chief's promotions. It was the casting of the first stone, one of many to be hurled during the next two years.

Dyke, who had yet to warm up to me, ran for re-election in April. I had thought he might lose because I knew what had happened in the county elections five months earlier. At that time, Dane County voters (including voters from Madison) had swept most of the conservatives off the county board and elected liberals to leading positions in the county: county executive, district attorney, and sheriff. The first winds of change had already blown through Madison. Everyone was waiting for the spring election in the city for the second wind of change to blow.

During Dyke's campaign speeches, he often made fun of me by making light of my use of the term "conflict management" to describe the way we were now going to approach protest in the city. He made every effort to challenge me, undermine me, and underplay my authority within the department. Looking for continued support from officers in the

department, he had continued to refuse to meet with me, and everyone in town knew it. It was a tense four months.

Soon, Ald. Paul Soglin, a university student representing the campus district, announced he was running for mayor—and appeared to be holding his own against Dyke. Now, being aware of the shifting preference of Madison voters and my popularity with the media, Dyke became less hostile.

As election day drew closer, it looked like Dyke was going to be beaten, and I could feel the tension within the police department. Most of the officers were formidable Dyke supporters, and hardly anyone within the department voiced support for Soglin. They knew him from his earlier days on campus. He was a rebel, a student activist. He had the additional credentials in the student district he represented of being arrested and jailed by Madison police during a campus demonstration. His long hair had been shaved while he was in custody—one more way to demean those who were causing trouble for the police. It had to be done, the former sheriff said, for "health" reasons.

Soglin was overwhelmingly elected mayor. Understandably, he didn't hold positive feelings about police. But because I was younger, had some interesting ideas about policing the city, and wasn't from the department, he was more than willing to work with me. We first met the day after his election. I had wisely stayed out of the mayor's race. Of course, I wanted to see Dyke ousted. I had my preference and felt empowered on the morning of election day when I cast my vote for Soglin.

I had remained apolitical since I arrived, and I worked to maintain that position throughout my years in Madison. Instead, I worked on the issues—

community relations, peacekeeping, and conflict management.

And I worked with the local media to gain support for my ideas in the community. The majority of the members of the media were in agreement with me that the police department needed to change. And it was evident, overall, in most of their reporting.

Looking back, I used the same tactics I used in dealing with hostility: move closer, closer is safer. While it may appear paradoxical, getting close to a crowd *is* safer. In close proximity to others, officers are not depersonalized. It is when they stand back or hide behind shields and face masks that their job becomes dangerous. So when I came under fire in Madison, I stepped up my public contacts and appearances—closer is safer. I sought out interviews, called press conferences, and offered to give talks to community groups about my vision and plans for the department. As I moved out into the community, I felt much more comfortable. I felt the community supported the direction I was taking the department.

A young, liberal police chief was one thing in Madison, but when Paul Soglin was elected mayor, there was a firestorm from conservatives in town. These folks, including many officers on the police department, were outraged by his election. Now, there wasn't only open disagreement with me, but also with our new mayor. After Soglin's election, Chicken Little would have had a great time in Madison crying out, "The sky is falling, the sky is falling!" The winds of change had now blown through Madison as it had through the county five months earlier.

The war inside the police department now began in earnest. Those who opposed me knew they could muster three votes from the commission to

oppose my policies or even get rid of me in a few months. Very soon, a petition was circulated by some officers who asked those in the department who didn't agree with me or my policies to sign on and indicate their displeasure. One hundred and fifty-three officers did—slightly less than a majority. The petition was forwarded to the PFC in August, 1973.

The internal and external opposition forces were now joining together. Each and every change in the police department was now described as my criticism of the department. While the opposition couldn't get rid of Soglin until the end of his two-year term, they could get rid of me—the six-month probationary clause that I'd thought unimportant now became their target.

I survived the probationary period, but the war continued for the next three years. There were investigations, hearings, depositions, trials, orders, and restraining orders as forces within the department, aided by conservatives in the community, came together in an attempt to oust me.

The atmosphere within the department was often cold and brittle. I'll never forget two early and significant department staff meetings. At the first meeting with my new staff, Thomas, my second in command, turned to me and said in a loud voice, "Chief, your mustache does not conform to our grooming code."

I couldn't believe what I had just heard. Was he joking? No, he wasn't. He never joked. Silence filled the room. All eyes turned on me. What was I going to do? "Well," I remember slowly and carefully replying, "Thanks for bringing this to my attention. I guess we will just have to change the grooming code, won't we?" And it was done.

I had the grooming code relaxed to permit officers and employees of the police department to look more like the rest of the community in hairstyle, length, and also the wearing of moustaches. My thinking was that if the department was going to become part of the community, it should start *looking* like the community. My mustache stayed.

A second challenge soon followed. This time the stakes were much higher than hair length and moustaches. It was during a joint meeting of my staff with command members of the sheriff's and university police departments. We had come together to plan a response to a large upcoming march and protest. My department was the lead agency, and as I started the discussion, Thomas interrupted and again asked me another pointed question: "Chief, we want you to know that we have fought long and hard to enforce our policy that the students must walk on sidewalks and not in the street during these protests. I hope you are not going to change that policy." Again, all eyes on me. Silence in the room. Now, for the second time in as many weeks, Thomas had openly and publicly challenged me.

But I began to see that these challenges could be turned into teaching moments. I again carefully replied, "Gentlemen, I know you have had a struggle over the past years with students, with protests, and many of you have suffered injuries. I know it has not been easy. But I want you to know that I tend to look at these things differently. I don't think our job is to keep the students out of the street. Instead, I think our job is to see that they have a safe environment in which they can exercise their rights to free speech, assembly, and petition. I don't want to fight over the street. It's not that significant. But what is significant is that we help them exercise their rights without anyone being hurt or property being damaged. We will no longer fight to keep protesters on the

sidewalk."

I sensed a feeling of relief from many in the room, especially from University of Wisconsin Police Chief Ralph Hanson and our new sheriff, Bill Ferris. Hanson, with many others from the university administration, had struggled with the harsh and often combative street policies of the Madison Police Department. And Ferris—a young liberal, basically inexperienced, and newly elected—also seemed relieved. Many of the officers sitting around the table that morning knew that the policy of keeping marching protesters out of the street wasn't only dangerous but foolish. I even sensed some support from my own staff—but not from Thomas. I now knew he was dangerous and that I needed to keep him off the street and away from protesters.

So, that became our street policy and practice for over 20 years: people matter more than property, and civil rights have precedence over local traffic laws. From that day forward and into the years I was chief of police, Madison never suffered property damage or had any of its police officers injured during a protest, on or off campus.

It didn't take me long to know what needed to be done; by listening to community and department members, I knew what I had to do. What I didn't know then was how long it would take. Over the years, I have questioned whether the size of a police department is a barrier to its improvement. I think it is. Police departments with more than 500 officers are difficult, if not impossible, to initiate lasting change. Their size, span of control, and internal culture simply prohibit any lasting improvements from being made.

The Madison department had fewer than 500 employees. It had an intelligent and well-trained

workforce and no history of internal corruption. Or so I thought until I stumbled upon a very dirty little operation in Madison—the undercover work of Herman Thomas' Affinity Squad and its secret files. And when I set out to tackle this problem, it helped me tackle another big one: the man who created the squad, kept its files, and was now trying to oust me – Assistant Chief Herman Thomas.

The problem identified to me by many members of the community was the secret reports the squad was generating. I doubt if the prior chief, Bill Emery, knew the range of its activities. Thomas had organized a focused intelligence-gathering effort staffed by police officers who dressed as hippies, students, or street people to infiltrate and gather information in the student community regarding campus protests.

Their ability to infiltrate came from their long hair. Cops didn't wear long hair—remember the department policy on hair length?—but long hair could gain them acceptance from those in the student community. But I soon found out there was a much darker side to the Affinity Squad than this almost comical description.

Officers assigned to the unit would join campus groups and submit reports based on who was there and what was said. These undercover officers attended as many community and student activities as they saw fit and reported their activities directly to Thomas. To keep the identity of those officers secret, even from other members of the department, many of the officers after being hired immediately went undercover, without formal training. Their names were even kept out of city and department personnel records. Some of them were students willing to inform on other students.

When I first heard about the squad and how it worked it reminded me of what I saw earlier in Berkeley. I witnessed how police had used undercover officers to make arrests on campus. I saw how much animosity it created with the students. I vowed then that I wouldn't use this kind tactic if I ever was a chief.

I terminated the program and these undercover officers came in from the cold, attended the police academy, and became regular police officers. I, of course, was wary about them, especially the negative impact this early experience might have had on their attitude about policing. I worried that the department had created a group of officers who though their role in society was to spy on people, rather than to serve and work with them. When these officers finally came back from undercover duty and became uniformed officers in the ranks of the police department, many seemed to have considered Thomas to be their leader and not me. Very few of them were supporters of what I was trying to do and the changes I was bringing to the department.

The actual work of this undercover effort, the reports they produced, contained more gossip than fact. Years later, I had to publicly disclose the contents of those files under the Wisconsin open records law after a number of community activists had filed a request. In order not to damage the reputations of those on whom the squad reported, I went to great length to see that names were edited out of these files prior to release. And on the long-anticipated day the media was waiting for, those edited files actually turned out to produce more of a whimper than a bang except for one thing. Someone on the editing team had overlooked one of the informant's names in the report, a woman who lived in the student community and provided information on people she knew to the police. Her name was not

blacked out in a report that was released. This resulted in the city having to pay a large cash settlement in 1980. I'll always wonder if the failure to edit her name was accidental or not.

One report in the files documented an encounter between uniformed and undercover police officers. After a street demonstration in which undercover officers had infiltrated the crowd, unknown to uniformed officers, the undercover officers were standing on a sidewalk near the campus when police assigned to the protest approached them.

Even though the protest was over, they were set upon and beaten by uniformed officers. There was a code word the undercover officers were to use. They told me they had shouted the word, but none of the uniformed officers said they heard it.

The interesting thing is that none of the undercover officers had done anything illegal—they were just hanging out in the area and they all received a sound beating. Two of those young undercover officers who got a beating that day later became outstanding command officers. They, of all people, personally knew things needed to change.

But there was a much darker and evil side to the Affinity Squad. It wasn't very long after my appointment that I heard from community members that they strongly believed the department had dossiers that contained negative and personal information on members of the community, including elected officials. This, of course, was a serious charge and not unlike charges that have been made about the FBI during the tenure of Director J. Edgar Hoover. It was alleged that Hoover used his secret files to keep members of Congress in line and supporting him.

When I would ask Thomas about this, he told me that the documents in his files were not about individuals but about illegal assemblies. He maintained there were no dossiers, no personal files on individuals. Still, the rumors abounded that personal information had been illegally gathered and used to force support from local politicians regarding police department matters—essentially to blackmail them into supporting the police department. This was a very serious allegation. But at the time, no one seemed to have any specific evidence. I would soon find out Thomas was lying. He was in a bind. If he told me the truth, he and his intelligence officers would have been subject to not only internal discipline but also the possibility of criminal charges.

Early one Saturday morning, I had read in the newspaper there   was going to be a campus march into and through the city. It was a celebration of an international event called China Day. I went to the planning meeting, and some students asked who I was. I told them I was the new chief of police. I don't think any of them believed me because they ignored me and went on talking about the demonstration. Their leaders even announced that they were going to try to take the street in opposition to   city rules and that some of them might be arrested. When the march began, I gravitated to the front. I wanted to see what was going to happen.

The demonstration went well until we approached the corner of Park Street and University Avenue. At that location, Madison officers from the day shift had assembled and formed a barrier to prevent the students from moving forward into the street. The tension was high as I walked up to the officers, identified myself, and asked them to let us pass. I asked them to help us get to the South Student Union a half-mile down the street. The officers stepped aside and the rest of the march was

uneventful, and the demonstration ended when we arrived at our destination.

My first protest demonstration in Madison had ended without incident. After the demonstration, reporters contacted me and asked what had happened. Why hadn't I stopped the students, as the department had always tried to do in the past? Why weren't they kept out of the street?

It was again a teachable moment of the type I would frequently take advantage of during my career. I told the reporters I believed it was the job of police in a democracy such as ours to protect demonstrators and, if necessary, to facilitate their right to protest as guaranteed in our Constitution. Rather than to block or suppress these events, the role of the police is to assist and protect. What I said made headlines in the *Wisconsin State Journal.* Not everyone in the city was pleased with what they read.

I later found out that I wasn't the only police officer at that student meeting. An undercover officer, unknown to me, was present. I was about to be the subject of an intelligence report submitted to Thomas. What concerned me most was what the officer reported about the nature and atmosphere of the meeting. At best, he didn't know what was going on. In the worst case, he submitted a false report.

At work on Monday, Thomas informed me he had received a report that said I was in physical danger during that meeting. It was from that undercover officer. Thomas went on to say that there were people there who were planning on physically harming me and that I shouldn't be out there in the community like that. This was strange, but even stranger because I was personally present and it was in direct contradiction to what I experienced at the meeting. The students present at the meeting were

cordial, friendly, and respectful, and I was never at any time in any danger.

I reminded Thomas that I had been a street cop for many years, and knew danger and what that felt like. I told Thomas he needed to evaluate the intelligence he was receiving, because it wasn't correct. In fact, I said, what was written in that report was false. I also reminded him that while I was the new kid in town, I wasn't stupid—and that group had not been dangerous to me or anyone else. What I didn't tell him was that he was the one I felt was most dangerous—not those students.

What was Thomas trying to do? Control me? Keep me in my office and off the street? Yes, I concluded, that's what he was trying to do. Just like he had done to Mayor Dyke. If I stayed in my office, I could be watched, isolated, and controlled.

I later learned that the police department, under Thomas, had, in fact, used these same kinds of tactics on Dyke. During those intense years of street protest, a police officer would be periodically sent out to check the undercarriage of the mayor's car for a bomb. This would, of course, cause the mayor to be more worried and dependent upon the police department and Thomas for his safety. Wouldn't this cause the mayor to begin to fear the community? Maybe to stay out of the community? To see the police as the only ones he could trust?

If a police leader or mayor is kept in fear and encouraged to stay in his or her office, then the police department can, perhaps, be free to do whatever it wants without supervision. But Thomas's scare tactics were not going to work with me.

All this intrigue came to a head a few months later just before the spring election. I had heard still

another rumor about the dossiers. Even though I had
served as chief only a few months, if it was to come
out that the department was gathering dossiers on
citizens, it could be a mark against my leadership.
That night, I ordered one of my assistants to enter
Thomas's office with a master key and check whether
or not those files kept in his office contained dossiers
on individuals or not. He reported to me later that
night that there were dossiers, about people by name,
containing information about non-criminal matters—
matters that essentially could be used for blackmail,
just as had been alleged.

I specifically remember him telling me the
contents of one file. It involved a prominent member
of the city council. It contained damaging
information about the alderman's daughter.
According to the file, she was working as a prostitute
in a city in California. This kind of information,
should the police threaten to release it, could become
an instrument of political bullying. Its release, during
those days, could significantly damage or end the
career of a local politician. Worse yet, it could be used
to influence voting in a way favorable to the police
department.

By the time I moved to grab the files, they were
gone from Thomas's office. I then received a report
that Thomas had been seen during election night
loading boxes of files into his personal vehicle. Later,
I learned he had taken these files to his home and
hidden them in his basement.

The next morning, I went to his home with
investigatory officers and questioned him about the
files. He said he had them in the basement of his
home. His defense was that he was afraid that the
newly-elected mayor would take control of them and
release the names of undercover officers, thereby
endangering them. When I asked about dossiers, he

again denied that he or any officers under his control had compiled information on people, only events. He then turned the files over to me. When I returned to the station and examined the files, the dossiers were gone—including the one about the alderman's daughter.

The act of taking, hiding, or destroying official police files, even if they were improperly gathered, is a criminal act. This was an indication of a serious ethical breach within the department, an instance of corruption.

Therefore, I took the information I had to the district attorney for his review and for a decision on whether to criminally prosecute Thomas. After reviewing the matter, the District Attorney, Humphrey "Jerry" Lynch, declined to prosecute. I still wonder today if that was the right decision for the Madison community. Thankfully, Thomas immediately resigned and the files were locked away in a bank safety deposit box for a time in the future when a decision would be made by a court concerning their disposition. Two problems had now been solved—Thomas and the files.

It was now time to forge ahead. I didn't find any other major ethical breach within the police department as potentially deep and destructive as Thomas' operation. Thomas had stayed around for the first four months of my administration, instigating trouble for me within the ranks, sowing seeds of discord that were to grow during the coming months and have an impact on me long after his retirement.

When leaders focus on the little things like dress codes and street use, it's easy for them to be distracted from what they really should be doing. Even when leaders get tied up on the big things like

illegal intelligence gathering, it is easy for them to get sidetracked. But the job of a leader is always to move forward. There is truth in the saying "When you are up to your rear end in alligators, it's difficult to remember that your initial goal was to drain the swamp!" Alligators surrounded me, but I still had to drain the swamp.

A few months after the spring election, I had a key opportunity to share my ideas with the community about draining the swamp. I was asked by Madison's Downtown Rotary Club to talk about the policing needs of our city. The Rotary Club brought together men and women each week from business, education, and government. It was a stellar opportunity for me to share my vision with them and the rest of the city through the various media outlets sure to show up on that day.

I titled my talk "The First Seven Months and the Next Seven Years." In it, I attempted to set forth my vision for the police department— where Madison's police needed to go. That day, I felt a real sense of urgency as opposition continued to build against me within the police department and in some segments of the community. I knew I needed to lay out an exciting future with lots of enthusiasm on my part, then be able to convince Madison residents that I could deliver on it. Two of my closest advisors in the community, Professors Remington and Goldstein, gave me wise advice: "David, this is a time when the community needs to know what will be lost if you are forced out and leave. You need to tell them now."

I laid out three directions that I planned on taking the department in the coming years. I told the Rotarians that I needed their help and support in doing so:

- *Decentralize police services and develop neighborhood and team policing. The police department has been centralized since the mid-1800s. We need to get out of a centralized location and work closer to the people we served.*

- *Build a people orientation—a sensitivity to, and understanding of human behavior. I would be recruiting high-quality, educated police officers and training everyone, especially those in leadership positions, about this broader role for police. Traditional policing responded to problems but was not interested in finding their cause. We would work with community members to prevent, diminish, and even eliminate crime and other community disorder.*

- *Develop our capacity for conflict management and crisis intervention in addition to our traditional law enforcement duties. Reduce the acrimonious relationship that now exists between the police and students. After years of fighting about the war, new strategies and tactics needed to be taken to handle public protests by means other than tear gas and a nightstick.*

This was where we needed to start heading now. But I went further and outlined a visionary goal for us seven years into the future. I needed to do this to let the community know what they would most likely miss if I wasn't around to lead the police department. I was, in fact, fighting for my life and my career:

[Eight years from now] we should have successfully made the quantum leap necessary to field a behavior and human services expert which shall be known as a professional police officer... Police officers of the future will be human behavior experts as well as community workers... These future police officers will also have an advocacy role within our communities. They will identify government and social problems and solve them with the resources of the government and the community.

At the end of my talk, I think everyone present, those watching television that evening, and reading about my comments in the *Wisconsin State Journal* and *The Capital Times*, the city's morning and afternoon newspapers, began to realize that the Madison Police Department wasn't going to be their grandfather's police department. Their new chief was calling not just for organizational improvements, but also for a massive transformation: creating a new breed of police officers, in a new department, to serve the community in new ways.

Mayor Soglin stood by me during the trials of those early months. I'm still thankful to him. In spite of having a hippie-liberal mayor in charge of the city, the city still ran well, and the police department finally came together and did its job. The city didn't fall apart. Soglin had a clear-cut service ethic, having been a city alderman, and he had a deep sense of equality and fairness. I worked closely with him and his team of city managers.

Just about everyone in the city and the police department came to know the two very large posters prominently hanging on the wall of my office. They were pictures of Dr. Martin Luther King Jr. and Mahatma Gandhi. The caption under King read: "No man is free until all men are free!" and the one under Gandhi read: "In a gentle way you can shake the world." They continued to be two crucial office companions during my life in Madison—constantly reminding me about freedom and the practice of nonviolence. They stayed there for my entire 20-year tenure.

But when I showed up at a vigil for peace in Vietnam one evening in the city and a news photographer snapped a picture of me holding a candle after the peace march was breaking up, another firestorm broke out. The picture of me

appeared on the front page of the morning paper. Again, some people related to it and expected this of their police chief, while others didn't. Later, it became one of the charges leveled against me – leading a peace march.

At first, I couldn't understand the controversy among my officers. I was a cop; they were cops. Why weren't they supporting me? I was their chief. The proposals I was making and the vision I was casting would enhance their jobs, lead to more respect for them from the community, and even put more money in their pockets through an educational incentive plan. When I had been the chief in Burnsville, I hadn't gotten that kind of resistance and we'd made larger, and quicker, strides. Burnsville officers and I had agreed we would work together to make Burnsville a world-class department, and all of us would benefit. Why wasn't this happening in Madison? When I was in Burnsville, I never felt I was an outsider—I was a cop just like the rest of them even though I came from the Minneapolis department. But in Madison, things were different. I was beginning to feel like an outsider, and it didn't feel very good.

When I showed up with my family at the summer police union picnic soon after I came to Madison, we were shunned. Hardly anyone would speak to us. When the Madison Fire Department heard about it, the head of the firefighter's union, Ed Durkin—who would later become chief of the department—invited me and my family to their picnic. I soon began to realize that my tenure wasn't going to be assured by senior members of the police department, nor the police union. If I were to survive in this job, it would be because the community supported me and wanted me to stay.

In light of the situation created by a proverbial

war at home, enlisting the full support of the police department itself may have been impossible. I had to make a decision. Should I get my support for change and improvement from police officers or community members? The answer was now obvious to me—the Madison community. After all, nearly one-half of the police department had signed a petition against me.

Soon the media began describing the conflict within the police department in sports terms—an "A" team and a "B" team. My supporters were, thankfully, described as the "A" team. The war at home had now established a beachhead within the department. I didn't consider myself an outsider, but I was one. To be an insider, one of the boys, I would have had to accept and bless all that had gone on during the antiwar years. This I couldn't do. And my choosing not to do that meant that a long, protracted internal battle was about to be waged. I had a fight before me, a fight for my life as a police leader. I knew I was going to have to push back hard in order to survive.

I had to find out who in this police department would join me. I knew who wouldn't. The police union leadership at the time and many officers still in the ranks who held deep-seated and antagonistic feelings about students would most likely not join me. Slowly, I was able to build a small, but solid, coalition of support. I found officers who wanted change. They were mostly younger and few in number. I needed the finest and the brightest in leadership positions where they could affect and support change, and that meant shortening seniority requirements for promotion and rapidly bringing them into the command structure. These officers, now deemed the "A" team, understood and shared my vision. They knew the department had to change, and they stepped forward to make it happen.

I went about building a team of willing players and bringing women and minorities into the department in large numbers. I don't think those on the "B" team understood the power of the term they chose for themselves. In a big football town like Madison, it's the "A" team who plays the game. They are in the game because the "A" team consists of the elite players. Those whose skills need more development are on the "B" team. The "B" team sits on the bench. The "A" team plays the game.

Demographics were also on my side. I came to Madison just about 30 years after World War II. Those who joined the department during or after World War II were now close to retirement. Within a few years, almost everyone in the top command ranks retired, and that permitted me to fill their places with officers who wanted to work with me and shared my philosophy. When Mayor Soglin went about filling vacancies on the police commission, I went from having two votes in my favor to three, then four and, finally, all five votes in favor of what I was trying to do.

When I met Morlynn Frankey, she was one of six policewomen in the department. All six worked in the juvenile bureau. In order for a policewoman to be hired in Madison, she had to have a four-year college degree. While these women received detective pay and possessed arrest powers, they were prohibited from carrying a firearm or standing for promotion. One of the first changes I made was to permit them to function fully as police officers—to be able to carry a firearm, to be eligible for promotion as the men were, and to be able to work in other department units if they so choose.

When these changes were approved by the commission, Frankey stepped forward and competed for promotion to lieutenant. Over the years, I

promoted her to higher and higher levels of responsibility. She worked closely with me in moving the department. She was a powerful advocate for women on the department, championed my vision, and retired as an assistant chief.

One of first things I had to do along with instituting major changes within the department was to try to manage the uprising against me. The things I needed to immediately do took a considerable amount of my time when I first arrived. I needed to establish written policies and practices regarding how we would go about policing and share them with our community; especially policies regarding the use of deadly force and the pursuit of fleeing motor vehicles. I also had to hire high-quality applicants, both men and women, along with people of color. I needed to bring not only women into the department but remove the restrictions on the women who were already there. So there was a lot of internal conflict during those early days, part of it the youth rebellion within our society and part due to the age difference between older and newly-hired officers. My willingness to relax the department's grooming code created some allies for me and my policies. On the other hand, it irritated many of the older officers. Even so, on any one given day, if a vote had been taken, I would have had difficulty getting 50 percent of the internal vote. In the overall community, on the other hand, I was confident I would have fared much better.

As in most organizations, senior employees in the department controlled its union. Many of those officers sought to get rid of me by any and all means possible. During my first two years, I had to fight numerous charges they brought against me and my administration.

The conflict escalated from the filing of the

petition with the police commission to formal charges being filed against me by seven officers who were looking for more than a review of my leadership. They were hoping to get me fired. It took two years to finally be acquitted of the major charges. Afterward, a newspaper story carried this quote from an officer who had signed the original petition against me:

So what if you don't like him. The department has leaped forward the past 20 months more than it did in all the 10 years I've been here.[48]

An editorial in the *Wisconsin State Journal*, two days later under the headline, "Chief Couper Vindicated," correctly observed,

They resented Couper's style, his philosophy. They were men who thought the polish on an officer's shoes or the length of his sideburns more important than his relationship with the community, the total community... Resentment against Couper was generated by a handful of veterans who saw Couper's progressive law enforcement philosophy as a direct challenge to their viewpoints... Too many smears have been leveled, too many unsubstantiated charges have been circulated, too much vindictiveness has been voiced, to be completely happy over the dismissal of the major charges against the chief.[49]

Those 20 months were a frontal assault against not only my philosophies but also against me and my family. It is one thing to have to go through an ordeal like this and still another thing to see your children suffer. I had six and four of them were attending school during those years. They suffered, too.

Yes, these were hard times; yet predictable given the job I knew I had to do. Somehow, in my

---

[48] 49*Wisconsin State Journal* newspaper, September 7, 1974.
[49] *Ibid.* Editorial, September 9, 1974.

youth, I thought I could convince the department that what I was doing wasn't only necessary but essential for their future. While I was able to do that in Burnsville, it didn't initially happen in Madison.

Those years took a personal toll on me as I often spent a full working day in the office followed by a full evening of hearings, investigations, and courtroom battles. John Bowers and Jack Carlson, from the Lawton and Cates law firm, were the two outstanding lawyers who doggedly and expertly defended me. Eventually, I was able to get back to police department business. I wish I could say that the internal conflict ended after this litigation was finished, but it didn't. Even so, as my tenure went on and a number of these adversaries either left the department or retired. I was able to replace them with educated and more flexible officers. Slowly, it all began to change. We were progressing.

Still, during those years of acrimony, I was relishing the day the hearings would be over and the charges against me resolved. I held a deep grudge against the officers who had taken action against me, and was convinced that many of them had given false testimony. I was going to fire them or put them in jail. That old police saying kept ringing in my ears— don't get mad, just get even.

My top staff were behind me on this, and we often talked about the sweetness of revenge. The night I was exonerated, I knew my next step was to go after them. However, my legal team had other thoughts for me to consider. That evening, they asked to speak with me alone. They reminded me that they were longtime residents of Madison and that what they had to say came from them as members of the community, not just as my lawyers. They advised me not to take action against those who had filed charges against me. They went on to say that from

their perspective, the city was sick and tired of all the conflict and acrimony within the department. Moving against a number of police officers would prolong the internal conflict for months, if not years. It was time, they said, for me to get on with moving the department forward.

When I heard their advice I was numb. I thought this was now fight time. I had never considered not retaliating. I wanted to go on the offensive, now it was my turn. But I sincerely respected these two men and I took their advice. Looking back, it was wise counsel, superlative advice. I thought about it that night and simply knew what I had heard was right.

When I didn't take action against those officers, many on my staff intensely disagreed with me. They, too, had been affected; they, too, wanted to get even. I had to take the high road and not let my feelings affect the job I now had to do. I had to shift from being a victim to being a leader.

I have to admit that when I first came to the department and began to encounter trouble within the ranks, my leadership style became more and more top-down, relying on force to get the job done. I felt threatened, and I fought back in the way I knew at the time – coercion. I now know coercive force might be the *easiest* way for leaders to operate when they encounter resistance. But it isn't the most effective way in the long run.

At a national police chiefs meeting in the late 80s, I distinctly remember a former commissioner of one of the largest police departments in America say he wanted to have leaders that were like junkyard dogs. He wanted bosses who got things done because their officers feared them. I knew he was wrong because the kind of police department I envisioned

wasn't going to be led by junkyard dogs that were feared and quick to bite. They may keep intruders out of the junkyard, but they didn't do much of anything else. You wouldn't want to bring them to a school or a senior center. I didn't want junkyard dogs—I wanted leaders: effective, educated men and women who taught and directed others by being competent and caring.

Thankfully, my inclinations toward using pressure to lead didn't carry over into my interactions with the community. I never felt I was in a struggle with them; instead, I considered them to be my primary supporters and allies in what I was trying to accomplish. So, I worked hard to encourage and activate the community to get involved in the police department. Early on, I established a number of community advisory committees consisting of civic, religious, educational leaders who agreed to give me advice on critical police-community issues. These committees were vital to maintain the support I needed to have among them. I never had to convince them that the department needed improvement.

Beginning in 1978, I had raised the stakes by asking the department to make a firm commitment to what I called a "Decade of Developing Organizational Excellence." I was trying to distinguish differences between the military organizations in which many of my officers had served and those of a modern police department. It was here that I began to see many links between business, industry, and government, few with the military style that was dominant in most police departments. The police were different than the military; they had more things in common with both public and private organizations that deliver customer services. These businesses were asking questions of their customers; finding out what they needed to know to improve.

While policing isn't a competitive business (at least so far), police departments do have customers, community residents who use their services, pay taxes, and act as shareholders—not unlike those in the corporate world. I told the community we needed to de-emphasize the paramilitary traditions of the police – to be more like other organizations in society and to develop enhanced relations with other agencies and the people we serve.[50]

More specifically, I addressed the need to decentralize police services and to be more neighborhood-oriented in our work. I told them we also needed to raise the department's educational standards and to begin to look at crime as a social problem—one that is intensified by causal factors such as poverty, unemployment, racism, and lack of education or job skills. I wanted police officers to use their minds as much as their muscle.

I think it is fair to say that my vision first became the community's and then the department's. I did it by constantly selling my ideas both internally and to the community and selecting and promoting those who shared my vision. I learned that organizations committed to sustainable improvement must have a clear vision, mission, and definition of which they are, where they are going, and what they will look like when they get there. In Madison, our vision was simple and clear: *Closer to the people. Quality from the inside out.*

This simple vision statement was intended to capture the thrust of the change effort: to improve the *inside* of the organization first—the men and women who work in the police department. I decided to do it this way because I had come to the conclusion that most efforts by police organizations

---

[50] Speech to the Madison Downtown Rotary Club. 1978.

to change had failed, even though the ideas involved were good. They failed because leaders didn't prepare and train the men and women who worked for them, and they used force or intimidation to implement the change. Coercive leadership wasn't effective nor sustainable. It didn't work.

Instead, the methods of a more collaborative style of leadership do work and can be sustained if top leaders in the organization are able and willing to first practice the new model and then teach others in the organization what they have learned. Too often, change in a police department has been portrayed to elected officials and the public as something as easy as issuing an order.

We know today that isn't the way it is done. Police departments today are complex organizations, and things don't just happen because the chief orders it. Any effort at changing the police must take into account the power of the organization to drag its feet; to resist. That is why any effort to change police must begin *inside* a department and, ultimately, be able to answer this question from the rank and file: "What's in it for us?" If a change-oriented chief and his or her staff cannot effectively answer that question, what is proposed most likely will fail. I advocated that the department take a path that meets the needs of the officers as well as the community—change and self-interest need not be mutually exclusive.

The model I used essentially centered on a clear, highly visible and shared mission. Leaders were expected to walk their talk; to be believably committed to where we were going. The success of the model would ultimately be based on how well they empowered their employees – that was a key.

Police chiefs can improve the quality of our nation's police if they are willing to be persistent in

developing work systems that empower their employees, listen to the community, and have the time to accomplish it.

For a city and its leaders to desire the kind of excellence I'm outlining in this book without giving the chief tenure is foolish, short-sighted, and sure to fail. I certainly would have failed if I didn't have both time and tenure.

Michael Scott, director of the Center for Problem-Oriented Policing (CPOP) and a law school professor, once served with me as a Madison police officer. He went on to work in various police line and executive positions in a number of cities. He made a noteworthy observation about transformation:

How can it be that such a large effort to transform the demographics, education, training and management of American police personnel... cannot be demonstrably linked in improvements in police practices in the field?... No matter who is employed to do the policing job, and how they are educated and trained, so long as the police job remains so challenging, so much in conflict, and so wedded to fundamentally flawed strategies, police performance will remain wanting. Put another way, changing the players won't make much difference if the game remains the same. [51]

The job of a leader is, and always had been, to change the game; particularly if the results are not acceptable. That's what happens at halftime. If you are behind, you change how you are playing the game. In Madison, I changed the game and others can do it, too. Scott's question is still valid today: can police really change? Or was my experience in Madison just an anomaly?

---

[51] Michael Scott. "Progress in American Policing?: Reviewing the National Reviews." *Law and Social Inquiry*, vol. 34, issue 1, Winter, 2008.

Chapter 5
How Many Chiefs Does It Take To Change a Department?

TOO MANY PEOPLE believe that our police cannot change, they cannot improve. It's just the way it is. I believe police can improve if certain factors are present. I thought those factors were in place when I retired in 1993. I thought police were on a new path toward improving the way they did business. But they weren't. They were once again going back to old practices; circling around and not moving forward. I was invited to join a number of our nation's leading police chiefs at a summit meeting on police improvement in Washington, D.C. in March, 2005.[52] The conference was sponsored by the Police Executive Research Forum; an organization in which I was an active member for many years; an organization that had a history of helping police improve.

What I heard and saw there that day caused me to reflect on my career in policing and all that I had hoped for. Had I retired too early from the game? I looked around the conference table and wondered why my former colleagues had not moved on from the point I had left them when I retired. Overall, things were not improving; it was the same-old, same-old. On the other hand, that day in Washington

[52] Chuck Wexler, Mary Ann Wycoff, and Craig Fischer. *Good to Great Policing: Application of Business Management Principles in the Public Sector.* U.S. Department of Justice, Office of Community Oriented Policing Services: Washington, D.C. 2007.

was a turning point that motivated me to put my thoughts together and write this book.

The purpose of this gathering was to discuss what Jim Collins had written concerning successful business organizations in his widely acclaimed book, *Good to Great: Why Some Companies Make the Leap and Others Don't.*[53] When I received my copy and read it, I was excited about what Collins had uncovered. I thought there were some things police could learn and apply from what he had found about high-performance companies. Why do some police departments make the leap while others don't? Why can't all police departments be great—exceptions to the mediocrity that seems to dominate the field?

But when I got to the meeting, it didn't take me long to realize that few of the chiefs in attendance had read the book. Fewer still were interested in engaging in the content of the book or discussing it. Even fewer suggested that Collins' work could possibly be applied to their departments.

Now, I knew many of the chiefs sitting around the table that day in Washington, and I have to say that my expectation was that by this time in their careers they would be willing and eager to discuss a provocative book such as this. I was wrong.

What Collins did was look for the principal factors that made good companies exceptional ones. He examined organizations that for 15 years tracked or performed *worse* than the stock market, and then went through an internal transition and subsequently outperformed all their competitors. That is where he started to see some remarkable differences. Some companies were good, but there were a few that were

---

[53] Jim Collins. *Good to Great: Why Some Companies Make the Leap and Others Don't.* New York: Harper-Collins. 2001.

great.

Collins found 11 companies that were "outperformers" and so he went on to study them in depth and compare them to their competitors. He wanted to know what these companies did that enabled them to transform and outperform their competitors. One of his key findings, naturally, had to do with leaders.

He called Level 5 Leaders those who were able to create companies that outperformed their rivals. These leaders were found to be humble, willful, diligent, and hard workers. They knew how to put the right people in place in the organization (and also how to remove those who were not). These leaders could almost effortlessly find the accurate information needed to make the necessary decisions. Board members of these companies shied away from selecting celebrity leaders because they knew they failed, in the long run, to create sustained results.

All this, by the way, is contrary to the popular image in America of the business leader (and police chief) who goes into an organization with guns blazing, negotiates a big salary, fires a bunch of people, puts together impressive quarterly performance reports, and then leaves. These leaders are not effective. And whatever they did accomplish wasn't sustainable. They were short-term leaders, and the organizations they led suffered.

The problem of applying what Collins found to a police department is an old one. It is one I had often encountered during my career. It made little difference whether or not a case study was from the Harvard Business School or the International Chiefs of Police; police leaders have difficulty accepting findings from other areas of work. Even good practices from other police departments. Over the

years, I can't tell you how many times I have heard these responses from police leaders: "Yes, but it doesn't apply to *my* department" or "We tried that, but it didn't work."

The lack of a foundation of rigorous academic training makes it difficult for police leaders to digest any kind of research or case study. This is the continuing and oppressive effect of anti-intellectualism in the police field and why it remains a major obstacle.

Needless to say, this meeting disappointed me. I had expected more, and not much seemed to have changed. A closed mind regarding new ideas and concepts continues to be one of the most dangerous impediments in the police subculture.

On that day in Washington, I sat back and listened to the conversation. It soon drifted away from Collins' book and became a sharing of anecdotes—war stories from the chiefs about *their* department and the fine work *they* were doing. They didn't listen very well to either the presenters or to each other.

When academics are willing to meet and talk with police leaders about their work, they often come away finding the police interesting but uninterested, gregarious but lacking serious engagement. This was the atmosphere I found in that conference room, and it was unsettling. I came away thinking that police were still in trouble and few people in America were aware of it. Something needed to be said and done about their arrested development.

I feared that other matters, like the economy, jobs, health care, immigration, and wars in Iraq and Afghanistan would be more pressing than any need to improve our nation's police. I thought nothing

would highlight the problems that continue to plague them.

But then came the Occupy Movement in 2011, and our police were once again on the street responding to public protest in many of our cities. While many citizens didn't know how police should respond to public protest, they knew that what they saw in some of our cities wasn't right. They thought police could do better.

Most citizens may not be able to conceive why highly-trained and competent police are needed, choosing to believe that good is good enough. For many others, at least before the Occupy Movement, police didn't bother them, so what's the problem? But what we are finding today is there are many citizens whom the police do bother and bother them daily as Nicholas Peart reminded us earlier. Most of these Americans are poor and/or people of color. As middle-class citizens in this country become less economically advantaged, they may find themselves in similar situations.

Worse yet, some people may feel that building a high-quality police department is simply not worth the effort or cost. Even citizen- activists can be timid about pressing for reform in a police department that isn't supportive of it. In such cases, they fear the push-back that can come from police who define them as troublemakers and know-nothings.

At the same time, American police leaders don't spend much time or effort raising the public's knowledge or expectations of their police either. It is about time to realize that our nation needs police leaders who can initiate and maintain a public conversation as to what citizens should expect from their police. Leaders who ask their communities to partner with them will be able to meet those

expectations.

As it stands, police have a tendency to tell citizens what their problems are, instead of *asking* them. For example, police may feel there is a problem with burglary in the community only to find out when they get to a community meeting the real issue is the department's aggressive stop and frisk tactics; the burglaries are few and far between, but the department's aggressive tactics are something citizens have had to deal with on a daily basis.

In the meantime, our nation's police drift further away from their commitment to solving community problems, working closely with citizens, and zealously protecting their rights. It is my belief that left alone, things won't develop. As our nation becomes more populous, undergoes economic downturns, energy shortages, struggles with immigration, and an increasing diversity of race and culture in our nation's cities, a higher level of policing will be sorely needed. Good simply won't be good enough.

The challenge to police today, if policing is ever going to be considered a profession is rather clear: they will need to develop a system of sustained leadership along with a body of knowledge that is able to fluidly incorporate research findings, be willing to experiment with this new knowledge, and effectively turn it into field practices. This is what professionals do. Thus, every police officer trained anywhere in the country would learn tried and tested methods, best practices and, in turn, would be expected to practice them during his or her career.

My point is that police leaders have a critical role to play in this society as guardians of our rights. This must never be forgotten by them or by us. Until American police forge and claim that unique role in

our society, they will continue to be viewed in the dim light of the past—as somehow being an ongoing part of the problematic historical legacy that I outlined earlier. For without a commitment to, and practice of, the values I have emphasized in this book, police will continue to be bogged down by a combination of poor performance and low expectations from the public. And that is a tragic situation.

Since that time in Washington, I've thought about the things I had learned during my career. Why hadn't these police chiefs learned the same things? I had written books and authored a score of professional articles about change and leadership. I had taught courses around the country in which I shared what I had learned in Madison about leading police and delivering community-based police services. Why wasn't organizational fairness and effectiveness commonly sought among our nation's police leaders? Why were police so slow to improve?

I have no doubt that the attitude which distains formal education and research along with a reliance on coercive leadership are their primary hindrances. I have concluded from my experience and continued observation that this has restrained and arrested their development. It isn't that there has been no improvement; I began police work without a college education, formal training, body armor or a personal radio. My point is that given the organizational improvements of other institutions in our society, the police have fallen disgracefully behind.

Before any institution can improve, it must identify the obstacles in its way. Some of them I've already identified, such as the power of the police subculture, the negative legacy of their history, and over-reliance on physical force in the field and in the police station. But there are other major impediments

American police must also deal with if they want to catch up and stay in front.

Overcoming these obstacles won't be easy. They are sturdily imprinted into our police. Doing so will require a commitment to intellectual excellence, civility, and the rule of law under even the most trying circumstances. It will require police to exhibit a high degree of awareness and self-control as they internally examine and police themselves. It will require that they actively seek to accurately match their communities' complexions and values with the officers they hire and promote.

From time to time, cities and their police have tried to overcome the effects of one or more of these historical, in-bred impediments. Most of the time, they have not applied well-thought-out strategies in doing so, or their efforts have been seen as merely cosmetic. Few attempts have been sustained.

Changing police isn't just about changing a few things, but everything: hiring, training, leadership, solving problems, community- orientation, and evaluation. It is about changing the very nature of the police function itself and the multiple ways that will have to be put in place to raise the intellectual capacity of police, curtail their use of excessive force, drive out the vestiges of corruption and racism, and implement a new culture of courtesy, customer focus, and restraint in using physical force. They will also have to learn how to properly handle protesting people not only singularly but in large crowds and develop on- going formal relationships with academic institutions.

After my graduate education, the University of Minnesota awarded me a grant to study police departments in Europe. It was a vital and essential part of my career development as I began to see

police on a larger scale and in different, but democratically-influenced, surroundings. I chose to study police departments in the cities of Stockholm, Copenhagen, Amsterdam, Hamburg, and London. The university's grant helped me identify and clarify the four obstacles that stand in the way of police improvement in America.

Obstacle 1: Anti-Intellectualism

It's 1971; I'm sitting in the office of the commissioner of police in Copenhagen. My eye catches the large oil paintings hanging high on the wall of the office. The paintings are very old, some from a century ago or longer. The commissioner, noticing my interest, says, "I see you are looking at the former commissioners of police in our city. The one over there, on your left, is Police Commissioner Romer. He was also a scientist—in fact, the first to calculate the speed of light." He concludes, "We come from a long line of educated police commissioners."

That moment, with my own recent college education not far from my thoughts, crystallized for me the notion that if we are to have a democratic and effective police institution in our nation, it *must* have higher education as its foundation.

Later, I was to learn more about the police commissioner who also was a scientist. Ole Christensen Romer (1644–1710), took the first quantitative measurement of the speed of light and was the second commissioner of police in Copenhagen, a position he held until his death. Upon assuming the office of commissioner, Romer fired the entire police force. He did so because he was convinced that morale on the force was so alarmingly low that every police officer needed to be replaced.

Romer didn't abandon his inventive qualities when he joined the police—he used his skills to invent and put into operation the first street lights and worked to improve the lives of the city's disadvantaged residents: beggars, prostitutes, and the unemployed. He established rules for building new houses, improved the city's water supply and sewage systems, developed new equipment for the city's fire department, and was the moving force behind paving streets and establishing town squares.[54] The police commissioner with whom I was speaking that morning in Copenhagen had not only big shoes to fill but an enormous intellectual legacy to uphold. I thought, if our nation's police leaders were all educated and as creative as Romer, where would we be today?

The negative spirit of anti-intellectualism presents itself in a number of ways in American policing. It begins with low educational standards for police applicants. Then in police training as the classroom curricula are more oriented towards high school than college. Within police operations, new ideas and creative approaches are neither sought nor encouraged. When it comes to police operations, traditionally-based past-experience is valued more highly than research or experience gained by others outside the field—even if it works.

The only way this obstacle is going to be overcome is requiring our nation's police to have an academically rigorous four-year college education before they are sent into the field. In addition, police departments must have an on-going academic relationship with a college or university in order to bring together academics and practitioners. The two can then work together to develop, test, and share the

[54]http://www.amnh.org/education/resources/rfl/web/ess aybooks/cosmic/p_roemer.html; January 1, 2011; 1112 hrs.

most effective methods of policing. This would eventually result in police officers spending time in classrooms and doing research and academics teaching in the training academy and walking a beat.

Obstacle 2: Violence

When I came to Amsterdam in 1971, I noticed their police force's remarkable restraint in handling protests and demonstrations. They had a huge population of hippies, migrants, and street people that had settled in their city. I was commenting on their tolerance to a couple of senior officers when one of them said, "You must realize that many of us were prisoners ourselves. We were arrested and put in prison when the Germans invaded our country. That experience made a difference in how we treat people."

A few weeks later, in Germany, I was amazed how that country's police tried creative ways to prevent having to use force during protests and demonstrations. At the time, the only method used in my country was physical force. The police in Hamburg, however, had developed other methods and strategies. For example, they would field a powerful sound truck when a protest was scheduled. Police in the truck played popular music and bantered with the crowd. They felt it tended to set a positive tone and reduce tension in the crowd. The police officer in the sound truck served as a disc jockey, communicating, and sometimes cracking jokes— all of which had a very positive effect and tended to reduce tension and anti-police sentiment within the crowd.

When I related to them what we in America did to control crowds and demonstrations, they looked at me as if I came from another planet. I resolved at that time that I would try to experiment with

different methods of crowd control—to use force only as a last resort. That was in the 1970s, and the methods we use today in our country to manage crowds and protests have changed little since then. In fact, they have gotten worse, as police now overly depend on technology to handle crowds and protests.

It is conceivable that we may even see a new device on our streets to control people who protest. The army has developed large microwave transmitters that literally heat people up. I'm not joking. Such a unit can be used as a non-lethal weapon to move people away from an area, or deny them access to it.[55] This technology could create a situation in which police no longer have to form a line or even be present. The power between police and protesters has dramatically shifted during the past 40 years. There is no need for police to talk to protesters anymore. They don't even have to be close.

Removing the obstacle of violence does not just pertain to handling collective gatherings—it must also apply to police officers' daily interactions and the way they make arrests. Rather than quickly resorting to physical force to accomplish their work, police need to be consistently trained to always use the *least* amount of force necessary to overcome resistance. The abuse of force by police does not only hurt those who are on the receiving end, because when the public determines that police have used unnecessary force, police lose their respect, which ultimately results in less cooperation, thereby diminishing the effectiveness of the police function.

If police should ever be expert on any subject it should be persuasion and the use of force. For

---

[55] 56 "60 Minutes," CBS television news magazine on June 19, 2009 on new, non-lethal Army crowd-control weapon. You can see the video at:
http://www.youtube.com/watch?v=kkGHgsgc6es.

example, many police use-of-force manuals rank pepper spray below that of using a pressure point to gain compliance. The thinking here is that the pepper spray leaves no permanent damage or continued pain to a person while a pressure point (like a wrist lock) could. This has permitted police to use pepper spray in situations of passive resistance. But the question is, should they? And should they do it in highly public protest situations like many of us recently witnessed on the campus of the University of California at Davis?[56]

Again, whenever police have to use force it must be carefully used and always within the bounds of public approval. Until the use of force is considered a public trust granted to them by the people they serve, it will continue to be a major point of contention between citizens and their police.

Obstacle 3: Corruption

Whenever police act above the law it is damaging to their effectiveness because it erodes the trust of the people. There are acts of corruption that involve stealing things and money for personal use. There are acts of corruption in which evidence is tampered with and testimony is untrue. Corruption in our nation's police departments and among its officers is another obstacle to police improvement. We all know that fallible humans like you and me staff public and private organizations. Police will make mistakes.

But what can be done is to significantly reduce

---

[56] 57 See an article and video of this at: http://www.guardian.co.uk/world/2011/nov/21/uc-davis-police-chief-leave?newsfeed=true). January 5, 2012; 1010 hrs.

the occurrence of both honest mistakes and willful acts. Law-breaking by the police should be an uncommon event. Citizens should always rightfully expect their police to first be honest. Police departments must be committed to effectively and intensively train their officers in the skills necessary to serve as public servants in a democracy. Selecting good people and training them, however, is only the first step. The organizations in which police work must also be supportive of and practice the values they espouse. This means a police department that is truly committed to openness with the public and transparency in its operations. It means police officials who treat their employees with dignity and respect, and a thorough, fair, and trustworthy system for investigating and resolving complaints of misconduct.

Incidents of corruption and acts of dishonesty were not unknown in the European cities and police departments I visited; yet they appeared to be few and far between. There was an expectation of citizens in those cities that their government and its officials, including the police, conduct themselves within the rule of law. There was an atmosphere and expectation among the police in each city that I studied that their business was to be conducted in a legal and ethical manner. Suffice it to say that a dishonest police department cannot continue to exist without dishonesty being a deep-seated part of the political culture of that city. If there is widespread corruption in a state, county or local government, it will be unusual to find an honest police department in that situation and *vice versa*.

Maintaining a culture of honesty is dependent upon police being adequately compensated as law enforcement professionals. A city doesn't save money by under-paying their police. Perhaps the finest advice for police officers regarding ethics is the two

commandments I was given as a young recruit: "Remember, everything that was illegal and wrong before you pinned a badge on your chest is still illegal and wrong. Never break the law in order to enforce it."[57]

Obstacle 4: Discourtesy

Simply put, while it will not leave citizens physically battered, police discourtesy still harms them and the community. This psychologically harmful act means not acting civilly and respectfully toward others.

It was in London, the final city I visited during my study, that the practice of civility was most evident. One day in busy downtown London, I watched a pair of young police constables standing on a corner answering numerous (and sometimes agonizingly repetitive) questions from passersby concerning directions and local landmarks. Each and every time, I noticed they were respectful and courteous.

Everyone who approached them had their attention, was listened to, and went away feeling that their question had been answered—and done so in a polite manner. In turn, I noticed that the citizens asking the questions showed a tremendous amount of respect for the officers. Police and citizens were practicing the art of civility.

Now, I know the British police have their problems, just as every police department does; but discourtesy does not seem to be one of them. It is true that civility or politeness is highly valued in

[57] I believe I received these words of wisdom from Deputy Inspector Edward Farrell, Minneapolis Police Department. Ed was the training director of the first formal police training academy I attended.

British society, and so it is with their police. But isn't civility also one of our values? In our encounters with governmental workers, don't we expect courtesy and politeness from them? A police department that practices civility in its encounters with others will soon find that they, in turn, will be treated civilly. But civility must also be practiced *within* the ranks of the department—how police treat each other and how leaders treat rank-and- file officers is especially crucial. When leaders treat employees with respect they soon find it is reciprocal. It is then much more natural for employees to treat those outside the organization the same way.

I made a commitment to myself that day in London that any police department I would be in charge of would focus on politeness and courtesy as a dominant organizational value. I also knew that if civility was to be an operational value within a police department, it also meant that its *leaders* needed to have polite and courteous interactions with their officers.

Civility is an essential ingredient in both the practice of internal leadership and the conduct of external community relations. Without public cooperation police have little chance of accomplishing their mission, and a discourteous police department much less. This means that a culture of respect and politeness must be created, nurtured, and maintained. While citizens may be expected to react negatively to verbal abuse, the same cannot be expected from a professional police officer. The standard is this: police must be courteous *to a fault*. By that I mean police should never over-react, return insults, or in any way be discourteous – *regardless* of the provocation, situation, or individual.

So far, you may have some doubt as to whether or not, given the historical background of our

nation's police, they are able to adjust to modern times. At one time, I viewed the police as the mythical Sisyphus— reliably going forth each day to push a heavy rock up a hill only to have it slide back down when the day was finished; never being able to push the rock over the hill—only to begin again the next day doing the same thing.

I no longer hold that view. I'm convinced that police can take their place among our most respected public officials. They can push that rock over the hill and move forward. As I will relate in the following materials, we did it in Madison and that improvement continues today, years after my retirement. With the right leadership and a progressive government, it can happen in any city. With the right conditions and the right support, it will only take one chief to change a police department.

Chapter 6
The Seven Improvement Steps

Step One: Envision

Police leaders must cast a bold and breathtaking vision to ensure a distinguished future for policing.

A GOOD VISION statement should be short, bold (even breathtaking), and those hearing it for the first time should be able to clearly remember it the next day. One quickly learns, however, that this is the easiest step. In order for a vision to work, it must be shared with others whom it affects. But having something shared with you is much different than having your vision become theirs.

For leaders to have their visions become owned by others takes time and commitment. They must also have passion and persistence. Peter Drucker, one of our nation's most influential thinkers on the subject of management theory, once described these kinds of leaders as *monomaniacs with a mission*.[58] If we ever learned anything about people in organizations is that to change anything takes time and commitment, passion and persistence.

Like most chiefs new to a department, I came with a vision that was, at first, a set of expectations as

---

[58] *"Whenever anything is being accomplished, it is being done, I have learned, by a monomaniac with a mission."* Peter Drucker. *Adventures of a Bystander.* New York: John Wiley and Sons. 1994.

to how I wanted the men and women of my department to conduct the business of policing. These expectations came about through my own learning and experience—the things I thought important.

From day one as a chief, I began to describe my expectations for the department at every opportunity. I was in the business of selling organizational change. I found that one of the top opportunities to do this was at the graduation of a class of new police officers. This was always a big event in Madison. I wanted my new officers to know who I was and what my expectations were—but most of all, how passionate I was about them.

- *Employ your full skill at all times and to all persons.*
- *Prevent, manage, or intervene in situations requiring police service.*
- *Be open, accept change in this changing world, develop and maintain a broad perspective of your function and the society in which you work, be flexible and develop the ability to grow with the people you serve.*[59]

Expectations matter. I would continue to use the same set of expectations over my years in Madison because they were what I expected of myself and from every police officer with whom I worked. These expectations would be the foundation of the Madison Vision. But before my expectations became the driving vision for the Madison department, there was a lot of work that first needed to be done.

---

[59] At the graduation ceremony of the Madison Police Recruit graduation, August 8, 1974.

The Madison Police Department

VISION

We are a dynamic organization devoted to improvement, excellence, maintaining customer satisfaction, and operating on the principles of quality leadership.

"Closer to the People; Quality from the Inside Out"

MISSION

We believe in the dignity and worth of all people.
We are committed to: providing high-quality, community-oriented police services with sensitivity, protecting constitutional rights, problem-solving, teamwork, openness, planning for the future, continuous improvement, and providing leadership to the police profession.
We are proud of the diversity of our work force, which permits us to grow and which respects each of us as individuals, and we strive for a healthful workplace.
(1986)

If a vision is going to be sustainable and last beyond the leader who casts it, the process is as important as the product. First, police leaders are needed who are not only monomaniacs with a mission, but who are willing to stay around long enough and to suffer through the pain that inevitably comes with an organization in the process of change.

Second, there needs to be constant and ongoing support by the community including elected officials—those outside the organization—to help

make the vision a reality. Leaders must cast their vision outside the department as much as they do inside of it.

Third, those within the organization must know their leader is willing to engage in a process with them to develop the vision. They, too, must be willing to participate in the work to make the vision become a reality and do all that they can to operate under its direction.

The Madison vision statement gained more traction within the department as each class of new officers took to the street. Time was on my side. And working closely with members of the department, I began to develop, with them, a more formal vision and mission statement that reflected the values that I sensed we all were beginning to share. The vision and mission statements brought out in 1986 had that support. It defined who we were, what we wished to become, and what our citizens deserved. It laid the groundwork for even bolder steps ahead.

My job in creating a shared-vision from a set of my expectations would have been more difficult if corruption had been extreme within the Madison department, the internal management mechanisms in disarray, its officers excessively violent, or the existence of seething racial resentment within the minority community. This kind of situation would have set my vision back by years—perhaps so far back that nothing else could have been accomplished except to try and turn around these impediments. I could, therefore, with some confidence, say that my job in coming to Madison was to pursue excellence in policing. I did not dwell on the department's shortcomings.

A leader must be able to encourage and enlist a substantial cadre of supporters within the organization, both junior and senior, who will stand

up, move out, and help make their leader's vision *their* vision. Unless that happens, a vision will never become a reality.

In Madison, a major amount of my time was spent establishing the value of an operating vision and the steps needed to make it happen—that is, its mission. The process of doing so is called *catch-ball*.[60] The term comes from the quality improvement days of Deming. The leader is to form a vision and pass it to members throughout the organization. They look at it, consider it, talk about it, and bounce it back. The leader receives their input. They may even have added new ideas and information. The leader ponders and incorporates their feedback, and passes it back again. And so it goes until the vision becomes shared. This is an effective organizational technique in which not only visions, but also ideas and methods, can be passed back and forth within the hierarchy of the organization with the purpose of developing shared visions, ideas, and methods.

I continued to promote my vision whenever I had the opportunity. As chief, I was in the sales business. And selling involves knowing your product and what your customers need. But if you don't have a desired product, no matter how hard you sell, buyers will be few.

---

[60] The Japanese developed this concept after World War II to develop highly-efficient policy management. The term is "Hoshin Kanri;" literally translated as: "point the direction and motivate everyone to achieve the vision." The way this is done is by what we in America call "catch-ball;" that is, pass concepts, goals, objectives, and strategies back and forth throughout the entire organization—from top to bottom—in order to improve and share them. See: http://cokepm.com/pmbok3/KnowledgeBase/qualitycorn er/700WorkingTogetherUsingCatc h-Ball.pdf, and http://www.realinnovation.com/content/c080623a.asp. January 23, 2012; 1035 hrs.

Step Two: Select

Police must encourage and select the best and the brightest to serve as police officers.

IN THE NOT-SO-DISTANT past, nepotism was rampant within police departments. This was a protective response by police to make sure that those who joined them were just like them—reinforcing the subculture and the *status quo*. Police encouraged their friends and relatives who held the same worldview as they did to join their ranks.

The goal today is to continue to staff the ranks of the police with persons who reflect the community served. To a large extent, that has happened in our nation's bigger cities. But it didn't happen overnight. In most instances, it didn't happen through police leadership, but by the changing color and gender of the electorate in our nation's cities.

What may have been the most difficult task of police administrators came about through legal mandates and civic elections, not because they were seeking diversity in their ranks. The forces behind those court decisions and electoral politics were that of a nation weary and angry at the injustices of racial segregation and keeping women out of all-male workplaces. So it didn't take long for elected officials to see that women and racial minorities were moved into the ranks of their police departments in our nation's larger cities in spite of police resistance in the ranks.

During the early 70s, our nation's law and culture were rapidly changing. There is no doubt in my mind that President Johnson's adding "gender" in 1968 to the anti-discrimination list of "race, religion, and national origin" was a huge opportunity for

women to serve in non- traditional jobs. This executive order assisted one of the most fundamental goals of a professional police—diversity. It enabled women as well as minorities and, eventually, those with different sexual orientations, to come to see the police as representing them, their interests— something that before had been almost unimaginable. But again, with a small number of exceptions, it didn't come about from police. Even today, most departments are sorely deficient in numbers of women police and even more so in the top ranks.

During this period, there was also opposition to raising educational standards for police, because of the fear that this would make the hiring of minorities more difficult. The argument was that minority applicants didn't have equal access to higher education and, therefore, a higher educational requirement would be another barrier to diversifying the department. At the time, this was partially true.

Today, however, the argument is no longer valid, but I do remember the struggle back in the 1970s. My efforts to get the police commission to set a baccalaureate degree requirement were always thwarted by the access-to-education argument. There was fear that a highly educated police would shut out people of color. Looking back, even though the Madison department didn't have a formal four-year college degree requirement, I was still able to attract and select a large number of applicants with college degrees–including many from minority backgrounds. Through aggressive recruiting and the compelling image we presented that we were a place for college graduates and the obvious visual change in the complexion and gender of our officers, we were still able to quickly integrate the department, raise the educational level, and receive praise from our community for doing so. Madison police were seen as educated men and women.

Assisting my commitment to hire police officers with degrees, I had a powerful educational incentive program in place. Madison's incentive program paid baccalaureate degree holders 18 percent over and above their base pay, and master's degree holders 22 percent. This meant that a police officer with a master's degree—and we had a number of them—was paid a salary equivalent to a lieutenant with a high school diploma. It was quite clear to all how Madison felt about the importance of education for its police.

At the time I retired, more than 25 percent of sworn officers in the department were women, and 10 percent were from racial minorities. In the years since my retirement, I'm proud to report that these numbers have increased, respectively, to 32 and 16 percent.

I'm confident that one of the more enduring things I did in Madison was to bolster the image of the police officer. It took a good 10 years before the image changed from police being seen as narrow and uneducated to that of being intelligent and highly trained.

One morning in the mid-1970s, I remember attending a briefing of senior day-shift officers, most all of whom were males older than I was. A number of them soon began complaining about the changes going on within the department—hiring women, new policies that restricted the use of deadly force and the requirement that a supervisor call off high-speed chases if they became too dangerous to the community.

I listened as the grousing continued. Then I asked them, "When I came to the department, many of your wives told me they were embarrassed to say

their husbands were police officers. They shared with me that those days of riot and turmoil took a toll on them and your children, as well. Now looking back, think -- is that the case now? Or are your wives and children proud that you are a Madison police officer?" It was quiet in the room. I had made a point. These senior officers knew they had gained respect under my leadership. Everyone had benefited from our effort to professionalize—to be a first class police department. They knew they were now viewed as respected professionals in the community.

Many of our new officers had broad backgrounds. They had worked before coming to Madison as teachers, nurses, social workers, and even lawyers. Anyone who heard about the education and background of these new officers couldn't help but consider them to be not only interesting and likable, but also educated and talented.

Removing the stigma of policing wasn't easy. It took time and persistence. Other police departments can learn from this—it isn't impossible to repair the damaged image of a police department. But it must be substantive and not just public relations work. And once it happens, the value of the effort will become clear: citizens and police both benefit from a competent, ethical, well-run police organization. There are superior relations with the community, effective problem solving, openness, good operational decisions, and a sense of safety and well being permeates the city.

A police department in America should be, at a minimum, as good as our nation's most successful business organizations. It should develop a workplace that encourages good ideas, listens well, and is willing to receive input from both insiders and outsiders. A professional organization values diversity of its personnel and considers it to be a strength, not a

weakness. A department like this has little trouble attracting good people to join their ranks.

But how should such people be selected? And how should they be prepared and trained? I have outlined the many functions and responsibilities we should expect of police officers in a free and multicultural society such as ours. It would be foolish to think that all the functions identified earlier by the American Bar Association could be brought to a high level of competency in a shorter time than what is done in the case of other important jobs in our society.

Nearly 50 years have passed since President Lyndon Johnson's commission recommended a standard be set that required police officers to hold a four-year baccalaureate degree. I'm sad to report today that only one *percent* of our nation's police departments have that requirement in place.[61] Today, more than ever, our nation needs an educated police. It is shameful that we don't.

The commission also made an observation that I never forgot. It found that most states in our nation require more training to become a barber than a police officer. At the time, I was struck by how odd that was. Are we more concerned as a society about how we look than how we are policed? I know the quality of a haircut is important, but so is the quality of decisions made by our police as they make inquiries, settle disputes, investigate crimes, arrest suspects, and give testimony in a court of law.

So I decided to check whether that observation still held true today. Using my home state of

---

[61] See http://utsa.edu/swjcj/archives/7.1/Bruns%20Article.pdf, May 6, 2011; 1207 hrs.

Wisconsin as an example, I found that to practice their trade, barbers and cosmetologists in my state must first graduate from a licensed school of barbering or cosmetology and then participate in an additional 1,800 training hours, all of which must be completed in not less than 10 months. On the other hand, the required training for police officers in my state is 400 hours. The observation made by the president's commission in 1967 still holds true. Wisconsin barbers and beauticians have a higher standard of training than that required of police.

The Wisconsin Law Enforcement Standards Board (LESB) requires police applicants to have either a two-year associate degree or a minimum of 60 college credits. But while it may be a standard, it isn't a *requirement*, as newly appointed police officers may practice until the end of their fifth year of service before having to meet this standard. We don't permit our barbers and cosmetologists to cut our hair without being properly trained and licensed, but we permit police officers to enforce our laws without training. This strange situation is reflected not only in Wisconsin.

There is something even more necessary to alter the present course of policing: how police candidates are attracted to the job. I would maintain that until policing is seen as a job for a college graduate like it is in Madison, there will continue to be few college graduates willing to serve as police officers. As an example, I recently read this description concerning employment opportunities on a website directed at those who may be considering a police career. It stated this about police training academies:

They are usually very disciplined and regimented. You will walk in formation and line up for inspection. During the week you are usually required to spend all of your time at the academy. On Friday night, you may be granted "liberty" and

allowed to leave the academy for the weekend, returning on Sunday night.[62]

Who would be attracted by the above introduction? Very few of the kind of people I was looking for. I found the most effective recruiting results were obtained by likening police work to joining a domestic Peace Corps and describing it as an essential job in our community in need of people with solid backgrounds in social work, conflict resolution, and helping professions like teaching, law, nursing, emergency medicine, psychology, and business. We must never forget that it is the people— the police officers—that make the difference in the quality of a police department.

So, why would an educated person want to join the police? When I was in Madison, the first thing I would mention was the opportunity for both personal and professional growth. Second, I would tell them we were an organization that is committed to listening to and acting on the valued ideas of its employees; that is, in Madison, a police officer isn't simply a cog in the organization wheel, he or she is a player. Third, as a member of this department you will have the privilege to serve, protect others, help those who are disadvantaged in our society, and contribute to the social good.

In being committed to developing a quality, world-class department from the inside out leaders must always begin with proper selection of the best and brightest applicants to serve as police officers. The future demands no less.

---

[62] 63http://www.policejobsinfo.com/hiring-process/training/ January 1, 2011; 1407 hrs.

Step Three: Listen

Police leaders must intently listen to their officers and members of the community.

THIS BOOK IS about more than change – it is about transformation. And transformation involves conversion, inside work, not just a change in appearance. The transformation of a police organization first begins inside its members. Much of what I have written here may be new and startling to some. But it shouldn't be foreign to those who are watching and listening to what is happening in the world today. The non- hierarchical pro-democracy movements around the world are really harbingers of the future. In order for the American police to attain the high level of professional excellence that I believe they are capable of, they will have to undergo this kind of total transformation.

By 1980, with eight years under my belt in Madison, I was getting content with how far we had come. The job seemed too easy, I had promoted the people I wanted and had them in place throughout the department. The community seemed satisfied with how the department had changed—we were more diverse and we effectively and fairly kept peace on the streets. The perception of citizens was that crime was under control. And I was reminded of the old adage, "If it ain't broke, don't fix it."

I had stayed on message, cast a bold vision and was selecting outstanding police officers. But what about their senior leaders? Had the vision transformed them as to their leadership style? What more did I need to do?

As I noted earlier, a new and growing movement was on the American horizon. It was a movement to increase the quality of our products and

services. Government was an agency that provided a service—not a product—however, taxpayers didn't seem like customers. But the American economy was in recession, and ideas like continuous improvement, reducing our costs, and increasing customer/taxpayer satisfaction looked like possible solutions to our problems.

This was the environment in which I found myself mid-career in Madison. During this time, an image came to me. It was that of the wagon trains which carried homesteaders west during the 19th century. On their journey, they had to cross oceans of virgin prairie. When approaching this sea of grass, the wagon master would intentionally stop the wagon train, stand on top of one of the wagons, then look, and listen. He would scan the horizon, then get down and put his ear on the ground. He looked and listened for signs of danger. He looked for telltale smoke of a deadly prairie fire raging through the high grass. He listened for the sound of a stampeding herd of bison that could capsize and crush the wagon train and cause injury or even death to those in his care. Good wagon masters did this because they needed information in order protect those who followed him. I found myself in the same place in 1980 when I thought about my career in Madison and the future of the department. The stress and conflict of the past eight years had hit me hard.

While things were stable within the department, everything else around me seemed to be tumbling down. A long-term marriage had broken apart and my children were angry with me. I needed a break. At this time, I remember telling colleagues that it was my belief that most of us could handle a crisis at work, or a crisis at home, but not both at the same time. I now found myself with both.

Joel Skornicka was mayor at the time and I

requested a six-month leave of absence without pay. I was tired, and I think he knew it.

Thankfully, he approved. When I was asked why I requested a leave, I said it was to write a book. I even had a title, *The Consumer's Guide to Police*. But others around me knew I was hurting. The speculation was that I was done. I wouldn't return. It was a fair prediction, as an anonymous source within the police department was quoted in the newspaper as saying,

Couper won't be back. He has talked a lot about teaching and writing, and I don't think he'll be back."[63]

The article in which this quote appeared also reported that I had filed for divorce the previous week and had moved out of the family home. Assistant Chief Edward Daley would be in charge during my absence. A day later I had to defend my request to inquiring reporters.

After eight years, I think six months is a reasonable rest for a police chief in Madison… It's a question of whether the people of Madison want a police chief with a heart attack, a police chief with a lot of other problems. I need this rest to be more creative and an even better executive. I am in tune with myself enough to know when it was time to take a break.[64]

As it turned out, writing, skiing, connecting with friends I hadn't seen for a while, and meeting some new ones, made all the difference in the world. It was time to recharge my batteries.

During this sabbatical time, one of the new friends I made was the woman who was to change my life. She was a new officer in the department, just

---

[63] *The Capital Times*, December 11, 1980.
[64] *The Wisconsin State Journal*, December 12, 1980

out of recruit school. I ran into her one day while on leave out walking on the Capitol Square. We talked and had coffee together. We decided to pursue a relationship. As it developed, she offered to leave the department prior to my return and continue her police career elsewhere so we could see where we were going. She did so and a year later, we were married.

Later, I remember asking her why she agreed to have coffee with me that day. Sabine looked at me seriously,

> *"Because I wanted to know if you were as big a jerk as some people say you were."*
> *"What did you find out?" I asked.*
> *"You were," she said smiling, "but you changed."*

Three months later, I surprised everyone and returned to full duty.

Upon my return, I started thinking about leadership—my leadership. Couldn't I do better? I needed to find out. And the optimum way to find out was to ask those whom I was responsible for leading. Was I a jerk?

After talking with Sabine, who was very familiar with the workings of the department, she suggested I hold a number of employee meetings in which I would be there not to talk, but to *listen.* I did so and asked each and every member of the department in these groups what they thought the biggest problem facing the department was. The answer was clear, direct, and unanimous—me. I was the problem, along with a lack of communication department-wide. Those small group meetings with every employee of the department were brutal, but absolutely necessary. If I had not done it, I never would have seen my vision come to fruition. And without this scanning

and listening to employees, the changes I implemented never would have lasted beyond my tenure.

I began to follow-up on what I had learned. I began responding to the communication problem. I did that by establishing an Officer's Advisory Council (OAC). I committed to meeting with the council once a month and thoroughly discuss with them the things they identified as important. It was to be a 10-person council with members elected throughout the department to represent both officer and civilian ranks.

After the first election, despite our growing diversity, all those elected turned out to be male and white. At the first meeting, we discussed this problem. Rather than take an attitude of tough luck, that's the way it is, those elected officers and employees decided that until women and minority representatives were sufficient in number to be elected, we established two more elected seats on the council—one for r a female police officer and another for an officer who was a racial minority. This was a significant step for these officers to take. I knew then that the time was right. It was a signal to me that the race and gender wars were over.

As a department, we were now ready to become more than just a good police department.

The OAC came to play a major role in the leadership and administration of the police department. Its members were given the responsibility for deciding issues like uniforms, types of weaponry, and criteria for the purchase of new patrol vehicles. Today, the OAC continues as a vital player in the Madison Police Department, and it will soon celebrate its 30th year of existence.

At the time I considered changing my leadership style, I had to ask myself what it was that I expected from those with whom I work. I knew that I wanted to work with people who were competent and worthy of my respect. I wanted work that was interesting and challenging. I wanted to work for leaders who listened to my ideas, recognized me when I did good work and kept me informed about what was going on. And I wanted to be able to grow and develop in my job.

I have to admit that leaders on the departments in which I served as an entry-level officer did not usually meet these work expectations. This was primarily because these work desires cannot be met in a coercive, top-down organization.[65]

When I personally asked the members of my own department regarding the kind of leader that would help them in their work, they described the very same things. They wanted to work for leaders who:

- *Respected them.*
- *Cared about them.*
- *Had confidence in their ability to do their jobs.*
- *Trusted them.*
- *Spent time with them.*
- They also said that those leaders needed to be:
- *Competent (knew their job).*
- *Champions (walked their talk).*
- *Fixers and improvers.*
- *Visible and involved.*
- *Willing to take risks and initiate action.*
- *In touch with them, understanding, and*

---

[65] *The Wisconsin State Journal*, December 12, 1980

giving support.
- *Open about what was going on.*

When I started to understand what I was being told, I realized that I must be the first person to be this kind of leader – to change myself and how I acted. Then, I had to help other leaders in the department to do the same thing. I knew that we were all creatures of habit, and that changing to this new way wasn't going to be easy—it would take time and would require a lot of training, patience, and hands-on coaching. It would also be, at times, painful.

In the past, I had set some things in place that were now helping me institute this new leadership style. The first was that I eliminated the military-style atmosphere of the police academy. When I was introduced to the academy class that was already in training before I was appointed, the class stood at attention when I entered the room. In fact, I found that not only did they stand at attention when I entered, but that they did so for every supervisor who came into their class. I also found that their method of teaching left much to be desired. This was more like middle school than a police academy. This, I knew, wasn't how adults learn.

So, I not only had to relax the training atmosphere to make it more suitable for adult learning, but also to find an academy director who shared my thoughts about this. I wanted the police academy to be run like a college or university. If I was going to begin to build a new future for police officers, it had to begin with their first police experience -- the training academy.

I was now in the next step. I wanted department leaders to use an adult-oriented leadership model—police officers were not children

and, therefore, were not to be treated as if they were. A coercive, top-down leadership model had no place within a police department that was seeking highly educated people to come and join it. Some of the people we were trying to attract into a police career were currently in business, law, social work, or teaching. And most of them wouldn't choose to remain in a police department that ran like an 18th century British warship.

I need to clearly say that these changes were not easy for any of us.

We all had, over the years, found comfort in the old leadership model. When I began as a leader, I made a lot of mistakes—but I kept on trying to get it right. I expected the same from others. I came to learn this about organizational change: it should never be imposed from the boss to the workers, but rather from the inside out—that is, after listening, input and study from within the organization. While everyone may not agree with the final direction taken, they need to understand why it is being taken. And once the change is internalized within the department, it can be introduced to the community.

What I began to see is that if I change myself—that is, "walk my own talk," or "practice what I preach"—I teach in a most significant and lasting way. I became the lesson I wanted to teach. In order to do it myself, however, I had to clearly explain, specifically, what I was talking about, why the new approach was necessary for our future, how we would begin to practice it. Then I had to deeply and intently listen to their feedback— how they understood what I was trying to communicate.

I found that the way to begin was for me to get out of my office. I had always believed in an open door policy. But I thought the open door was to

permit my employees to come in and talk with me. How wrong I was. The door to my office was open so that I could get out and listen to them.

This became one of my first experiments in what Tom Peters in the 1980s would call MBWA: Managing by Wandering Around. I started to make a weekly (and sometimes daily) habit to get out of my office and into the workplaces of the department. Each summer I booked a month on the street. I worked nights, in uniform, driving a marked squad car and took calls.[66] My job was to model the street behavior I expected from my officers and to find out what needed improving. I was beginning to learn that transformation begins at the top. Not the other way around.

When department leaders started *listening* to their officers, and avoided strong-arm tactics to get

---

[66] In researching this idea, I found that I was, in fact, "managing by wandering around;" a concept first championed by Tom Peters and Nancy Austin in 1985 after they saw it in operation at Hewlett-Packard. [See Peters, T. and Nancy Austin, "A Passion for Excellence: The Leadership Difference", Collins, 1985.] It was there that Peters saw this technique used by Bill Hewlett and Dave Packard who pioneered the open-style of management. See online article in *The Economist* magazine: http://www.economist.com/node/12075015;7/29/11,114 9 hrs. Today, it is still viewed as one of the "more influential business-management ideas." However, reflecting back, I first started this practice in 1980 at the urging of my wife, Sabine, who was then a rank and file police officer. It just seemed to her that it was a good practice for anyone in a leadership position and detached from the daily and critical work done by police officers and detectives. I remember Dr. Deming once saying that if managers wait for employees to come to them they will only bring managers small problems. The big problems, he said, need to be sought out and found. It is a leader's primary job to do so.

work done, change started to happen. The same thing can go on within the communities police serve—listening works.

Step Four: Train and Lead

Police leaders must implement professional training and a collaborative leadership style.

TO TRAIN IS to lead, and to lead is to train—the two are inextricably linked. Good leaders are good trainers and *vice versa*. When I embarked on the huge task of improving the Madison department from top to bottom, I started thinking about the valuable role rank-and-file officers could take in being an active part of this transformation.

Therefore, I had to be able to attract, hire, and promote to leadership positions the finest people I could find. I knew the kind of people I was looking for and that such high-quality people would only be attracted to serving in an organization that considered them to be of high value and a future leader.

To build a quality department, commanding officers—up to and including the chief—must themselves exhibit a willingness to learn, to alter their own behavior which works against change, and begin to lead by example. Police officers must listen to and respond appropriately to their communities, but the most optimal way to learn this is by what they see going on in their own departments. They can only learn to serve their communities if their own leaders *first serve them.* In this respect, there is much police can learn from the private sector and the academics who work with and define successful leaders in business and industry.

It took me years to develop a style of leadership

that was based more on coaching than on compulsion. In my early years, it seemed as if it was the only way to get officers to do what I wanted them to do. I often wonder today if I took on the role of coach earlier would it have reduced resistance. At the time, I feared that if I did it would have been even greater. I'll never know.

Where did I learn to use coercion? It was in the Marines, and it seemed normal. Everyone else was using it. But you don't have to serve in the Marines to learn strong-arm tactics. It's all around us – in our families of origin and in our workplaces. In the Marines, I did what I was told and made sure that those for whom I was responsible did what I told them to do–or else. That was how I saw my leaders operate. But I also was learning something else: the importance of organizational history and tradition, of courage, honor, and steadfastness in the face of adversity. The Marines taught its recruits all that was noble about the Corps. We all learned the motto: *Semper fidelis*, "Always faithful." I believed I would fight just as fearlessly and ferociously as Marines in the past had done, from the Revolutionary War to the present day; that's what Marines did and who they are.

When I joined the police, I found that most of the men I worked with were veterans like I was; many were former Marines. We had a common language and a common set of leadership expectations as we came together in the police. I remember as a police officer in Minneapolis I was put in charge of training a large group of officers (including supervisors that out-ranked me) in civil disturbance training. One of the sergeants challenged my instruction, and I remember clearly using the leadership style I had learned as a Marine: "Knock it off! I'm in charge here. And if I were you, I wouldn't want to challenge that." He backed down, but looking back, I'm

embarrassed about how I handled that situation. I already knew there were other ways to handle this than the way I did.

Today, many police departments still continue to run their training academies like boot camps. These departments have training officers who look and act like Marine Corps drill instructors. They even wear the familiar Smoky Bear hats of a Marine drill instructor. As I became more acquainted with police work, I couldn't understand why police were using the same training model I had been subjected to as a Marine. There was no similarity whatsoever between being a Marine infantryman and a police officer—the two job functions were as different as night and day.

Later in my career I began to understand that leadership is more than giving orders. I realized that most people, me included, don't like being subjected to pressure in their workplaces. And when we are, our reactions are far from positive. Tom Gordon taught me to reconsider my use of it as a primary leadership style. At the midpoint of my career, I was beginning to have huge doubts about the value and effectiveness of putting people under duress; that is, using coercion. Then I read Gordon's book, *Leader Effectiveness Training*. It provided me with the rationale I needed to avoid it whenever possible.[67] Gordon was widely recognized as a pioneer in teaching communication skills and conflict resolution methods to parents, teachers, youth, organizational managers, and employees.

Gordon was a licensed clinical psychologist on the faculty of the University of Chicago and he served in the Army Air Force during World War II. His target audiences were parents, teachers, and

---

[67] Tom Gordon. *Leader Effectiveness Training*. New York: Bantam Books. 1978.

organizational leaders; now it would be my department and me.[68] In his book, Gordon describes how people react to pressure or intimidation when their leaders use it:

The use of coercive power causes people to reduce their upward communication in an organization. It can also cause people to engage in rivalry and competitiveness, and to rebel and withdraw. The use of coercive power costs the leader in time, enforcement, alienation, stress and, eventually, diminishing influence with employees.

Gordon is saying that when leaders use coercion, they are faced with two immediate problems: they must now make sure their decisions are followed (and that takes extra work), and the quality of these decisions will be less than if they had asked their employees for input. That is because workers will naturally withhold essential information from those who coerce them. This, of course, could be information critical to a high- quality decision. Gordon goes on:

We can all think of situations in which we were coerced into having to accept a superior's decision without our input… [It] also has a negative impact on ideas, creativity, innovation, and motivation.

---

[68] For more information on Tom Gordon and his work, see:
http://www.gordontraining.com/leadershiptraining.html.

A leader is best

When people barely know he exists

Not so good

When people proclaim and obey him

Worse when they despise him

But of a good leader

Who talks little

When work is done His aim

fulfilled

They will say

We did it ourselves

Lao Tzu. 6th century, b.c.e.

The coercive method, nevertheless, became the way most of our industrial, governmental, and educational systems operated—including our police departments. It is the way many of us have experienced leadership in our adult lives. The historical legacy of this, as I mentioned earlier, goes back to Frederick Taylor and his *Scientific Management*.

The cumulative negative effect of using intimidation to lead our nation's workers, especially police, no doubt is incalculable. I cannot say this any clearer: the use of it to lead is wrong and shouldn't be tolerated in any organization. There are more effective ways to lead—and the finest leaders will know this. Along with avoiding using this tactic, there is being a leader who helps, coaches and develops others—a servant leader.

That brings me to Robert Greenleaf. Greenleaf first used the term servant leadership in 1970:[69]

The servant-leader is servant first... That person is sharply different from one who is leader first... The leader-first and the servant-first are two extreme types. Between them there are shadings and blends...[70]

According to Greenleaf, servant leadership is primarily having a focus on *others*, not oneself. It is that focus on others that makes a talented leader. The preeminent leadership test, Greenleaf noted, is for leaders to be able to ask themselves three questions:

- *Do those under my leadership grow as persons?*
- *Do they become healthier, wiser, freer, more autonomous, more likely themselves to become servant leaders?*
- *What is the overall effect of my leadership on those who are under-privileged and will they benefit by my leadership or not?*

These three questions can, of course, be used to evaluate our leaders—but first they should be used to evaluate our own leadership style. Most all of us will, one time or another, be put into some kind of leadership position where others will be dependent upon our direction. This may be in our home, work, or in a volunteer community group.

According to Greenleaf there are also two other serious maladies that confront our society:

---

[69] For more about Robert Greenleaf's work see http://greenleaf.org.

[70] Robert Greenleaf. *The Servant as Leader.* An essay. 1970. Larry Spears, ed. and R.K. Greenleaf. *Servant leadership: A journey into the nature of legitimate power and greatness* (25th anniversary edition.). New York: Paulist Press. 2002.

widespread alienation and the inability or unwillingness of persons to serve. No two attitudes could be more disastrous to any society than these two—a sense of disconnection and the avoidance of serving others. I sense that even today those two maladies continue to confront our society as our economy and place in the world falters.

Greenleaf also foresaw the chief institutional problem of most of our public and private organizations, too high a priority on telling others and too low a priority on doing.

I came to find that these ideas of leadership were not new. I see it today in the motto of the British officer training school at Sandhurst – *Serve to Lead.*[71] Yet, the concept of a servant leader is much older than Sandhurst. It emerges cross-culturally in the writings of the ancient Chinese philosopher Lao Tzu. While some historians disagree as to whether Lao Tzu was an actual historical figure or not, the sayings attributed to him have stood the test of time.

Servant leadership, therefore, isn't a new idea. An essential aspect of the concept is that people who wish to lead must first serve—that is, they must know what it is like to serve others rather than increasing their own wealth or power. The benefit of servant leadership is that those who receive it experience personal growth as they become involved in the working and decisions of the organization, are listened to, and consulted as to what can be done to improve the work they do.

Many of today's management consultants, like Stephen Covey, build on Greenleaf's concept when they highlight the important characteristics of good

[71] Royal Military Academy at Sandhurst, UK. http://www.army.mod.uk/.

leadership. These kinds of leaders:[72]

- *Inspire trust by building relationships.*
- *Clarify purpose by creating goals to be achieved.*
- *Align systems so that there is no conflict between what they say is important and what results they measure.*
- *Able to unleash talent in other people.*
- *The world is vastly different today and ever-changing. If we can develop leaders who can withstand and embrace the changing times by deeply rooting themselves in these principles of great leadership, then we can develop great people, great teams, and great results.*[73]

This brings me to the third influence on my leadership development—W. Edwards Deming.[74] In the case of Deming, his teaching was more personal because I got to know him over the years. I attended his lectures and worked with some of his closest disciples, like Peter Scholtes, Brian Joiner, and Bill Hunter,, and others who came with Deming to participate in the Hunter Conference, an annual quality improvement gathering in Madison.

Later, Deming invited me to a series of Saturday morning discussions he held at the University Club in Washington, D.C. This was a time when many of us in Madison city government were intensely involved in bringing Deming's concepts into our work in city government. I found his personal touch and coaching to be extremely helpful to my own personal growth.

---

[72] http://www.stephencovey.com/blog/?p=6 May 28, 2011; 1124 hrs.

[73] Steven Covey. *Seven Habits of Highly Effective People.* New York: Simon and Schuster. 1992.

[74] 75 For an overview of Deming, see the W. Edwards Deming Institute website at http://deming.org.

Under then-Mayor Joseph Sensenbrenner's leadership (1983-89) there was a total involvement by city employees in this movement. He called it QI: Quality and Improvement. They were the golden years of quality in Madison as government, business, and educational institutions all found wisdom in Deming's methods and then worked together to make quality a lifestyle in Madison. His approach helped me see police work as a system capable of being continuously improved along with the importance of collaborating with others outside the police department. But more importantly, this changed the way I saw myself as a leader.

Deming's ideas first took root in Japanese industry after World War II. Many years later there began a growing movement in our own country to use his methods not only in American industry and business, but government as well. The Madison Police Department was a part of that movement

How was a 90-year-old professor able to impact business both in Japan and the United States? During World War II, Deming worked as a census statistician in Japan for General Douglas MacArthur. In Japan, Deming's expertise in statistical quality control techniques, combined with his involvement in Japanese society, caught the attention of Japanese industrialists. He was invited to join the Japanese Union of Scientists and Engineers (JUSE), whose members had studied the statistical control methods of one of Deming's former teachers, Walter Shewhart. Like Shewhart, Deming believed that a worker's lack of information profoundly hampered the process of improving products and delivering services.

Shewhart, who had worked for Bell Laboratories, developed an improvement cycle that

will be familiar to anyone who has studied problem-oriented policing. The cycle contains four continuous steps: *Plan, Do, Study, Act.* Shewhart and Deming both believed that if this cycle of improvement is maintained, and if management is willing to disregard unsupported ideas, the quality of work, products, and services will consistently improve and costs will be reduced.

As part of America's post-war reconstruction efforts in Japan, that country's industrial leaders wanted to learn more from Deming. During the 1950s, Deming trained hundreds of Japanese engineers, managers, and scholars in his methods. The message was plain and direct; if Japan improved the quality of their products, they would reduce their expenses, increasing both their productivity and market share.

Almost immediately upon hearing Deming's message and learning his methods, a number of Japanese manufacturers applied his technique and soon achieved almost unheard of levels of quality and productivity.

They not only raised the quality of their products, but also did so at reduced cost—and it created an international demand for Japanese products.

Within a few short years, Japanese products moved from being considered junk to the legendary high level of quality and customer loyalty they enjoy today. These Japanese manufacturers who listened to Deming are now familiar household words around the world: Honda, Sony, Toyota, and Mitsubishi.

After the Japanese occupation ended, Deming returned to the United States and began a small consulting business out of his home in Washington,

D.C. And without the startling first decline of the American automobile industry in the late 1980s, along with the energy crisis, Deming most likely would have spent the last years of his life quietly advising a few businesses on the East Coast and writing his memoirs. Then in 1980, he was featured prominently in a now-legendary NBC documentary titled *If Japan Can...Why Can't We?*[75]

This documentary lit a fire in America. It was a question many of us asked. And it deserved an answer. Why couldn't we? The television program that night highlighted the increasing industrial competition we were facing from Japan. It documented how Japan had gone about a process of continuously improving their products, reducing their costs, and dramatically improving the quality of their products. At the time, these were two things our huge, but failing, automobile industry was struggling to achieve.

I remember sitting at home the evening the program aired and feeling something stirring within me—a fire was being lit. Central to the NBC program was an interview with Deming about what he had taught Japanese industrialists after World War II. As a result of the broadcast, the demand for Deming's services increased dramatically. Ford Motor Company was one of the first American corporations to seek help from him.

To the automaker's surprise, when Deming began teaching at Ford, he didn't start out by talking about quality, but rather about poor management at Ford – their leadership. He told them that their

[75] "If Japan Can, Why Can't We?" Television special by NBC TV on June 24, 1980. See Vanderbilt University Archive: http://tvnews.vanderbilt.edu/siteindex/1980-Specials/special-1980-06-24-NBC-1.html.

managers were responsible for *85 percent* of all the problems they were experiencing in developing higher-quality and lower-cost products. The problem wasn't American workers—the problem was their leaders.

Less than four years later, Ford came out with more profitable and higher quality vehicles. Ford chairman Donald Petersen said,

We are moving toward building a quality culture at Ford, and the many changes that have been taking place here have their roots directly in Dr. Deming's teachings.[76]

Leadership cannot be separated from training. How any worker is trained is directly related to the quality of their work. If leaders don't provide quality training to their employees, how can they expect their employees to be able to deliver the high-quality services they demand?

When I came to Madison I knew that I must immediately adopt a two-fold approach to my work. The first goal was to improve training, both pre- and in-service, within the police department. The second was to develop its leaders.

I knew that it took more than the four weeks of police training I received in 1962 to effectively prepare a new police officer; my guess was, it took at least a year. And I knew that I had to immediately put an end to the authoritarian model of leadership Madison was using to train and lead its police officers – old and new.

Top-quality leaders and competent instructors who are themselves modeling the coaching and

[76] http://www.bbh.ro/pdf/EW-Deming.pdf January 1, 2011; 1320 hrs.

mentoring style of thoughtful servant-like leadership must staff the academy. And an academy must be of sufficient length to be able to train officers in the basic skills necessary to be a competent and effective police officer. It must also acculturate them into a new style of policing and embrace its values. I needed to stress to Madison recruits that the most powerful weapon they had out on the beat was their brain, not their firearm.

Currently, police recruit training in the United States averages about 16 weeks in duration. Larger departments—those with more than 100 officers—train their officers only slightly longer: an average of 21 weeks. As to in-service training, while over 80 percent of our nation's police agencies report that they conduct it, it averages fewer than five days a year.

Police have argued back and forth for years about the time necessary to adequately train a police recruit and the amount of time that should be committed to in-service training after they are sent out on the beat. Many factors come into play here. On one hand, there is intense pressure from elected officials and citizens on police leaders to deploy newly hired officers as quickly as possible. Often, political squabbling and financial restrictions within a city have delayed the police department's hiring plans, and as a result, pressure comes from within the police ranks as well, to get newly hired officers on the street as soon as possible.

Yet a clear and present danger exists, both in terms of safety and liability, if police officers are deployed who are not adequately prepared. Unfortunately, most police trainers are given a set period of time in which they are expected to turn out competent police officers. The inclusion of new topics in the curriculum to meet current trends,

needs, or expectations—such as learning how to care for an increasing population of homeless or mentally ill people—is often neglected in favor of the traditional curriculum. And when new courses are proposed, police trainers are left with a decision as to which current courses they should be reduce or even eliminate in order to keep within the timeframe they have been given.

Even more unsettling is to learn that well over half of our nation's police academies train in an atmosphere police trainers themselves identify as stress-based; that is, intimidating, even bullying. This makes half of American police academies more like military boot camps or correctional facilities than places in which college-educated young men and women are prepared to be professional police practitioners.

Looking to other occupations that are similar to police work, from paramedic work to psychology, we find statewide requirements for their practitioners' education and training, methods of examination and licensing, independent reviews of their conduct, and required continuing education. In comparison, what is required of the police seems grossly inadequate.

In recent years, police have learned the benefits derived from a supervised field training experience for their new officers. Such a program enables a department to continue the training and evaluation of their recruits in the actual environment in which they will work. Coupled with an 18-month probationary period, a structured field training experience with a senior officer helps ensure that new officers are not only well-coached but also capable of making the crucial day-to-day decisions required of them. But for that to work takes well trained and prepared field trainers who are also able to be effective trainers and leaders.

In-service training—or continuing education—is necessary for veteran police officers and can be met in a number of ways. There should be a formal annual in-service training for all police officers for at least a period of two weeks. There should also be various short roll-call training topics supervisors can cover before officers go on duty; this sort of on-going training will also model leaders as teachers. And there can be formal coaching programs, specialized schools outside the department, and encouragement of police officers to increase their formal academic education in related fields, such as criminology, public administration, psychology, counseling, and law.

Given what other professions in America are doing, primarily through their governing bodies and state licensing boards, it wouldn't be unreasonable to expect police officers, including those in supervisory and command positions, to meet an annual two-week training requirement of at least 80 hours of continuing education credits.

When citizens in our society have contact with most vocational practitioners, from physicians to plumbers, they have a set of expectations. They expect the practitioners to be competent and to solve their problem to the best of their ability, and to do so at a fair and reasonable price. They also expect that practitioners will behave respectfully and competently.

And when it comes to police, these expectations should be no different. In fact, given the authority given to police in our society, citizens have the right to expect even more—the very highest level of respectful treatment and competent practice.

While the improper practice of some

professions may result in inconvenience or monetary loss, improper practice on the part of police may result in not only the loss of one's liberty, but also life. With so much at stake, it shouldn't be unreasonable to expect that each state have a politically independent police standards board with the authority to set minimum standards for police selection and training. Equally reasonable would be a requirement that police actually be licensed by the state and their conduct subject to review like other licensed professionals as some forward-thinking states are now doing.

Historically, trying to make police be more accountable to their communities through the courts has been unsuccessful. Any change that is court-ordered usually isn't sustainable. Therefore, it can in no way be considered an effective method for organizational transformation. I would also place on the ineffective list training curricula or programs like community and problem-oriented policing that are implemented top-down, without officer input, or without consideration to the other organization- wide changes that also need to be put in place.

More recently, two American criminology professors, Allison Chappell and Lonn Lanza-Kaduce studied a police academy in Florida. They looked specifically at storytelling as a way for leaders to help implement community-oriented policing. I found it to be very interesting because storytelling was one of the primary leadership tools I had used in Madison years earlier. There is power in a story.

When I began to teach other police leaders around the country what we were doing in Madison, the stories I told seemed to be the most effective way I had to get my points across. Those who attended my classes wanted to hear the stories. In effect, the storytelling that goes on within a police academy or

department are usually the real things that an organization values. That's why they are so essential; through story, police officers begin to understand the nature of policing, how they are supposed to act, and what seems to be important.[77]

Unfortunately, in most police organizations there are more stories about the successes of traditional practices than community policing. In fact, the culture of traditional policing is full of stories that range from high-speed pursuits to drug busts and shoot-outs. Stories are effective; they capture a listener's attention and, with regard to traditional policing, invariably involve the physical, not the service-oriented, side of policing. Chappell and Lanza-Kaduce found out that police called those traditionally oriented stories war stories:

The context of war stories shifted the setting; it became informal and relaxed—both for the storyteller and the listeners. War stories were "times out" from the usual discipline that was expected. The recruits were allowed to laugh and enjoy themselves. The relaxed storytelling defined what was truly valued in police work and in the police culture.[78]

I found, however, that a department transforming to a more community and problem-oriented culture can find just as many interesting and captivating war stories as those told about traditional policing.

A case in point would be a neighborhood foot patrol officer in my department who worked very closely with her community. In the process of doing

[77] Chappell, Allison T. and Lonn Lanza-Kaduce. "Police Academy Socialization: Understanding the Lessons Learned in a Paramilitary-Bureaucratic Organization." *Journal of Contemporary Ethnography.* Sage Publications, December, 2009.
[78] *Ibid.*

this, she found that quite a large number of residents on her beat had outstanding warrants for a variety of offenses. She went back to the office and developed a list of those in her neighborhood with outstanding warrants; their home addresses, mug shots, and phone numbers. Rather than forming a traditional task force to go out in the early morning hours and raid these residences, she did something different. She started making phone calls. "Hello, this is your neighborhood police officer, I work in your neighborhood and I understand you have an outstanding warrant. It is necessary that you get this cleared up, and so I expect you to satisfy this warrant within 10 days. Can you do that?"

When she started this, the number of open warrants in her neighborhood diminished significantly. People came in and took care of them in ways a traditional police crackdown could never have accomplished. Of course there was criticism from some of her peers. "She has no authority to do this. Only the court can grant an extension, and her job was to go out and arrest these criminals." But the proof of the pudding is always in the eating, and the power of this story is that she cleared up more warrants than anyone else, or any special task force had. And she did it in a very creative and effective way.

Another officer in another neighborhood across town (who is now Madison's chief of police) put together a computer skills class for unemployed, low-income women in his neighborhood. These women had lost their jobs because their clerical skills didn't include computerized word processing. His efforts resulted in many of these women finding employment again.

Still another officer found empirical data to support placing highly visible traffic cones in

restricted speed school zones. As part of this experiment, he clocked the speeds of vehicles in zones that had the more- visible warning cones versus those that didn't. There was a significant reduction in the speed of traffic in school zones with the traffic warning cones present. This officer took a chance in doing this because one of the city attorneys had previously stated the police had no authority to put objects like traffic cones into the roadway and said we couldn't do this.

Since that time, however, the practice he recommended has become standard not only in Madison but throughout the state. He, too, suffered some peer criticism, "How could he not have ticketed those speeders? His job is to write tickets, not do speed studies." Perhaps, but this officer saw his job as more: ensuring a lasting method of safety for children in the community. To him, the most effective way was to develop a method to reduce the speed of automobiles in school zones throughout the city. And he was able to prove that his system actually worked.

Another officer responded to complaints that cars were speeding in his district in this way: the traditional approach was to run radar, write a bunch of tickets, and then go on to other business. This officer, however, thought there might be a better way. He decided he would work with the neighborhood association. He called neighborhood leaders together and asked for help. Together, they developed a plan.

After notifying the media about what they were about to do, they set up radar and waved those who were speeding into a large parking lot and off the street. It was there that neighborhood residents approached the speeders and requested that they slow down for their children's sake.

The officer was present in the parking lot but didn't make the initial contact after he stopped the vehicle. No tickets were issued. The entire city heard of the traffic safety project in the local news, and people began not only to slow down at that school crossing zone, but it was reported that speeding was reduced throughout the city.

Yet another neighborhood officer, assigned to an area with a high concentration of Hmong, took the time to learn their language so she could be a more effective police officer in their neighborhood. This skill was critical when she had to inform community leaders that cultural practices like abducting underage women for purposes of marriage wasn't permitted here. She paved the way for our first Hmong officer who was hired in 1991.

For new police, these can be powerful stories because in each case the officers involved stepped outside the traditional policing box to alter an established practice of the department. In each case, what they did resulted in sturdier bonds with the community. In each project, officers were willing to work informally and outside established hierarchies to get the job done. These stories soon became the new stories; stories that could reinforce principles of community policing and compete with the old war stories.

In concluding their study, Chappell and Lanza-Kaduce made some specific recommendations to integrate community or problem-oriented policing within a police organization. They suggested three crucial changes:

The academy should re-examine its paramilitary structure (marching, posting, dress, discipline, war stories); especially consider introducing the horizontal and less-formal

relationships that occur in many community-policing activities.
The academy must find ways to align informal
instruction with the formal curriculum (blending traditional
and community-oriented policing).

The academy should re-examine its culture in terms of
how it defines police work and in regards to the us vs. them
mentality... all members of the public, including the suspects
and the perps, should be dealt with professionally.[79]

Department leaders must know, experience and
be able to relate stories that support the new
direction the department is going. And this
storytelling must not only be done within the
department but within the community as well.

As I have sharply argued, the education and
training of police isn't a subject that can be discussed
separately from the structure and style of leadership
of the police department (including storytelling). The
practice of educating and training employees is part
and parcel of an effective city government—a
government that will also make sure that the chief of
police of their city is also able to meet specific
professional expectations.[80]

The following story comes from a time when I
was teaching three- day leadership courses for police
chiefs and their staffs across the country. I developed
this course in order to share what I had learned about
leadership and community-oriented policing in
Madison.

One particular morning I was at a large urban
police department in Nevada. As I was setting up my
classroom at their training academy, I looked out the
window and observed a formation of their new police

[79] *Ibid*
[80] See Appendices E and F.

recruits. I decided to go outside and get a closer look. The recruits were standing in three ranks—it was an inspection, a situation I could easily relate to from my days as a Marine.

Suddenly, the training instructors started yelling at the new officers. Some were ordered to do push-ups by way of the familiar military command: "Drop and give me ten." In addition, I heard the instructors calling the young officers "assholes." I returned to the classroom in time to greet the chief and his command staff. I introduced myself and the curriculum for the next three days, and then asked, "Are your officers permitted to call citizens names?"

They seem shocked, "We have rules against doing that. Why do you ask?"

"Well," I replied, "I was watching your new officers outside this window and observed your trainers calling them very derogatory names. You know, it really doesn't matter if you have rules against such conduct because when their teachers call them names, they will think that it's okay for them to do the same to citizens. And if you ever try to discipline them, their defense will simply be, 'That's what the department taught me.'"

I recently learned that the department never did change. Their academy remains stress-based, military, and intimidating. I don't know if their training officers ever stopped calling recruit officers names. But one thing I do know, is that if they don't stop, I predict they will continue to have problems with officers disrespecting citizens. How could they expect any different kind of an outcome? [81]

---

[81] That department recently was identified as using "harsh" recruit training methods in the *Las Vegas Review Journal*, "Police Academy Recruits Endure Harsh Road," http://www.lvrj.com/news/a-new-day-a-new-life-

From insights like this, I was able to develop a new style of leadership in the early 1980s that was closely aligned with the teachings of Gordon, Greenleaf, and Deming. I called "quality leadership." Now I had to start walking my talk. It had to start with me, but it also needed to be practiced by other leaders in the department. Needless to say, not every leader in the department was enthusiastic about changing their leadership style.

But I stayed on message, trying to demonstrate that those of us who were the leaders of the department were the first people who had to start. In police work, senior leaders didn't (and still don't) typically rise to a level of authority by being more open, good listeners, or supportive of the men and women they are responsible to lead. Instead, traditional police leadership was and is more known for being closed, not taking input from subordinates, and not being supportive of them—coercive—more about controlling than coaching.

After I trained department leaders, the next step was to conduct something I called the *Four-Way Check*, It required every department leader, including myself, to participate. Briefly, the check required leaders to get feedback on their performance from four directions—1) those whom they supervised, 2) peers with whom they worked, 3) the person to whom they reported, and finally 4) an in-depth self-evaluation and meeting with me.

112139069.html, January 1 2011; 1151 hrs. It didn't note whether recruit officers were still called "assholes" or other derogatory names during their training.

Principles of Quality Leadership

1. *Believe in, foster, and support teamwork.*
2. *Be committed to the problem-solving process; use it and let data, not emotions, drive decisions.*
3. *Seek employees input before you make key decisions.*
4. *Believe that the most effective way to improve the quality of work or service is to ask and listen to employees who are doing the work.*
5. *Strive to develop mutual respect and trust among employees; drive out fear.*
6. *Have a customer orientation and focus toward employees and citizens.*
7. *Manage according to the behavior of 95 percent of employees and not the 5 percent who cause problems. Deal with the 5 percent promptly and fairly.*
8. *Improve systems and examine processes before blaming people.*
9. *Avoid "top-down," power-oriented decision-making whenever possible.*
10. *Encourage creativity through risk-taking and be tolerant of honest mistakes.*
11. *Be a facilitator and coach. Develop an open atmosphere that encourages providing and accepting feedback.*
12. *With teamwork, develop with employees agreed-upon goals and a plan to achieve them.*

As you might expect, all of this aroused and stirred up headquarters. I had some people on my top command staff that were digging in their heels. They had supported me and been with me since the early days of the 1970s. Many of them felt they didn't need to change, and they didn't particularly want to do this. Some of them were not interested in asking their employees how they were doing as a leader. They were quite comfortable with the control style of leadership we had all invariably used for years.

The reluctance of my command staff (all of whom had tenure) was troubling, but I knew this was a noteworthy moment of truth for me and for the future of the department. Was I really committed to this new process, or would I back off when the people who reported to me showed reluctance?

At a meeting of the department's highest commanders I talked about why I thought the new process was crucial for us and why the future of the department was dependent upon it. I wanted them to reach a consensus before I went further. But as we went around the table that day, I knew I didn't have one—in fact, only a few were in favor of what I was proposing.

What was I to do? Well, I had learned that one of the major benefits of following Deming's teachings was that it would help us build relationships with leaders in other fields who were trying to do the same things we were. And at a quality training session a year or so earlier, I had met a man from Milwaukee who was in the manufacturing business.[82] I remember him saying that he had struggled with getting buy-in from his managers. So I gave him a call and went to

---

[82] I can't remember the date, though it was quite early in our change efforts, probably the early 1980s. I only remember his name was "Bill" and that he was the quality person for Falk Gear in Milwaukee.

visit him.

He turned out to be extremely helpful. He said that in his experience, if the principal leaders in an organization waited until everyone got on board, they would never get to where they needed to go. Instead, he suggested, if I could get 25 percent of my staff willing to move with me, I should do so.

At first that sounded dangerous. Just 25 percent? Didn't I need to have a majority? Would I dare move with less and leave a lot of my people behind? Even those who had been my stalwarts?

He replied, "No, you don't leave them behind. You tell them you are leaving, going to a new place, because you intensely believe it is the right thing to do. You need them. You want them to come with you—but you can't allow them to stay back. They have to come along now."

He went on to share with me a compelling image:

Your boat is about to cross a wide river and land at a new place. When the boat leaves, it won't return. It's a one-way trip. You want your whole team to come with you, but you won't be able to come back later for them. You want everyone to come on board with you because you value them and their contributions, even if they are not fully committed to making the trip. Later, you tell them, they will become more comfortable with what you are asking of them and willing to do yourself. You commit to helping, coaching, and teaching them so they will be successful in this new way. You won't leave them hanging out. You remind them this is also a new and difficult way for you. But you need them to come with you—now.

So when I determined that I had at least a quarter of my topmost commanders on board, I gave the boat speech. I could tell it was very

uncomfortable for some to hear, but for others it was a sign that I was really committed to the direction we were about to go. There was electricity in the air—invigoration for some and shock for others.

As the boat left the dock, it was a stormy journey—but what my friend in Milwaukee told me that day turned out to be excellent advice. And eventually, it worked.

But when leaders who reported directly to me were not seen as supporting this effort, or were unwilling to make personal changes, I had a big problem on my hands. Remember, I worked within a civil service system of tenured leaders. Would I formerly discipline them? What was I going to do? These were my team members, men and women I had promoted and worked with over the years. Now some were refusing to change.

All in all, this era became the second major transformation I introduced in the department. We all had survived the first, but would we survive this one? The first transformation was to address our training needs, recruit more educated and talented personnel, and alter the way in which we were responding to public protest. Now, almost 10 years into the job, I made the decision that we must develop a work environment that was able to listen and tap into the intelligence and experience of our officers and other employees. It was a difficult time.

As it turned out, most tried. And even though their employees didn't consider them as true leaders, as adopting the new leadership style, they were given credit for trying. Other command officers simply waited me out. Waited for retirement eligibility and left. The officers who replaced them, however, were those who not only adopted the new leadership but also were enthusiastic about it. These new leaders

were viewed by department employees as being honest practitioners—they practiced what they preached. We now were into the second transformation.

One of the more effective steps I took to get reluctant command officers on board was to have them identify three to five things under their command that were in need of improvement, for which they would take personal responsibility, and then work on them. They were to submit their list to me for approval. Then share it with their officers. Periodically, they would report to me as to how their efforts were progressing.

The main factor, of course, was that they were to use our new methods of leadership to do so. And when members of the department saw the department's highest commanders working to improve the things for which they were responsible, and using the new methods, it made a big difference. They became more effective leaders. Leaders were now teaching by doing. This is the crucial relationship between leadership and training in operation. The two are not separate. Leaders train and trainers lead.

Step Five: Improve Continuously

Police must unceasingly improve the systems in which they work--everything they do.

IMPROVEMENT OF OUR nation's police is possible, but it has got to be a constant and not sporadic occurrence. It is going to take some work from each and every one of us. It is possible to engage police officers in a pursuit of excellence, which is essentially what this is. In the long run, this commitment to improving the systems in which police work is good for them and all of us: police will

have more support from their community, they will feel nobler about themselves and the work they do, and their workplaces will be more comfortable, gratifying, and engaging.

It will be so for citizens, too, because police themselves will be treated with dignity and worth within their own workplaces, and have leaders who respect and listen to them. The method I used was that which Deming proposed – all work is a system; all systems can be improved.

While this isn't the only method available, it was one that found persuasive resonance with me. But one thing must be clear: whatever system is used in the organization, it must always exist to help them excel, and to do so *incessantly*. What is isn't good enough, because what is can and should be done better, whether it is processing traffic tickets or responding to public protest.

An organization that is committed to, values, and engages in making things better, is a more effective and exciting place to work. Citizens will feel safer and more in control of their problems when they have a department like this in their community.

Additionally, citizens will benefit by being policed by men and women who are committed to protecting their rights. There will be more ease in the minority community as many of the police officers will be, themselves, people of color. But most significant of all these characteristics, officers will treat everyone fairly and respectfully and be willing to work with community members in solving problems.

The reality, however, is that even if you begin today, it will take years to do this. The first place to start is in your city, county, town, or village and the time is now. For the most part, good police

departments come from having people working inside of them who hold the values I have identified in this book. It is a truth that good policing, on the way to being distinguished policing, happens not so much because of the techniques, tools, or structures of a police department, but because of the values held by the men and women who do the work. Those police departments are found in communities that hold dear the basic values of our society: liberty, justice, fairness, equality, and participation.

I have always said that I could pick first-rate officers and leaders, if I knew whether they thought people were basically good or bad. If they believed people were essentially good, then they could be trained and developed to be good police officers and leaders of police. If they believed otherwise—that people were essentially bad or evil—it was a very difficult task to train and develop them into the kind of police and leaders I wanted in my department and you want policing your community.

Officers who believe everyone is just waiting for a chance to do evil are not able to be caring or compassionate. I say this not to deny the existence of evil, for there surely are terribly evil people out there, but rather we must see things in balance: there *are* evil people in the world, but they are small in number compared with those of us who try to follow society's rules and help others.

As these critical steps of casting a bold vision, selecting the finest, focusing on training, listening, collaboratively leading, and working to continuously improve, are taken they will begin to show results both inside the police department and outside in the community.

The next step is to evaluate and to measure what has been done – are there data to show that

things have, in fact, turned around? Can the department measure its stated achievements?

Step Six: Evaluate

Police must be able to critically assess, or have assessed, the crucial tasks and functions they are expected to perform.

MY FIRST EFFORTS to evaluate how we were doing were rudimentary. I knew I had to have frequent and on-going contact with the Madison community I was hired to serve and protect. I should say its *communities* because no city is just a community by itself; a city today consists of many diverse communities. But for the most part, I became the sounding board for the department. Listening was my first attempt to try and determine how we were doing in realizing our vision and staying on mission.

This caused me to always be willing to talk to just about any group in the city or journalist from the media and tell my story—my vision for our police department—and listen to what they had to say in response.

Another effort came about as we evolved into a community- oriented organization. I came to understand that I needed a more official and systematic way to find out how we were doing. To find a way beyond just listening at community meetings, receiving comments from elected officials, or reading letters to the editor in our daily newspapers. I needed to find some way to directly ask citizens as to their level of satisfaction with our services.

From my own experience, I knew this: citizens who have had no contact with their police tend to rate us quite high; out of sight, out of mind.

Conversely, those who have had contact with us don't rate us quite as high as those who have not. And, disturbingly, the more contact citizens have with us, the lower they tend to rate us (remember what Nicholas Peart said earlier about what he thought about repetitive stop and frisk tactics by police in his community).

What I intended to do was create a survey of people who had contact with us – I called it a customer survey. A contact could be, for instance, making a verbal complaint, being the victim of a crime, or even being arrested. As it turned out, the results of this monthly survey became a valuable source of information. It helped me to more realistically evaluate how we were really doing.

Think about it: without an ongoing survey, how will any police department know how it is doing? In the business world, customer feedback is essential. It should be no different in a police agency. How else will police know what their citizens think of their services? But more critical, how else will police know what services or functions need to be improved?

I decided I needed to have this kind of feedback. I wanted to hear from those with whom we had actual contact; not those who just have an opinion about us. I wanted to know how we were doing from those with whom we actually had dealt face to face. If I was requiring department leaders to get feedback from each other and their employees, why not from those who used our services?

After a number of things were considered, such as cost, the number of surveys we needed to send out, and to whom we'd send them, I began to mail out a survey form with a self-addressed, stamped envelope. It was sent from me to the people identified in every 50th police incident (as determined

by randomly-selected case numbers). Each survey was enclosed with a personal letter explaining why I was doing this, why I thought it was necessary, and asked for their feedback.[83] The survey asked them to rate their experience with us on a scale from one to five (one being poor and five being excellent) in seven categories:

- *Concern*
- *Helpfulness*
- *Knowledge*
- *Quality of service*
- *Solving the problem*
- *Putting you at ease*
- *Professional conduct*

At the end of the survey, I asked the critical question: how can we improve? And those who answered were not hesitant to tell me.

The survey also asked respondents for personal information about where they live, their age, race, gender, and income level. I made a commitment in the letter I sent out to read *every* returned survey and publish the results in our newsletter, whether the commentary was good or bad. I also made it clear to both officers and the citizens who received the surveys that they wouldn't be used to initiate disciplinary action against any officer. There was another way to do that. If a citizen had a complaint against a particular officer, they were directed to contact our Internal Affairs Unit. I had to make it clear this survey wasn't about discipline, but about gathering important information as to how we were doing.

---

[83] At that time we were assigning about 100,000 case numbers each year; therefore, a 1-in- 50 sampling meant we mailed out an average of 160 surveys each month.

We had a very respectable return rate of 35 to 40 percent. I used the results to report to the mayor and city council how the department was doing in personal hands-on contacts. During the seven years I used the survey, we made steady progress in improving overall citizen satisfaction each and every year. I put together and published a line graph showing the rate of citizen satisfaction officers were achieving. It was a clear, visual indication that Madison officers were continuously improving. And they did it on the street with all types of people and in all kinds of situations.

Traditionally, police departments have learned how they are doing by paying attention to the wrong things. Police leaders gathered information by reading newspapers, watching television news, attending city council meetings, civic gatherings, reviewing formal complaints, and talking with community leaders, just as I had done for years. All of these things need to be done, but they won't tell a police chief how his or her department is *really* doing. Only a broad survey that pays attention to age, gender, race, and socioeconomic level can do that. The only effective way to know whether the people who use police services feel their police department is doing a good job is to ask those who have had *direct* contact with its officers and employees.

My next step was to seek an outside evaluation of our efforts. Did continuous improvement really happen? Were they effective? I needed to know the answers to these questions as well, not just from my gut, or from a survey, but from empirical data. I decided to ask the National Institute of Justice to formally evaluate us. A research proposal was developed and the contract awarded to the Police Foundation in Washington, DC. After a three-year study, this is what they found:

- *Job satisfaction among police employees was high.*
- *Teamwork went on between shifts, especially in officers' approach to problem solving; it also included detectives and neighborhood officers.*
- *The burglary rate in the community was lowered.*
- *There were reduced sick leave and use of overtime.*
- *There was high citizen satisfaction with police services.*
- *A work environment was established that empowered police employees to be creative in their duties.*[84]

The findings were significant. A transformation had occurred.

They found that our new style of leadership was apparent throughout the department as well as in the experimental police district (EPD). (The mission of the EPD was to experiment with new patrol and investigative strategies including an intense experiment with quality leadership.)

An interesting additional finding was that even though the number of officers in the department had not increased during the four-year research period, citizens reported seeing *more* police all over the city; an outcome, perhaps, of getting closer to the community and encouraging motor patrol officers to get out and walk their neighborhoods.

The three-year study examined the efforts undertaken by us to create a new organizational

---

[84]*Community Policing In Madison: Quality From the Inside, Out. Technical Report*, Mary Ann Wycoff and Wesley G. Skogan. Washington: Police Foundation. 1993.

design—both structural and managerial, built to support community- and problem-oriented policing. Notably, researchers found the department's attempt to bring progressive, comprehensive change to our operations was successful:

- *Employee attitudes toward work and the organization improved.*
- *Physical decentralization was achieved.*
- *Residents believed crime had become less of a problem.*
- *Residents believed police were working to resolve issues of importance to the neighborhood.*

In the conclusion of their report they made a statement that I believe captures Madison's 12-year effort to raise the fairness and effectiveness of the police function in their community; a second major effort during my 20-year tenure.

[I]t is possible to change a traditional, control- oriented police organization into one in which employees become members of work teams and participants in decision- making processes... This research suggests that associated with these internal changes are external benefits for citizens, including indications of reductions in crime and reduced levels of concern about crime.

All of the above methods of evaluation are ways that communities and their leaders can attempt to determine how well their police are doing. But no matter what I did, the methods I devised to measure and evaluate how my department was doing paled in comparison to the public influence created by publication of *Crime in the United States*, the annual report of the FBI as part of the national system of Uniform Crime Reporting (UCR).[85] I vowed early on

---

85 86 http://www.fbi.gov/about-us/cjis/ucr/ucr;

in my career that I wasn't going to allow this to be the sole measure by which my department and my leadership were going to be evaluated.

In a recent interview, veteran journalist Bill Moyers talked with David Simon, creator of the popular HBO series *The Wire*, Simon, a former journalist and police reporter, talked about evaluation. Simon mentioned the propensity of corporations, governments, and their agencies to "juke their stats"—that is, to alter data so that it appeared that they were doing well, even when they weren't. The following dialogue is from an episode from *The Wire*, in which "Prez" Pryzbylewski, a cop turned teacher, has an exchange with the school principal about numbers and teacher evaluation:

Principal: So for the time being, all teachers will devote class time to teaching language arts sample questions. Now, if you turn to page eleven, please, I have some things I want to go over with you.

Prez: I don't get it—all this so we score higher on the state tests? If we're teaching the kids the test questions, what is it assessing in them?

Teacher: Nothing—it assesses us. The test scores go up, they can say the schools are improving. The scores stay down, they can't.

Prez: Juking the stats. Teacher: Excuse me?

Prez: Making robberies into larcenies, making rapes disappear. You juke the stats, and majors become colonels. I've been here before.[86]

In his interview with Moyers, Simon further

December 13, 2011; 0932 hrs
[86] *The Wire.* Home Box Office miniseries, Season 4. 2006.

reflects on his life as a journalist and police reporter:

> *You show me anything that depicts institutional progress in America, school test scores, crime stats, arrest reports, arrest stats, anything that a politician can run on, anything that somebody can get a promotion on. And as soon as you invent that statistical category, 50 people in that institution will be at work trying to figure out a way to make it look as if progress is actually occurring when actually no progress is… a police commissioner or a deputy commissioner can get promoted, and a major can become a colonel, and an assistant school superintendent can become a school superintendent, if they make it look like the kids are learning, and that they're solving crime. And that was a front-row seat for me as a reporter. Getting to figure out how the crime stats actually didn't represent anything, once they got done with them.*[87]

I spent a good deal of my time as police chief trying to teach members of the media, as well as elected officials and community members, what exactly crime was and what it meant. To remind them that a numerical increase or decrease didn't necessarily mean that crime was *actually* up or down. I didn't juke the stats nor pressure my officers about reducing these imaginary numbers.

A reported numerical increase (as the UCR shows) could instead mean citizens have more confidence in the police to solve crime, and therefore are now reporting it. On the other hand, a decrease in the rate of reporting could indicate not that crime is down but that police are underreporting various crimes by labeling them as lesser offenses; a practice that many believe to be standard operating procedure in most American cities today.

For example, an attempted burglary might be

---

[87] Bill Moyers. PBS interview with David Simon (producer of the critically acclaimed HBO series *The Wire.*) April 17, 2009.

classified as a vandalism; a forcible rape as an assault; a homicide as a sudden death. Each of these instances of downgrading would move a crime from the UCR's closely watched eight Part I Offenses category to the lesser considered category of Part II Offenses.[88] A decrease in reported crime could also mean that citizens have less confidence in the police to do anything about it and, therefore, simply don't bother to report it.

The fact is that none of us can make a valid judgment one way or another when it comes to analyzing *reported* crime as the data are presently collected. However, there are more valid statistical methods in existence to determine *actual*, not simply reported, rates of crime. This method uses a statistical sampling of citizens, rather than relying on offenses that are reported to the police and that the police in turn report. Yet America and their police still are wedded to this archaic method of data collection and evaluation in spite of the existence of more effective and truer methods of measurement.

That said, and despite my years of educating the media, I don't think many of them wanted to abandon the simplistic aspect of being able to report crime being either up or down—the data released by the UCR. Remember, when you hear crime is either up or down, it really isn't a very good way to evaluate how your police are doing. You need to ask more questions.

Social and economic factors have an enormous influence on the nature and levels of crime in any community.[89] In fact, even the UCR lists factors that

[88] Federal Bureau of Investigation. Annual Uniform Crime Report.

[89] David Couper. *How to Rate Your Local Police*. Washington: Police Executive Research Forum. 1983.

can influence crime: the size of the community, how crowded an area is, the composition of the population, with particular regard to age, the stability of a community; economic conditions, job availability, climate, and various emphases of local law enforcement agencies.[90] What wasn't anticipated at the time the UCR was created was that police agencies themselves would manipulate the data for their own purposes— that is, juke the stats, to show the supposed effectiveness of a particular mayor or police chief.

But, of course, we should have. The problem of how we count things isn't a new one. Nearly a century ago, a British public servant had this to say about reporting statistics:

The governments are very keen on amassing statistics. They collect them, add them, raise them to the nth power, take the cube root, and prepare wonderful diagrams. But you must never forget that every one of these figures comes in the first instance from the [village watchman], who just puts down what he damn pleases.[91]

It is true that citizens who live in a community where the police are respected and responsive are more willing to report crimes than those who live in communities where police are not respected or not thought to be effective. The result can be that a police department that is negatively viewed by the community will have a *low* incidence of crime reporting and therefore a low crime rate, while a police department thought to be highly effective and responsive would experience a high reporting rate. In these cases, reported crime will be up because citizens believe their police can and will do something about

[90]http://www2.fbi.gov/ucr/cius2009/about/variables_affecting_crime.html , May 25, 2011; 0907 hrs.
[91] Josiah Stamp. *Some Economic Factors in Modern Life.* London: King and Sons. 1929.

it.

Additionally, the *kind* of criminal activity that often threatens a community and causes widespread fear isn't often captured by many of the eight Part I UCR Crimes. These are criminal activities that affect the quality of life in our cities, such as street drug dealing, weapons offenses, littering, graffiti, noise violations, and other alarming and unsettling events. Simply stated, the current system isn't a good method to either know the amount and extent of crime in your community or to evaluate your police department, there are other ways to do this.

One way would be to expand the National Crime Victimization Survey (NCVS), which has been collecting data on personal and household victimization in America since 1973. It provides an ongoing, statistically sound sample of residential addresses. Twice each year, data are obtained from a nationally representative sample of roughly 49,000 households, comprising about100,000 people, as to the frequency, characteristics, and consequences of criminal victimization in the United States. The U.S. Census Bureau on behalf of the Bureau of Justice Statistics administers it.

The NCVS provides the largest national forum for victims to describe the impact of crime on them and the characteristics of violent offenders. It was designed with four primary objectives in mind.

- *To develop detailed information about the victims and consequences of crime.*
- *To estimate the number and types of crimes not reported to the police.*
- *To provide uniform measures of selected types of crimes.*
- *To permit comparisons of crime over time and*

types of areas.[92]

The survey categorizes crimes as personal or property crimes. Personal crimes are rapes and sexual attacks, robberies, and aggravated and simple assaults, including purse-snatchings and pocket picking. Property crimes are burglaries, thefts, auto thefts, and vandalism.

We also must remember that even though we have a statistical method to more effectively uncover unreported crime through the NCVS, a substantial number of crimes still take place that will remain unknown to either police or those who conduct the surveys. It is crime that neither reporting nor surveying discovers.

Victimization studies frequently reveal that *less than one-half* of the crimes that occur are reported to the police. The reason for this is that victims often feel there is little the police can do about a crime or the crime involved an activity they don't wish others to know about such as a man who gets robbed in a park known for being frequented by homosexuals.

Because his family and co-workers don't know of his sexual orientation, he may choose *not* to report the crime. This can also be true in other assaults, including forcible rapes after which the victim does not wish to either be identified or testify as a witness against his or her offender.

Victims often do not report certain crimes to police because they are ashamed, embarrassed, or feel that they somehow caused their victimization.

Here are some things we have learned about crime from studies like the NCVS:

---

[92] *Ibid*

- *Most crimes go unreported to the police.*
- *Most are not serious.*
- *Most are thefts.*
- *Most victims of serious offenses know their attacker.*
- *Most rapes happen indoors between people who know each other.*
- *Most crime is between persons of the same race.*
- *Most are unsolved.*
- *Children (people under 18 years of age) are responsible for almost one-half of all arrests for serious crimes.*
- *Crime may or may not be increasing. (We cannot tell unless we know the actual amount of crime.)*
- *The reduction of crime will primarily be a function of demographics. As the percentage of people under age 25 rises or falls in the overall population, so will crime rise or fall.*
- *The reduction of crime is not largely dependent upon governmental techniques to control it.*

With the rise or fall of reported crime often being the major issue impacting the leadership of police departments in most American cities, it isn't difficult to understand why police would try to underreport crime.

This is often done by redefining a criminal incident—labeling an attempted burglary as a broken window— therefore putting it in the damage to property category so that it no longer counts as a major offense. This means the declassified incident will not add to the city's formal crime rate.

So is crime increasing or decreasing in your community? Without knowing the results of a

victimization study, you cannot know. You cannot take the UCR as an indicator. If you read in tomorrow's newspaper, see on television, or hear on the radio that the number of rapes in your city is rising, you must first ask: is the seeming increase in rape due to an increase in the reporting of these crimes to the police, because victims have more confidence in the ability of the police to do something about them? And might such confidence in the police department be due to training and hiring practices that have placed female police officers in patrol and investigatory roles? If so, the increase in the number of reported rapes would be a positive indicator of police competence, not negligence.

Or on the other hand, is a decrease in the number of reported rapes due to the reluctance of victims to report these offenses to the police because they see the police as not being caring or sensitive in these matters? In this case, a seeming decrease in the incidence of rape would be an indicator of police incompetence.[93]

The way out of this confusion is for the nation's police leaders to either refuse to participate in the UCR program and, in lieu of this, to call for a victim-based survey in their city. Local departments can supplement these data by partnering with local colleges and universities to gather these data, which

---

[93] An internet search of "manipulating crime statistics" reveals a number of sources to emphasize this point. See http://www.huffingtonpost.com/len-levitt/adrian-schoolcraft- enter-_b_714484.html?ref=email_share ; December 5, 2011; 0243. Also, listen to an interview with Officer Schoolcraft at: http://www.thisamericanlife.org/radio-archives/episode/414/right-to-remain-silent ; December 5, 2011; 0250. Of course, the New York City Police Department is not the only department that has struggled with charges of "jukin' the stats."

would provide more accurate crime statistics to the police and the community. Currently, one of the major problems with the NCVS data is that it is collected from a national sample and cannot now be broken down city by city. If it could be, American police and citizens would know the actual amount and extent of crime in their communities.

In addition, there are a number of other surveys that should be conducted on an ongoing basis, such as surveys of people who have contacted police either as a complainant or victim, or who have been stopped and frisked, or arrested by police. Communities and their police departments need to have an idea of how these recipients of police action have been treated, especially with regard to their age, race, ethnicity, immigration status, or sexual orientation. Surveying community members as to how fair and effective they believe their police to be is vitally necessary in a democracy and would provide police leaders and citizens with critical information.

Step Seven: Sustain

Police leaders must be able to maintain and continue improvements to their organizations.

AS I MENTIONED, a leader should always be thinking ahead, scanning and listening. And this should be with the intent to sustain the good work and improvements that the organization has accomplished. It turned out that what I was developing almost unknowingly in Madison was something Peter Senge later came to identify in his book *The Fifth Discipline: The Art and Practice of the Learning Organization.* When I first read Senge's excellent definition of the learning organization, it made clear that what we were attempting to do was just that:

Organizations where people continually expand their capacity to create the results they truly desire, where new and expansive patterns of thinking are nurtured, where collective aspiration is set free, and where people are continually learning to learn together. [94]

An organization that is learning to learning together can sustain itself. It is also an organization that should be practicing the new leadership because that's what the leadership I have described in this book does. It frees people to learn together. While there are varying definitions of a learning organization, there remains a core principle in all of them.

They are organizations that facilitate the *growth* of all their members and continuously work to transform themselves. [95]

My experience taught me the benefits of such an organization. This kind of organization is able to learn from its successes as well as its mistakes. It can innovate, be competitive, respond to external pressures, link and adjust its resources to meet customer needs, continue the pace of change, and bolster its image in the community; that is, to sustain itself. I can say this was our experience and that every one of the characteristics of a learning organization should be present in all the places in which we work—in factories, corporate offices, schools, churches, not just police departments.

One of the many outcomes of the quality

---

[94] Peter Senge. *The Fifth Discipline: The Art and Practice of the Learning Organization.* New York: Bantam-Doubleday. 1990.
[95] 96*The Learning Company: A strategy for sustainable development*, M. Pedler, J. Burgoyne, and T. Boydell (1997) and "Managing Learning: what do we learn from a Learning Organization?" *The Learning Organization*, D. McHugh, D. Groves and A. Alker (1998).

movement in Madison was developing teamwork and organizational skills in group facilitation. This gave us a tremendous edge. Within a few years, no one in the police department wanted to attend a meeting that didn't have a trained facilitator present. Meetings went so much smoother when trained facilitators were present. They assisted not only decision-making but also relational processes – how the group works together. By having trained group facilitators within the ranks of the department, we were able to more effectively conduct the business of committees and work groups within the department.

The job of a team leader is to help the group accomplish its agreed-upon tasks, to make the necessary decisions. The job of a facilitator, on the other hand, is to work in concert with everyone in the group, including the team leader, but primarily be concerned with process, how the group works together—practicing its values, ensuring participation of everyone regardless of rank, making sure all information is shared, and helping members of the group grow.

The powerful concept at work here is that *everyone* in the group is responsible for the group's success and growth. This means that anyone in the group has the authority to call the group back on subject, identify and interrupt patterns of conflict, offer clarifying comments, summarize activities, and provide feedback.

The other big step was identifying our future. Within a year or two after launching the Officer's Advisory Council (OAC), I decided we needed to look ahead toward the future—to stop, look, and listen like the old wagon masters did, scan for dangers and challenges. We needed to think about the kind of department in which we wanted to work and the kind of department the community wanted. This was the

direction I was going. Now I needed people to help me look to the future. It became the Committee on the Future of the Department.

The requirement for participation on the committee was that members had to have at least 15 years left to serve before retirement. I wanted those who were to do this futuring work to have not only experience but also time left to participate in making that future real—to be a stakeholder in that future.

The officers who served on the committee met two to four times a month for a year before they issued their report. This kind of work is immensely significant for the success of sustaining any organization. For us, it set in motion the energy to think about tomorrow, how we might need to alter or change the organization, and how we might keep our effort going. In their report, the committee made three formidable recommendations with supportive material:

- *Move closer to the community.*
- *Make better use of technology.*
- *Improve workplace wellness.*[96]

Those recommendations gave substance to my dream for decentralized neighborhood patrol districts that I first envisioned when I came to Madison. This now would more effectively move our officers closer to the people they served.

Very soon construction was begun of our first decentralized police station—the Experimental Police District. The EPD was to be our field laboratory.

---

[96] *The Learning Company: A strategy for sustainable development,* M. Pedler, J. Burgoyne, and T. Boydell (1997) and "Managing Learning: what do we learn from a Learning Organization?" *The Learning Organization,* D. McHugh, D. Groves and A. Alker (1998).

Their recommendations also caused us to examine our structure, internal practices, and the overall direction in which the department was moving.

Ultimately, that early effort to create a future vision for the department resulted in complete decentralization of patrol and investigative services into four stand-alone district stations that serve the City of Madison. The origins of this idea first began with my vision back in 1973 and the creation of a neighborhood patrol unit in the early 1980s, which assigned foot patrol officers to a number of our city's key residential and business areas.

This was a new idea for Madison. Our department had always operated out of one centralized building in the downtown area. The EPD, however, was located on the far south side, in one of the most active policing areas of the city. The officers who volunteered to work out of it had a hand in not only deciding the location but also the new station's building design and cost.

But the most remarkable move made was to let officers who volunteered to work there select their leaders. This would be the place where the new leadership style and problem-oriented policing methods would be solidly exercised. Years later, the ability of the Madison department to sustain a number of changes made nearly two decades earlier was highlighted in a national publication of the Police Executive Research Forum (PERF).[97] The document surveyed the application of business management principles to the public sector, particularly police departments. In it, Chief Noble Wray and Captain

---

[97] Chuck Wexler, Mary Ann Wycoff, and Craig Fischer. *Good to Great Policing: Application of Business Management Principles in the Public Sector.* U.S. Department of Justice, Office of Community Oriented Policing Services: Washington, D.C. 2007.

Sue Williams of the Madison department highlighted the leadership academy, which was still operating nearly 20 years after its inception. They wrote:

In the 1980s, then-Chief David Couper instituted the Leadership Promotional Academy in the Madison, Wisconsin Police Department. The academy was initially open to anyone who wished to compete for promotion, with the approval of the individual's supervisor. Work performance during the previous 12 months must be judged satisfactory. A person wishing to be promoted is required to have attended an Academy within the five years prior to the current promotional process.[98]

The publication went on to describe the process in which each attendee was expected to identify, analyze, and suggest the improvement of a current practice or function of the department. In doing this, attendees learn about the direction of the department from the chief and meet leaders they might not previously have known. Moreover, the department gains by ensuring all aspiring leaders acquire basic leadership skills and gain knowledge of, and strategies for, improving department work systems. The end result was that the Madison Police Department was able to learn how to sustain itself and its effective practices.

---

[98] "Good to Great Leadership Summit" conference, Washington, DC, sponsored by the Police Executive Research Forum, March 29, 2005.

Chapter 7
Person of the Year: 2011

The proper handling of public protest is a unique and special requirement for police in a democracy.

IN MY EXPERIENCE, one of the biggest transformations I made in Madison was to move the department into a professional stance with regard to handling public protest. The way in which police in a democracy respond to public protest is often a defining moment for them and the community. At the end of 2011 *Time Magazine* named the protester as its "Person of the Year." Doing so not only highlighted the centrality of protest today in America, but the important role it is taking throughout the world.

In the long run, police will ultimately be judged by how well they do this—how they do it fairly and effectively, without regard to whether they agree with the people in those crowds or not. Overall, police officers should always treat everyone they encounter respectfully, with courtesy, and without regard to their race, gender, national origin, political beliefs, religious practice, sexual orientation, or economic status—and that goes for people in crowds, too. It's a big job, but the primary function of police is always *relational*, whether they are responding to a domestic dispute, investigating a crime, enforcing a traffic regulation, helping an elderly person cross a busy street, or handling a crowd. Once this is understood, it is a lot easier to figure out what it is police need to do and how they should do it when it comes to handling public protest.

Early on, I envisioned a police department in

which the officers would become experts in human behavior because much of what goes wrong in policing happens when police are unable to effectively respond to people. Therefore, it is vital that police have access to and understand current research regarding the field of human psychology and established methods to deal with people who are disturbed, angry, grief-stricken, or intoxicated, without having to resort to physical force—or, if physical force is necessary, to use it wisely and humanely.

Robert Peel knew this 150 years ago when the field of psychology was in its infancy. He knew that the proper handling of people by police resulted in public approval of their actions and cooperation. He also knew that when police don't do this well it works against them. The proper handling of people simply made the job of policing a lot easier. Peel believed that police in a democracy should exercise absolute impartiality and develop a relationship with the public that gives reality to the historic tradition that, within a democracy, the police are the public and the publics are the police. This is also something I have believed since my earliest days in policing.

For police to become experts in human behavior, they need to cultivate an ongoing and formal relationship with academics in this area and should be eager and willing partners with them. In the past, this has not been the case—new information and research seldom trickled down to police, and police tended not to seek it out. It is precisely the lack of these kinds of connections with academia that has severely limited the growth and ability of police in this crucial area of their work life. In fact, it is one of primary things that has arrested their development.

A good example of how police methods can be

made more effective can be found in how they have tended to handle hostage and barricaded-suspect situations over the years. I use this as an example because there are few instances of the method of continuous improvement being used with regard to protests. Perhaps it is because protests have tended to be less frequent in occurrence.

Nevertheless, In the 1960s, I recall police were all over the response chart with regard to responding to hostage-taking situations and barricaded-suspects. At first, whoever arrived first at the scene just charged in. Shortly after I became a police officer, I assisted the Minneapolis police at a tense situation in which two officers had been shot. Thankfully, their wounds were not life threatening. We weren't organized. No one seemed in charge as I took up a position at the rear of the building where the suspect was holed up. We exchanged gunfire, and later I found that the round I had fired from my shotgun had driven the suspect into the basement of the building. I didn't have radio communications with the Minneapolis dispatcher and knew little of what was happening. I saw the suspect, fired, and later went home. No questioning. No reports.

When catch-as-catch-can situations like this didn't work very well, police responded by training a special team of officers to do this work.

This was how the concept of SWAT—Special Weapons and Tactics— came about in the late 1960s in the Los Angeles Police Department. This only happened after scores of officers throughout the country were shot while operating independently and without a plan or training.

The next development was to bring in special hostage negotiation teams (HNT). These were officers trained to make contact with the hostage

taker(s) and, if possible, negotiate—talk suspects into surrendering without harming their hostages. Police chiefs quickly learned that the objectives of SWAT and HNT units could conflict when a SWAT team commander argued for action and an HNT leader wanted more time to negotiate. This tension worked well for police and citizens as police became more deliberate in their actions. Tacticians and negotiators could effectively work together.

None of these strategies were developed through the social sciences; instead, they arose through trial and error. In one situation, something worked. Another time, it didn't. Why not? What were the different factors? What should we do next time? Finally, police settled upon a strategy that bought time. It slowed things down.

That worked until what appeared to be a hostage situation at Columbine High School in Colorado in April 1999, turned into a mass killing spree and the killers were willing to die. After the shootings at Columbine, which resulted in the deaths of over a dozen students and a teacher and two dozen more being injured, a new strategy had to be developed. Officers could no longer wait and get organized, but had to take immediate action to save lives that could be in jeopardy.

The new strategy was that if there was shooting going on at the scene, the first four officers who arrived were to enter and to stop the shooter. Again, this strategy was developed more through trial and error than intensive study and incident research. This is strategy by trial and error. Police learned that if they were willing to be flexible, open, evaluate their actions, and make the necessary changes, things could be made better. If there were as much effort placed in developing protest response strategies as there has been with regard to hostage takers and barricaded

suspects, our nation's police would be far more capable today in handling protest.

Of course, that wasn't the atmosphere I worked in as a young police officer. Those readers who are in or beyond the baby-boomer generation might remember the lyrics of a song from the late 1960s called "For What It's Worth," that I found so unsettling. The rock band Buffalo Springfield sang it: for me, these lyrics capture the protest movement that I found myself in the 60s and 70s.[99]

> *There's something happening here.*
> *What it is ain't exactly clear.*
> *There's a man with a gun over there*
> *Telling me I got to beware.*
> *I think it's time we stop, children, what's that sound?*
> *Everybody look what's going down.* [100]

This song reflects the chaos and craziness of that era. At the time, I worked on that street and *was* the man who would come and take them away. Stephen Stills wrote the song not, as some assume, in response to the shootings at Kent State (which took place later in 1970), but in reaction to the growing tension he saw between police and street people on the West Coast. The song has come to symbolize that challenging time in our nation when many young

---

[99] The rest of the song: *"There's battle lines being drawn/Nobody's right if everybody's wrong/Young people speaking their minds/Getting so much resistance from behind/I think it's time we stop, hey, what's that sound/Everybody look what's going down. "What a field day for the heat/A thousand people in the street/Singing songs and carrying signs/Mostly say, hooray for our side/It's time we stop, hey, what's that sound/Everybody look what's going down. "Paranoia strikes deep/Into your life it will creep/It starts when you're always afraid/You step out of line, the man come and take you away/We better stop, hey, what's that sound/Everybody look what's going down."* "For What It's Worth," Steven Stills, 1967.
[100] *Ibid.*

people questioned the behavior of their government and the police, took to the streets in protest, and began to view police no longer as friendly public servants, but as the enemy—stop, everybody look what's going down!

Now fast-forward to the present day. The British Home Office has been concerned about the behavior of their passionate football (soccer) crowds; a thousand people in the street and the confrontations that frequently occur between those crowds and police. Commendably, the British consulted academia for some help and found Dr. Clifford Stott, a social psychologist who studied crowd behavior.

Stott is one of Europe's leading researchers regarding crowd behavior. But he advocates a different approach for police to use when handling crowds. His studies found that:

[L]arge-scale disorder tended to emerge and escalate because indiscriminate, heavy-handed policing generated a group mentality among large numbers of fans that was based on shared perceptions that the police action was illegitimate. This had the effect of drawing ordinary fans into conflict with the police.[101]

When a crowd perceives the police as overreacting or being heavy-handed, its members have a tendency to stop observing and start taking action. It is exactly what I had experienced early in my observational studies in Berkeley and

---

[101] Clifford Stott. "Crowd Psychology & Public Order Policing: An Overview of Scientific Theory and Evidence" in a submission to the HMIC Policing. Public Protest Review Team. September 14, 2009 and http://www.timeshighereducation.co.uk/story.asp?storyCode=189237&sectioncode=26. December 27, 2010; 1101 hrs.

Minneapolis. To prevent this from happening, Stott advocates what he calls a "softly-softly" approach—a low-key approach in which officers mix with and relate to crowd members on the basis of their behavior, rather than their reputation.

If police approach a crowd with the *expectation* that its members are going to make trouble, it often turns out that way. Even so, most police around the world have continued to use the traditional hard methods of the past when responding to crowds.[102] For the most part today, communicating, relating, or dialoguing with people who are protesting isn't what police do. The soft approach is precisely what I developed and used years before during my time in Madison. It worked then and, as Stott suggests, it works now.

However, in many cities, and for a short while in Madison after I left, the soft approach has for the most part been neglected if not abandoned. Instead, protesters, and others assembling in crowds, are met by large numbers of police organized into crowd-control teams, outfitted with full body armor, shields, batons, gas masks, and large amounts of liquid pepper spray at the ready. What do you think the expectations are here? Of the police? Of protesters?

Whatever soft approaches police had been willing to use in the past were quickly abandoned soon after 9/11. At that time our nation entered a new era in which police wore soft body armor like medieval knights, carried shields and sword-like batons, but used 21st-century chemical technology— the hard approach. The result of that approach is that

---

[102] This is most likely because of how Seattle police were caught off guard by protesters at the meeting of the World Trade Organization in Seattle in 1999. This seems to be the point in time when American police started to shy away from a "soft" approach.

today almost every public protest police arrive outfitted and with the expectation of violence, and—as if it were a self-fulfilling prophecy—it happens.

In the spring of 2009, *The New York Times* reported the aggressive actions of crowd control police at that year's London G-20 meeting:

The police say they acted appropriately in a chaotic situation, despite having officers with little experience in crowd control. But the circulation of videotape taken by protesters and passersby does not help their arguments.

The images—of police officers charging at and striking apparently peaceful protesters, among other things—have horrified lawmakers and members of the public and prompted demands for a review of police policy.104

The actions of the police in London that year prompted David Gilbertson, who once formulated national policing policy in the U.K., to remark about hard crowd-control tactics:

The attitude used to be that the British police acted more or less with the sanction of the public. That attitude has been abandoned. The public is regarded as the enemy.[103]

This is precisely what Robert Peel didn't want to have happen when he developed his principles of policing over 150 years ago. Police need to operate with the permission and approval of the public, and the public should never be regarded as the enemy.

The harsh tactics our nation's police have recently used have created a psychological and physical chasm between them and protesters. The distance between police and protesters is a critical

---

[103] "Critics Assail British Police for Harsh Tactics During the G-20 Summit Meeting," *New York Times*, May 30, 2009.

factor: as I mentioned earlier, closer is more effective. When police are physically in close proximity to protesters, the tendency will be for the crowd not to depersonalize them. When police are not depersonalized it becomes much easier, and safer, for them to enter into a crowd of people and dialogue with them.

It appears today, with the new equipment police have received; the balance of power has shifted to them. In crowd situations today, police no longer see any need to negotiate or make compromises with protesters.

They no longer have to wait to see how a crowd will behave; instead, they can suit up for battle expecting one to occur and knowing they will ultimately win. These are dangerous practices.

There were four events in my career that profoundly influenced me about how police should behave in crowds. They happened many years ago, but as I now reflect, they were pivotal points. They changed the way I would later come to approach crowds and protesters in Madison.

The first event happened nearly four decades ago in Sproul Plaza on the campus of the University of California at Berkeley. This was at the height of the free speech movement and antiwar protest on campus. We, in Minneapolis, had correctly assumed that we would soon be experiencing this on our own campus. Berkeley was the place where it was all beginning to happen. On my return, I was to train police officers in my department about what I had learned.

As it turned out, I didn't learn what to do there but rather what *not* to do. I saw questionable police tactics and behavior that were very upsetting. After a

few days of observation, riding with police, witnessing arrests, monitoring demonstrations, and attending police debriefings, I vowed after that if I ever became a police leader, I would do things very differently.

The second event was the antiwar protests that soon came to my own campus and organized by my friends from the SDS and other campus protest groups. Those protests suspended my classes at the University of Minnesota for a number of days until the governor sent in National Guard troops to restore order. Rather than being on the street as a police officer at the time, I was on a leave from my department finishing up my graduate work. I now found myself again as an observer of police tactics. But this time it was from the perspective of being a student.

What I saw during those days caused me to revisit that vow again—if I ever became a police leader, I would do things a lot differently. I saw no dialogue, no negotiation, and little creativity beyond a massive show of force by police and military that included the presence of armored vehicles. It seemed strange to be on the receiving end for the first time. The attitude from the police and military that were present was clear: "Shut up. We are not going to listen to you. We are in charge and we have the power to make you stop and go home."

Remarkably, no one was killed or injured during this strike. While only a year or so later, in May, 1970, a similar strike at Kent State led to the deaths of four students after National Guard troops, who were on campus, shot at unarmed student protesters.

I came to understand more that there were a variety of ways to effectively—as well as morally and legally—police a city and properly handle people. In

each and every case, the argument for relationship could be made: relationships between police and their communities, relationships between individual police officers and citizens (including those who are angry, victimized, mentally ill, or impaired by alcohol or other drugs), relationships between police officers and their leaders, and, finally, relationships between police and protesters—those who are unhappy with the government.

I also began to study research concerning crowds and their behavior. It was and is quite limited. I learned that Sigmund Freud believed that people in crowds behaved differently than individuals.

Gustav LeBon, a 19th century social psychologist noted for his work on crowd psychology, observed that a crowd fosters anonymity in people and can generate collective emotions. Elias Canetti, a 20th century Nobel Prize winning author, classified crowd behaviors ranging from mob violence to religious assemblies. What I found was that effective methods of crowd- control were not only about force and tactical maneuvers, but also about dialogue, negotiation, and reduction of fear.

The last influential event took place after my retirement from the police. Again, I'm again observing police from the outside. Like most people in the United States, I witnessed the tragic day of September 11, 2001. But unlike many other citizens, I was paying close attention to the effect it had on our nation's police. All of us in America since that fateful day have lived in fear. And our police, for the most part, have done so as well.

Our nation's police have been unable or slow to return to the community-oriented role they were in the process of working through— such as soft methods of crowd control, neighborhood policing,

and focusing on solving community problems. Too many of our nation's police are busy looking instead for terrorists in the community rather than support from it.

This new militarism has gripped police and turned them away from the pursuit of community policing to focus on technology to solve their problems and antiterrorism as their new focus. It isn't that the threat of urban terrorism should be ignored, but rather, who should have the primary responsibility? I see the police as community workers—not urban commandos.

The Madison Method

- *Facilitate and protect the right of people to assemble and petition their government.*
- *Always use restraint and care in the use of force.*
- *Dialogue before, during, and after the event.*
- *Be effective and noticeable peacekeepers.*
- *The focus should be on the protest, not the police.*
- *Be open and communicate with the media.*
- *Continuously improve this method. (1990)*

Police officers, working closely with their communities in our nation's cities, should take advantage of their unique role to guarantee fairness and effectiveness in their practices. This is the paramount local strategy to prevent domestic terrorism. I have often thought that negative contacts, day in and day out, with the poor and people of color have done more to erode our nation's security than any international threat.

The state National Guard, not the police, should be the primary organization to respond to situations that are beyond the capability of local police departments. They have the logistics, intelligence, and weaponry to do so. The guard is local, and has the equipment and support systems to do this. While our local guard units have been deployed to Iraq and Afghanistan, police in many cities have had to fill the gap. It will be difficult for police to give up that role when they return. In the meantime, there has been a substantial regression in their progress toward community policing.

My tenure as chief in Burnsville, Minn., from 1969 to 1972, gave me the time to integrate what I had learned in the academic world and what I had experienced as a city police officer. With few opportunities for handling crowds in Burnsville, I was given the chance to think about and develop my ideas about crowd control when I interviewed for the chief's job at the University of Minnesota and in Madison. Handling crowds and protest was one of the major, and most controversial, tasks police had to do in that day. And to many observers, the police in Minneapolis and on the campus of the University of Minnesota had not done it skillfully. My approach as to how I would handle protest became a defining strength for me in becoming the top candidate for these positions. It is no less important today.

I had newer and more effective ways in mind regarding how to handle people than beating them up. These ideas didn't just come from the classroom, but were a blend of academic and direct experience. Every good street cop knows that communication matters—you talk *with* the person or people you're dealing with, not *at* them. Good police officers always exercise their verbal skills more than their physical ones. What was different is that I believed you could also do this with people in crowds.

One of the primary reasons I survived in Madison was that the new (soft) crowd control measures I brought in worked. During the next 20 years, we never lost control of a crowd, and that included hundreds of protests and demonstrations at the state Capitol building, on the campus of the university, strikes by state workers, teaching assistants at the university, and local meatpackers.[104] The method we used has recently been called *The Madison Method* by police officers outside of the city.[105]

This method is just as noteworthy today because of the Occupy Movement and the varieties

---

[104] For a general listing of those protests and demonstrations see references regarding the history of protests and social action from the 1970s to 90s at: http://archives.library.wisc.edu/uw-archives/exhibits/protests/1970s.html.
[105] In March and April, 2011, government officials in Madison effectively used many of these techniques in handling a multi-week demonstration and occupation of the state capitol building as a result of the governor-elect proposing to end collective bargaining in Wisconsin for most public employees. See: http://www.policeone.com/Crowd-Control/articles/3361291-The-Madison-Method-for-crowd-control/and http://www.cityofmadison.com/police/specialunits/specialEvents.cfm; January 26, 1750 hrs.

of police response we have seen. What is it we should expect police to do in these situations? What is the role of the community and elected officials? Are the police to be mere instruments in the arm of government, or not?

All things aside, how police handle public protest in our nation is one of the most noteworthy measures of the quality of a department's policing. When police do this well and without violence they move from good to great.

Three Examples of Effective Protest Management in Madison

1. Student Block Party With a History of Violent Conflict With Police

Less than five months after my appointment, newly elected Mayor Soglin and I were confronted with a request from the residents of Mifflin Street for a street use permit. Mifflin Street was close to the university campus and was the preferred residential neighborhood for many students and activists. The residents wanted to hold their historical annual spring party again. But the prior two years before I came to Madison, the gathering had resulted in a drawn-out battle between residents and police.

Though two years had passed since that blow-up, there still was lingering resentment in the community of how the police had responded to the previous gathering. It ended with arrests, and use of tear gas, and liberal application of nightsticks. When the permit came before the city council, the community wondered what the new mayor and I were going to do. Were things going to be different? This was my first test and much was at stake, and I

knew I needed help with training, planning, and staffing.

I wisely looked inside the department and asked my officers for help in creating a new, and intensively trained, unit called the Special Operations Section (SOS). The SOS would now have primary responsibility for crowd management. This unit would model the new behaviors I was seeking to instill among all my police. Fortunately, a large number of junior officers jumped at the chance. It would be an opportunity to try something new and creative. To this day, I don't know what I would have done had so many officers not volunteered for my experiment.

Many of them already knew the old ways had not worked very well and had generated considerable animosity and disrespect toward them and the police department. Looking back, my request enabled officers within the department to stand up and define themselves as being open to change and willing to progress. Many of them went on to be department leaders.

My plan was to put together a training experience for them on conflict management. I found help from Prof. Robert Shellow of Carnegie Mellon University, through a grant from the Police Foundation. Shellow had who had studied the soft methods in which I was interested. Dr. Morton Bard, a licensed psychologist, and former New York City police officer, who had also done considerable work in crisis management, joined him.

At the end of the training, officers in the new unit developed their own crowd-control strategy based on the new information they had just learned. Here's what we know, now what would you do? All of the officers had had prior experience using

traditional methods of crowd control—declare an unlawful assembly, make a show of force, display batons, disperse tear gas, move the crowd, and arrest those who remained. Now they were being pressed to think of other ways.

Surprisingly, the officers chose to use none of the old methods; instead, they decided to use techniques of low-key action, increased visibility and dialogue with residents and those coming to the event. The plan they presented to manage this potentially explosive gathering was to assign themselves, individually, as single officers, on the perimeter of the area in which the block party was to occur. They would be on-site early in the day to greet and speak with those coming to the party.

They chose to wear uniforms for identification, but not hats. This was more of a change than it might appear—Madison police officers had always been required to wear their hats when on duty and were disciplined when they didn't. The young people coming to the block party would quickly see that the police department wasn't conducting business as usual; something was different. And we, if course, wanted them to know this wasn't business-as-usual.

The volunteer officers also requested permission from me *not* to wear firearms during the event. This recommendation set me back. This was the one recommendation from the unit that I had to veto—it would have generated tremendous pushback from the rest of the department. It would have made headlines around the country, but I had to think about bringing the rest of the police department along with me. I thanked the officers for their creative thinking, which was commendable and courageous, but it was simply too early in my tenure as chief to approve it; too risky. If I had sent unarmed officers to the block party, and one of them

had been injured, I would have lost whatever support I had from the rest of the department and the community.

This early experiment in sharing decision-making with rank and file officers proved to me that they, given information and responsibility, could make good decisions. This was a lesson I wouldn't forget. When the backlash happened within the department, I put this lesson on hold. But I didn't forget it, and in later years it was what helped me and the department make that quantum leap in the early 1980s.

The day of the block party was tense as we gathered early on that Saturday morning for briefing. The media and the community were expecting another confrontation between police and students. Some were anticipating this happening. But it didn't.

It turned out that the officers were outstanding—they talked and joked with those who came to the party and were quickly seen as being at the party to help and not hinder the day's events. They were seen as peacemakers, not agitators. I don't think we made any arrests that day. The party ended late that night, and groups of young people were seen cleaning up the day's trash from the streets and bagging it for pickup by city crews.

This was my first real test using a soft style of crowd management, and it worked. It would serve me well during the coming years.

Not everyone, of course, saw what we did as a good thing. Within the department there were a number of officers, including those in command, who were casualties at the Dow protests and the earlier Mifflin Block Parties. They saw this in a much different way. They saw my strategy as giving in to

the students—even capitulating to them—and being weak. Many of those officers had old scores to settle. And while there injuries had healed on the outside, there remained deep, unhealed wounds inside.

2. Large Protest Regarding Public Policy at the State Capitol Building

The second major example of the department's new and evolving crowd-control methods occurred years later in April, 1986, when a large, organized protest was held on the grounds of the Capitol protesting public investments in South Africa. In the years since the Mifflin block party, we had handled hundreds of protests, demonstrations and large crowds such as the annual Halloween celebration downtown that at its height had more than 100,000 revelers in attendance without noteworthy incidents.

This protest was against also the apartheid policies of South Africa. While the Madison police normally don't have jurisdiction over state property, we were called in to assist the Capitol police. Governor Tony Earl had called Mayor Joel Skornicka for aid, who then called me. By the time I arrived on the scene to make an assessment, many of the demonstrators, who now filled the Capitol grounds, had begun constructing wooden shanties; symbols of the segregated townships outside the larger cities in South Africa.

I saw that a large number of the demonstrators were not from Madison but had come from other cities in Wisconsin and throughout the Midwest. The initial attitude of the demonstrators wasn't friendly toward the presence of police. They were not the usual protest people we had worked with over the years. At first, neither of us knew what to expect from the other.

I needed to talk to the governor before we got involved in this emotionally charged situation. I told him that it would be preferable if we kept things low-key and didn't make any immediate demands on the protesters. I asked that my department be the lead agency in handling the situation. The governor agreed.

I wanted to avoid a confrontation for as long as possible, but even as I spoke, protesters had entered the Capitol building and staged a sit-in in the central rotunda. The Capitol chief and I had agreed that his officers would handle the inside of the building and we would handle the outside. At the end of the day, the Capitol police would follow their standard practice of locking down the building. When that happened the demonstrators would be asked to leave. And some did. Those remaining were carefully escorted outside and the doors locked behind them. This happened without incident or arrests.

While we had used our soft strategy effectively during numerous demonstrations and sit-ins during the past decade, this crowd was by far one of the largest and most diverse we'd ever dealt with. I saw this as another opportunity for us to put into practice and highlight what we had learned about handling crowds and how police in a democracy operate.

I presented our plan to the governor. We would assign uniformed police officers, without hats, batons, or any riot control gear, to enter the crowd and dialogue with the protesters. But this time we went beyond merely talking with them and calming them down—we instructed these officers in some of the alternatives to divestment and how divesting might severely impact everyone in South Africa, blacks and whites. We encouraged protesters to form discussion groups in the crowd. Those assembled came to see the police as not trying to prevent protest

but rather to facilitate it; they soon realized that the police who present were informed, smart, and willing to engage in political discussions.

This protest was an occupation and, literally, a massive sit-in and campout on the Capitol grounds. This meant that a large number of the protesters were doing more sitting than protesting. The point of contention, I knew, would be when some legislators got tired of all this and ordered us to expel the protesters from state property. If that happened, the businesses and government buildings on the Capitol Square and downtown area would be vulnerable to damage and vandalism. It was a waiting game on both sides.

We briefed our officers on these issues and reasserted to the protesters that our role was to *facilitate* the protest, not prevent it. We also let them know that we, too, were against racism and any system of discrimination. The presence of our diverse workforce in terms of gender and race also spoke a clear message that day. The protesters knew we were here to stay and not in any hurry to end things.

Our strategy was always to keep *us* from becoming the issue, and to keep talking. The protest went on for six days. As time went on, we started negotiations with the leaders concerning dismantling the scores of illegal shanties that had been constructed on the lawn of the Capitol building. The presence of the shanties was, of course, an issue of enormous contention, as people are not generally allowed to build structures on the grounds of a state capitol and many members of the community believed the police needed to do something about it. We often heard, "Look at this mess, who's going to clean it up?"

Everyone expected that if we moved to dismantle the shanties, it would create the issue that

could ignite the crowd. It never happened. We were able to negotiate a smooth withdrawal and permitted a few symbolic shanties to remain standing for a few more days. It was a win-win ending. A positive ending brought about by police willing to be patient and withhold action.

I believe the overwhelming majority of the demonstrators went home feeling that they had made a powerful and well-heard protest against apartheid, petitioned their government for redress, been heard by that government, and witnessed a democratic police in action; police who served as facilitators and protectors, who acknowledged their right to assemble and protest the actions of their government.

Now, you may ask how you get police officers to enter a potentially hostile crowd without protective gear. One of the strategies we used was having a reserve force in readiness. A few blocks away, out of the view of the public and media, was a team of police officers kept in reserve with helmets, batons, and tear gas. They were on standby in case any person, including police officers, in the crowd was in danger of harm. That was how I could justify asking officers to enter such a large crowd. Again, speaking softly and carrying a big stick works effectively for police when the stick is out of sight. The difference here was our big stick wasn't our first or only strategy. It was only one of our strategies—and only one of last resort.

3. Protest Regarding Foreign Military Intervention

Over the years, we had gained a lot of experience in handling people in large groups—it demonstrated that our soft methods of crowd control and conflict management worked, and we continued to hone our skills. We handled many more block

parties, celebrations, labor strikes, protests and attacks on medical clinics during anti-abortion actions, more demonstrations at the Capitol and in the campus area, and a host of other gatherings, and assemblies—one of which resulted in 100,000 motorcyclists descending into our city to protest a proposed law which would require them to wear safety helmets.

After the spring of 1975, when the Vietnam War ended, we didn't have any more antiwar protests. That lull ended in 1990 when the first Gulf War broke out, and Madison citizens and university students again took to the streets in protest. We wondered if we'd be able to use the same tactics we had used for nearly two decades. Would the fact that this was a war, with a potential like Vietnam for a draft, make it a different kind of protest? I again remembered what Stuart Becker had told me about Dow Chemical. I didn't want this event to be about the police.

The atmosphere in the city was very tense as the war began. We still had some officers working in the department who had been at the Dow protests. We saw many of the antiwar folks from the 1970s back on the street again—years older and now with their children in tow.

As expected, there was also a very intense pro-war attitude in the community and a feeling that we all needed to support our troops and reservists. This attitude was also sharply prevalent in the ranks of the police department. We had veterans like myself in the department and also officers who were members of local military reserve units. I had to make sure that a Dow situation didn't happen again. I wanted any protest that occurred to be about governmental policies and not the police.

As was our practice, we gave the SOS the initial responsibility to work with the community organizers

who were planning the protests. Like almost every group we had worked with over the years, they agreed to meet with us. I also called a meeting of my management team and suggested we develop a statement of expectations regarding what citizens could expect from us. The statement was printed on pocketsize cards, which we distributed to those who showed up at the scenes of the protests. It was, of course, also given to the media, who gave it front-page play.

A problem that occurs at most protests is that citizens don't know what to expect from their police. That situation causes a tremendous amount of tension. So, why not tell them?

At the first protest, I walked with my officers through the crowd of a hundred or more protesters and distributed the cards to those who had assembled for the march. Throughout the various Gulf conflicts, the issues stayed focused on what Washington was doing and not on us. We had learned much about handling people, applied what we had learned, continually tried to enhance and fine-tune our method, and shared what we had learned with the community and other police departments.[106]

---

[106] In February, 2011, protesters again occupied the state capitol in Madison to protest Governor-elect Scott Walkers proposed budget legislation that, if implemented, would effectively eliminate collective bargaining for all public employees except police and firefighters. The protest went on for a number of weeks in February and into April. Crowds approaching 80 to 100,000 filled the capitol square and building. Republican officials used a "soft" approach by not forcing the demonstrators out of the capitol building and were very tolerant of crowd behavior. The tactic worked as the crowds eventually diminished   and the protesters left the capitol building. (For further information see *Wisconsin State Journal* article at: http://host.madison.com/wsj/news/local/govt-and-politics/article_9f189108-4cbc-11e0-b9b8-

The proper handling of public protest was a major goal of mine before and during my time in Madison. What we did in Madison is illustrative of the process a professional police agency is to use in responding to any community problem. It is what professional police do.

Epilogue

Chief Couper today.

IT IS POSSIBLE to bring sound and lasting change to the police so they reinforce and uphold the traditions and values of our society. It isn't only possible, but essential, to change the direction they are going today.

We need moral police organizations; staffed by men and women who reflect the community they serve, and see their function as community leaders in blue. They will become not only the police we want, but also the police we deserve as they work to overcome the historical obstacles I mentioned earlier: anti-intellectualism, violence, corruption, and discourtesy.

The Madison experience has made me even more confident that these obstacles can not only be overcome on a broader scale, but be sustained beyond the tenure of an individual police chief or political entity. Through a solid commitment to

education and collaboration with the academic community, police will no longer be seen as narrow-minded and bigoted technicians. When police officers are trained in the proper use of physical force, the community will no longer view them as out-of-control and untrustworthy. Because of what was accomplished in the past, the Madison community today sees their police as thoughtful, knowledgeable, and restrained—that is, professional.

Corruption and other illegal behaviors have, as I documented earlier, been with us throughout police history. It is true, power corrupts.[107] Whether real or perceived, this is the albatross that will forever be around the neck of our nation's police. That said, when the overwhelming majority of officers in a department are stalwartly committed to obeying the law while they enforce it, and sanctioning those who don't, a culture of honesty and candor will prevail.

Finally, courtesy and civility can be trained and maintained even in an organization in which the core of its role is the capacity to use force. Even physical force can be used in a civil manner if it becomes a professional tenet in the police ranks and officers believe that all people are worthy of being treated with dignity.

Throughout this book, I have attempted to illustrate the vital role that leadership plays. The chief must have vision, passion, education, and tenacity; and those on the front line, the same things—vision, passion, education, and tenacity. Developing leaders in all ranks, from the top to the bottom of the organization, will assure that a quality police

---

[107] This popular saying is attributed to John Acton (1834–1902), a historian and moralist who was known as Lord Acton. He expressed this opinion in a letter he wrote to Bishop Creighton in 1887: *"Power tends to corrupt, and absolute power corrupts absolutely. Great men are almost always bad men."*

department will be sustainable.

It was my life-long passion for the art of policing that moved me to write this book. However, with that passion came many mistakes and bad decisions. Is there anything I wished I had done differently along the way? Of course—who doesn't wish life had a re-wind button? I literally grew up and into this job. I had my share of struggles.

My life as a chief would have been easier if I had learned and practiced the following earlier in my career: listening more, speaking less, managing by walking around, working more closely with the police union, knowing more about the personal lives of my employees (there is no way police officers can leave their personal lives in their lockers when they come to work and strap on a gun). I wish I had more understanding and empathy when my officers were suffering from depression, a divorce, or a death in the family.

This book, therefore, has been both practical and personal. Every transformational police leader pays a personal cost trying to make a bold vision become a reality. Whether or not this can be avoided by a future generation of leaders remains to be seen. Perhaps what I have suggested about paying attention not only to the interior lives of my officers, but my own as well, may help. In my own case, my survival depended on maintaining my physical health, exercise, balancing work and family, and having social, recreational and intellectual interests outside the police. This is because the subculture of police is very powerful and can easily subvert the finest intentions—even the moral structure—of its practitioners, if it isn't recognized and controlled.

It is my hope that the seven steps I described in this book will be discussed, shared, and put into

practice, not only by the police, but in their communities as well. I'm not suggesting here anything that police are not able to do. Transformation isn't an exercise in capital, but in brainpower. It doesn't cost money to cast a bold vision, or to raise the hiring standards, or to internally train officers and their leaders with existing resources. It doesn't cost money to listen, and it doesn't cost money to continuously upgrade the systems in which we work. It may cost some dollars to do outside research, but in the meantime, police chiefs can do their own surveying just like we did. And it doesn't cost money to sustain an outstanding, community-oriented police department because with the changes I am suggesting comes trust, cooperation, and community support—things no money can buy.

But, it will take time. It will require bold leadership from the police themselves. It can't begin in the squad room; it has to begin with the chief. A mayor cannot do it, nor can a city council. Citizen committees cannot do it (just look at the miserable track record of police review boards around America). If police are to realize their potential as Constitutional officers, their leaders will have to take and be the first step. Perhaps one of them is reading *Arrested Development*.

Every time I visit Madison I see the results. I see a police department that is highly educated, many of the officers with graduate and law degrees. I see a police department that is extremely representative of, and responsive to, the community it serves—nearly 30 percent of the officers are women, and over 10 percent are men and women of color. But most of all, I see a police department which is respected, effective, fair, supported, and appreciated by the community.

My life has gone on. I retired into a second and,

I might say, equally challenging and fulfilling career as a clergyman. The shift was relatively easy. I moved from protecting people to caring for their souls. And that which I learned serving with the police applies there as well— including the seven steps.

For many years, I thought I had left the police behind me. But I was wrong. I kept coming back to them. I kept thinking about them, and I soon found that my concern was as enormous as it ever was. They are the constitutional officers who now protect me and my rights and the rights of my children and grandchildren.

Again, our nation faces an epic challenge in how its police are responding to protest. As we have seen from Cairo to Moscow, protest among people isn't a thing of the past, nor something only democracies face. In every nation, police are being tested.

I hope and pray that this book will be read, and those who read it will learn from my experience and my mistakes. I hope everyone will find inspiration and direction here no matter where they work. I also hope that young men and women will continue to have the desire to contribute to their society as I did, and join the police. Join them in order to improve them, and be the kind of police officer I have described in this book— smart, restrained, honest, and courteous.

To learn more about contemporary police issues and how to improve our nation's police I urge you to follow my weblog at http://www.improvingpolice.wordpress.com.

--Soli Deo gloria—

Acknowledgments

LET ME START from the beginning. Wayne Bennett was chief of police when I joined the Edina Department a few months after I was discharged from the Marines. I quickly learned that education mattered in Edina and professional ethical values were central to them. Chief Bennett set the standard. It was a good beginning.

When I left Edina for Minneapolis, I met Deputy Inspector Ed Farrell who was an educated cop and director of the training academy. He, too, left a positive impression on me and the necessity of an educated police. Later on in Minneapolis, Inspector Don Dwyer (later chief) was one of the few college-educated officers on the department and someone I respected and tried to emulate.

When I joined the police, I also began my studies at the University of Minnesota. My two mentors were Professors David A. Ward and John Clark. They inspired me as I saw the valuable link between social research and practice in policing.

It was Patrick McInnis, the Burnsville City Manager who gave me my first chief's job. We both were young. As a city leader, he was creative and innovative. He took a chance with me and let me build Burnsville into a highly professional police organization and require a college degree for all police officers. To this day, Burnsville is among the one-percent of the police departments in our country that require a baccalaureate degree as an entrance standard.

Three close personal friends and colleagues

shared my dream for policing: David Gorski, Bill
Mavity and Jack Morse. David and I were both
Marines. He worked with me in Minneapolis and
Burnsville and went on to head police departments in
Golden Valley, Minn., Harvard University, and then
Appleton, Wisc. from 1977-1995. Sadly, he died of
cancer in 2000. To this day, I miss his wit and
counsel.

Bill Mavity and I attended Minneapolis recruit
school together. He was a great cop. After a number
of years, he left the department and headed up the
criminal justice section of the Metropolitan Council.
While he was there, he stood election for Hennepin
County Sheriff. He then went on to law school at the
University of Minnesota, graduated and was admitted
to the bar. The rest of his career was spent as a
working lawyer representing many police clients. He
and I remain in close contact to this day.

Jack Morse was the chief of police in New
Hope, Minn., when we began our professional law
enforcement fraternity in Minneapolis. He was an
educated chief and one of our first members. He
served as assistant chief to David Gorski during his
Harvard years and eventually retired from there as
second-in-command. Jack lives in Hull, just across
the bay from Boston. He and I also remain close
friends.

I must also mention the national effort to
improve police. There was Gary Hayes at the Police
Executive Research Forum, Hubert Williams with the
Police Foundation, and other like-minded colleagues:
Chiefs Lee Brown who served in New York, Atlanta
and Houston, and Joe McNamara, who served in
Kansas City and San Jose.

In Madison, there is much to be acknowledged.
Assistant Chief Edward Daley and Policewoman

Morlynn Frankey were the first officers to support my ideas and welcomed me to the department. They were soon followed by a number of others who, along with them, soon became members of my top command staff: Ted Balistreri, Jeff Frye, Jack Heibel, Tom Hischke, and Rick Wallden.

I must also mention the three outstanding administrative assistants over the two decades I was in Madison that I was blessed to work with: Eileen Scrivner, Luisa Prey, and Sharon Kittle.

Three months after my appointment, a young student-councilman, Paul Soglin, was elected mayor of Madison defeating incumbent mayor, Bill Dyke. Dyke never was in my corner. Paul's support was vital to my tenure in Madison. I also want to thank Mayor Joel Skornika who had the insight to grant me my leave of absence in 1980.

On the nearby University of Wisconsin campus, two professors from the Law School standout: Frank Remington and Herman Goldstein. They both became close friends and mentors of mine. Herman continues to serve in that capacity. Sadly, Frank died in 1996. The Frank J. Remington Center continues his legacy of restorative justice and law-in-action.

A decade later, a newer breed of officers emerged to share my second effort in the transformation of the department – Deming-oriented quality improvement and a collaborative form of leadership. Of significant help and encouragement at this time was our forward-thinking mayor, Joe Sensenbrenner, along with other quality champions in city government: Tom Mosgaller, Pat Natzke, and Dorothy Conniff. In the police department, Cheri Maples, Noble Wray (now chief of police), Mike Masterson (now chief in Boise, Idaho), Joe Balles, and others became instrumental in continuing to help

me move the department during this significant period in the department's history.

It was also when I met my wife, Sabine Lobitz. She has continued to be the light of my life during the past 30 years we have been married.

As a police commander herself with the State Capitol Police Department, she wasn't only an unsurpassed friend and confidant, but also a noteworthy sounding board, and a loving, confidential critic. Together, we wrote books and articles and shared a common vision for policing a democracy.

Finally, I'll never forget the many Madison police officers who, without their sturdy support, my years in Madison would have been difficult, if not impossible. I chose to hire these men and women because I was impressed by not only their education and intelligence, but also by their compassion and commitment to serve others.

Gratefully looking back, most of what I did in Madison has been sustained. As we all should know by now, change does not come easy to the police – but sustaining those changes beyond the tenure a change- oriented chief is almost unheard of. Some would say it is a miracle.

I also want to thank my first editor, Josh Wimmer, my final editor, Rob Zaleski, and my youngest son, "Zeke" Joshua Couper, who helped with the final manuscript review. Gwen Walker from the University of Wisconsin Press also gave me prodigious help, advice, and encouragement during this project.

Thank you, each and every one of you.

Appendices

Appendix A
Major Recommendations
National Commission on Law
Enforcement and the
Administration of Justice (1967)

1. *Citizen advice:* In each police district that has a minority-group neighborhood, there should be a citizens' advisory committee that meets regularly with police officials to work out solutions to conflict problems that arise; it should include those who are critical or aggrieved.

2. *Community relations:* Police departments should have community relations machinery that plans and supervises the department's community relations programs. Such machinery is a matter of the greatest importance in communities with a substantial minority population.

3. *Minority recruitment:* It should be a high-priority objective of all departments with a substantial minority population to recruit, deploy, and promote them fairly.

4. *Citizen complaints:* Every jurisdiction should provide adequate procedures for full and fair processing of all citizen grievances and complaints.

5. *Written policies:* Police departments should develop and annunciate policies that give police personnel specific guidance for the common situations requiring exercise of police discretion.

6. *Three-tiered entry:* Basic police functions should be divided among three kinds of officers, here termed the community service officer, the police officer, and the police agent. The ultimate aim of all police departments should be that all personnel with general enforcement powers have baccalaureate degrees.

7. *Recruitment:* Police departments should recruit far more actively than they now do, with special attention to college campuses and inner-city neighborhoods.

8. *College degree:* Police departments should take immediate steps to establish a minimum requirement of a baccalaureate degree for all supervisory and executive positions.

9. *Selection:* Until reliable tests are devised for identifying and measuring the personal characteristics that contribute to good police work, intelligence tests, thorough background investigations, and personal interviews should be used by all departments as absolute minimum techniques to determine the moral character and the intellectual and emotional fitness of police candidates.

10. *Criteria:* The appointing authority should place primary emphasis on the education, background, character, and personality of a candidate and less on present employment standards of age, height, weight, visual acuity, and prior residence.

11. *Compensation:* Police salaries must be competitive with other professions and occupations that seek the same graduates.

12. *Promotion:* Promotion eligibility should stress ability above seniority.

13. *Lateral movement/pension transfer:* To encourage lateral movement of police personnel, a nationwide retirement system should be devised that permits the transferring of retirement credits.

14. *Probationary period:* Entering officers should serve probation periods of, preferably, eighteen months and certainly no less than one year. The probationary officer should be systematically observed and rated. Chief administrators should have the sole authority of dismissal during the probationary period and should willingly exercise it against unsatisfactory officers.

15. *In-service training:* Every general enforcement officer should have at least one week of intensive in-service training a year. Officers should be given incentives to continue their general education or acquire special skills outside their department.

16. *Improvement:* Each state should provide financial and technical assistance to departments to conduct surveys and make recommendations for improvement and modernization of their organization, management, and operations.

17. *Police legal advisor:* Every medium- and large-sized department should employ a skilled lawyer full time as its legal advisor. Smaller departments should arrange for legal advice on a part-time basis.

18. *Management team:* Every department in a big or medium-sized city should organize key ranking staff and line personnel into an administrative board similar in function to a corporation's board of directors, whose duty should be to assists the chief and his staff units in developing, enunciating, and enforcing departmental policies and guidelines for the day-to-day activities of line personnel.

19. *Maintaining integrity:* Every department, regardless of size, should have a comprehensive program for maintaining police integrity.

20. *Team policing:* Police departments should commence experimentation with a team policing concept that envisions those with patrol and investigative duties combining under unified command with flexible assignments to deal with the crime problems in a defined sector.

21. *Deadly force:* A comprehensive regulation should be formulated by every chief administrator to reflect the basic policy that firearms may be used only when the officer believes his life or the life or another is in imminent danger, or when other reasonable means of apprehension have failed to prevent the escape of a felony suspect whom the officer believes presents a serious danger to others.

22. *Records and communications:* States should assume responsibility for assuring that area-wide records and communications needs are provided. In every metropolitan area there should be laboratory facilities for all the

communities in the area. Specialized personnel from state or metropolitan departments should assist smaller departments on major investigations and in specialized law enforcement functions. Each metropolitan area and each county should take action directed toward the pooling, or consolidation, of police services...that will provide the most satisfactory law enforcement service and protection at the lowest possible cost.

23. *Police standards:* Police standards commissions should be established in every state and empowered to set mandatory requirements and to give financial aid to governmental units for the implementation of standards.

Appendix B
Madison's Improvement Plan

Step 1: Educate and inform employees about our vision, our goal, and the quality improvement method.

- Begin discussion with top management team and train them.
- Discuss and ask employees; get feedback from them.
- Share feedback with the chief and his management team.
- Get buy-in from top department managers.
- Survey external customers—our citizens.
- Ask, inform, and keep the Officer's Advisory Council up to date on all this.
- Tell, sell, and persuade through the department newsletter and during employee meetings.

Step 2: Prepare for the transformation.

- Appoint an internal Quality Coordinator to help with the transformation.
- Form an internal Quality Leadership Council to work through problems and barriers encountered during implementation of the new leadership.
- Require all who seek to be promoted to leadership positions to have both the knowledge and ability to practice the new leadership.
- Actively and strongly tie our quality improvement efforts in with the city's efforts in this area.

Step 3: Teach quality improvement and the new leadership skills.

- Train all supervisors and managers in the new leadership and methods of quality improvement.
- Train all employees in the new leadership and methods of quality improvement.

Step 4: Start practicing the new leadership.

- Require department leaders to begin to implement the new leadership, principle by principle.
- Begin a system of employee feedback to all department leaders.
- Top leaders are required to identify three to five things that need improving, work on them, and take responsibility for them.
- Top leaders are to develop a plan to demonstrate their advocacy for quality improvement methods and start practicing the new leadership.
- Top leaders start identifying and sharing with each other and their employees each week the improvements they are working on and those they have accomplished together with their employees.

Step 5: Check progress and make corrections.

- During monthly meetings for sergeants and lieutenants, the chief asks them how they are doing and they report in.
- Make changes, if necessary, to make the department more responsive to the new leadership; use quality improvement methods to do so.

- Add an elected police officer to the chief's management team.

Step 6: Make continual organizational improvements.

- This step is to be an ongoing process—it is continuous improvement within the organization. It is understood that if an organization stays as it is, it is, in reality, falling behind the rest of the world.
- To get a snapshot of what went on within the Madison department during this time of intense organizational transformation and change, Appendix C captures ten years of organizational effort (1981 to 1990) and indicates the various steps we took, and when we took them.

Appendix C
Madison's Improvement Timeline

1981

- An elected Officer's Advisory Council created

1984

- Committee on the Future of the Department created

1985

- Committee on the Future of the Department issues its report

1986

- Neighborhood Service Officers created in six city districts
- Mission statement developed by management team
- Experimental Police District (EPD) planning team created
- EPD begins to survey internal and external customers
- City of Madison under Mayor Sensenbrenner begins Quality and Productivity (QP) program
- Principles of Quality Leadership (QL) developed within the police department
- Employee information sessions held on QL—everyone attends; chief teaches
- Team leader/facilitator training begins

1987

- Top management, lieutenants, and sergeants trained in QL (five sessions of six days each)
- Customer survey form developed, pretested, and sent out to randomly-selected citizen-customers who have had police contact
- First department Quality Coordinator appointed
- Quality Leadership Council (QLC) formed champions throughout the department to help the chief keep improvements going and support the change in leadership style
- QLC begins work on number-one problem identified by police officers: the promotional system
- OAC given final decision-making authority—patrol vehicles and weapons

1988

- Experimental Police District established in South Madison.
- Three-day quality training for all employees
- Reorganization—top staff and bureaus of the department organized into working teams instead of bureaus and sections
- Chief holds progress checks with lieutenants and sergeants during one-day quality training sessions

1989

- Four-way check expanded requiring leaders to solicit input from subordinates, peers, the chief, and to do a self-assessment as to how they are doing
- Chief's check-ins continue with lieutenants and sergeants
- Planning for the skills portion of the Quality

Leadership Academy begins
- Emphasis on practicing what we have learned so far
- Police union president joins the chief's management team as a full voting member

1990

- Quality Leadership Academy begins for all promotional aspirants and is one of the recommendation of the QLC
- Field operations decentralized
- Stressing teamwork and use of quality improvement methods

1991

- Focusing more intently on who our customers are
- City-wide customer surveying
- Detective check-ins with the chief and begin to discuss how their work can be improved
- Neighborhood foot patrol officers increased

1992

- Revised Quality Leadership workbook published based on what we have learned. Other departments purchase the workbook and send their members to look at what we are doing.
- More neighborhood foot patrol officers added increasing to thirteen the number of independent, district foot patrol assignments in key city areas
- A citywide cross-functional team with other city departments established the way various city departments can begin to learn from one another. Facilitators are shared between

city agencies.
- Neighborhood Intervention Task Force created to address growing gang and drug problems
- Customer surveys analyzed by neighborhood

1993

- Reorganization of the detective team into four districts with a central support team
- National Institute of Justice Report *Community Policing in Madison: Quality from the Inside, Out: An Evaluation of Implementation and Impact* is released.

Appendix D
The Twelve Principles of Quality Leadership

1. Believe in, foster, and support teamwork.

Teamwork is working together—working to solve crimes and conduct investigations, as well as to resolve problems that arise at work or in the community. It is helping each other, being one team. It is taking pride in our collective achievements. It is belief in the ability of the group over anyone's individual effort—that is called synergy. We should try to do our work with teams whenever possible.

2. Be committed to the problem-solving process; use it and let data, not emotions, drive decisions.

Use the problem-solving process: Identify the nature and scope of the problem, seek a number of alternatives that will solve the problem, choose the most effective alternative, implement the chosen alternative, follow up on its implementation (correct, if necessary, to make it better). Too often we use our emotions or feelings to choose a course of action. This principle encourages the use of data, figures, information, and facts to drive that decision-making. Soliciting input isn't data—it is necessary, but let's not call it data. You should know the data tools: how to gather data, how to show it graphically, and how to look at variation of data. Let data do the talking. When employees ask for new things or new ways of doing things, encourage them to use data to support their recommendations—not use of power (We have all decided that...) or use of feelings (You know this is the better way of doing that...). Collecting data is using statistical tools o understand, bring into control, and correct a process. Using data will help our

decision-making because we will be able to answer that extremely crucial question: How do we know this is true?

3. Seek employees' input before you make key decisions.

This is a commitment to ask your employees about what the key decisions are in the workplace. They may be staffing levels, assignments, transfers, or taking time off. Whatever they may be, they are things that the employees feel are decisions on key matters—not things you or I think. The commitment is to ask before these decisions are made. It does not mean that you have to do what your employees believe you should do. (This is a very fundamental point in the principles: Our commitment is to input. We may, in fact, do what our employees want; or we may choose to delegate to them our authority to make the decision; or we may simply take their input under advisement; but we promise to ask them before we make the key decisions.) Key decisions are those that affect the three to five things that are essential to workplace satisfaction *as defined by employees*. They may be determined either by individuals or by groups of employees. Key decisions should be discussed and an agreement reached as to what constitutes these key decision areas. Leaders should then agree to ask for employee input on these key decision areas before they make any decisions regarding them. Employee input does not mean decision- making by taking a vote without group discussion. It is the power of group discussion, hearing everyone's point of view, understanding and deliberating on what has been discussed, that makes group decision- making far more effective than one person's decision or a group of individuals voting on solutions without discussion. When employee input is requested, it should be clear at the beginning of the process how the decision will be made and who will

make it.

4. Believe that the best way to improve the quality of work or service is to ask and listen to employees who are doing the work.

As supervisors and managers we don't do the front-line work. We depend on others to do the job of responding directly to the customers, the citizens of our city. It has been a long time since most of us have performed this job. Therefore, we depend on the men and women who do this job to tell us what they need to do get the job done. As bosses, one of the most fundamental things we can do for our employees is to ask them what they need and listen to what they have to say. Listening is the difficult part for those of us who have spent years learning how to tell people what to do. Active listening is a skill that can be learned and developed. Using the inquiry process, which is about asking the right questions, is also a skill that can be learned. Quality leaders refrain from telling; they ask the right questions: How do you know that? What have you learned through this effort? What kind of help do you need from me? The power of this is that an individual comes to his or her own solution with the help—not the direction—of the leader. Listening and questioning are crucial skills to develop as a supervisor or manager. Employees want bosses who are willing to listen, and we need employees who will honestly tell us about what's going on.

5. Strive to develop mutual respect and trust among employees.

How do we develop respect and trust in the workplace? One of the keys is to do unto others as you would have them do unto you. People want to be respected and trusted. Bosses who show respect and trust have respected and trusted employees. We must

come to the workplace with the basic belief that our employees deserve respect and can be trusted—that's why we hired them in the first place. For example, when checking out a complaint regarding an employee, there are ways to do it that may not compromise the respect and trust of the individual involved. In many cases, our attitudes have a more lasting impact than our words or the processes we use. Our employees have a right to know what's going on, when the process has been completed, and what our findings are. In every case, except those in which a serious offense has occurred, we want to correct and rehabilitate employees and get them back to duty. We must all be committed to driving fear out of our workplace.

6. Have a customer orientation and focus toward employees and citizens.

A customer orientation and focus means that we listen to our customers. Customers may be citizens, elected officials, employees, or interest groups. As supervisors and managers, we have as direct customers our employees, who provide service to their customers, the citizens and taxpayers. Listening and being responsive to citizens is our ultimate goal. There are, of course, a number of parameters—the law, ethics, and budgetary constraints. In this new era of community policing, listening to the customer is a vital part of the job. It is a change. Professionals today don't have the exclusive market anymore of knowing what is best for their patients, clients, or customers. Today, people want to be heard and participate.

7. Manage the behavior of 95 percent of employees and not the 5 percent who cause problems. Deal with the 5 percent promptly and fairly.

This is a fundamental principle regarding people. It should help us to look at how we view our employees. Do we believe that they can be trusted, are mature adults, and want to do a good job? Or do we believe that they are untrustworthy, immature, and want to avoid work? This principle causes some supervisors and managers a great deal of difficulty. They have trouble accepting the notion that they should trust their employees. Let's look at how many of your employees are in the first group and how many are in the second. We believe 95 percent of our employees fall into the first group and 5 percent or fewer falls into the second group. For too long, the actions of the 5 percent have dictated the rules and policies and how the organization is run. We believe that the actions of the 5 percent shouldn't dictate how the rest of the employees are treated in the workplace. Five-percenters should be responded to in a prompt and fair way. Rules shouldn't be written based on the behavior of the 5 percent, nor should the department be run as if all employees were in the 5 percent group. The 5 percent must, however, be dealt with and not ignored. We have all heard a great deal about the need for consistency and fairness in the disciplinary process. Being fair is more important.

8. Improve systems and examine processes before placing blame on people.

Continually monitor the systems you are responsible for to enhance them and, ultimately, the quality of the output. Leaders have responsibility for the performance of systems—this is creative and valuable work. In the past, we have emphasized that the job of a manager was to watch over, maintain, and inspect systems. No more. Our job today is to enrich these systems—continually, incessantly, and forever. If we see our job as inspecting systems, a machine—a computer can replace us. Our employees also see that kind of work as being not essential or necessary. If

we see our job as the improvement of systems, a machine cannot replace us—only creative and caring people can do this kind of work, and our employees know it. This is also a good human behavior rule. People don't like to fail. When they do, it is wise to look at systems first. Only after systems are examined is it fair and safe to examine how people may have failed. We should be trying to get at the root of the problem, not attempting to fix blame on an individual. If a system is out of control, it is only a matter of time before the next employee gets in trouble. The solution is to fix the system. Leaders work on the system; employees work in the system. Standards need to be set, feedback given, and control limits established. There will be variation in performance, but it should be within the established upper and lower control limits. Variation is a fact of life and to be expected. Those who fall below acceptable performance shouldn't be punished. Our job is to ascertain what they need from us—training, encouragement, support, and feedback—in order to get them into the range of acceptable work performance.

9. Avoid top-down power-oriented decision-making whenever possible.

We should avoid the use of coercive power whenever possible. When we use it we should remember that we all pay a cost in its exercise—giver and receiver. The finest decisions are those in which we all participate and concur. The next are those decisions in which everyone is asked for their input before something is decided. Of course, we will have occasional no discussion decisions in our work. When we do, we should make a commitment to our employees that we agree to critique those decisions whenever possible. Tom Gordon, in his book *Leader Effectiveness Training*, illustrates the costs to leaders who use coercive power to get the job done: costs of

time, enforcement, alienation, stress, and diminishing influence. There is also the cost of making a less-than- quality decision, because communication between employees and leaders who use coercive power is greatly reduced.

10. Encourage creativity through risk-taking, and be tolerant of honest mistakes.

We will never get creativity and innovation from our employees when we tell them they cannot make mistakes. All that we know about people tells us that creativity is chilled and repressed in such an environment. It isn't easy to accept honest mistakes. The price we pay for zero defects, however, is zero creativity. Many of us have been working together for many years. We all remember each other's mistakes and failures. Without forgiving and forgetting, we will never be comfortable in the workplace. If we don't permit honest mistakes, new ways and ideas will never be tried. It's simply too risky in an authoritarian organization. Quality and creativity is the result of a constant process of trying and improving.

11. Be a facilitator and coach. Develop an open atmosphere that encourages providing and accepting feedback.

A leader's job today is different. It is challenging and gives us opportunities for personal growth because it offers so many new options. Being an effective quality leader means being a coach, teacher, student, role model, and, most significant, and a champion of the new philosophy. We are in the business of helping people develop and experience personal growth. Our employees' goal is to deliver a quality service to our citizens by being responsive and sensitive to those citizens' needs. We can model this behavior by being responsive and sensitive to our employees' needs. All this can only be accomplished

in an atmosphere of trust, honesty, and openness. Part of this process is honest feedback. An honest feedback system is essential for the creation of a quality organization. Feedback is for the receiver. It isn't designed to make the giver feel better by venting. Venting is sometimes necessary, but don't mistake it for feedback. Leaders have consistency of purpose—a vision as to where they are going. Leaders develop the competence of their people. They are committed. Their employees know where they stand.

12. Use teamwork to develop agreed-upon goals with employees, and a plan to achieve them.

This principle tries to capture the importance of progress and moving forward as a team. We plan where we are going and establish agreed-upon ways to achieve that goal with input from and discussion with our employees. We help create a vision. Our job is then to align that vision with our practices. We can do that by coaching our employees toward excellence—not by trying to control them. Long-term goals are essential to the performance of a quality organization. Once goals are set, it is critical for leaders to follow up and—at least weekly, if not daily—to coach employees to success. There is a technique used to achieve maximum performance from individuals, frequently adopted by athletes who want to capture world records. It is called visioning— mentally picturing you, yourself, achieving something. For example: jumping higher or running faster or farther than you ever have before. Organizations need to create similar visions and plan accordingly (1992).[108]

---

[108] *Quality Leadership Workbook.* Madison Police Department. 1992. An updated and revised *New Quality Leadership Workbook for Police: Improvement and Leadership Methods* (2014) by the author and Sabine Lobitz is available at www.createspace.com/4515020.

Appendix E
Outline and Key Questions:
How to Rate Your Local Police

Leadership Characteristics

1. What kind of person is the chief?
- Clear vision
- Willingness to challenge the status quo
- Take risks, be innovative, and build a coalition of support for change
- Self confidence
- Personal integrity
- Respect of community and elected officials
- Ability to inspire and motivate

2. What tone does the chief set for the agency?
- Coherent crime control strategy
- Concrete crime prevention strategy
- Defend rights of unpopular groups
- Equal delivery of community police services

3. Does the chief articulate the policies of the agency clearly and understandably?
- Speaking out and taking a stand
- Spokesperson on crime control and public safety
- Advisor on personal security
- Preserver of due process guarantees
- Defender of minority rights
- Protector of the weak and injured
- Manager of a complex bureaucracy

- Guardian of the rule of law

Policy Characteristics

4. Does the police agency have a clear sense of its objectives?

American Bar Association: Standards Relating to the Urban Police Function:
- Are there written policies for all operational practices?
- Does the police agency select the finest individuals to be police officers?
- Does the police agency provide high quality training for its officers?
- Does the police agency reinforce the minimum requirements for a good police officer?
  - Effectiveness
  - Integrity
  - Civility and courtesy
  - Health and physical fitness

5. Does the police agency guide, train, and supervise police officers in the restraint of the use of force?

6. Is the police agency willing to investigate and discipline officers engaging in misconduct?

Organizational Characteristics

- Do police officers respect individual rights?
- Does the police agency address crime and order problems by using all community resources?
- Does the police agency cooperate and

coordinate with neighboring law
enforcement agencies and with other
agencies in the criminal justice system?

- Does the police agency communicate well
with the public?

- How does the police agency approach the
media?[109]

---

[109] David C. Couper. *How to Rate Your Local Police.*
Washington, DC: Police Executive Research Forum, 1983.

Appendix F
Professional Leadership
Expectations: Chief of Police

Tenure. A binding employment contract of at least seven years. A police department that needs improvement must be assured that there will be a continuity of top leadership. To think about transforming a police department in less than this period of time is foolhardy.

Leadership. The department leadership style must ensure the growth and development of its members. Not only must the chief officer be assured of an appropriate amount of time necessary to do the job he or she was hired to do, but the style of the chief's leadership (and that of his or her subordinate officers) is critical. To permit a chief officer to coercively lead the department and instill an atmosphere of fear within it is to shut down the kind of open and collaborative communication that is necessary for any organization seeking continuous improvement of its operations and functions.

Training. Even if the chief officer has tenure and is committed to an open, participative leadership style, the department must also be committed to providing high-quality training for everyone, and also have the same commitment to providing on-going training through an officer's career. Training is what develops and maintains the skills expected of a professional police officer.

Experimentation. Police in a democratic society must be willing to experiment with new ideas and concepts. This means that a police organization must develop a culture that encourages innovative thinking and challenges current practices. This is a rapidly changing, technologically oriented world and those

who serve as police must be aware of social and cultural trends and understand the diverse thinking that holds a free society together. In today's world, to remain in place is to fall behind.

Evaluation. A commitment to experimentation must be concurrent with a commitment to evaluation. A department must be willing undergo constant self-evaluation and open itself to outside research and evaluation as well. It must have a way to evaluate the results of well-thought experimentation and be open to new ideas and practices that this kind of evaluation will suggest.

Appendix G
The Law Enforcement Code of Ethics

As a law enforcement officer, my fundamental duty is:

- To serve mankind.
- To safeguard lives and property.
- To protect the innocent against deception, the weak against oppression or intimidation, and the peaceful against violence or disorder.
- To respect the constitutional rights of all men to liberty, equality, and justice.

I will keep my private life unsullied as an example to all.

I will maintain courageous calm in the face of danger, scorn or ridicule.

I will develop self-restraint and be constantly mindful of the welfare of others.

I will be honest in both thought and deed in both my personal and professional life.

I will be exemplary in obeying the laws of the land and the regulations of my department.

Whatever I see or hear of a confidential nature that is confided to me in my official capacity will be ever kept secret, unless revelation is necessary in the performance of my duty.

I will never act officiously or permit personal feelings, prejudices, animosities, or friendships to influence my decisions.

With no compromise for crime and with relentless prosecution of   criminals, I will enforce the law courteously and appropriately without fear or favor, malice or ill will, never employing unnecessary force or violence, and never accepting gratuities.

I recognize the badge of my office as a symbol of public faith and I accept it as a public trust to be held so long as I am true to the ethics of the police service.

I will constantly strive to achieve these objectives and ideals, dedicating myself before God to my chosen profession...law enforcement.

(Adopted by the International Association of Chiefs of Police, 1957)

Appendix H
Twelve Qualities of Police

Michael Scott and I developed the following document in mid-2012. We felt there was a need to clearly build on earlier works defining the police function and develop what we believed to be the essential qualities of police in a free and democratic society. This document was put on the Internet site GoPetition.com.

TWELVE QUALITIES OF POLICE IN A FREE AND DEMOCRATIC SOCIETY:

An Invitation to Our Nation's Police Leaders

We are two former chiefs of police who are inviting our nation's police leaders, present and former, to support twelve specific policing values.

Some background

David Couper began his career as a police officer and detective in the Minneapolis Police Department and then served as chief of police in two departments, Burnsville, Minn. and Madison, Wis., for over 25 years. Michael Scott was a police officer in Madison, Wis., and went on to serve in various administrative positions in the New York City; Ft. Pierce, Florida, and St. Louis Metropolitan police departments and then as chief of police in Lauderhill, Florida. Together, we represent two generations of American policing.

David retired a number of years ago and pursued a career in pastoral ministry and has recently written a book about his career in Madison and improving police. Michael continues in the criminal justice field as a clinical professor at the University of Wisconsin Law School and director of the Center for Problem-

Oriented Policing.

Even if you do not know who we are, we would like you to know that we have devoted a good share of our lives toward improving the police profession through practice, management, writing, and teaching. We care about police. Now we feel the need to set forth a description of the critical qualities of policing in a democracy. And we ask you to join us in this grassroots effort to articulate our professional values.

We believe that police can be leaders in our nation by modeling and protecting our democratic values. We know police can do something about crime when we work collaboratively with those whom we serve. And police chiefs can initiate a new kind of modern leadership within our ranks that respects the men and women we are privileged to lead and listens to their good ideas about how we can improve policing.

We believe we are at a moment in our nation's history when police leaders need to stand up and define who we are, what we do, what it is we are trying to accomplish, and above all, to what values we are committed.

We have drafted the statement below that articulates those qualities of policing that we believe are essential in a free, open, and democratic society. We invite you who are current or former police leaders to read the statement and, if you agree with it, to endorse it by signing your name to it electronically and listing the names of the police agencies which you have led or now lead.

We are indebted to the police scholars, police officers, professional police associations, police unions, lawyers, elected officials, and citizen advocates who have also shaped our profession's values, but we envision this statement coming from

the men and women who now serve or have served as leaders in the police field.

At this time, we have no objective or plan for this statement, other than to make it. We have no political or personal agenda, only a professional one. If you choose to endorse the statement, we ask that you do so on the assumption that this is an open and public document, one with which you would be proud to be publicly associated. If it turns out that many police leaders, past and present, from across the nation, representing many types and sizes of police agencies, sign the statement, we might well consider issuing a press release about it and/or inviting our professional associations to make what use of it that they can in their own work. And, regardless of what we do with it, we invite you to use it as you see fit within your own police agency and community.

Thank you for taking the time to read the statement and to consider endorsing it.

POLICING OUR NATION

Qualities of Police in a Free and Democratic Society

Preamble

We the undersigned, current and former leaders of police, know that policing a democracy is a difficult business. It is mainly so because the government assures its citizens certain rights that limit, and even challenge, the power of the state. This is especially evident in assuring those who live in a free society the right to protest, to be secure in their persons and homes, and the right of due process.

In establishing our nation's Constitution, the founders wrote they were doing so "to form a more

perfect union, establish justice, insure domestic
tranquility, provide for the common defense,
promote the general welfare, and secure the blessings
of liberty." Although set forth nearly four score years
before the establishment of the first American police
agency, these aims could well be understood as the
foundational statements of our system of policing. To
a large extent, the American police institution exists
to advance these goals and help society honor its
social contract. Therefore, the quality of a democracy
is heavily dependent upon the quality of its police.

Since 1829 when Richard Mayne, Charles Rowan
and Robert Peel first proposed principles of policing
for mid-19th century London, principles that
continue to shape American policing, we believe
there is ever a need to revisit these first principles and
to reaffirm or adapt them, as appropriate, for the
present times. Those original principles are
paraphrased as follows:

1. Police exist to prevent crime and disorder.
2. Police ability to perform their duties is
   dependent upon public approval of police
   actions.
3. Police must secure the willing co-operation
   of the public in obeying the law to be able
   to secure and maintain the public's respect.
4. Police ability to secure public co-operation
   diminishes the need to use physical force.
5. Police preserve public support not by
   catering to public opinion but by
   demonstrating impartial service to the law.
6. Police use physical force to enforce the law
   or restore order only when persuasion,
   advice and warning is insufficient.
7. Police and the public share policing
   responsibilities.
8. Police should never appear to take on the
   powers of the judiciary.

9. Police effectiveness is to be measured by the absence of crime and disorder, not the visible evidence of police action in dealing with it.

In our own country, several major efforts sought to clarify the police function and to set broad standards for our nation's police. Each effort responded to widespread public concern about crime in America and the police role in addressing it.

The 1967 President's Commission on Law Enforcement and Administration of Justice described the complexity of the police function, the need for police to improve their relationship with the public, the need to improve the quality of police personnel and training, and the need for police to operate with greater restraint under the law. The 1973 National Advisory Commission on Criminal Justice Standards and Goals Report on Police extended the President's Commission's work by publishing more specific police organizational standards.

The 1971 American Bar Association's Standards Relating to the Police Function jointly developed and endorsed by the International Association of Chiefs of Police, were especially helpful in articulating the broad and sometimes conflicting policing objectives. In summary, they are to:

- Prevent and control conduct threatening to life and property, including serious crime.
- Aid crime victims and protect people in danger of physical harm.
- Protect constitutional guarantees, such as the right of free speech and assembly.
- Facilitate the movement of people and vehicles.
- Help those who cannot care for themselves, including the intoxicated, the addicted, the

mentally ill, the physically disabled, the old, and the young.

- Resolve conflict between individuals, between groups, or between citizens and their government.
- Identify problems that have the potential for becoming more serious for individuals, the police, or the government.
- Create and maintain a feeling of community security.

Since police- and victim-reported crime rates peaked in about 1980, they have fluctuated and then, beginning in about 1990, steadily and dramatically declined to their present historically low levels. History tells us that unless fear of crime becomes a major public concern, little attention is paid to our nation's police and to what they are or are not doing, and little effort is put forth to improve the institution. But we believe that discussing our core policing principles is best done in an atmosphere that is not clouded by a national sense of alarm or panic about crime.

While our country's police are presently challenged on one hand by increasing demands upon them to address such issues as terrorism and illegal immigration, and on the other by declining fiscal resources, the relatively low crime rates allow some greater space for public discourse about the police role in society. Equally compelling is the need to reconcile core principles of democratic policing with the fast-evolving nature of information, forensic, and surveillance technology. Out of concern that some of our nation's police are undergoing a slow and persistent erosion of trust, fairness and accountability, we believe it is time to state clearly what it is police should do and be in our society.

We believe the following 12 qualities of

democratic policing set forth a template that police as well as citizens and their elected representatives can use to evaluate the police institution and, if found wanting, use to guide the quest for continuous improvement.

This statement of principles is not intended to be critical of our nation's police but rather to help all of us clarify the nature of our function, public expectations, and the central importance of the police role in a society that professes to pursue justice fairly, equally, and without bias.

Qualities of Police in a Free and Democratic Society

1. Accountable

Police recognize the nature and extent of their discretionary authority and must always be accountable to the people, their elected representatives, and the law for their actions, and be as transparent as possible in their decision-making.

2. Collaborative

Police must be able to collaborate, as appropriate, with community members and other organizations in settling disagreements, choosing policing strategies, and solving policing problems. This collaborative style must also apply to the way police departments are led and managed. This means police leaders must actively listen to their officers and work with them in identifying and resolving department and community problems.

3. Educated and Trained

All police officers with arrest powers should begin their career with a broad and advanced education in the sciences and humanities. Training should consist of rigorous and extensive training courses in an adult-learning climate that teaches both the ethics and skills

of democratic policing.

4. Effective and Preventive
The mark of a good police department and the officers who work within it is that they continuously seek to handle their business more effectively and fairly, emphasizing preventing crime and disorder and not merely responding to it, and applying research and practical knowledge, using problem-solving methods, toward that end.

5. Honest
Honesty and good ethical practice are essential. The search for and cultivation of these traits begin with the selection process and continue throughout an officer's career. Only those police candidates who have demonstrated good decision-making so far in their lives should be selected.

6. Model citizen
Police officers must not only be good police officers, but good citizens as well, modeling the values and virtues of good citizenship in their professional and personal lives.

7. Peacekeeper and Protector
The police role is, above all else, that of community peacekeepers, and not merely law enforcers or crime fighters. Their training, work, and values all point towards the keeping of peace in the community. As gatekeepers to the criminal justice system, police must see themselves as defenders and protectors of Constitutional and human rights, especially for those who cannot defend or care for themselves in our society.

8. Representative
The members of police organizations must be demographically representative of the communities they serve, both because it reflects fair employment

opportunities and because it enables the police to be more effective in achieving their objectives.

9. Respectful
Police officers should treat all persons with unconditional courtesy and respect, and be willing to listen to others, especially to those without social power or status. Likewise, police leaders should treat their workers with courtesy and respect their employment rights.

10. Restrained
The preservation of life should be the foundation for all police use of force. Police officers should continually prepare themselves to use physical force in a restrained and proper manner, with special training in its application to those who are mentally ill. Deadly force should be used only as a last resort and only when death or serious injury of the officer or another person is imminent. Less-than-lethal force should be preferred where possible.

11. Servant Leader
Every police officer, regardless of rank, must simultaneously be a good leader and a good servant, to the public and to the police organization. Servant leaders use their authority and influence to improve others' welfare.

12. Unbiased
Although some bias is inherent in human nature, police officers recognize that they can and should train themselves to reduce their biases and deal with all people fairly and without regard to their race, ethnicity, gender, socio-economic condition, national origin, citizenship status, or sexual orientation.

On this we stand, we who are present and former leaders of police in America. If you are in agreement, we ask you, as a police, to go to

http://www.gopetition.com/petitions/policing-our-nation.html and join us in signing this important statement.

David C. Couper and Michael S. Scott

Bibliography

Albrecht, Karl and Ron Zemke. 1985. *Service America: Doing Business in the New Economy.* New York: Dow Publishing.

Bayley, David, H. 1988. "Community Policing: A Report From the Devil's Advocate." In Jack R. Green and Stephen D. Mastrofski (eds.) *Community Policing: Rhetoric or Reality?* New York: Praeger.

Bennis, Warren and Burt Nanus. 1985. *Leaders: The Strategies for Taking Charge.* New York: Harper & Row.

Bittner, Egon. 1970. *The Functions of Police in Modern Society.* Chevy Chase, MD: National Institute of Mental Health.

Bolman, Lee and Terrance Deal. 2002. *Reframing Organizations: Artistry, Choice, and Leadership.* San Francisco: Jossey-Bass.

Braiden, C. 1987. "Community Policing Nothing New Under the Sun." Unpublished manuscript. Edmonton Police Department.

Brassard, Michael and Diane Ritter. 1987. *The Memory Jogger: A Pocket Guide of Tools for Continuous Improvement and Effective Planning*, Metheun, MA: Goal/QPC.

The Challenge of Crime in a Free Society: A Report by the President's Commission on Law Enforcement and the Administration of Justice. 1967. Washington, D.C: U.S. Government Printing Office.

Chappell, Allison T. and Lonn Lanza-Kaduce. 2009. "Police Academy Socialization: Understanding the Lessons Learned in a Paramilitary- Bureaucratic Organization." *Journal of Contemporary Ethnography.* Sage Publications.

Coens, Tom and Mary Jenkins. 2000. *Abolishing Performance Appraisals: Why They Backfire and What to Do Instead.* San Francisco: Berrett-Koehler.

Collins, Jim. 2001. *Good to Great: Why Some Companies Make the Leap…and Others Don't,* New York: HarperCollins Publishers.

Couper, David C. 1971. "The Need for Excellence in Campus Policing." *The Police Chief* magazine. Washington, DC: The International Association of Chiefs of Police. January issue

_____1972. "The Delivery of Neighborhood Police Services." The Police Chief magazine. Washington, DC: The International Association of Chiefs of Police. March issue

_____ 1974. "Remarks of David Couper as Director of Public Safety, Burnsville, Minnesota." Changing Police Organizations: Four Readings. United States Conference of Mayors. Washington DC: National League of Cities._

_____ 1983. *How to Rate Your Local Police.* Washington, DC: Police Executive Research Forum.

_____. 1990. "Police Department Learns Ten Hard Lessons," *Quality Progress* magazine, Milwaukee, October, 1990.

_____. "Seven Seeds for Policing," *FBI Law Enforcement Bulletin,* March, 1994.

Couper, David C. and Sabine Lobitz. 1987. "Quality Leadership: The First Step Toward Quality Policing." *The Police Chief* magazine. Washington, DC: International Association of Chiefs of Police. April issue.

_____. 1991. *Quality Policing: The Madison Experience.* Washington, D.C.: Police Executive Research Forum.

_____. 1993. "Leadership for Change: A

National Agenda." *The Police Chief* magazine. Washington, DC: The International Association of Chiefs of Police. December issue.

Covey, Stephen. 1992. *Principle Centered Leadership.* New York: Simon and Schuster.

_____. 1990. *Seven Habits of Highly Effective People.* New York: Simon and Schuster.

Crosby, Philip B. 1979. *Quality is Free: The Art of Making Quality Certain.* New York: Mentor Books.

Deming, W. Edwards. 1986. *Out of the Crisis.* Cambridge: MIT Center for Advanced Engineering Studies.

Eck, John and William Spelman. *Problem-solving: Problem- Oriented Policing in Newport News.* Washington, DC: Police Executive Research Forum. 1987.

Fullan, Michael. 2005. *Leadership and Sustainability: System Thinkers in Action.* Thousand Oaks, CA: Sage Publications.

Goldstein, Herman. 1990. *Problem-Oriented Policing,* New York: McGraw-Hill Publishing Company.

_____. 1987. "Toward Community-Oriented Policing: Potential, Basic Requirements, and Threshold Questions." *Crime and Delinquency*, 33, 1:6-30.

_____ 1979. "Improving Policing: A Problem- Oriented Approach. *"Crime and Delinquency*, 23, 2:236-258

_____and Charles E. Susmilch. 1982. " Experimenting with the Problem-Oriented Approach to Improving Police Service: A Report and Some Reflections on Two Case Studies." Madison, WI: University of Wisconsin Law School.

Gordon, Tom. 1978. *Leader Effectiveness Training.* New

York: Bantam Books.

Guyot, Dorothy. 1979. "Bending Granite: Attempts to Change the Rank Structure of American Police Departments." *Journal of Police Science and Administration* 7 (3)

Heifetz, Ronald. 2004. *Leadership Without Easy Answers.* Cambridge: Harvard University.

Hickman, Craig R. and Michael A. Silva.1986. *Creating Excellence: Managing Corporate Culture, Strategy, and Change in the New Age.* New York: Plume.

Imai, Masaki. 1986. *The Key to Japan's Competitive Success.* New York: Random House.

Isenberg, Jim. *Police Leadership in a Democracy: Conversations with America's Police Chiefs.* New York: CRC Press. 2010.

Johnson, David R. and Frank P. Johnson. 1987. *Joining Together: Group Theory and Group Skills*, 3rd Ed. New York: Wadsworth Publishing.

Kanter, Rosabeth Moss. 1983. *The Change Masters: Innovation and Entrepreneurship in the American Corporation.* New York: Simon & Schuster.

Manning, Peter and John Van Maanen, eds. 1978.*Policing: A View from the Street.* New York: Random House.

Naisbitt, John and Patricia Aburdene. 1985. *Re-inventing the Corporation.* New York: Warner Books.

National Advisory Commission on Civil Disorders. 1968. Supplemental Studies for The National Advisory Commission on Civil Disorders. Washington, DC: U.S. Government Printing Office.

National Research Council. 2004. *Fairness and Effectiveness in Policing: The Evidence.* Committee to Review Research on Police Policy and Practices. Wesley Skogan and Kathleen Frydl (eds.), Committee on Law and justice, Division of Behavioral and Social Sciences and Education. Washington, D.C.: The National Academies Press.

Neiderhoffer, Arthur. 1969. *Behind the Shield.* Garden City, NY: Doubleday.

Peters, Tom. 1987. *Thriving on Chaos: Handbook for a Management Revolution.* New York: Knopf Books.

_____and Robert H. Waterman. 1984. In Search of Excellence. USA: Warner Books.

_____and Nancy Austin. 1985. *A Passion for Excellence.* New York: Warner Books

Prenzler, Timothy. 1997. "Is There A Police Culture*?" Australian Journal of Public Administration,* 56.

Reiss, Albert. 1971. *Police and the Public.* New Haven, CT: Yale University Press.

Roberg, Roy, Kenneth Novak, and Gary Cordner. 2009. *Police and Society,* 4th edition. New York: Oxford University Press.

Rubinstein, Jonathan. 1973. *City Police.* New York: Farrar,   Straus, and Giroux.

Scholtes, Peter. 1998. *The Leader's Handbook: Making Things Happen, Getting Things Done.* New York: McGraw-Hill.

_____, Brian Joiner, and Barbara Streibel. 1988. *The Team Handbook.* Madison: Oriel Inc.

Scott, Michael. 2000. *Problem-Oriented Policing: Reflections on the First 20 Years.* Washington, DC: Office of Community Oriented Policing Services, U.S. Department of Justice.

_____. 2006. "Implementing Crime Prevention: Lessons Learned from Problem-oriented Policing Projects." *Crime Prevention Studies,* vol. 20.

_____. 2008. "Progress in American Policing?: Reviewing the National Reviews." *Law and Social Inquiry,* vol. 34, issue 1, winter.

Sensenbrenner, Joseph. 1991. "Quality Comes to City Hall." *Harvard Business Review* (March-April), 64-75.

Sergiovanni, Thomas. 2007. *Rethinking Leadership: A Collection of Articles,* 2nd ed. Thousand Oaks,

CA: Sage Publications.

Skolnick, Jerome H. and David H. Bayley. 1986. *The New Blue Line: Police Innovation in Six American Cities.* New York: The Free Press.

_____. 1988. *Community Policing: Issues and Practices Around the World.* Washington, D.C.: National Institute of Justice.

Skolnick, Jerome. *Justice Without Trial: Law Enforcement in a Democratic Society.* 1966. New York: John Wiley and Sons.

Sparrow, Malcolm K., Mark H. Moore and David M. Kennedy. 1990. *Beyond 911: A New Era for Policing.* USA: Basic Books.

Tichy, Noel M. and Mary Anne DeVanna. 1986. *The Transformational Leader.* New Jersey: John Wiley and Sons.

Toch, Hans and J. Douglas Grant. 1991. *Police as Problem Solvers.* New York: Plenum Press.

Trojanowicz, Robert C. 1982. "An Evaluation of the Neighborhood Foot Patrol Program in Flint, Michigan." East Lansing: Neighborhood Foot Patrol Center, Michigan State University.

Walton, Mary. 1986. *The Deming Management Method.* New York: Dodd-Mead.

Walker, Samuel. 2005. *The New World of Police Accountability.* Thousand Oaks, CA: Sage Publications.

Wycoff, Mary Ann and Wesley G. Skogan. 1993. *Community Policing in Madison: Quality From the Inside, Out.* An Evaluation of Implementation and Impact. Technical Report. Washington, D.C.: Police Foundation.

Wycoff, Mary Ann. 1982. *The Role of Municipal Police: Research as Prelude to Changing It.* Washington, D.C.: Police Foundation.

_____. 1988. "The Benefits of Community Policing: Evidence and Conjecture." In Jack R. Greene and Stephen

D. Mastrofski (eds.) *Community Policing: Rhetoric or Reality?* New York: Praeger.

Weisburd, David, and Anthony A. Braga, eds. 2006. *Police Innovation: Contrasting Perspectives.* Cambridge, U.K.: Cambridge University Press.

Index

A

B

D

Lynch, Humphrey "Jerry", 137

M

Madison Professional Police Officers Association
(MPPOA), 119, 120
Madison, Wisconsin, 7, 11, 241
Madison's Improvement Plan, 5, 277, 283
Madison's Improvement Timeline, 5, 277, 286
Madison Method, protest and crowd control, 255
Mahatma Gandhi, 7, 140
major cities, 68, 72, 107
Malcolm X, 76
manage the uprising, 144
managers, 46, 140, 190, 193, 200, 202, 216, 283, 284,
292, 293, 294
Manage by Wandering Around (MBWA), 190
Maples, Cheri, 274
Marine Corps, 8, 193
Marine drill instructor, 193
Marines, U.S., 9, 52, 94, 96, 192, 272, 273, 2
marriage, 183, 210
martial arts, 117
Mavity, Bill 273
MacArthur, Douglas, 199
Masterson, Mike, 274
McInnis, Patrick, 102, 272
mentally ill, 24, 204, 252, 310, 313
Murton, Tom, 101
Metropolitan Police Act, 59
Mifflin Block Parties, 259
Mifflin Street, 256
militarization, 48, 104, 188, 253
Milwaukee, 14, 216, 218, 316
Minneapolis, 7, 8, 9, 10, 11, 18, 26, 27, 28, 29, 44, 57,
94, 95, 96, 98, 101, 102, 103, 111, 112, 114,
119, 141, 167, 192, 244, 248, 250, 254, 272,
273, 305, 3
Minneapolis City Council, 44
Minnesota Chiefs of Police, 107
minorities, 11, 33, 106, 117, 143, 175, 176, 177

P

T

U

Z

Photo Scrapbook

Above: Sgt. David Couper, U.S. Marines.
Serial No. 1518984.
Below: Couper at a field exercise, 1960s.

Above: Photo for Minneapolis Police
defensive tactics manual.
Below: Teaching at police recruit school.
Attacking recruit was David Gorski.

Above: With Attorney Stuart Becker during a hearing in the early 70s.
Below: With Mayor Paul Soglin during first successful Mifflin Block Party, Spring, 1973.

Above: With Nobel Prize winner Howard
Temin, Governor Patrick Lucey, and
Supreme Court member (and new Chief
Justice) Shirley Abrahamson.
Below: Some of the Dane County Chiefs of
Police, 1970s.

Above: With his office poster of Dr. Martin
Luther King, Jr.
Below: Madison recruit class, 1980.

Above: With Dr. W. Edwards Deming at a conference in Madison.
Below: Madison Police command staff at ropes course teamwork training in the early 1990s.

Above: Photo for Parade Magazine with
Chiefs Lee Brown (Atlanta) Hubert
Williams (Newark), and Joseph McNamara
(San Jose).
Below: Teaching Quality Leadership to
Kettering, Ohio police.

Above: At a conference with his friend, Herman Goldstein in the 1990s.. Below: Washington, DC, receiving the national police leadership award from the Police Executive Research Forum. Left to right: Jeffrey Frye, Noble Wray, Ted Balistreri, and Mike Masterson.

Above: With his wife, Sabine Lobitz,
Captain, Wisconsin State Capitol Police.
Below: Horse Patrol at the Holiday Parade,
circa 80s.

Above: Officiating at a baptism at St Peter's
Episcopal Church in North Lake, Wisc.
where he currently serves as a priest.
Below: At his desk writing a blog for
"Improving Police."
(http://improvingpolice.wordpress.com)